HOLIDAY HEROINE

HOLIDAY HEROINE

SARAH KUHN

BOOK SIX OF HEROINE COMPLEX

DAW BOOKS, INC.

DONALD A. WOLLHEIM, FOUNDER

1745 Broadway, New York, NY 10019

ELIZABETH R. WOLLHEIM

SHEILA E. GILBERT

PUBLISHERS

www.dawbooks.com

First Printing, August 2022
1 3 5 7 9 10 8 6 4 2

DAW TRADEMARK REGISTERED
U.S. PAT. AND TM. OFF. AND FOREIGN COUNTRIES
—MARCA REGISTRADA
HECHO EN U.S.A.

PRINTED IN THE U.S.A.

For Amber,
my constant in many things—including this book.

CHAPTER ONE

IF THERE'S ONE thing I've never been able to do, it's blend in.

Take my stint playing Christmas Tree #7 in my fourth-grade holiday pageant. Prior to this tragic bit of casting, I was positively elated at the *very idea* of a holiday pageant. I am one of those people who unabashedly loves the many festive markers of winter: gingerbread and cozy sweaters, mulled cider and mistletoe, jaunty snowpeople and jingle bells. Every time a movie starring multiple Christmassy Vanessa Hudgenses pops up in my Netflix queue, my heart sings just a little bit louder.

My big sister Evie thinks this is because there's so much spectacle associated with the holiday season, so much pomp and circumstance, so many of those famed silver bells jangling their way into people's ears in the most ostentatious way imaginable. It *is* true that I never miss a chance to be as extra as possible . . . and I suppose the holiday pageant ended up being a prime example of that.

I was pissed because Clara Montrose was cast as the lead—the Sugar Plum Fairy who dances in front of the shuffling line of boring Christmas trees, blessing them with her sparkly magic wand. Our teacher, Mrs. Sasser, claimed it was because she was the best dancer in class, a notion I protested mightily. Clara had taken all of three beginning ballet lessons when she was six, but to hear her tell it, you'd think she was a principal with the Joffrey or some shit.

I later overheard Mrs. Sasser admit to another teacher that she'd actually cast Clara because she "looked the part," being blonde and blue-eyed and teeny-tiny. Whereas I, with my snarl of unruly dark hair, my gangly limbs that were already too long for my body, and (let's be real) my Asian face . . . apparently did *not*.

So I resigned myself to being a tree, but could never quite manage the one bit of direction I was given, which was—you guessed it!—*blend in*.

First, I got a little *too* into the costuming, sprucing up my blah cardboard tree outfit with not just one but three different shades of green paint, superglued tinsel accents, and a metric fuckton of glitter. Then, at the actual performance, my little tree self danced so aggressively in the background that I totally upstaged Clara, who just kind of swayed around and unenthusiastically waved that magic wand while I twirled, leaped, and emoted like my heart depended on it.

My performance was all the other parents could talk about for weeks.

That Bea Tanaka . . . she's going to be trouble.

I can't say they were wrong.

But now that I was on the cusp of full-fledged adultdom, I was trying really hard to be more of a proper grown-up, and it had actually been many, many days since I'd gotten into *any* kind of trouble—a new record for me! Six months ago, I'd made the very mature and responsible decision to up and move from my San Francisco home to the beautiful Hawai'ian island of Maui, catapulting myself across an entire ocean to take an exciting new job with the area's fledgling Demonology Research Group. This meant leaving Team Tanaka/Jupiter, the superheroing outfit my aforementioned sister Evie ran with her best friend and partner in all things world-saving, Aveda Jupiter (aka Annie Chang).

I know ditching my entire family and a plum superheroing gig might not *sound* mature and responsible on the face of it, but I'd hoped to find purpose, independence, and myself. After my supernatural adventures had led me to a way-too-intense flirtation with villaindom, I'd realized I needed to figure out who I was apart from my overbearing, overprotective family—where I was always Evie's tempestuous little sister, the forever baby of the team. And then this potentially thrilling new job had come along, promising actual demonhunting and the kind of on the ground research I adore—not to mention the chance to work with Dr. Kai Alana, founder of the DRG and owner of one of the biggest, coolest brains in the demonology field (and honestly, in the *world*).

At last, I'd be on my own for the first time in my entire life, doing stimulating work that spoke to my very soul, and figuring out what kind of superheroine I wanted to be.

"You've got this, Bebe," my best friend Leah Kim had said right before the move. "Like a butterfly emerging from its chrysalis, Bea Tanaka 2.0 is going to be epic: confident in her abilities of emotional projection, kicking ass in her scintillating new job, and definitely *not* heading down the nefarious evil villain path at all!"

I appreciated her vote of confidence. And thus far, my efforts hadn't been going too badly. Unlike my little Christmastree self, I was doing my best to not make a scene everywhere I went—to finally *blend in*.

Of course, there were still moments wherein this was an epic challenge.

Take today, which started off as a gloriously peaceful morning, then quickly devolved into the kind of chaos I'm generally known for.

I popped out of bed at my customary 9 a.m., admired the ridiculously blue Maui sky, and wandered down the street from my teeny bungalow to K Okamoto Bakery, a legendary establishment that concocted fresh malasadas and other delectable pastries every morning and stayed open until they sold out (usually a matter of hours). The bakery was the kind of no-frills, no-nonsense joint that always felt just a little bit magical to me—the lighting was dim, the decorations were minimal, and the faded letterboard menu behind the counter hadn't changed in decades. No need for extra bells and whistles, because the sweets were the absolute stars, and the bakery's dedication to craft and sheer passion for pastry provided all the flair required.

I was waiting patiently in line with my friend Keala, like I did every morning. Said line was already out the door, but no one was in any hurry—the comforting buzz of idle chatter filled the space as customers meandered forward, everyone stoked to attain their morning sugar rush. The humidity in the air was already strong enough to make my untamable snarl of hair cling to the back of my neck, but I barely noticed. I was fully entranced by the parade of sugary treats jostling for attention in the massive glass case that took up most of the front of the store. Yes, I saw it every morning, but I never failed to be warmed by its welcoming glow.

"Ahhh, the cream puff," I breathed reverently, studying the pile of fluffy golden-brown delicacies that had been placed front and center this morning. "Why have I never considered the potential majesty of the cream puff? Maybe I'll try that."

"You had one guava malasada the day you arrived and never looked back—you were all pau!" Keala countered, her eyebrows disappearing under her fall of choppy reddish-brown bangs. She gestured to the glass case, which led to a battered old-school cash register perched on a small square of counterspace jammed with gum and dusty trinkets for sale. "So many of these treats are still waiting for Bea Tanaka to pronounce them so 'ono, but that malasada will always be your one true queen."

"Facts," I said, gazing mournfully at the untasted cream puff. "Sorry, cream puff, but the contrast between donut-y sweetness and that signature tang of guava jelly is an unreal level of perfection, and I must pay tribute whenever I can."

"Your expression is sooo dreamy right now," Keala teased, her impish dark eyes sparkling with amusement. "I love that you've maintained a passion for the guava malasada, even after ingesting approximately five million of them."

"You know how people say 'absence makes the heart

grow fonder'?" I said, as we shuffled forward in line. "For me, it's the opposite: *excess* makes the heart grow fonder. I can't wait to eat at least five million more."

"This explains so much!" Keala exclaimed. "Like how you've purchased enough of my rings for your fingers, toes, and possibly other appendages even though you've lived here for less than a year."

"You're complaining about me being a super regular customer?" I protested, brandishing my hands—which were fully festooned with Keala's beautiful creations, rings constructed from raw pearls and shattered bits of shells woven into complicated twists of gold and bronze wires. She sold her jewelry at the outdoor market a few doors down from the bakery, and we'd met because I'd been drawn to her table full of shiny things like the little magpie I am.

Keala had been intrigued by my very Californian magical goth girl aesthetic—messy blue-and-purple-streaked waves of hair swirling around me, black slip dress soaking up all that sun, eyeliner just shy of "human raccoon" status. In turn, I'd complimented her obvious sartorial panache—she was always wearing the most casually perfect vintage Levi's cut-offs, which she paired with an array of loudly patterned silk blouses, an armful of her own jewelry, and a rainbow of pastel eye shadows that popped against her glowing bronze skin. We'd ended up talking for hours about our shared love of romance novels and *Sailor Moon*, and my first real friendship in Maui was born.

"Not complaining, eh?" Keala said, her mouth quirking into a crooked smile. The eclectic pile of bangles gracing her right arm jangled as she wagged a teasing finger at me. "On the contrary, I—"

"Excussshhhheee me!"

Keala and I whipped around to see a very loud white lady tourist crashing her way through the bakery's charming wooden doors, her eyes overbright and slightly unfocused, her plastic tiara askew. Judging from the rumpled, bedazzled sash twisting itself across her chest and proclaiming her a

BRIDE TO BE in glittery silver letters, I was guessing she was doing a whole destination bachelorette thing.

"Excuse me!" she called again, snapping her fingers. "Me and my girlsh . . . girlshes . . . have been partying alllllll night! We need breakfasssssshhhhhht!"

"Yeah!" another belligerent voice rang out—and then a cavalcade of similarly disheveled white blonde women crashed in behind The Bride like a topple of dominos, their BRIDESMAID sashes a Pepto-worthy shade of pink. "We saw on TikTok that this is one of Maui's most foodielicious hidden gems," the bellowing bridesmaid continued. "And we just had to try it!"

"Jennifer B. is gonna be *pissed*!" another, even blonder bridesmaid gloated. "That's what she gets for missing out on the bach of the century to stay home with her gross old dying cat!"

"*Hiss*," Keala grumbled, and I covered my hand with my mouth, transforming an errant giggle into a fake cough. One of the things I loved about Keala was that she always said things like "hiss" or "snort" instead of, you know, doing the actual action. "'Hidden gem,' my ass, this place is a fucking hundred-year-old institution and therefore always swarming with dedicated locals and lolo tourists."

"As evidenced by the very long line they all just bypassed," I agreed. "But hey, if it's on TikTok, it must be true."

"Tell us about your shh—secret menu items!" The Bride demanded, ignoring the rest of the line to stumble her way up to the counter. A vaguely disapproving murmur ran through the line—not a scandalized or surprised murmur, however, given that rude tourists were part of life round these parts. The Bride, of course, took no notice of any kind of murmur. The bridesmaids followed her lead, shuffling behind her in an unruly parade of pink sashes, hairspray, and entitlement.

"We want only the most exclusive tastes of aloha, with the most *exotic* ingredients!" The Bride continued, slamming a hand down on the counter hard enough to make one of the dusty gum displays jump, as if surprised to be disturbed after all these years of just sitting there.

"We heard you have a guava mass . . . mal . . . *pastry donut thingy*!" yelped the bridesmaid who hated Jennifer B. "That sounds, like, sooo authentically Hawai'ian."

"Guavaaaa," agreed another bridesmaid, her eyes widening into big blue saucers. "I'm gonna grow my own in the community garden when I get home! I can probably buy, like, some seeds while we're here, right?"

Auntie Iris, the stone-faced elder who worked the counter nearly every day, gave The Bride and her entourage a blank look. "Out of guava malasadas," she said, slicing a definitive arm through the air. "You need come earlier."

"Don't worry, she's got a couple for us stashed behind the counter," I murmured to Keala. "We *could* make do with a donut stick, which is awesome, but as I just established: nothing is quite as awesome as a guava malasada."

"You've got that dreamy look again," Keala said, giving me finger guns. "And I can't believe you got Auntie Iris to accept you into her inner circle so quickly. It's usually a decade-long process involving passionate statements of fealty and elaborate tokens of appreciation."

"What can I say, I have a gift," I said, offering a faux-modest shrug. "Senior Aunties love me the most."

"What do you mean you're out?! Make sh-some mooor-rre!" The Bride slurred, drunkenly stabbing a finger in the air.

Auntie Iris gave her the stink-eye. Given that so many tourists who wandered off the fancy resort grounds expected locals to drop whatever they were doing and play friendly-faced tour guide, that stink-eye had been honed into a razor-sharp blade of devastation.

"And where's that beautiful aloha spirit I keep hearing so much about?!" The Bride bleated.

"God," I muttered, rolling my eyes at Keala. "Do you think she can hear the actual words she's saying, or . . . ?"

"I think she can, and I think she fucking loves it," Keala said, her eyes narrowing and transforming her elfin appearance into something more malevolent. "Major colonizer energy, eh? Like those of us who live here are smiley animatronics that only come alive to cater to these lolos' every whim. Like I always say: eat, pray, shove it up your ass!"

I twisted my pearl rings around my fingers, trying to ignore the prickle of anger in my gut, the hum of irritation running over my skin—and the whisper of darkness that told me to go unleash unholy hell on The Bride and her minions.

That was, after all, what Past Bea would have done.

"Growl," Keala huffed, shaking her head at the standoff that was now happening between Auntie Iris and the bridal crew. "Speaking of gifts, though, why not use your actual superpower on Girl Boss and her squad?"

"Nah," I deflected, even as that hum of irritation grew louder, like a swarm of mosquitos was suddenly crawling all over me. "Auntie Iris has so got this."

I twisted one of my rings around my finger in an especially aggressive manner, trying to squelch the panic that was now rising in my chest—the one prompted by Keala's mention of my *other* gift.

Yes, it's true. I have an actual superpower, just like Evie and Aveda. But whereas Evie's is "yeah, so I can shoot fire from my hands" and Aveda's is "yeah, so I can do a bit of telekinesis, but my *real* power is being a total badass at absolutely everything I do," mine is more like . . . "yeah, so I can project my emotions to make you feel whatever I want you to, and maybe this leads to me mind-controlling you a little baby bit. Or *a lot* baby bit. We'll just have to see!"

At its base level, I thought of my emotional projection power as akin to one of those scent diffusers you can buy at Muji, or a really awesome aromatherapy candle—a subtle way of shifting the atmosphere and massaging someone's mood. This had come in super handy at my previous customer-service job at an adorable indie bookstore. And yeah, okay, sometimes I had projected a little more strongly than *strictly* necessary when a customer was super annoying or condescending or needed to be convinced that they *did* actually need to purchase every single volume of a sexy wereporcupine shifter series in order to adjust their atrocious attitude toward the romance genre and become a better person.

Um, just for example. I guess "subtle" is generally not in my wheelhouse.

But things had taken a sharp turn down the supervillain path during my last San Francisco escapade before the big move. I'd made contact with an evil demon disguised as my late mother and started leaping into the supernatural dimension known as the Otherworld. Suddenly, my power had morphed and changed, and my little aromatherapy candle had turned into something more like straight-up mind control—a feeling so intoxicating, I'd started getting too comfortable with my power's evil-adjacent tendencies. I found that I could basically make people my puppets if I wanted to.

Obviously I hadn't wanted to.

I mean, for the most part.

But there was no denying it could be super satisfying to exert that kind of control over, say, a middle-school archnemesis who swans into your place of work and treats you like the lowliest of bugs simply because your current gig involves serving them coffee.

Given my cartoon character appearance, my various intersecting marginalizations, and my status as the forever baby of Team Tanaka/Jupiter, I was used to being dismissed, underestimated, and not taken seriously—but when I felt that power thrumming through my veins, when I sent a projection spinning in some particularly heinous person's direction and saw that smug smile obliterated from their face—

Well. It made me feel like I was actually *powerful.* As worthy of the superheroine mantle as Evie. But obviously taking away someone's free will isn't exactly on the good-guy side of things.

Even if that someone is a total jerkwad.

Anyway, I wasn't entirely sure what effects still lingered

from all my brushes with the Otherworld, but I'd been *very careful* about using my power since then. I figured this was all part of my newfound dedication to maturity, responsibility, and blending in.

And then there was that incident a month ago that had convinced me I needed to stop using my power altogether.

I thought about that now as I studied The Bride and Auntie Iris, silently pleading with my heady mix of panic and rage to *retreat*. But even as I breathed deeply—inhale, count to seven, exhale, repeat, repeat, repeat—I felt that undeniable tug, that *need* to save Auntie Iris and put The Bride in her place. The intoxicating darkness that had called extra loudly since that incident a month ago whispered to me now, reminding me of how *good* using my power would feel. Especially on entitled assholes with big Karen vibes.

"Stop keeping the exclusives from us!" The Bride squawked, finally ending the standoff with Auntie Iris. "I'm a customer, and I do *not* approve of your attitude! I need to speak to the manager!"

"Why is it *always* the manager?" I groaned, attempting to shove the beckoning call of my power to the side, even as my irritation ticked up about a thousand fold. "Auntie Iris is one of the freaking *owners*!"

"If Auntie looks could kill, Karenzilla would be dead," Keala muttered, nodding toward Auntie Iris's stink-eye, which was now dialed up to max levels.

"Let's get some *service* up in here!" one of the bridesmaids bellowed, sashaying over to a tower of pre-bagged donut holes. "Or we're gonna have to start leaning in, practicing self-care, and being our best, most empowered selves!"

And with that, she swiped at the bag of donut holes teetering precariously at the top of the tower of treats. It fell immediately, setting off a donut-hole avalanche as bags and bags of sweets crashed to the floor in violent succession.

"Hey!" a voice barked from the line. "What the fuck?!"

Oh, crap. That was *my* voice. And now *my* feet were carrying me over to The Bride and her minions, propelling me toward the mess I just could not seem to ignore. I blew out a long breath and reminded myself to *calm down*, to rein in all those pesky emotions. To *not* exert my control over this infuriating white girl gang and their demands.

Don't do it, I thought to myself, even as my feet kept up their indignant stomp. *Don't project all over them and force The Bride to film a TikTok where she confesses to being a flaming asshole and then wires all of her earthly assets to Auntie Iris and the bakery, where they will be properly used for good instead of wasted on "exotic" bachelorette parties and guava seeds, which I'm pretty sure will not fare well in this lady's pretentious "community garden" anyway. You're trying to be* responsible, *remember?! And mind-controlling people is not responsible!*

I finally reached the squad, who weren't even attempting to clean up the spilled donut holes, and planted myself in front of them—hands on my hips, blatantly blocking their view of Auntie Iris.

And remember your whole thing about not making a scene!

Right. Okay. I breathed deeply again. There were other ways to handle this.

I mean, probably.

"Hey, um, bridal squad," I said, forcing my shoulders to relax and ordering the seductive pull of my power to just shut the fuck up already. I even managed to school my features into something that resembled "friendly."

"Hey," The Bride said, looking me up and down. I clocked and analyzed that look in two seconds flat. She was definitely fascinated by my "exotic" biracial appearance, and was moments away from either negging or complimenting my hair (or maybe both—I'd started to grow the blue and purple out as part of my "blend in" initiative and had dark roots halfway down my head at this point). This would be followed by unprompted gushing about her deep love for anime and/or

K-pop, and then she'd be trying to adopt me into the squad as her token pet—like one of Gwen Stefani's Harajuku Girls.

In the past, I would have embraced my first impulse without a second thought, made her into my perfect puppet, and forced her to grovel at Auntie Iris's feet. And yeah, maybe filmed the whole thing for the internet's viewing pleasure.

But now, I firmly shoved that instinct down.

"You seem like ladies of very, ah, cultured taste," I continued, keeping my benign expression in place. "Like you're seeking out some of the most authentic experiences the island has to offer, hmm?"

"Exactly!" The Bride huffed, tossing her golden locks over her shoulder and straightening her tiara. "We're just trying to support struggling, family-owned local businesses and this is the treatment we get?!"

"So ungrateful," one of the bridesmaids murmured, sounding truly aghast.

"Struggling?!" Auntie Iris hissed behind me. "We make enough in yesterday's sales alone for me to go to Disneyworld this summer! I gonna go on Space Mountain at least five times."

"That sounds soooo frustrating," I said, tamping down hard on my urge to unleash every single negative emotion I was having upon this girl. I couldn't help but briefly fantasize about what her face would look like if I used my power to erase that infuriating smirk. "But y'know . . ." I leaned in, all conspiratorial-like. "This place has kinda blown up since all the TikToks. It's pretty well-known now, practically *mainstream*." I lowered my voice like this was a particularly dirty word. Which, to this crew, it probably was.

They all reacted as I thought they would, recoiling in horror.

"Oh no," The Bride lamented. "What will we do *now*?"

"As it happens, I've got the inside line on the hottest new underground foodie sensation," I said. "It's so secret, it doesn't even have a name. Just an address!"

"What?!" The Bride had her phone out already, rabidly scanning her maps app. "Ugh, why can't I get any reception on this shithole island!"

"It's cool, I can put it in your notes app," I cooed, holding out my hand.

The Bride hesitated, glittery nails wrapped protectively around her phone. "I have a lot of confidential information on here," she said, looking down her nose at me. "You'll need to sign an NDA."

"That . . . I really don't care about anything that's on your phone," I blurted out, unable to keep the annoyance out of my voice. "Just give it to me."

She hesitated again, locking me in a standoff much like the one she'd just engaged in with Auntie Iris.

Come on, I thought, irritation thrumming through my entire being. *Seriously. Just give it. To. Me!*

I was calculating my next move—maybe it would be easiest to sign the freaking NDA?!—when The Bride's shoulders suddenly relaxed, her gaze softened, and she handed over the phone.

"Um, thank you," I said, taking it from her.

"Do they have guavaaaa?" the obsessed bridesmaid demanded, trying to peer over my shoulder.

"Tons of it!" I assured her. "My god, so much guava! You're gonna have such an *authentic* experience."

I typed an address into The Bride's phone, making a big show of screwing my face up in concentration. I resisted my supervillain urge to also program in a tiny virus that would cause her phone to self-destruct whenever she did something offensive.

"Thank you!" the guava-loving bridesmaid squealed, stepping in and snatching the phone before The Bride could get to it. "Damn, my buzz wore off—we gotta grab more booze on the way. Right, Allison? Allie . . . ? Are you okay?"

I focused back on The Bride—Allison—who looked like she was frozen in place, her eyes taking on a glassy sheen.

"I . . . fine," she said, her voice robotic. "Just fine."

She frowned and shook her head a little, as if trying to shoo cobwebs from her mind. I noticed then that her shoulders hadn't just relaxed—they'd totally slackened, slumping so low she was barely holding herself upright.

Oh no.

Oh *shit*.

Please tell me I didn't just—

"Come on," the bridesmaid said, looping an arm through The Bride's. She gave The Bride a concerned glance, then started dragging her toward the door. "Let's go, girls!" the bridesmaid called out, waving a hand to rally the rest of the squad. "Man, all those mai tais are giving me major gas—we should score some Skinny Girl marg mix! At a much friendlier establishment than this one, of course."

I swallowed hard, unable to take my eyes off The Bride as she was marched to the exit. She still looked stiff, blank—a shell of the self-righteous malasada crusader who'd tried to go to war with Auntie Iris.

When exactly *did her demeanor shift?*

What had I done?!?

I let out a gusty exhale, replaying The Bride's suddenly robotic voice in my head over and over, trying to pinpoint and analyze her abrupt change in mood. Maybe I'd fantasized too hard about how good it would feel to see her go all docile—but now that it had actually happened, it didn't feel good at all.

Probably because I'd been trying so freaking hard to *not* do exactly that.

I turned back around, expecting to see the line proceeding in orderly fashion as I had my silent freak-out, Auntie Iris selling donut sticks to less disruptive customers.

But . . . no. I'd been so wrapped up in my little moment with The Bride that I hadn't noticed the entire bakery falling silent.

Every single customer was staring at me. And yes, their expressions were mostly amused and/or grateful—a few even clapped. Yes, Auntie Iris was giving me an efficient head-bob—which, coming from her, was the equivalent of throwing a massive parade. Yes, I'd just taken down a boss-level Karen. And I'd *tried* to do it without giving in to the darkness that pulled so insistently on my soul.

But what no one here knew was that I had very possibly failed at that last bit.

And I'd *still* managed to make a scene. I saw a couple of the line denizens holding up their phones—they'd clearly been filming the whole thing, and that would make its way to the internet, where Evie and the rest of my family would see me taking center stage in the latest edition of Karens Gone Wild.

Nothing mature, responsible, or oh-so-grown-up about that.

And if I'd accidentally used my power in an undeniably villainous fashion to mind-control The Bride? Well. Even worse.

Past Bea would've absolutely savored this moment—she would have preened a bit, flashed the crowd a dazzling grin, and encouraged the scattered claps to turn into a rousing round of cheers and applause. She would have basked in these folks' admiration and approval, perhaps riling them up enough to start chanting her name. And yes, she would have felt truly powerful.

Even though she'd just done something very bad.

I scurried over to rejoin Keala in line, keeping my head down as my cheeks warmed. The line reset a bit, reverting to light chatter and a dutiful shuffle forward.

"Nice work! You prevented this place from going totally hamajang," Keala chirped, bumping her shoulder affectionately against mine. "What did you type into that girl's phone?"

"The address for the Kahului 7-Eleven," I said. "I have it memorized because Pika always wants me to take him there for Berry Blast Slurpees."

"Not even an ABC Store. How fucking *exclusive*!" Keala cackled. "They're gonna love it."

I forced a smile and tried to squash the thread of panic slithering through my gut yet again.

Dammit. No matter what I did, I *still* couldn't manage to blend in. I could grow my hair out all I wanted, but that didn't change what was inside of me.

That Bea Tanaka . . . she's going to be trouble.

Perhaps I was incapable of being anything but.

CHAPTER TWO

AFTER THE KARENING, Keala and I secured our guava malasadas and I walked her the few remaining steps to the bustling outdoor market that housed her jewelry stand. She gave me a jaunty wave with her last bite of malasada and told me to stop by later. I waved back and stretched a smile across my face like I was a totally normal person and not a chaos monster caught up in a sudden thought spiral of doom.

What just happened, what if I accidentally mind-controlled that girl without even trying, what if Evie's already seen the video and realizes her wayward little sister is destined to be a supervillain, what if I am destined to be a supervillain and there's nothing I can do to stop it—

I shook my head vehemently, as if to shoo the thoughts away, and tried to refocus on my hard-won malasada. I forced myself to home in on the sheer decadence of that perfect jelly—sweet and tart all at once, that irresistibly tangy finish dancing across my tongue. And beautifully surrounded by a pillowy donut shell bathed in crumbs of cinnamon and sugar that I licked from my sticky fingertips.

I told myself to just keep walking down the street, the same street I'd traversed every day since moving to Maui. One foot in front of the other—that's all I could do.

I suppose "street" was perhaps overstating the matter a bit. The three most important locations to my daily Maui existence—home, bakery, office—were all located in the little enclave called Makawao. The center of town consisted of one big paved road running through lush countryside, the main drag dotted with shops, convenience stores, and an outdoor market where local artists like Keala sold their beautiful creations. Most of the storefronts were done up in a way that recalled oldey-timey saloons or minuscule barns, charming wooden structures painted shades of brick red and sage green, topped off with white trim and rustically lettered signs. This made sense since Makawao was known as the home of the paniolo, or Hawai'ian cowboy—there was even a rodeo parade every year, horses and their human minders strutting up and down the street and showing off their best tricks. The town was also perched on the slope of the famed Haleakalā volcano, which meant we got a fair number of tourists passing through, though certainly not as many as the fancy resort areas on the island.

The bakery was at one end of the street, and the Demonology Research Group's office was at the other. This usually made for a peaceful malasada-laden stroll, a time when I could be alone with my chaotic mess of thoughts, drink in the endless blue of the island sky, and feel the sun strengthen itself for its daily duties.

But today, my thoughts were just a little *too* chaotic for that.

I sped up my pace, making my walk brisk and to the point—even as jittery nerves frolicked around the malasada crumbs that were now safely stored in my belly. When I reached the office, I spotted my friend Roger lingering on the porch, wearing a distinctly cranky-looking expression.

"Sorry, Rog," I said, crouching down to his level and making my eyes all sympathetic. "I didn't save you any this time—Pika keeps lecturing me about feeding y'all sweets. And also I got caught up in an existential spiral that took me to a place so grim, I needed every single bite."

Roger's glare intensified as he opened his mouth to let out a hearty *caw*.

Oh yeah—Roger is a chicken.

That's another cool thing about Makawao, it's swarming with wild chickens. They flounce down the street, unbothered by all the humanity. Gather around the dumpster behind the little musubi shop on the corner. Glare at you balefully if you even try to get in their way.

Makawao chickens, as the old saying goes, do not give a fuck.

Roger and I had reached something of a détente, however, once I'd started slipping him malasada bits in the morning. Pika, the cantankerous elderly chef who owned the charming café next door to my office, claimed that human sweets were bad for chickens. But I swore Roger's feathery rooster's coat—brilliant flashes of green, gold, and red—was much more lush these days, so glossy it looked like a painting.

Roger let out another protesting *caw*, pulling me out of ruminations on his feathers.

"Okay, okay, I'll bring you a bite or two tomorrow," I relented. "And I'll make sure they still have guava jelly attached, I know you love that shit."

Roger cocked his head at me. If chickens had eyebrows, his would've been raised sky high.

"No, I'm fine, Rog," I said, flashing a quick smile. "It's just . . ." I looked around quickly, as if to make sure no other chickens were eavesdropping on us. "I had a weird encounter this morning, and it's made me all panicky, and I feel like I can't actually tell anyone about it because I've managed to convince Evie that upending my life and moving was the exact best thing for me, and that I'm totally a mature adult who can handle her business, and I can never admit that I was maybe, possibly, just a little bit wrong, because it will only confirm that I'm still the same old Bea Tanaka: flighty, irresponsible, and lacking in my commitment to sparkle motion. Or my commitment to *anything*."

Roger made a softer cooing noise that sounded almost sympathetic.

"You're right," I agreed. "I'm trying really hard to not be

that Bea Tanaka—you know, the one that was also totally on the supervillain track. I gotta try *harder*."

I sat down on the porch next to Roger and leaned against the office's sturdy exterior, the sunlit planks warm against my back.

"You know how it is with me and Evie," I murmured to Roger. "Well. Actually I guess you don't, since we maybe haven't reached that level of deep human-chicken connection in our relationship just yet. But to give you an idea: I think Big Sis has been worried about me for the entirety of the twenty-three years I've been alive. I mean, she was about that age when she had to start taking care of me, when Mom died and Dad took off. And much as I want to convince her that her shaky parenting hasn't fucked me up for life ... I actually haven't done the best job refuting that notion."

Roger made a little clicking sound with his tongue. Like even he knew I was an eternal problem child. I couldn't help but feel a little more relaxed in his presence, though, so I decided to hang on the porch for a few seconds more. The other members of the DRG usually got in closer to ten, so I could spare a moment to chill with my best chicken friend.

I slipped my phone out of my pocket and checked my various messages, half-wondering if my encounter with the Karen Squad had already gone viral. But there were no random social media alerts, nothing from Evie going on and on about how she was oh-so-disappointed in me.

Still, I could practically hear her scolding voice in my ear: *Beatrice Constance Tanaka! What have you managed to get yourself into this time?!*

My email was jammed with a bunch of things I immediately snoozed for later—but mundane things, ordinary life things. This made my shoulders relax a millimeter or two. I saw chirpy notifications from mailing lists I never remembered to unsubscribe from, forwards from my friend Lucy Valdez (Team Tanaka/Jupiter's fight trainer and weapons expert) about some new British murder show she wanted me to watch, and a travel itinerary from my brother-in-law—Evie's half-demon husband Nate Jones, who also served as Team Tanaka/Jupiter's demonology expert.

Evie was currently six months pregnant, and she and Nate were headed my way for a much-needed babymoon. They'd be arriving in a week, and they were staying in a hotel—my adorable bungalow was barely big enough for me and the occasional guest who didn't mind pretzeling themselves to fit into various nooks and crannies. But I still needed to make the place spotless, organized, and presenting as the exactly right level of lived-in for their visit. Evie was convinced that I was *hashtag thriving* in my brand-new, totally grown-up life, and I really wanted to keep it that way.

Evie and I were finally in therapy these days—we'd never had the chance to process our grief, or our relationship that changed forever when both of our parents went away. So now, we were trying to do all of that. And yet, I still felt the need to prove to her that I was totally okay. That I was indeed thriving. That she could at last check me off of her neverending list of things she had to worry about, a list that had quadrupled in size since she'd become pregnant.

I switched from email to my camera roll, idly scrolling through so I could start making a list of places I wanted to show Evie and Nate on their trip, all the wonderful food I was eager to introduce them to. A slight smile tugged at the corners of my mouth as I relived my first few months in Makawao. I thumbed through snaps of me, Keala, and her girlfriend Giselle diving into massive plates of spicy garlic shrimp and frosty POG (passion fruit-orange-guava) slushies. Stopped to admire a lovely portrait of me and the other members of the Demonology Research Group posing in front of our brand-new office. Lingered on a nice beach shot I'd taken of Lucy and her wife Rose, who had come to Maui for their honeymoon. And finally landed on a crooked selfie I'd tried to take with Roger, wherein he'd insisted on skittering out of frame and therefore showed up as a feathery multicolored blur.

"Hey, look at us, Rog," I said, showing the screen to him. "You know, when I first got here . . ." I frowned at my collage of shiny, happy pictures. "I *did* feel like I was on the thriving cusp. The new gig was so damn cool, and I was enjoying all that stimulating demon-based research and getting out in the field—just like I'd always wanted. Plus, there were new friends and a constant stream of incredible food to try, and I also felt like . . ." I trailed off, scrutinizing the photo of Roger and me. My mermaid waves had still been fully blue and purple at that point, brighter than the sun.

I didn't really know how to vocalize the next part, even to a trusted friend like Roger. I mean, I hadn't been able to vocalize it to any of my human friends either, so I supposed that was par for the course.

But when I'd arrived in Maui, I'd been filled with the weird, giddy freedom of being truly on my own for the first time in my entire life. I'd sensed I was finally finding something like *purpose*—Evie was always droning on and on about how superheroing her way through San Francisco had done that for her, how it made her realize what she was meant to do with her life and helped her find a way to live, period. And while one of my major issues (according to my therapist, anyway) was the fact that I always seemed to be looking for some kind of magic bullet that was going to "fix" everything that was wrong with me, I'd thought I was *at last* on my journey toward self-actualization. After all, Doc Kai—aka Dr. Kai Alana, the aforementioned awesome demonologist who'd created Maui's Demonology Research Group—had been oh-so-impressed with what she called my "big weird brain," and had enthusiastically offered me the job that brought me out here. To have someone I admired so much see that kind of potential in me wasn't something I was used to, and it felt like a sign that I was on the right path.

Doc Kai created the DRG after a series of incidents on the island that seemed to point to supernatural activity. This was a big deal since, up until that point, demon activity had been pretty firmly concentrated in San Francisco.

It all started fourteen years ago, when the very first Otherworld portal opened up in the city. Said portal had actually been opened by aspiring demon queen Shasta—who, in a soap operatic twist worthy of our most legendary daytime divas, was also Nate's mom. Shasta had been attempting some sort of invasion situation, but her portal was so freaking shitty, it snapped shut immediately, killing her raiding party of humanoid demons—and sending their powers directly into the bodies of various San Francisco residents, like mine and Evie's and Aveda's.

That original portal led to aftereffects that Evie and Aveda were still dealing with all these years later. They were constantly battling things like evil cupcakes and literal bridezillas, and they'd even slugged it out with demonically powered versions of ghosts and vampires. We'd also recently learned that the walls between our world and the Otherworld had rubbed perilously thin in certain spots, giving the demons all-new ways to cause trouble—and they seemed to be expanding their radius, bringing supernatural escapades to other parts of the Bay Area and Los Angeles and . . . well, we'd *thought* Maui. That was another reason the job had been so intriguing to me—if there were about to be demons in a whole other location, that meant much new research to embark on, and I'd thought me and my particular mix of talents might be able to offer superheroic assistance.

But nothing much of the supernatural variety had happened in Maui since I'd moved out here. Doc Kai had set up a tip line of sorts, an email address where anyone could write to us after observing or experiencing something that seemed out of the ordinary. It was always crammed with overexcited tourists, claiming some really big waves they'd seen while lounging on the beach sipping fruity umbrella drinks were *definitely* demons. Their imaginings were sometimes so vivid, we couldn't help but wonder if something *was* happening and we just kept missing it. I enthusiastically threw myself into the work, traveling to the site of every single reported incident and doing a thorough exploration, investigating any area that might be catnip for demons, and conducting extensive interviews with anyone who claimed to have seen something.

After a few weeks on the job, I'd started to miss Evie and the rest of my family more than I'd ever admit to them, so I'd done what I usually do and cheerfully inserted myself into their business, assisting in several of the team's recent investigations from across the ocean. This had been fun initially, a way for me to stay connected to the team while still pursuing my own independence—and I'd even come up with an idea for a very special supernatural side experiment.

But I'd needed help with said idea, so I'd called up yet another important member of Team Tanaka/Jupiter.

"Just hear me out, Scott!" I'd crowed, launching right into my pitch as soon as he'd answered the phone, no time for hellos. Scott Cameron was Team Tanaka/Jupiter's resident mage, as well as Aveda's endlessly sweet husband. He'd known me since I was a disaster-prone toddler. "I'm talking to *you* about this because I know Evie and Aveda will just rain all over my parade with the instant and unnecessarily emphatic *NO*s," I blathered on. "I want to, like, see if you can create a new spell—wherein superpowered individuals can temporarily fuse their powers into one *mega-combo power*. There were all these reports of a possible demon attack on a local beach this weekend—and yeah, the attack ended up being the fevered imagining of some particularly drunk tourists, but what if it had been real?! The only person with superpowers currently located on Maui is *me*, and I don't know that I can handle a full-on demon battle all by myself. So, what if—*what if, Scott!*—we could do a spell that would fuse the powers of every member of Team Tanaka/Jupiter and host them in my body, thereby turning myself into a badass, bulletproof Voltron of doom?!"

I'd waited for a moment, holding my breath as he considered. I used to construct elaborate, glittery posterboards for every single genius idea I wanted to present to the team—but these days I was relying on the sheer force of my motor-mouthed enthusiasm.

Luckily, said motormouthing can be quite convincing, even when I'm not using my power.

"That sounds equal measures terrifying and incredible, Bug," Scott had finally replied, voice laced with unconcealed amusement. "Where do we start?"

That was what I loved about Scott—he was infinitely good-natured, and therefore always up for my most outrageous ideas. (And this was why he was the only living person who could get away with calling me by my hated childhood nickname.)

We'd done some experimenting with the concept, and had eventually deployed it about a month ago during a fraught battle against some demonically powered vampires who'd gone after Evie and Aveda. The whole thing was revealed to be a plot by Shasta, who we'd learned was after Evie's baby. We still didn't know what her ultimate goal was, but she claimed the baby was the key to building a permanent bridge between our world and the Otherworld, which we were assuming Shasta wanted to use for evil invasion-type purposes.

Scott and I had managed to do a successful version of the power combo spell, merging Scott's magic with my emotional projection and Aveda's telekinesis. Together, we'd taken down Shasta and her human minion and basked in the triumph of teamwork.

But there was something I hadn't told anyone.

That battle, that spell . . . *that* was when everything changed for me.

I could still remember the moment when my elation turned to terror—all within a matter of seconds.

Scott had been on the scene with Aveda, preparing to face off against a swarm of vampires at an LA comic book convention (yes, the adventures of Team Tanaka/Jupiter are never anything less than totally ridiculous). I'd been here in Makawao, waiting for the spell to take hold. Scott had cast the spell, giving us a mental link, and then merged our three powers together—all hosted in Aveda's body.

Scott's power drew on Otherworld magic, bits he was able to access to do his spells. As soon as our brains linked up, I'd felt that brush of magic against my mind—bright and weird and wild.

You okay, Bug? Scott had thought to me.

Yes, I'd thought back. *I . . . wow. This feels* so *cool. Like my brain is suddenly made of motherfrakkin' rainbows! Do you feel that, too?!*

I don't think it's exactly the same for me, he'd thought, a bit of a chuckle in his voice. *Each of us will probably experience the mental link differently, depending on our power.*

Well, I currently feel like those rainbows are beaming through me and making me glow like the most powerful disco ball ever created, I'd thought. *So let's go kick some vampire-demon ass!*

I'd reveled in my rainbow-disco-ball sensation as Scott and I used our powers to bolster Aveda's telekinesis, delighted in watching through her mind's eye as she duked it out with all those pesky vampires.

Our mental link with Aveda was temporarily broken when she'd turned into a giant swarm of bats and flown to the vampires' underground lair (I told you our adventures are ridiculous!), but we'd managed to re-establish contact just in time.

Aveda! I'd thought at her, exhilarated that we'd been able to link up once more. *We lost you for a minute when you turned into the bat swarm thingy—which was majorly cool by the way, do you think you can teach* me *how to—*

Bea, Scott had interrupted, that chuckle threading through his voice again. *Later. We've got stuff to do right now.*

And we'd done it. I'd felt that telekinetic pull from Aveda as she finally took down Shasta's human minion—as part of our plan, she'd pulled Otherworld energy from said minion's body, and I could feel it swirling around the magic of Scott's spell. So much incredible power that was not of this world.

I swore I could see all that Otherworld magic dancing through the air, sparkly iridescent colors bathing the shadowy vampire lair in fantastical enchantment. I luxuriated in that sensation again, that alien brightness that dazzled me so much, and felt it wrap around my mind.

I rejoiced in our heroic triumph, in Scott and Aveda's exultation. I'm not sure how to explain this, but I felt the same kind of satisfaction and power I'd experienced in the past when I'd mind-mojoed someone who was being a total dick—only now, it was because I'd successfully used my power for *good*. I'd been able to superheroically change things for the better, and all that magic was flowing through me and cheering me on.

I *was* the sparkly rainbow disco ball. Nothing had ever felt so right.

And then suddenly it was all *wrong*.

The magic was still humming through me, Scott's spell still in effect. But in an instant, right after the climax of our battle, instead of merely brushing against my mind . . . it felt like the magic was enveloping it. *Consuming* it.

And I was overtaken by a sensation I hadn't felt in months.

It was the same intoxicating darkness I'd experienced when I'd jumped into the Otherworld during my adventures with the evil demon who had impersonated my mother. It was a siren song, a call to temptation, a whisper that echoed through my mind telling me that *this* was what I needed, *this* was the life-changing purpose I was looking for, *this* was what I finally had to give in to.

It told me I had to embrace that dark magic in order to feel whole.

And I knew that was a direct one-way ticket to supervillaindom.

Prior to my battle against Mom-Demon, I'd established a personal code to regulate my power. I told myself I'd only use it for the greater good. If I had to mind-mojo a particularly difficult customer at It's Lit, the Bay Area bookstore where I used to work, it wasn't just for my personal gain—it was for the community at large. But I'd never persuade somebody to do something they straight-up did not want to do. At the time, anyway, that had been out of my power's scope.

Of course, as I mentioned before—my code could be a bit, ah, flexible. I did sometimes exert a little more control than necessary when I really wanted to convince someone of something, or to stop fools from acting like *complete* fools. And when my power morphed and changed during all the Otherworld jumping, I'd started to take advantage of the mind-control aspect in ways that were definitely in line with the bad-guy side of things. I'd turned the supremely annoying siblings of my beloved boyfriend, Sam Fujikawa, into mindless puppets, forcing them to apologize for all their condescending transgressions. I'd tried to kidnap my former BFF and childhood nemesis, Nicole, nearly making her a human sacrifice and dragging her to a bleak prison dimension in the Otherworld, simply because my Mom-Demon had told me that was what was necessary in order to get everything I'd ever wanted (including the resurrection of my dead mother, which I'd longed for more than anything).

And hell, way back when, before I'd even known I had a superpower, period . . . I'd actually offered myself up to Shasta as a willing minion following a supreme blow-out fight with Evie. I'd been a rebellious, grieving teenager, and Shasta had made me feel like I could finally be important and respected—if only I sold my entire soul to her.

Yes, I'd eventually come to my senses in all the instances described above. But these experiences led me to one undeniable conclusion: I simply couldn't be trusted with a certain level of power. I was too impulsive, too mercurial, and I'd always end up making the wrong choice.

After my Mom-Demon adventures concluded, I'd decided I needed to redefine my code. I would never again seek out that kind of seductive magic. And I'd be *extremely* careful about using my emotional projection so that I never got close to that sort of temptation ever again. I thought maybe this wouldn't be too hard since some of the more extreme boosts my power had gotten from the Otherworld seemed to have lessened or fully disappeared with time—I could no longer jump into the evil demon dimension, for example, and I knew that was for the best.

Working on the power combo spell with Scott had seemed like something that would help me find a new code. It was cooperative superheroing, after all, and would allow the powerful aspects of my projection to be used in a constructive way. No need for mind control, because hey, mashing together three very different yet ultimately complementary powers was way cooler.

But when that Otherworld magic started to envelop my mind, when it suddenly morphed from "sparkly rainbows" to "sparkly rainbows, but it make it as dark and goth as Bea's excessive eye makeup," I'd felt its call all over again.

I'd hoped this feeling would vanish once we finished the spell and severed our powers from each other.

But it hadn't. It had actually *grown*.

That Otherworld darkness stayed inside of me—and now it felt like a living, breathing piece of my soul. It was a constant hum underneath all my thoughts, jagged shadows that enveloped every feeling I had. I tried to shove it down, to ignore it in the hopes that it would just go away.

And . . . it didn't. I swore I could feel that darkness merging with my power, turning it into something warped and twisted. So I'd decided it was time for an all-new code: I would have to stop using my power altogether. Quit cold turkey. Lock it down and stuff it into a safe buried somewhere deep inside of me, so it could never hurt anyone again.

So *I* could never hurt anyone again.

But sometimes . . . sometimes I felt like the darkness that lingered inside of me was pushing my power in new and unpredictable directions. Even though I was trying not to use my power at all, I sensed my emotions occasionally spilling all over people of their own accord, causing me to project without even meaning to. Like the day a couple weeks ago when I'd expressed a deep-seated desire for the chocolate peanut butter mochi from Maui Specialty Chocolates, and Doc Kai had bought out the whole store during her lunch break, showering me in boxes of sweets. I swore her eyes had gotten that blank, glassy look, sending those tendrils of panic swirling through me.

And this morning . . . I mean, hadn't The Bride looked the same? Her eyes had that exact glassy sheen all of a sudden, and then she'd gone weirdly docile and handed me her phone.

"Fuck!" I blurted out, prompting Roger to send a protesting *"Caw!!"* my way. Roger did not believe in the use of excess profanity.

"Sorry, Rog," I said, stuffing my phone back in my pocket. "I know I have to do better. I have to *be* better. And I have to keep my power on complete lockdown."

I couldn't tell Evie and Co. about any of my fears—not if my goal was to be a true grown-up, handle my business, and *not* make her worry. She was so freaking happy about my #thriving state, and I didn't want to do anything to destroy that. If I was going to have any hope of graduating to responsible adultdom, I needed to learn how to control my own power. I couldn't rely on the actual responsible adults in my life to step in and save me at every turn. Part of figuring out who I was apart from them meant actually being *apart* from them.

I just had to work harder on the control part. I had to remember my new code. That was all there was to it.

I took one last deep breath and stood, trying to power myself forward with newfound determination.

"Good talk, Rog," I said, attempting to embody a confidence I did not feel. "And I promise: guava goodness coming your way tomorrow."

CHAPTER THREE

I ENTERED THE office, ascertained I was the first person there, and settled in at my desk, trying to shake off the last vestiges of my morning doom spiral and my confession to a chicken.

I can do this. I can be better. I can control my own power, goddammit. I mean, Leah always says my brain is huge and full of science!

I could practically hear my best friend's bubbly voice delivering a perfectly timed pep talk directly into my ear. Leah was the one person I probably would've been able to confide in about my current dilemma. She had a sunny, effervescent way of being that always made me immediately want to spill the beans—I'd pretty much told her my deepest, darkest secrets about five minutes after we first met.

But this felt too deep and dark to share with anyone.

And as I'd just determined: I was handling it.

It would be nice if she were here, though. Or . . . actually, maybe it wouldn't. I'd pulled back quite a bit from the feverish level of texting and calling I used to keep up with both her and my boyfriend, Sam—I just knew they'd be able to tell something was wrong with me.

Sam and I had also been having some communication issues. Long-distance love is hard and awkward and involves way too many nights obsessing over why someone couldn't find time in their entire day to text you back.

Anyway, my main form of contact lately had been to mail the two of them actual paper letters documenting, in great detail, my favorite Christmas movies. It had started out as a fun lark, a not-so-stealthy scheme for me to convert Sam—the world's biggest Christmas-hating Grinch—into a holiday freak. Leah, my partner in crime in all things, had supported this heartily. Over the past month, the letters had also become a way for me to keep in touch without inadvertently revealing too much about what was going on with me.

I felt a pang of longing, missing them both. And the silence in the empty office was suddenly way too loud.

"Hey Bea, howzit!"

I yelped, jumping out of the way of the door that was now swinging open to let in Doc Kai. The jump was necessary, as our office was a fairly intimate affair, owing to the fact that the Demonology Research Group consisted of three people: me, Doc Kai, and our assistant-type person, Tosh.

Doc Kai (a nickname I'd coined that delighted her, because most things delighted Doc Kai) had located the office space all by herself when she'd decided the DRG needed to be its own independent entity, completely separate from the Maui PD and other law enforcement–type agencies. Because Doc Kai had a big weird science brain of her own (part of why we vibed so well), she'd managed to secure generous funding from various academic grants and institutions. So far, our work hadn't required anything major like an actual lab, but Doc Kai had a vision that we'd eventually be able to expand.

Our office space wasn't much, but it fit our trio perfectly. It was a small unit that had probably once been a residential home—the exterior had the oldey-timey cowboy look that dominated the street, wooden planks painted the same brick red as the most classic of barns. The interior mostly consisted of one large-ish room, so Doc Kai and I had positioned our desks on opposite sides, facing each other. Tosh had their own desk right near the entrance, and there was one narrow additional room that we'd turned into a teeny kitchenette.

Some people would've found this setup cramped, but I loved it—it made me feel like the three of us had our own scrappy detective agency or something (an observation I'd gleefully shared with Lucy to feed her British murder mystery obsession. She'd immediately demanded detailed photos of the office, which I'd been extra amused by since most people wanted to see beaches and volcanos and beautiful Maui nature things).

"Morning, Doc Kai!" I said, hustling across the room to my desk. "I'm doing okay, just a little discombobulated this morning."

"Mornings, what are they good for, yeah?" Doc Kai exclaimed, flopping down at her own desk and toying idly with her choppy hair. She'd tried bleaching it a few weeks ago and the results had been predictably orange. So then she'd tried cutting it off, and things had pretty much devolved from there. Doc Kai had the eccentric, absent-minded aura of Doc Brown in *Back to the Future*, if Doc Brown had been a curvy Native Hawai'ian woman in her thirties with a predilection for vintage aloha shirts, ratty high-top sneakers, and anything that contained a metric ton of sugar. Tosh, meanwhile, stuck pretty much exclusively to a wardrobe of glamorously rumpled linen jumpsuits and was the only person I knew who subsisted on blended green juices purely because they liked the taste.

The three of us made quite a team.

"I'm sending you the latest reports to analyze," Doc Kai said, booting up her laptop. "May head down to Lahaina to investigate some new sightings—unless you want that gig?" She raised an eyebrow at me. "Maybe this time, it'll be one actual supernatural thing, eh? What if there are, like, some kine demonic sea monsters existing in harmony with all the surfers and marine wildlife? How cool would that be?"

"Always the dreamer, Doc Kai," I said, laughing a little. "I'd love to see your vision of a harmonious ecosystem actually come true, but most of the demons I've personally encountered have been all the way hostile."

"Ya never know," Doc Kai insisted, her dark eyes shining

behind the hot pink plastic frames of her clunky glasses. "Today could be the day!"

I truly admired Doc Kai's vision. We'd met because she'd gone to grad school with Nate, they'd stayed friends, and he was the first person she'd contacted when possibly supernatural occurrences started popping up on Maui. Doc Kai's deepest passions were protecting her community and preserving the island, and she held out hope that if demons did start washing up on the shore . . . well, maybe they'd be friendly and she could bring all her impressive knowledge together to help them become a thriving part of the local wildlife. Her doctoral dissertation had actually explored a controversial theory around this idea. Because many of the Otherworld demons over the years had shown signs of adaptability—like the puppy demons who took the form of the first earthly object they saw—Doc Kai wondered if they would be able to adapt enough to organically incorporate into an ecosystem, diversify it further, and ultimately bolster it.

"Imagine if we had one Otherworld demon round these parts who ate all the pampas grass cloggin' up the forests, yeah?" she'd say, grinning away as she scribbled down her latest theory. "Or what if there were sea demons who could absorb the toxic, non-reef-safe sunscreen that gets dumped in the ocean? Think of the possibilities, Bea!"

Even though I didn't foresee the invasion-happy Otherworld demons being particularly open to such things, I enjoyed brainstorming with Doc Kai on all of her innovative hypotheses—I loved the way her science brain worked, the way she always looked at things from an unexpected angle.

"Soooo, you sure that's a no on Lahaina?" Doc Kai asked, snapping me out of my thoughts. "I'd love your on-the-ground insight."

"I . . ." I hesitated, toying with one of the many fidget-spinner contraptions I kept on my desk.

When I'd first arrived in Maui, I'd been so ready and raring to go, excited for supernatural happenings to start . . . well, *happening*. I was eager to get in there, get my hands dirty, maybe even figure out how to use my power to help Doc Kai with her various missions. I'd always been the first to suggest going out in the field—Doc Kai still ribbed me about the time I'd begged to go investigate hints of demon activity brewing in Hāna, the end point of the famous "Road to Hāna," a long, twisty highway that curved through breath-taking landscapes and waterfalls. Doc Kai had correctly suggested we go later in the afternoon, but I'd been way too eager for adventure and had ultimately convinced her to leave first thing in the morning—only to spend the entire day stuck in an endless traffic jam behind tourists who didn't understand that a journey through so much untouched terrain requires serious driving skills, respect for the long-suffering guides, and a vehicle way more robust than some dinky rental car.

Still, even though the reports that arrived in our inbox usually ended up being a whole lot of nothing, I'd been thrilled every time we got a new email, a new report, a new thing to investigate.

But after the power combo incident, I'd had to lock that down as well. Who knew what would happen if I got out in the field and there was real demon-type stuff happening . . . and I lost control of my power and destroyed something? Or someone? Or—

Well. Best not to go down *that* spiral.

Now I did everything I could to stay in the office, meticulously reviewing reports and writing up my own. That was the only kind of work that seemed safe enough.

"I really want to cross-reference the reports from last week," I finally said, pulling a regretful face. "Tosh and I have talked about building out an actual database, but I need to do a bunch of organizational background work first."

"Well, okay," Doc Kai said, giving me a puzzled smile. "You do what's calling ya, Bea, I don't want you getting bored. Science should be fun!"

"No chance of boredom here." I manufactured another smile and glanced around the office, searching for an easy subject change. "Hey, I don't know if you noticed, but I added one of Giselle's new paintings to our wall décor—I thought it looked especially fetching next to Carmelo's latest wrestling pennant."

"Yeah, shoots!" Doc Kai exclaimed, her eyes widening with delight as she admired our wall hangings. "Look at those colors together—cool enough to give me chicken skin. Our walls are definitely the best-looking on the block. Or maybe just the loudest, but . . . eh. Same thing."

Doc Kai and I had gone to great lengths to dress up the aggressively bland beigeness of the office's interior. I'd hung several of Giselle's art prints and kept an assortment of colorful toys and family photos on my desk. Doc Kai had added neon-accented swag from the local wrestling league (her boyfriend Carmelo was an enthusiastic competitor), tiny pennants and streamers weaving around the art prints. It was all very eclectic, and not the sort of décor that would've found its way into a Pottery Barn catalog, but it made perfect sense to me.

See? I firmly reminded myself as I settled in at my desk. *Look at the life you've built here. One little Karen-related slip-up isn't enough to destroy all of that! Just keep it on the straight and narrow and everything will be okay.*

I booted up my laptop, saw all the messages I'd just snoozed, and set a reminder to respond later—particularly to the itinerary, so Nate and Evie would know I was fully prepared for their visit. Then I clicked on the message Doc Kai had just sent, the one containing the newest reports.

A frisson of anticipation skittered up my spine as the message opened. It took a minute, because our office wifi was extremely slow and shared with Pika's café next door—I sometimes had to pound on our one common wall so he would stop clogging up the bandwidth watching old episodes of *Columbo* during his morning macadamia-pancake-making marathon.

As the email resolved itself into coherent formation on-screen, I skimmed through the words . . . and tried not to dwell too hard on the confusing mix of emotions that immediately bubbled up in my gut.

It was yet another set of thoroughly mundane reports, and I had to sternly remind myself that I should *not* be disappointed by that. The only emotion I should be feeling at the moment was *relief.*

But that disappointment was loud and clear, a klaxon blaring through my restless mind.

Stop it, I told myself. *You can learn to love this kind of work. If you set your mind to it, you can become the best damn boring report reviewer in the whole wide world.*

I repeated this to myself over and over again, even as my brain wandered and my body twitched with the urge to do something else, to seek out the adventure I'd always been so eager for. But at least the crushing disappointment started to ebb.

I blew out a long breath and rolled my neck, psyching myself up for the task—maybe if I acted like reviewing reports was the most epic thing in the world, it would magically become so.

I methodically went through my "let's get down to *business*" routine, silencing notifications on my phone, arranging the little quilted pillow I used to keep my posture straight, and sweeping my tangle of hair into a messy bun so it would stay off my neck as the afternoon turned even more humid. As a final touch, I slapped on my gigantic noise-canceling headphones. Sometimes I actually played music on them, but mostly they were there so I wouldn't get distracted (as an added bonus, they drowned out the dulcet tones of *Columbo* that were about to start echoing through the wall).

I glued my eyes to the screen and started to read. As usual, Tosh had helpfully streamlined all the emails that had come in, compiling everything into one cohesive report. It was still over fifty pages long, but whatever. The reports were in line with a lot of what we'd seen recently, tourists eagerly proclaiming they'd "definitely seen something really weird," only to later realize it had simply been a hallucination induced by too much sun and too many mai tais. Interestingly enough, the latest batch of hallucinations seemed to be taking monster movie-esque form, in line with the fantastical beasts I'd watched in all my dad's favorite kaiju movies as a kid.

Maybe Doc Kai will get her friendly sea monster demons after all, I thought, my lips quirking into an amused half-smile.

I focused on the screen and kept reading. I was right in the middle of a particularly scintillating description of "nature's foamy bubble bath decorating the wave's majestic crest" (this tourist must be an aspiring novelist or something), when a sweet, spicy, altogether delectable smell invaded my nostrils. I paused on the word "crest" as the scent washed over me, transporting me to a world of tinsel and ugly-but-cozy sweaters and silver bells sending their festive siren song out through snowbanks strewn with holly.

Gingerbread. Christmas time. An army of Vanessa Hudgenses!

I smiled and inhaled deeply, forgetting about the would-be novelist's purple prose for a moment.

"That's right, Bea!" a cheery voice chirped. "I made these just for you!"

"Blargh!" I exclaimed, looking up and ripping my giant headphones off. "So I guess I said that out loud?" I winced as a sharp stab of pain lanced through my temple. "And *so* loud that it apparently gave me a monster headache?"

"Shoots!" Doc Kai confirmed, beaming at me. She'd managed to sidle up to my desk without me noticing, and was holding out a plate of perfect little gingerbread people, each one bearing a cheery smile and a festive scarf and mittens.

"You did say it *really* loud—probably headache-worthy," Tosh retorted from their desk across the room. "I thought Pika might pause his episode and pop his head in to see what's going on, but—"

"But he's gotten to the 'just one more thing' part of *Columbo*," I said, cocking my head to listen. "And that's always his favorite." I turned back to Doc Kai and gave her a grateful-yet-confused smile. "Thank you, these are so cute! But how did you manage to sneak them in without me noticing?"

"Ran home, baked 'em on my lunch break!" Doc Kai crowed, waving the plate under my nose. "You were so engrossed in your work, you didn't even notice."

"Wow, lunchtime already . . ." I frowned, glancing out the window and noting that dusk was painting brilliant slashes of pink and orange across the sky. "Whoa, actually way past lunchtime. I *swear* I just started reading this report a few minutes ago. I think I managed to skip lunch entirely. And Tosh, I missed you coming in—"

"We know not to bother you when you've got the big cans on," Tosh said, miming placing headphones over their asymmetric black bob. "That's the do-not-disturb zone."

I snagged a cookie, rubbing my temple with my free hand. *Ow.* That was one big ol' monster of a headache. I must've been reading way too intensely. And had I really hyperfocused on this boring report for the entire day? Time had basically evaporated. Dammit, that meant I'd also missed my chance to visit Keala at the market.

Doc Kai flashed me one of her genial grins and left the plate on my desk before returning to her own. "I might have to do another batch to find the gingerbread balance," Doc Kai said, settling into the battered old office chair she refused to replace because she'd spent a full decade breaking it in just right. "I know it's a perilous spectrum of too sweet, too spicy, and too everything, yeah? But I'm dedicated to making all kine gingerbread until I get it *exactly* right. You deserve nothing but the best, Bea."

I froze, her seemingly innocuous words echoing through my head as the gingerbread turned to dust in my mouth.

It's nothing, I told myself sternly. My temple throbbed, as if trying to dispute that notion. *Doc Kai is a kind person who simply wanted to do something kind for you. Nothing more to it.*

I forced myself to swallow my suddenly tasteless mouthful of cookie as my gaze zeroed in on Doc Kai, scanning her for glassy eyes, a monotone voice, or anything that might indicate she hadn't made the cookies of her own free will. Had I expressed a desire for gingerbread recently? Had I mentioned that this morning, when she'd arrived at the office, and just didn't remember?

"Um, Doc Kai," I began, my voice way too high-pitched. "What prompted this little baking adventure? Not that I'm not grateful." I pasted a big smile on my face and saluted her with the cookie.

"I wanted to practice before Nate and your sister come to town." Doc Kai beamed. "They need to know that we're looking out for you, and will simply not allow you to ingest sub-par gingerbread."

"But where did that urge come from?" I said, trying to keep my voice smooth and even and *not weird*. "Like, were you inspired by something specific or did it come to you in the middle of reviewing reports or . . ."

"Truth be told, me and Carmelo were watching one of your Christmas rom-coms last night," Doc Kai said. "With all the Vanessa Hudgenses. And then we both got one craving for the stuff, and since you and Evie are doing your whole Christmas in the Spring thing during the trip—well, it seemed perfect!"

"Right," I said, pointing at her with the gingerbread person's foot and trying to ignore the unease that was still swirling through me. I ordered myself to focus on the cookie and savored another bite, enjoying the combination of spicy and sweet and the dark undertones of molasses.

Doc Kai was an excellent baker who'd been inspired by an outside force to do some baking. And her eyes looked perfectly fine—not glassy at all. There was no hint of that

robotic monotone I'd detected from The Bride. I snuck another look at her just to be sure. "I think you've already
perfected it," I said. "This is some top-level gingerbread
right here."

"Are you really not going back to the Bay for the holidays?" Tosh asked, arching a perfectly shaped eyebrow and
shaking their head so their impossibly cool silver earrings
jangled back and forth. "I know actual Christmas is still a
ways off, but we all already agreed to close the office for a
week, yes?"

"I . . . I could," I hedged, biting off the gingerbread person's left hand. "But since everyone else in my family is going somewhere . . ." I trailed off, shrugging.

For the first time ever, every single member of my family
back home had their own separate commitments for Christmas. Lucy and her wife Rose were going to have their first
extended familial holiday, bringing Lucy's mom and Rose's
parents (and Rose's cranky cat Calliope) together for a full-
out feast. Aveda and Scott were spending two weeks in LA,
where Scott had been working at a local youth center. Said
center always hosted a meal for holiday orphans and other
folks with no place to go, and Scott was happy to be in charge
of this year's edition. Leah, her girlfriend Nicole (yes, the
same Nicole who was also my former frenemy, but we'd been
forging a new bond), and her precious rescue dog Pancake
had planned an adventurous road trip up the West Coast
("We're gonna see so many fir trees, Bebe, and actual snow—
a *real* Christmas, not a California Christmas!" she'd enthused. "I bought a proper puffy jacket and everything!").

And Sam . . . well, we hadn't talked much lately, but I was
guessing he'd probably spend the holidays helping out his
parents. He was their youngest son, their obvious favorite,
and the only Fujikawa sibling who'd stayed in San Francisco
after graduating to adulthood. That also meant he'd become
responsible for fixing all their computers, doing all of their
shopping, and helping them out with various household

tasks. I didn't feel like it was fair to ask him to drop all of that for me—especially since, despite my best efforts, he still hated Christmas so much.

As for Evie and Nate, they'd be home with a new baby, barely six months old. And though I knew Evie would insist otherwise, I was guessing my presence would be more intrusive than anything else. I'd actually made up the tiniest of white lies, claiming that the holiday season would *definitely* be the busiest here at the DRG, what with all the hapless tourists in town, just waiting to be tasty demon snacks. So there was no way I could make it back. That's why she'd suggested the Christmas in the Spring visit in the first place— no, it wouldn't be with the whole family, but she and Nate and I could decorate cookies and watch movies and exchange gifts.

"Maybe we can even modify a few traditions," she'd suggested during one of our recent FaceTimes. "What do you think of, like, snow angels, but in the sand? Or decorating a palm tree with some lights?"

I didn't have the heart to tell her that 1) environmentally, this was actually very bad for palm trees and could possibly start a fire when combined with the blazing island sun and 2) palm trees decorated with Christmas lights always seemed to end up looking like giant penises.

Honestly, it was sweet that she was trying so hard to make something work for me after I'd flat-out lied to her.

So I tried to shove down my guilt and general unease, my feelings of twitchiness and uncertainty. I needed to practice putting on a happy face. I needed to show her I was really okay, and that I appreciated her efforts to bring Christmas to me.

I practiced smiling in the reflection on my laptop's fingerprint-smudged screen.

"Damn, Bea," Tosh hooted from the other side of the room. "You look like you're about to eat someone."

"Just a cookie someone," I assured them, my eyes still

focused on my blurry reflection. I tried to summon all those Christmassy feelings, the festive demeanor I'd need for Evie's visit.

I *still* looked like I was about to eat someone.

I bit off the gingerbread person's head, relishing the defiant *snap* way more than I should have.

FROM THE SUPER EPIC ARCHIVE OF BEA TANAKA'S TOTALLY LEGENDARY HOLIDAY MOVIE LETTERS

Dear Sam and Leah,

As promised in our group chat, here is my first in what will surely be a legendary series of letters detailing ALL of my fave ever holiday cinematic classics! I have two goals here. One is of course to share my many wondrous words with y'all so you can feel as if I am still physically close enough to pop by for one of our epic movie nights, wherein Sam cooks his delectable katsu for us (and Pancake gets the leftovers) and then Leah and I make his head explode by pairing it with sugary pink alcohol that must—must!!!—come in a bottle with a twist-off top and a label featuring way too much calligraphy.

My second goal is to FINALLY convert Sam, my otherwise completely perfect boyfriend, from Total Grinch to Holiday Season Fanboy. This will not be an easy task since Sam has been dead-set on hating Christmas for as long as I've known him, and has even gone so far as to ban all holiday and holiday-adjacent films from our movie night watch list. Lee, you've gotta have my back on this! Together, we can turn the tide and show Mr. Sexy Grinch that it IS the most wonderful time of the year and should be respected as such!

I'm gonna start with my absolute favorite classic that does NOT star Vanessa Hudgens. That's right, it's A Kaiju for Christmas. And yes, I can already see both of you rolling your eyes. But allow me to make my case anyway, because I'm pretty sure neither of you have ever actually watched this one all the way through.

So as you may or may not know, A Kaiju for Christmas is a bit of an oddity as far as holiday rom-coms go. Not because of the kaiju, though! No, it's because this supposed rom-com does NOT have a happily ever after. (Yes, Leah, I know—that means it's NOT a proper romance. But I saw it when I was 11, it made a huge impact on my horny tween psyche, and it still gets me right in the feels. So please allow me to make my case!)

A Kaiju for Christmas is all about a regular human dude, Thomas, who falls for a mysterious woman named Sandrine who absolutely loves the fuck out of Christmas. At 11, I certainly fancied myself a lady of extreme glamour, sophistication, and mystery—and I was already a big Christmas stan myself, so obviously I became obsessed with her. Just like Thomas.

In short order, Thomas discovers that Sandrine is actually the nefarious Christmas Kaiju, a fantastical Godzilla-esque beast with claws and fangs and glowing golden eyes who is also the size of a massive city skyscraper! (I only wished I could relate to this part, because how cool would it have been if I'd been able to stomp through the playground at my aggressively white elementary school, terrifying all the tiny racists with my earth-shattering roars!)

The Christmas Kaiju swoops in to menace various cities during the holidays—a warlock cursed Sandrine to be in this monstrous form for part of her waking life, and she has no control over when she morphs into the kaiju. All she knows is that it always seems to happen during Christmas. (Sam, don't even—I know you're reading this like, "See! Bad shit happens during the holidays, and it's extra super magnified because everyone's drunk on eggnog and unhappily reflecting on the general state of their existence." While that might be just a little bit true, it's also a time when the world is alive with extra wonder, when everything glows brighter and hope springs eternal in our gingerbread-warmed hearts. And heightened levels of eggnog can also lead to heightened levels of joy!)

Anyway, Sandrine's unpredictable kaiju-ness means her holiday-set courtship with Thomas is extra awkward, and it all culminates in a pretty hilarious scene where Thomas has to hide Sandrine's kaiju form from his judgmental family during their over-the-top annual Christmas party. But the two really do fall in love (see, Lee! True love!!), and Sandrine figures out a way to full-on celebrate the holidays as the kaiju, turning herself into a benevolent sort of monster who brings joy and festive tidings to cities around the world—like an even scarier-looking Santa Claus. Now, instead of causing destruction and fear during this magical season, she's bringing the love! Sam, take note! This could be you if you'd only get over your Grinchiness!

But then—plot twist!—the warlock who originally cursed Sandrine comes to Thomas and tells him that the spell has a second part that's about to take effect (why do these freakin' spells ALWAYS have a second part?!). At the stroke of midnight on Christmas, Sandrine will either become one hundred percent kaiju or one hundred percent human—and her one true love is to decide what her ultimate fate will be. The warlock gives Thomas a special magic talisman—a medallion with a bunch of ancient-looking runes scribbled on it—that our noble hero will imbue with his decision. The warlock also informs Thomas that he is forbidden from telling Sandrine about any of this or offering the choice to her. He has to decide himself and keep it a secret, because that's just how magical curses work. As the warlock reminds Thomas: true happiness always demands a sacrifice. You can't have pleasure without going through some major shit first!

Of course Thomas is tempted to choose humanity for Sandrine so they can enjoy the holidays (and life in general) as a normal human couple. But he ultimately realizes that Sandrine's true calling is to be the world's official Christmas Kaiju, and that she'll be miserable if she's anything else. This is her fate, her destiny, the thing she was meant to do! She's finally found a way to be happy by embracing her truest self.

And that means she can't be with Thomas.

So, for love, Thomas makes the sacrifice—he chooses the kaiju form for her and leaves her behind forever.

Yes, it's a Christmas rom-com with a rare bittersweet ending. (I know, Leah! Not really a rom-com! I am only calling it that for simplicity's sake. Whenever this movie is featured in any kind of holiday marathon, all the hate mail starts pouring in to whatever network or streamer it's on—viewers feel understandably betrayed.)

I guess . . . I always saw the beauty in Thomas's sacrifice. He knew that ultimately, fate would never allow him and Sandrine to be together like a normal couple—they just weren't built for happily ever after. So he chose the thing that would allow Sandrine to finally fulfill the destiny she was always meant to have.

Tell me you aren't crying right now!! Even if the simple facts of the plot didn't get you, my appropriately dramatic telling of it surely did!

In the end, you've got two people in an impossible situation, and one person facing an impossible choice. And it makes me swoon every fucking time.

XOXO,

Bea

CHAPTER FOUR

THERE WASN'T MUCH left of the workday, so I called it after polishing off two more gingerbread people. I saved a small mittened hand for Roger, carefully tucking it into a napkin as I shut down my laptop and gathered my things. Tosh had already left for the night, but Doc Kai was still at her desk, reviewing a new series of reports. I bid her goodbye and left the gingerbread mitten in Roger's usual spot on the porch. Hopefully he'd find it in the morning and forgive me for my earlier transgressions.

I did one last phone/social media check before leaving, and was relieved to see that my face-off against Karenzilla and the Karenzilla army had *not* gone viral. In fact, I didn't see anyone posting about it at all. I supposed it had appeared innocuous enough—I hadn't yelled at them (even though they'd totally deserved it), and it's not like my emotional projection expressed itself in a visually flashy way, like Evie's fire. And hey, Karens Causing Trouble videos were a dime a dozen these days.

So maybe I hadn't made *too* big of a scene.

I also managed to do some virtual sleuthing and track down The Bride's social media accounts—my accidental projection appeared to have worn off eventually. She was restored to her bitchy, non-glassy-eyed state, and had posted a long series of TikToks detailing every nook and cranny of "Maui's best kept and most authentic secret!" . . . the Kahului 7-Eleven.

Maybe I could count today as a win.

Although I still couldn't help but wonder about Doc Kai and the gingerbread . . .

I tried to shoo my nagging existential crisis away as I stepped into the dusky cover of evening.

Come on, Bea—immerse yourself in the peace of the night! Immerse!!

The air was still warm, the lush heat of the day melting into a dreamy haze. The Maui sky tends to drift slowly into the evening, painterly pinks and oranges morphing to a gentle gray that looks soft as a kitten's fur. And I'd never quite get over how brilliant the stars were here, as if someone had scattered fistfuls of diamond shards everywhere. I always slowed my walk back home, wrapping myself in the gentle quiet of the dark. And trying to calm that wild instinct of mine that always felt like it needed to be somewhere else, that was never satisfied, that hungered for *more*. That urge had grown exponentially since the power combo spell incident, and refused to be quiet no matter how many times I told it to shut up.

I took a few deep breaths and tried to slow my steps again.

"Hey Bea, howzit? You all pau with work?"

I turned to the familiar sight of Pika sticking his head out of his café door, brandishing a grease-splotched paper bag emitting a heavenly scent.

"Yeah, done for the day and doing pretty good, Pika," I said. Despite his advanced age, Pika refused to let any of us refer to him as "Uncle," because it made him feel old. "How 'bout you? Oh, did you refill your heart meds yet? 'Cause I can drive you to the pharmacy on Friday, just remind me tomorrow—"

"I'm all fine," he insisted, waving a dismissive hand. "Shouldn't be your worry, eh?"

"Friday," I repeated firmly. "I'll borrow Doc Kai's car and pick you up at eight, you'll be back before the brunch rush."

"Maybe," he said, raising a noncommittal eyebrow.

"Pika . . ." I forced myself to pause and take a deep breath. Yes, I needed to convince him of this, but I had to make absolutely sure I did so in a totally non-supernatural matter. Even if that meant I spent the next several hours out here arguing with him. "I'll take you for Guri-Guri ice cream on the way back," I pressed. "C'mon, we haven't had any of that sweet, sherbet-y goodness in a whole month!"

"Don't need no Guri-Guri," Pika claimed—but I saw undeniable interest percolating in his eyes.

"We can each get four scoops! The extra large cup."

"Mmm," Pika grunted, in a way that I knew meant acceptance.

"How was *Columbo* today, did he crack the case?" I asked, switching to a topic he'd like better.

"You know he did," Pika snorted, waving the paper bag at me. "I got leftover plate lunch for you. Kālua pig, rice, mac salad with crab. And yeah, an extra musubi or two, 'cause I know you gonna ask."

"Thank you," I said, my heart warming as I accepted the bag from him. "You don't need to feed me all the time, Pika. Don't get me wrong, I love your food, but—"

"Just gonna throw it out otherwise," Pika insisted. "You want come in and eat, talk story for a bit?"

"I can't tonight," I made myself say, hugging the bag to my chest. In the past, I'd always jumped at the chance to unwind from a long day with Pika, listening to all his complaints about customers, his twisty theories about specific episodes of *Columbo*, and the latest gossip from his gang of "Car Uncles," a rag-tag group of elderly local men who spent their spare time restoring ancient automobiles. But after my encounters with the Bride Squad and Doc Kai's delectable gingerbread, I just didn't trust myself. I was tired and a little stressed and there was a strong possibility I wouldn't be able to keep my messy emotions from spilling all over him.

"I get it," Pika said, waving me off. "You call that non-local boy of yours. When he gonna come back and help with the old Dodge Charger I been tryin' to get running?"

"Soon, I'm sure," I said, my smile becoming forced as my thoughts flitted to Sam and our current difficulties. I hugged the bag more tightly to my chest, warding off any further questions I didn't want to answer. "I'll see you later, Pika. Hope Columbo cracks the case tomorrow."

"He will, you gotta have faith," Pika said, nodding at me. "And remember, you said we gonna get *four* scoops of Guri-Guri on Friday."

"Friday—four scoops," I agreed, waving good-bye to him.

My heartbeat sped up as I walked away, my brain locking itself more firmly into the spiral I couldn't seem to pull out of. Yes, I'd managed to avoid further conversation . . . but I'd still convinced him to do something he initially hadn't wanted to. Was that simply due to my natural, non-supernaturally-enhanced powers of persuasion, or—

It was the Guri-Guri—he agreed because of the four scoops. You didn't do anything. You didn't accidentally mind-control him. No mind control is more powerful than the promise of ice cream!

I tried to breathe slowly, to let the luscious scent of Pika's savory pork soothe my racing mind. Of course, the more I tried to calm myself down, the more my brain felt the need to spiral, loudly and helpfully reminding me of all the things I'd managed to rationalize away in the space of a mere twenty-four hours.

The Bride, Doc Kai's gingerbread, Pika . . .

And what if there was more? What if my emotions were spilling onto people so easily now that I wasn't even aware of it?

I sank to the ground next to the big dumpster behind the main drag, the one the chickens loved so much. My heartbeat sped up again as I plunged deeper into my spiral, my breath coming and going in little gasps as panic sliced through me.

Was the supervillain path my inevitable destiny?

Would I eventually have to separate from everyone, to remove myself from the office with Doc Kai and Tosh and never get ice cream with Pika or malasadas with Keala ever again?

In addition to my supervillain destiny, was I also meant to be totally alone?

I leaned my head back against the wall of the mochi shop, closing my eyes and forcing my breath to slow and even. Trying to immerse myself in the calming beauty of night once more. I imagined myself breathing through all of my confusing, out-of-control feelings—casting them aside and watching them evaporate into the air.

When I finally felt a sense of equilibrium returning, I carefully got to my feet and picked up Pika's bag of food again. Maybe I'd feel better after eating.

I took a step toward my bungalow, conjuring all of the encouraging, empowering thoughts I could.

You are strong and disciplined and have a shit-ton of self-control—Bea Tanaka 2.0! You are no longer an attention-seeking Christmas tree who's definitely going to be "trouble." You—

I was stopped in my tracks by a sudden rustling sound emanating from behind the dumpster. It was a faint rustling, like a mouse was rooting around in the random pieces of overflow garbage that always ended up back there. Or maybe it was one of the Makawao chickens seeking dinner.

"Everything okay?" I called out, feeling slightly ridiculous. "Roger, is that you?"

rustlerustlerustleRUSTLE

All that scrabbling around was growing more intense, like whatever was back there was really getting into it.

I probably should've just ignored it and gone home and eaten my delicious dinner from Pika. That would have been the smart thing to do, especially after the long, anxiety-inducing day I'd had.

But sometimes my natural instincts kick in before I have the chance to do the smart thing.

Suddenly I was stepping toward the dumpster and peering around the back of it, trying to home in on the weird sounds. If it *was* Roger, I could let him know there was a perfectly good gingerbread mitten with his name written all over it. No need to ingest actual garbage.

"Hello?" I said, blinking in an attempt to get the shadows behind the dumpster to come into focus.

I saw a faint shape, way too small to be a chicken. Maybe it *was* a mouse? But, no, it had a strange shape to it. It looked like it had . . . spikes? And that swoop right there, was that a claw of some kind?

What the hell was I looking at?

As if sensing my presence, the thing's movements got more frantic. It still appeared to be rooting around for something, and now it was doing so with more gusto, that shadowy thing that might be a claw slicing through the air.

"Hey!" I said, raising my voice. "I'm not sure if you're threatening me or waving hello, but, um . . . show yourself! Bea Tanaka, official demonology expert with Maui's Demonology Research Group, right down the road!"

Oh god. Why couldn't I ever sound cool and professional? Also, why did I think this creature needed to know our office location?

The creature went still, its claw pausing in midair.

Then it launched itself directly at my face.

"Fuck!" I screamed, leaping out of the way.

It soared past me and landed on the ground near the dumpster, its claw waving even more wildly.

I took a tentative step toward it, now able to make out its shape. It was tiny—no bigger than a mouse, really, but the similarities ended there. It was a minuscule monster that looked like some unholy mashup of a dinosaur, a lobster, and Godzilla. Spikes ran up its back, and its hands were those lobster-like claws—which were now snapping at me indignantly. Its eyes glowed bright gold, and when it opened its mouth to hiss at me, I saw that it boasted an impressive row of sharp fangs. Its skin glowed with an iridescent sheen, akin to a beetle's shell—murky blues shifting to violent neon pink in the dim light.

"Holy shit," I blurted out. "Are you a *kaiju*?! Only, like, way smaller than the ones in movies?"

The thing waved a claw again and growled at me, its bright gold eyes meeting mine.

scared scared SCARED

I gasped, jumping back. Was that this thing's *thoughts*? That were currently echoing through my head? Did we have some kind of weird mind-meld situation going on, or . . .

That Otherworld darkness inside of me pulsed, conveying satiated pleasure—as if I'd fed it a very tasty snack.

SCARED I can't please please scared please

I shook my head, trying to rid myself of the mini kaiju's intrusive thoughts.

Then it launched itself at my head again.

A scream bubbled up in my throat, but I clamped my lips shut and ducked, dropping to the ground. I slammed my hands over my ears and shut my eyes tight, my ragged breathing echoing in my ears.

And I tried like mad to shove down every bit of confusion and worry I'd felt throughout the day, even as those emotions coalesced into a gut-wrenching hurricane spinning its way through my bloodstream.

The louder my emotions were, the more I wanted to scream. I clamped my lips tighter, unwilling to let out so much as a peep. My power had a secondary characteristic, a small level-up I'd received during a supernatural earthquake years ago. It meant I could sometimes destroy things by vocalizing my projection—Evie called it my Canary Cry.

No matter what I was seeing, what I was feeling, I needed to keep it safely locked away. Who knew what could happen if I unleashed my currently heightened feelings all over the peaceful streets of Makawao?

I could not scream. I could not feel. I could not do *anything*. So how could I take on this mini kaiju?

I turned around slowly, lowering my hands from my ears, trying to figure out where the kaiju had landed.

All I saw was the dumpster. The bare ground. The bag of food I'd dropped, its enticing grease splotches glistening in the light of the moon.

There was nothing. No sign of anything supernatural. Just me and the garbage, hanging out in this peaceful-as-fuck alley.

"Bea?"

Yet again, I managed to stifle my scream as I whirled around to find . . . Pika. Standing over me and toting a big bag of garbage he was clearly about to throw out.

"What're you doing back here?" he queried, his bushy brows drawing together.

"N-nothing," I said, scanning the spot where I swore I'd just seen a tiny fantastical creature only moments ago—the spot that was now completely, irrefutably empty. Not a creature was stirring. Not even a freaking mouse. "I guess I'm doing nothing."

CHAPTER FIVE

I ASKED PIKA about five kazillion times if he'd seen anything weird. I did not specify that "weird" meant a freaky mini kaiju who I had possibly just communicated with in telepathic fashion. He insisted that the only thing he'd seen was "your fool ass muckin' round the garbage."

Goddamn frakkin' frakballs. Was I now hallucinating supernatural creatures out of *nothing*, just like all the drunk tourists who kept clogging up the DRG inbox with their fevered imaginings?! I mean, some of them had hallucinated kaiju-like creatures—so my own fevered imaginings weren't even that original! I hadn't overdosed on sun and mai tais, but I *had* been stressed all day, spiraling down my anxiety spirals extra hard . . .

I dashed off a quick text to Doc Kai and Tosh, explaining what I may or may not have seen and couching it in some jokey self-deprecation. I promised to write up a report on the probably imagined "incident" the next day, but added a hasty disclaimer that my subsequent interviews with the witness (in this case, myself) were unlikely to produce much in the way of helpful information.

I closed my eyes and took a few calming breaths—a practice I'd already engaged in so many times today. The harder I tried to stay out of trouble, the more it seemed to find me. The darkness inside of me pulsed, as if it absolutely loved that idea.

Calm down, I thought at the darkness, picturing it as a jagged shadow floating inside my chest. *At least let me eat dinner—that's a fairly benign activity, right? Not too many ways to get in trouble doing that!*

Luckily, Pika's bag of mouth-watering food had miraculously survived its action-packed journey home. I let myself into my bungalow, flicked on the light, and took two steps away from the door so that I was in the small kitchen/dining area. My bungalow, though a freestanding structure, was basically a studio apartment—almost everything was contained in the same space. The kitchen was steps from the entrance, my bed was steps from the dining table. I'd Tetrised a single cushy armchair somewhere in between. The wall behind said chair boasted one giant window, which served up gorgeous views of palm trees and green and the lush rolling hills that led up to the volcano.

Doc Kai had managed to get a housing stipend written into one of her grant budgets, and when she'd presented the bungalow to me as my official Makawao living quarters, she'd apologized for the postage-stamp size. But I'd loved it instantly. Yes, it was teeny-tiny, but it was also the first space I'd inhabited that was entirely mine. No one could complain about my haphazard décor, my penchant for staying up until 3 a.m. watching Christmas movies, or my messy jumble of tinkering projects that spilled all over the non-eating side of my kitchen table (I only had room for one table, so said table had to multitask). Right now, I was working on a motorized iPad stand for Pika, so he could move *Columbo* around more efficiently while he was cooking and avoid getting neck and/or eye strain.

I did sometimes miss the unique feeling of living in Team Tanaka/Jupiter's HQ back in San Francisco, a ramshackle Victorian in the lower Haight where the team lived and worked. There was always *something* happening in the Victorian, our messy found family spilling in and out of every room and making the whole place feel bright, bustling, *alive*.

I felt a little pang of loneliness as I spread my solo meal out over the eating side of the table. The whole family would have gone all in on this feast—especially Evie, who always relished finding the most delicious, soul-filling foodstuffs wherever she went.

Sometimes I missed my sister so ferociously, it felt like my heart was calling out to hers, all the way across the ocean. Of course I could never actually *tell* her that, since I'd spent so much of my life chafing under her rules, struggling for more independence, and trying to be as rebellious as possible. And now that I was trying to be all grown-up and out on my own . . . well. It felt like I *extra* couldn't tell her.

But I did miss her. I missed them all.

As if on cue, my phone buzzed with an incoming text—Scott, asking me yet again if we could try out another round of experiments on the power combo spell. I'd successfully put him off for the past month, replying with breezy messages claiming I was too busy at work. I was ashamed to tell him that I simply couldn't trust myself to do any kind of power combo spell ever again.

I texted back a bland deflection, blaming work once more. Then I focused on the very important business of snarfing down my dinner (superlative as usual, my compliments to Pika and the inspirational powers of Peter Falk) while scrolling through my phone, trying to chase my loneliness away.

Once I'd exhausted the wonders of social media and the puzzle game I'd already beat four times, my gaze wandered to the small shelf I'd rigged above the microwave. Said shelf held a haphazard mix of spices, sauces, and oils, but my eye landed where it usually did—on the small eraser propped up in front of a jar of furikake, the one shaped like a cheesy first-place trophy with an ostentatious #1 emblazoned across the front.

It was an eraser Sam had won during a Calculus Bee we'd competed in during high school, back when we were still warring academic rivals constantly trying to outsmart each other. We'd continued that dynamic into adulthood, although at some point, it had morphed into something like best friendship. He and Leah and I had become a perfectly balanced trio: Leah's sunny sweetness counteracting Sam's cocky assuredness, my penchant for chaos swirling around both of them in a way that ensured things were never boring. And Sam and I had maintained our constant, mostly good-natured bickering, keeping a running score going between us.

But then, during my drama-filled exploits with my Mom-Demon, we'd grown closer. We'd sort of accidentally kissed. We'd started sleeping together, no strings attached—an especially good idea since both of us tended to get bored easily and dated around with wild abandon. And we'd promised not to fall in love with each other.

We had, of course, failed spectacularly on that last one.

He'd given me the eraser as a symbol—he claimed he'd fallen in love with me *first*, and that meant we no longer needed to compete with each other. No more keeping score, because he wanted to give his heart to me freely. And I was surprised to realize that all I wanted was to do the same.

We'd only been officially together for about a month when I'd moved out to Maui, and for a while, we kept things going strong—furiously texting, sexting, constant FaceTimes. I'd discovered an addictive online game wherein you challenged your opponent to solve increasingly difficult math problems and equations, and we'd played that for weeks, getting so into it that Leah had teasingly asked me if we were using it as foreplay (I'd had to ask if she wanted a serious answer to her joke question, because *seriously* . . . of course we were).

The equations generated by the game had eventually proved too easy for us, so we'd started making up our own and set up a special version for the two of us on a private Discord server. Sam had even recorded his own take on the "reward" the game always bestowed upon the winner, which was a way-too-excited movie trailer–style voiceover guy declaring, "WOWIE, LOOK AT YOU—YOU JUST MATHED SO HARD!"

It never failed to make me laugh.

I'm not sure when things started changing, or if our daily texts dwindling and our phone sex sessions starting to feel more obligatory was just a natural progression for a long-distance relationship. But if I had to pinpoint one turning point, it would probably be last Christmas—my first in Maui, just three months after moving away.

I'd stayed on the island because at the time, work had at least *seemed* busy. We were still in the thick of investigating the supernatural-seeming incidents that had led Doc Kai to form the DRG in the first place, and I'd thought maybe Shasta would set her sights on Maui at some point. Me staying put had seemed imperative, both for my original mission of finding independence and excelling in my new job and my new mission to protect my sister and her future offspring.

Doc Kai and Carmelo had invited me over to their place for Christmas, and I'd eagerly accepted. I always loved the chance to experience something new, and all the friends I'd managed to make would be in attendance—Doc Kai and Carmelo had known Tosh for years, everyone in Makawao knew Pika, and I'd introduced the gang to Keala and Giselle. I figured that if I was missing some of the beloved traditions I'd built up over the last few years in San Francisco—stringing popcorn garlands with Nate while I forced him to watch an endless stream of holiday rom-coms, singing Christmas karaoke with Evie at the top of our lungs, helping Leah dress Pancake up as a very cranky elf—I'd be able to recreate them somehow, even though I was far from home.

And then sweet Sam had surprised me by showing up on my doorstep on Christmas Eve.

"How are you *here*?!" I'd shrieked, throwing my entire body at his, my arms wrapping around his broad torso and hugging him tight.

"Bea . . . *ow*!" he'd laughed, gently adjusting my arms so I wasn't squeezing the life out of him. "See, there are these things called airplanes—"

"Shut up!" I yelped, burying my face in his chest and breathing him in. He always smelled deliciously woodsy with just a hint of spice—sandalwood and cinnamon, like you were ensconced deep in the forest and had gotten a whiff of someone baking something mouthwateringly rich. "*God*. I miss you so much."

"I miss you too," he murmured, stroking my hair. "Though I'm surprised you admitted it first. Y'know, if we were still keeping track of points—"

"But we're not," I retorted, turning my face up to look at him. "Because you said I *won*, remember? Like, I won *forever*. No taking that back."

"I'd never dream of it," he said, his eyes searching my face in that way that made me go weak in the knees. He tapped my forehead, his gaze turning heartbreakingly tender. "I've missed this crinkle. The one you always get when you're thinking extra hard."

I let out a happy sigh. Yes, we'd communicated near constantly in the months since I'd been gone, but looking at a picture, hearing a voice over the phone—it just wasn't the same as getting to *touch* someone. To study every single one of their features as they went through the gentle quirks and subtle expressive changes of everyday life.

I did that now, greedily drinking him in like I'd been stranded on a desert island for a hundred years. His jet-black hair still had that perfect swoop to it, but it had grown a little longer, flopping rakishly over his forehead. His dark eyes still danced with irresistible mischief, but now there was a hint of something soft underneath that—like he was also paying extra special attention to memorizing my face, all the ways it had changed in the time we'd been apart. I noticed that he was holding me more tightly than usual, and that neither of us had let go yet.

"What are you wearing?" he asked, giving me an amused once-over. "Is this some kind of extreme elf cosplay?"

"It's a sleep onesie," I said, making a face at him. "Decorated to make me look like Santa's cutest little helper. I'm doing what I can to keep things festive. But seriously: I thought you were finally about to have the full Fujikawa family Christmas your parents have always dreamed of. I know any kind of holiday celebration is basically your worst nightmare, but weren't Ms. Bore and Mr. Brag actually deigning to pay y'all a visit this year?"

Ms. Bore and Mr. Brag were the nicknames Sam and I had given to his siblings, Emily and Alex. Both were very accomplished in classic overachiever Asian terms—Emily was a fancy professor, Alex was a fancy doctor. And they always made sure that everyone around them knew it.

One of their favorite pastimes was belittling Sam—in their eyes, his mechanic's job, his lack of a college degree, and his surface himbo tendencies made him the undeniable fuck-up of the family. It gave me more joy than it probably should have that Sam was actually his parents' absolute favorite. He was the child who took care of them—the child who stayed. And frankly, the way he approached life was way more fun than his snide, snobby, boring-ass siblings. (And yes, these are the same siblings I'd done a little light mind control on. I know it was wrong, but after hearing these descriptions, can you blame me?)

"Ms. Bore and Mr. Brag are indeed in the house," Sam confirmed. "Well, the house back in San Francisco. That's actually why I was able to get away. They can be on 'rent duty for a few days. And I really could not bear the thought of you, the world's biggest Christmas freak, being alone on the actual day."

"I wouldn't have been *alone*," I said, willing myself not to melt into a big pile of goo. "I'm going to a friend's place—"

"Let me rephrase." Sam pulled me closer. His gaze turned serious—another thing that always made my heart do backflips. "I couldn't bear the thought of being away from you on your favorite holiday."

Well, that did it—I was thoroughly goo-ified.

I leaned in, closing the last bits of distance between us to press my lips to his. He responded immediately, his hands sliding up my back to cradle my neck, stroke my face, tangle in my hair. His tongue swept my lips apart, igniting all my nerve endings and making me sigh against him.

"So I was planning on marathoning my favorite Christmas movies tonight," I murmured against his mouth. "But I know you hate that shit—"

"I hate the holiday itself," he said, his lips drifting to my neck. I closed my eyes and leaned into it, electrified to feel his mouth on me after all these months apart. "Growing up, it was never a good time. I had to deal with Emily and Alex acting like entitled little shits and hiding the one really cool off-brand Transformer my parents always saved up to buy for me. And then in adulthood, it's become about me figuring out how to keep my parents from being sad all day because their two eldest children can't be bothered to pick up the phone. So this . . ." He nipped the delicate flesh of my ear-lobe and I let out a little squeak. "*This* is a pretty big fucking improvement."

He pulled back and arched an eyebrow at me, Cocky Himbo Sam surfacing for a moment. "You know, this is our first actual Christmas together—like, as a couple. Maybe you can show me just how amazing the holiday is."

"I can *definitely* do that." I took his hand and led him inside my bungalow. "But first, let me give you the tour . . ."

He pulled me in for another long kiss. "No offense, Bea, but I don't know that your interior design skills are the thing I'm most interested in right now—"

"The bed's over there!" I managed between kisses. "End of tour!"

We didn't stop kissing as I led him to the bed in question, dragging him down into the fluffy mattress and letting it envelop us both like the softest of clouds.

"You know, I did have the perfect belated Christmas gift planned for whenever we were going to be together," I mused, trailing kisses down his jawline, delighting in the goosebumps peppering his forearms.

"Tell me," he said, his voice rough with wanting.

"Weellllll . . ." I nipped at his neck, my teeth scraping lightly against his skin in a way that I knew drove him wild.

"I was going to wrap my body in strategically placed yet very festive ribbons—"

"Strategically placed because you're not wearing anything else," he said, his hand drifting to the top button of my onesie, fingertips grazing the bare skin of my collarbone. I shivered.

"Of course. And then I was going to tell you to unwrap your present, use the ribbons to tie me to the bed, and—"

"*Fuck,*" he groaned, his hand sliding to my breast.

"Among other things," I agreed, trying valiantly not to completely lose my train of thought. "You know, I'm also not wearing anything underneath this elf onesie, which I'm guessing puts me on the naughty list."

He growled in the back of his throat, a sound that always reverberated through my whole body, nearly sending me over the edge. And I lost my train of thought entirely.

Later, snuggled up against him, feeling warm and cozy and yes, *very* naughty . . . that's when things started to go wrong.

"Baby," he'd murmured, toying idly with my hair. "I need to talk to you about something."

"What is it?" My spine straightened as nerves skittered through my gut. Yeah, so I was new to the whole couple thing, but I was pretty sure "I need to talk to you about something" never led anywhere good. Like, no one ever says "I need to talk to you about something—you've magically been granted a forever supply of ice cream!" or "I need to talk to you about something—I've invented a Star Trekkian transporter device so that we may now live in separate places while still managing to in-person bone as much as we want!"

One of the things that worked best about Sam and me was that we were both fully dedicated to fun. When we'd entered into our initial "friends with very sexy benefits" arrangement, we'd promised each other that we'd end it as soon as it *stopped* being fun. But the good times and sheer joy we got from being with each other never seemed to end, not even when we'd upgraded to committed coupledom. We hadn't had many "I need to talk to you about something" moments.

"The other reason I wanted to come out here," he said, his voice hesitant, "is because I don't know if I'll be able to do that for a while."

I adjusted my position next to him, tilting my face up to meet his eyes, my arm still slung across his chest. "What do you mean?"

"It's my parents," he said, brushing a particularly unruly lock of purple hair off my face. "They're getting older, and they need my help a lot more. My mom had a fall last week—"

"Oh no, is she okay?" I blurted out. "Why didn't you tell me?"

"There was nothing you could really do from here and I didn't want to freak you out. And that's not . . . I mean, when we talk, I want to enjoy it as much as I can since you're so far away. I don't want to dwell on stuff that's maybe not so fun. She *is* okay, but she tweaked her back and has to do physical therapy. We don't have any other family around, and Emily and Alex are never in town for very long. So . . ." He pasted on a cheesy, self-deprecating grin. "Lastborn son here, just trying to do his filial duty. You know how it is."

"I, um . . ." My cheeks heated. The truth was, I had no idea. Yes, Sam and I were both the babies of our families, and we'd both been happy accidents. But while he was the apple of his adoring parents' eyes, Evie and I were basically orphans at this point. I couldn't think fast enough on how to smooth that over, how to magically make his statement not awkward.

Sam was right, our calls were doses of pure pleasure, soaking up as much of the other person as we could before returning to the realities of our daily lives. We didn't tend to dwell on anything too heavy.

"Sorry," Sam said, wincing. "Shit. That was truly fucking thoughtless."

"No, no." I rubbed his shoulder in what I hoped was a reassuring manner. "That's so much, Sam, and I'm sorry I can't, like . . . empathize in a specific way? But I am here for you, whatever you have to do. I could come back with you to San Francisco—"

"No." He shook his head vehemently. "You're not giving this up, Bea—you *can't*. Evie keeps talking about how much you're thriving out here. You wanted this so bad, you *made* it happen, and I'm so proud of you. You wanted to make your world bigger, remember? And you're absolutely doing that."

"We both wanted that—to make *our* worlds bigger. Together," I murmured. But my voice was so quiet, I wasn't sure he heard me.

And then he was kissing me again and it didn't matter anyway.

When I think back to that moment now, I can't help but feel that we kissed more desperately after that, like we were trying to hold on to something that wasn't even gone yet.

We had an incredible few days together—Sam got to meet all my local friends, I introduced him to the best Maui cuisine, and we spent the majority of our alone time together naked. Shockingly, grouchy Pika took a particular shine to my "non-local boy," since Sam shared two of his primary interests: cooking and cars. He'd heartily introduced Sam to the Car Uncles, and they'd spent a whole afternoon working on the Frankensteined engine of an ancient jalopy. I'd hovered around, knowing they'd offer me any random spare parts for my tinkering projects when they were done.

My heart fluttered whenever I pictured Sam and Pika hunched over the engine together, Sam saying something that made Pika laugh so hard, tears streamed down his weathered cheeks. Sam looked up while Pika was laughing and gave me one of his sly, slow smiles, sweat beading enticingly down those muscular forearms that had been bronzed by the Maui sun.

But even though we'd rededicated ourselves to fun with a vengeance, there was still this *thing* that now existed between us. Maybe it was uncertainty. Maybe it was the sense that things were shifting, changing. Or maybe two supposedly reformed, easily distracted players simply realized they weren't the best fit to keep that long-distance love going. We'd possibly crossed over into the "this is *not* fun" realm, but we kept stubbornly hanging on to each other anyway.

And I didn't know how to fix it. Or how to describe what needed fixing. That probably bothered me most of all.

After Sam returned to San Francisco, the general tone of our communication was different. Every time I was about to text him about something silly, every time I thought about sending a flirty pic, I found myself plunged into a swirl of doubt. Sam was dealing with hard, serious things regarding his parents—their roles were inevitably flipping, so *he* was now taking care of *them*. As an almost orphan, I knew there were things about all that I could never hope to understand. And I didn't want him to feel like he had one more obligation, one more person to worry about. I wanted to be that fun harbor for him. But I worried that wasn't what he needed, either.

So after a fifteen-minute spiral wherein I'd scrutinize a sexy selfie, then wonder if sending a sexy selfie was goofy or shallow or just not what he needed right now . . . or if (horror of horrors) his phone screen was in view of his parents, who probably did *not* need to see a detailed photographic study of their beloved baby son's girlfriend's breasts . . .

Yeah, I'd just end up deleting the photo, never to be sent.

And since Sam had a lot of physical therapy and doctor's appointments to take his mom to, he was suddenly way more busy and almost never had a moment to talk. His calls, texts, photos started to dwindle as well.

Now I wasn't sure what was going on with us. I certainly hadn't mentioned my freak-out over the power combo spell, that Otherworld darkness that had taken up residence inside of me, or any of the weirdness that had happened since. And even though I didn't want to talk to him about it, I didn't want to talk to *anyone* about it . . . well, that made me feel farther away from him than just about anything.

I savored my last bits of kālua pig, still staring at the goofy eraser propped on my kitchen shelf. I glanced at my phone, and without even quite realizing what I was doing, clicked over to the Discord channel that contained our private math game. I clicked on the last message, which was from several weeks ago, and heard Sam's voice declare: "YOU JUST MATHED SO HARD!"

I couldn't help but giggle.

Impulsively, I tapped on his name under my contacts. Yes, it was three hours later in San Francisco, but maybe he was still awake. He used to stay up late. Did he still? Or was his current routine so exhausting, he fell asleep as soon as he set foot in his apartment? Hmm, was he even staying at his own place? Maybe he'd moved in with his parents—

"Bea?" There was his deep voice, echoing through the line. I instantly felt warm all over.

"Hey baby," I said, my gaze going to the eraser again. "I was just thinking about you—"

"Is everything all right?" he cut in, his voice tipping into alarm. "It's late—"

"Not that late here," I countered, a bit stung. He did *not* sound happy to hear from me.

"Right, the time difference," he said, almost to himself. Now he sounded harried, distracted. Like an ER doctor I'd callously pulled out of surgery for no good reason. "I sort of associate late-night calls with emergencies—"

"Even calls from . . . your girlfriend? Sam, I . . . I'm sorry if I interrupted something, I really just wanted to say hi. There's no emergency."

"Oh, good. That's good," he breathed out, relieved. I pictured his broad shoulders untensing as he ran a hand through his floppy swoop of hair. "Listen, I actually have to go—my parents have some of their friends over, and they're doing karaoke and . . . what?"

"I didn't say anything," I started—then realized he was talking to someone else, someone who was actually in the room with him.

"No, Auntie Chrissy already had seven bobas, do *not* let

her tell you—okay, okay, just give me a sec." I heard some shuffling around on the other end of the line. "Bea? Sorry, let me call you back," he said, sounding even more stressed. "I have to deal with a house full of unruly seniors."

"Oh, that sounds—" But he hung up before I could finish my sentence.

I stared at my silent phone and let out a long breath.

Would it be pathetic if I played that little clip of him saying "YOU JUST MATHED SO HARD" over and over again, pretended like he was right here saying it directly to me, his irresistible mouth quirking into a teasing half-smile?

Yeah, probably.

I released yet another dramatic sigh and swept my empty food carton into the trash (another perk of eating Pika's leftovers every night—no dishes). Then I moped my way over to the bed, busted out my laptop, and cued up my favorite holiday rom-com that does not star multiple Vanessa Hudgenses, *A Kaiju for Christmas.*

Hey, I'd already had one extremely disconcerting kaiju-riffic encounter tonight—might as well lean into it. And I was definitely in the mood for a melancholy ending, which was not something the rest of my holiday movie library tended to provide.

A Kaiju for Christmas sat at an interesting cross-section of my interests—Christmas and romance and the Japanese monster movies I'd grown up watching with my dad before he'd been consumed by his grief over my mother and left Evie and me behind. I used to long for him the way I longed for my mother, but our most recent encounter had showed me just how narcissistic and self-involved he'd always been. He was basically a nonentity in our lives now, but I thought about him occasionally—he'd actually been born and raised in Hawai'i, and was responsible for Evie's and my obsession with spam in all its glorious configurations.

Keala had asked me once if being here made me feel more connected to him, or if he was perhaps the reason I'd been drawn to Hawai'i in the first place. I'd thought about that

long and hard . . . and I'd had to say no. Doc Kai's big ol'
brain and the promise of adventure and monster-fighting
had brought me to the island, and I saw no scrap of my dead-
beat dad in the beautiful, generous Makawao community I'd
been lucky enough to become part of.

But sometimes I did worry that his inherent selfishness
lurked somewhere in me—right alongside that pesky darkness I couldn't seem to ignore. It was selfishness, after all,
that had powered many of the villain-esque decisions I was
now so ashamed of.

I thought about that as I watched the movie. I wondered
what choice I'd make, were I in Thomas's shoes. Would I be
able to let Sam go if it was truly what was best for him? Or
would I hold on at all costs because I wanted him so badly
and my own impulsive desires trumped all?

I turned that question over and over in my mind as the
movie unfolded, keeping one eye on my phone and hoping
Sam would call me back.

I was still waiting when I finally drifted off to sleep.

CHAPTER SIX

I WAS AWAKENED by the decidedly non-dulcet tones of a tropical rainstorm. Sheets of water lashed against my window, shaking the glass. Outside, the palm trees were being blown into swoopy diagonals, fighting hard to remain upright. I attempted to sit up in bed and was immediately hit with overwhelming pain stabbing directly into my right temple.

Ow. How did I have a hangover when I hadn't had anything resembling alcohol the night before? That seemed massively unfair.

I massaged my temple with one hand and felt around for my phone with the other—I swore I'd left it lying right next to my pillow, pathetically waiting for Sam to call back. I needed to see if Doc Kai had texted me. In the case of a full-on rainstorm, we usually decided to leave the office closed for the day and hunker down at home. Sometimes I braved the short walk over to Doc Kai and Carmelo's place so we could hunker down together. Carmelo would make his special "Filipino loco moco," which used longanisa in place of the hamburger patty. The hearty combo of sweet meat and rice smothered in thick gravy and topped with a perfectly runny egg was the ideal rainy-day meal. Actually, I'd argue it was the ideal meal for any occasion and/or weather condition.

I felt around some more, searching underneath my pillow, but my phone was nowhere to be found. And say, the laptop

I'd fallen asleep watching didn't appear to be on the bed, either.

I frowned, scanning the cozy space of the bungalow, and finally spotted both laptop and phone perched on the kitchen table, plugged in to charge. My frown deepened. I almost never remembered to plug in any of my devices at the end of the day, meaning I was fairly accustomed to waking up to my phone somewhere near my pillow, its battery at a pitiful three percent. Evie was constantly getting on my case about it.

I stood and crossed the room, still massaging my throbbing temple. Clearly I was groggy, and did not recall an unexpected bout of electronics-related responsibility from the night before. Maybe I'd snag an extra guava malasada today— the additional sugar boost would make me more alert.

But I stopped in my tracks before I even got to the kitchen, the scent of something wholly unfamiliar invading my nostrils. It was fresh, citrus-y, vaguely astringent . . . wait a second, was that *Lemon Pledge*? Like, a cleaning product? I sniffed the air more vigorously and scanned the bungalow again.

It was totally spotless. More spotless than when I'd moved in. More spotless than *ever*.

My forehead crinkled. Had I engaged in sleep *cleaning*? Like sleepwalking, but way more productive and completely out of character?

I forced myself to make the last three steps to the kitchen and unplugged my phone, glancing at the screen. No messages, nothing new from Doc Kai or Tosh. That was odd, especially since I'd texted them about my mini-kaiju encounter (well, probable hallucination) the night before. Even if we were having a rain day, I still needed to write up that report. I was about to send a message to our group thread, when there was a loud knock at the door.

I quickly shot off a text to my coworkers, eyes glued to the phone screen as I robotically headed over to answer the door, my foggy, aching brain trying to understand why I was suddenly living in a totally clean bungalow with fully charged devices. That really wasn't my style *at all*.

I opened the door and was pelted in the eye by rain streaking aggressively through the muggy tropical air. I threw an arm over my face and jumped back instinctively, throwing the door open wider.

"I'm assuming whoever's there is not a murderer, or if you are . . . well, you had to work pretty hard to get to my doorstep in this weather," I called out. "So while I'm not about to let you straight-up murder me, you can at least come in for coffee or whatever."

"That is extremely touching, Bea," a very wry, very familiar voice said. "But I *really* have to pee, so . . ."

I lowered my arm and swiped away the last bits of water that had just smacked me in the face. Evie, Nate, Aveda, and Sam were all standing in front of me—well, Evie was already booking it to the bathroom, Nate casting a worried glance at her retreating form. I blinked a few times, as if they were a mirage that was about to disappear.

"Oh!" I exclaimed. "You're all . . . here."

"We are," Nate agreed, stepping forward to give me a hug. "And we apparently picked the worst day to fly in, we were originally going to—"

"To surprise you!" Aveda piped up, beaming at me and tossing her trademark power ponytail over her shoulder.

"Surprise me by . . . being a week early?" I said, still trying to process what was happening.

"We're not," Nate said, pulling back from the hug and fixing me with a concerned stare. "Have you not been receiving the updated itineraries I've been sending you? This is when we were scheduled to come in—"

"And the surprise part is me and Sam!" Aveda crowed, her black eyes sparkling with excitement. She gave Sam a little shove. "For goodness' sake, greet your beautiful girlfriend! She looks like she's in shock!"

"She is," I said, attempting a slight smile as Sam wordlessly enfolded me in his arms. I closed my eyes and relaxed against him, breathing in his woodsy, spicy scent. Trying to ground myself in something real. "Sorry, y'all, I must have gotten the dates mixed up. I really thought you weren't coming until next week!"

"Classic Bea, always in chaos," Aveda said, grinning affectionately. "But don't worry, with this weather, we figured today was kind of a wash anyway . . ." She frowned at the rain that was still beating against my window. "Hopefully, things will clear up tomorrow so we can have a beach day and I can finally practice all my new surfing moves. Scott says I'm a natural—practically pro level after only a few weeks of his lessons!"

"The scary thing is, she's not exaggerating—she is actually that good," Evie said, exiting the bathroom. She crossed the room, and Sam let me go so she could envelop me in a tight hug. "Hey, Little Sister. I'm so happy to see you."

"Same," I said. "It's . . . it's so wonderful to see you all."

I hugged Evie back, trying to let go of every bit of confusion I was currently experiencing. My headache, at least, seemed to be easing, that sharp stab of pain dulling to a faint pulse.

How had I managed to completely fuck up the dates of the visit I'd been thinking about nonstop? Had my overtaxed brain somehow realized what was happening and instructed me to deep clean the bungalow while I was still asleep? And hadn't I just been talking to Sam the night before?

Maybe that was why he'd seemed so weird and distracted and had never called me back. He was trying to keep the surprise under wraps.

"Sorry," I said, lightly smacking myself on the head as I pulled away from Evie. "I just woke up, so I'm kind of disoriented. What do y'all want to do today, since nature may not be cooperating with the whole beach situation? We could manage some lovely indoor activities, though, like making cookies or watching movies or—"

"Evie needs to rest," Aveda proclaimed, giving an officious nod.

"Not gonna disagree with that," Evie said, letting loose with a monster yawn and rubbing her pregnant belly. "It was a long flight, and we should go settle in at our hotel. And we thought maybe you and Sam would want some quality time together. By yourselves."

"Oh . . . okay," I said, my gaze going to Sam.

He hadn't said a word since they'd arrived. I studied him, trying to assess what was going through his brain. He just stared back, his dark eyes unreadable. I gnawed on my lower lip, twisting my hands together. It wasn't unusual for Sam to be unable to get a word in edgewise amongst my overwhelming, loud-ass family. But usually this was when he gave me one of his sly, secret smiles, as if to let me know that he was still here, still present in the moment. That even if there was a lot going on, we were always in it together, and he'd always be there for me—the baby of the family, the one they wrote off as unreliable chaos.

But right now, he looked so *serious*. And like being here was causing him physical pain.

"We thought he could stay with you," Aveda piped up, gesturing to a suitcase I hadn't noticed before. "So you two can be all romantic while us boring adults stay at the hotel."

"We're also adults," I murmured, sounding like I was trying to convince myself.

"Er, yes. Of course," Aveda said, her brows drawing together as she looked from me to Sam and back again. "We'll be on our way, then!"

She grabbed Evie—whose eyelids were starting to droop—by the elbow and started to hustle out the door. Nate hung back, placing a tentative hand on my shoulder.

"Bea, are you all right?" he asked, his deep rumble of a voice hushed. "You seem a bit . . ."

"I'm totally fine!" I squawked, pasting on a big smile. "Just, you know, being my usual disorganized self. Sorry, I must've missed all your itinerary updates! But don't worry, we're gonna have so much fun! I'm already planning our Christmas movie marathon, which I know is your absolute favorite part—"

"Of course," he said, grimacing a bit. "We will call you later. I'm greatly looking forward to catching up with Kai as well."

"Bye-bye!" I trilled, giving them an expansive wave as they exited the bungalow. I shut the door behind them and turned back to Sam. "So. Um. What do you—"

I was interrupted by my phone buzzing insistently in my hand, reminding me that I still had other responsibilities. I looked at the screen and saw a message from Doc Kai in response to the text I'd sent earlier.

We are taking a Rain Day! Doc Kai had texted. *But Bea, you also have this week off anyway, so you can spend time with your family! I better not see you doing any work!*

Unless it's an emergency, Tosh helpfully added. *Then it's all hands on deck, or some other sailing metaphor I'm unfamiliar with*

Shush, T!! Doc Kai had responded. *And Bea, I'm not sure what message you mean—you didn't text us last night? Whatever report you're talking about can wait until your Christmas in the Spring vacay is over! You're supposed to be relaxing more, remember?*

I stared at the phone screen, frowning. Had my text about the mini kaiju not gone through? And how did everyone else know my schedule—and my family's schedule—way better than I did? I'd been *so sure* they were coming next week . . .

"Hey. Bea."

My head snapped up and I met Sam's gaze. He was still giving me that unreadable look, and he was making no move to get closer to me. And I swore I felt a chill in the air that had nothing to do with the dreary weather outside. (Given that it was a tropical storm, it was actually quite muggy.)

"I'm sorry," he said, finally taking a step toward me. My

heart lifted—he probably realized things were all weird be-tween us, and now he was going to mention how overwhelm-ing my family could be, that's all it was, but we were finally alone and he'd pull me into his arms and kiss me hello, and maybe we'd manage to stop kissing long enough for me to change into that festive elf onesie so he could take it off with as much relish as he had last time . . .

"I know this is weird," he continued. "And I tried to get out of it. But this whole 'surprise' thing has been in motion for weeks, and Evie and Aveda don't seem to be aware of what's going on with us, and you know how insistent they can be when they want to do something, and they *really* wanted to give you this surprise—"

"Wait." I held up my hands, my mind a whirl. "What do you mean by . . . you tried to get out of what? Seeing me? And what *is* going on with us? I don't think I know that either . . ." I shook my head, trying to get everything he'd just said to come into focus.

"Bea." He stepped toward me again, closing the distance between us, and took my hands in his. He met my gaze, doing an intense scan of my face. Now I could see flashes of emo-tion surfacing in his expression, but it wasn't desire or happi-ness or that whole "we're in this together, no matter what" thing.

No, he still looked like he was in *pain*.

"I can get a hotel or something if this is too much," he said, squeezing my hands. "I don't want to intrude on you, not after—"

"Sam." Tears sprang to my eyes. What was he talking about?! "Why would you get a hotel? Did I say something wrong when we talked on the phone last night? I didn't mean to interrupt your parents' karaoke night, or, like, deprive Auntie Chrissy of her eighth boba. I really just wanted to hear your voice, I was missing you so much, and I couldn't stop staring at that eraser you gave me, and then you didn't call me back—"

"Baby." He squeezed my hands again, his tone very soft.

"I didn't call back because I didn't think there was anything else to say."

"What do you *mean*?" I spat out, my voice breaking. Frustration roared through me as my tears started to spill down my cheeks. "Of course there was more to say, we barely got to talk—"

"Yeah, we barely got to talk," he repeated back at me, dropping my hands and blowing out a long breath. He shook his head, that pain in his eyes on full, heartbreaking display. "I guess we were too busy breaking up."

CHAPTER SEVEN

"WHAT?!" I EXPLODED.

I shook my head vehemently, my half-Technicolor hair springing into a rainbow hurricane of movement.

"Sam. Are you serious?! We did not *break up*—"

"We absolutely did," he insisted, crossing his arms over his chest and glowering at me.

"How?" I pressed, frantically replaying our talk the night before in my head. "I called, you were busy with your parents and their friends, you did *not* seem particularly happy to hear from me—"

"I was in the middle of something. And that apparently wasn't okay with you, and then we both seemed to come to the same conclusion at the same time—"

"Am I living in an alternate dimension?" I couldn't seem to stop shaking my head, like that was going to convince him. But seriously, where was he getting this? "You said you were going to call me back—"

"I'm positive I did *not*," he retorted. "So maybe you *are* living in an alternate dimension."

My eyes filled with tears again. "Okay, it sounds like we had diametrically opposed interpretations of this conversation, but all that aside . . . you don't actually want to break up. Do you?" That last bit came out plaintive, my voice cracking pathetically.

"I . . ." He trailed off, scraping a hand over his face. He crossed the room and sat down heavily on the bed, the silence between us growing weighty and uncomfortable. Outside, the rain lashed mercilessly against the window, as if trying to make this fraught conversation as dramatic as possible.

I stayed standing, shifting uncomfortably from foot to foot, hastily swiping at the tears in my eyes before they had a chance to make their way down my cheeks. How was it that only a few months ago, we'd started a visit unable to keep our hands off each other . . . and now we were *here*?

And why couldn't he answer me? He was supposed to say no, *of course* he didn't want to break up—sure, things had been a little awkward between us since his last visit. But we'd work it out, we'd fall into bed together, we'd have slow, delicious sex while the storm raged on outside, and then we'd snuggle close and eat gingerbread in our little cocoon, my heart glowing with contentment. We'd dedicate ourselves to *fun*, just like we always did.

None of that happened.

Instead Sam finally raised his head to look at me, his dark gaze inescapable. I squirmed again, desperately trying not to cry.

"Baby," he finally said—and his voice was all soft and gentle, which somehow made everything worse. "I . . . I don't know. We've been having a hard time, I feel constantly guilty I can't give you everything you deserve—"

"You *can*," I insisted, a stubborn whine making its way into my voice. "You do."

"And I don't think you can give me everything, either," he pressed on, ignoring me. "Look, when we got into this . . . I mean, we knew it wasn't the best idea. Because of how we both are."

"What is that supposed to mean?" I demanded, even though I already knew.

Flighty, easily bored, always looking for a good time . . . and deeply allergic to commitment. *That* was how we both were. That's why our initial Just Sex, Just For Fun arrangement had worked so well.

"You know what it means," Sam said quietly, echoing my thoughts. "Neither of us is exactly cut out for a relationship. And now we're both going through big life stuff, and maybe we just don't have the bandwidth—"

"The *bandwidth*?!" I spat out, my eyes widening in disbelief. "What the fuck, Sam, you don't even sound like yourself! This isn't a math equation. I know we both find math super romantic, but . . ." I bit my lip. "I *love* you. Like, big, wild, all-consuming love. I never thought I could feel that way about someone—that I'd actually *want* to feel that way about someone. It absolutely terrifies me, but it's true, and we both admitted it to each other, and we agreed we were going to try, and—"

"We did try," he cut in, his voice exhausted. "It didn't work."

"I *love* you," I repeated, sounding desperate—like those three little words were my life preserver, the only thing keeping me from drowning in this moment. "Isn't that the most important thing? Doesn't the kind of love we have conquer all?"

He met my gaze, his eyes full of so much hurt, it took my breath away. He looked hollowed out, a shell of his usual self.

"I don't think it does," he finally said.

I tried to say something, anything, but the words clogged in my throat, emerging as a strangled sob.

"I can't be here right now," I managed, tears building in my eyes again.

I whirled away from him, aiming myself at the door, barely hearing him calling after me, reminding me that it was pouring rain outside and I was still in my pajamas. I couldn't think, could only feel the vicious stab of pain that started in my chest and radiated outward, engulfing every cell of my body.

I catapulted myself outside and hastily threw an old blanket draped over the railing around my body, stuffing my feet into the plastic gardening clogs I always kept on the porch. The rain was still coming down like that was its only job (I suppose that *was* its only job), but the air was as muggy and humid as I thought it would be. My pajamas from the night before consisted of an old pair of sweats I'd cut into raggedy, uneven shorts and a stretched-out tank top with MATH-LETE emblazoned across the front.

I pulled the blanket more tightly around me, trying to keep from getting totally soaked, and started to clomp down the mostly empty Makawao street. I had no idea where I was going, and I was guessing almost everything was closed during the storm. But I had to get away from my confusingly Lemon Pledged bungalow and Sam.

Sam, my charming, cocky, upsettingly hot boyfriend . . . who no longer wanted to be my boyfriend.

I fought back tears again.

Maybe I could go hang in the Demonology office while we both cooled off. I straightened my spine, glad to have some kind of direction, and continued my trek. The contrast between today and yesterday was stark—the bakery was closed, the market wasn't operating due to rain. Even Pika had shut down, a cardboard sign with a hastily scrawled BACK TO-MORROW, YOU GO SOMEWHERE ELSE plastered across his café door. I glanced around fruitlessly for Roger as I reached the office and unearthed the spare key Tosh kept hidden under a loose wooden plank on the front porch. I of course hadn't thought to grab much of anything during my dramatic exit from my bungalow, including sensible outerwear. The blanket I'd tossed around my shoulders was now soaked, and my gardening clogs were dripping with excess water. The humid air outside kept me from being truly cold—I was mostly just sweaty and confused.

I let myself into the office, toed off my clogs, and swapped out my wet blanket for a threadbare quilt we all liked to use for power naps. Then I settled in at my desk, trying to figure out what to do next.

I parsed my fight with Sam, replaying his words in my mind and trying to figure out what the hell he'd been talking about. How had we managed to have two completely different conversations with completely different outcomes?

And did any of that even matter, since *his* conclusion was that he no longer wanted to be with me?

"This is the worst fucking fake Christmas ever," I muttered, narrowing my eyes at the remnants of a gingerbread cookie on my desk. I picked it up and chomped on it . . . and nearly felt my tooth crack.

"What the hell!" I yelped, spitting out the rest of the rock-hard cookie and massaging my jaw. Hopefully I hadn't cracked a tooth. And damn, maybe Doc Kai did need to work on her gingerbread recipe. The cookies shouldn't be that stale after only a day.

My gaze wandered to the one useful thing I had managed to take with me—my phone, which hadn't left my hand since I'd disconnected it that morning, right before Evie and Co. had arrived and derailed my entire day. Possibly my entire life.

And hey, for once it was fully charged.

I snatched it off the desk and hit Leah's name in my contacts, hoping she wasn't too wrapped up tending to Pancake's impressive list of daily demands or working a busy shift at It's Lit. I went with an audio call over FaceTime because I really couldn't literally *face* anyone right now. Especially someone who knew me so well.

"Bebe!" As soon as her voice rang out over the line, my shoulders relaxed a bit. There was Leah, my stalwart best friend, cheery partner in crime, and constant voice of reason. If anyone could help me untangle this mess, it was her. "Why are you calling me?! Isn't your family there? Isn't Sammy there? I thought you'd be hip deep in Christmassy things by now!"

"I . . . no," I managed, glumness washing over me. "Also, how does everyone know that my family moved their visit up a week except me? Am I really that bad at keeping track of email? Or itineraries? Or—"

"I thought it was always supposed to be this week?" Leah

said, and I could practically see her nose scrunching up the way it did when she was trying to work something out. "Eh, maybe I'm wrong! Anyway, back to my question, why don't I hear any jingle bells or, like, cookie-baking sounds?"

"Because Sam and I broke up!" I blurted out, tears welling in my eyes again. "Or he seems to think we broke up, I didn't think that at all, but the end result is that we're not together right now, so . . ." I trailed off as sobs clogged my throat once more, and let the tears stream fully down my cheeks. The darkness inside of me pulsed, as if to encourage such things. I'd been so careful lately, keeping my feelings contained, blending in as best I could . . . now I didn't have the strength to be anything other than what I usually was. Messy and mercurial and unruly, letting everything out and not giving it so much as a second thought.

"Bebe," Leah breathed. "Wow. I don't even know what to say. I'm so sorry! But why do you think you had such different interpretations of what happened? Usually y'all are very, like, same page!"

I took a deep, cleansing breath and tried to recap the whole mess for her, starting with my and Sam's truncated phone call the night before.

"And yet, he remembers this whole conversation we didn't even have!" I concluded, my voice escalating into a wail. "Or I don't remember us having it, anyway. Given that I can't seem to keep anyone's vacation dates straight, maybe we totally did and it's yet another thing that slipped my mind!"

"That doesn't sound like you, Bebe," Leah said, her voice very gentle. "And I know we've talked about the weirdness that's been happening between you and Sammy since his last visit, but none of it seemed like a breakup-level offense."

"Has he said anything to you?" I asked, my voice twisting into a hysterical shriek. "I mean . . . sorry. I shouldn't ask you that, I just—"

"No, it's okay. Let me think . . ."

I closed my eyes as she lapsed into silence, pulling the quilt around my body. I pictured her scrunching up her nose even more intensely, her eyes going to the ceiling as she scanned her memories. The very image made my chest tighten; I missed Leah so much. She'd been a constant part of my daily existence for five years now, and being so far away from her, I sometimes felt like I was missing part of myself. We'd had to negotiate our boundaries a bit around the topic of Sam, since we'd all been best friends previously and she obviously wanted to stay close to both of us after things between Sam and me shifted. I knew she heard about our relationship from both of us—and being Leah, she always tried to provide the best, most impartial advice.

"You know, Bebe, Sammy's been pretty busy taking care of his parents lately," Leah said slowly. "I've barely seen him in weeks—although I've also been super busy, I'm still trying to convince Charlotte to let me buy the store—"

"Wait, *what*!" I shrieked, momentarily diverted. "You want to take over It's Lit? Like, fully?" It's Lit, the adorable romance bookstore where I'd once worked, was actually where Leah and I had first met. She was now the manager, but the place was still owned by Charlotte Wilcox (sometimes known as Letta), an endlessly morose Bay Area business-woman. Though Leah was dedicated to It's Lit, I'd had no idea she wanted the store to be hers.

"Yeah? Kinda my main quest at the moment," Leah said, sounding puzzled. "But you know how Charlotte is, she's totally uninterested in the store these days, but she claims she just doesn't get my vision—I want to start by painting one of my murals of awesome mermaids on the wall behind the counter! One will be Blasian—Black and Korean, like me, and the other will be Japanese and Irish, like you. And that's just step one of my grand vision for the store! I wish I had your posterboarding skills so I could really show her!"

"I . . . wow," I murmured, feeling farther away from her than ever. How was it that I had no clue about such a key development in my best friend's life?

Of course, I already knew the answer. It was because the

mysterious darkness I now felt inside of me had caused me to pull away, only communicating through those damn letters. That darkness was really messing everything up.

"But anyway, I haven't seen Sammy in a bit and Pancake has been despondent," Leah continued. "You know Sam is the only one who will cook him his very own all-bacon dinner."

"I know," I said. The fact that Sam would prepare an entire separate meal for a tiny diva of a dog was one of the things that made me love him beyond all reason.

"I remember he seemed wrung out at our last dinner together," Leah continued thoughtfully. "You know how freaking vain he is—usually there's not a hair out of place! But that night, he looked haggard. Worn around the edges. I told him I was worried about him, but he shrugged it off, said he'd had a long day with his parents. I didn't push, but . . ."

"But apparently he was also haggard from thinking about how much he didn't want to be with me," I snuffled.

I tapped listlessly at my laptop keyboard, the screen coming into focus. A few new messages popped up, texts that had come through while I was on the phone with Leah.

Bea, seriously!!! No working! Doc Kai had written. *Pika called and said he thought he saw you running toward the office "like some fool chicken with its head cut all the way off"*

Pika's eyesight is questionable these days, Tosh countered. *But Bea, if you are thinking of going out, don't take your family on one of your "Maui rain walks," not everyone finds those charming*

"Bebe?" Leah said. "You still there?"

"Yeah, sorry, Lee," I murmured, clicking on a new message that had just come in. It was from Pika. Keala and I had been trying to teach him how to text properly, with mixed results. Maybe he was about to scold me as well.

This right? Our photo, the text read. I clicked on the accompanying image.

And my stomach dropped.

It was a fairly basic picture, but the image displayed

knocked my brain off its axis, sending it spinning into a spiral of confusion.

It was me and Pika—me grinning at the camera, him managing something that wasn't quite a smile, but also wasn't his customary scowl. We were both brandishing tiny paper cups stuffed with pink and orange swirls of ice cream—Guri-Guri, which I'd promised him the day before.

But we were going on *Friday*. Yesterday was Monday. Friday hadn't happened yet.

So how . . . ?

I zoomed in on the photo, blowing up every single detail, leaning forward in my seat so I could scan them more intently. Was this from a previous trip? No—Pika had his promised four whole scoops, which I'd never gotten for him before. And I was wearing a ring I'd just purchased from Keala over the weekend. And the date . . .

I frowned, the pit in my stomach deepening.

The date was *Friday's date*. Like, future Friday.

A disorienting haze descended over me, and I suddenly felt like I was moving in slow motion.

I looked at the date in the corner of my laptop. Frantically scanned through my email. Paged through all the texts that had popped up on my laptop.

All of them told me the same thing—that today was a Monday. A week after the Monday I'd only just experienced . . . yesterday.

"Bebe!" Leah shrieked, her tone verging on desperate. "What's going on? Are you okay?"

"I . . ." I gripped the edge of the desk, a sense of numbness overtaking me and shooting pins and needles into my fingertips. I felt like I was permanently stuck in that state of slow motion now, unable to move faster than a snail.

"I'm not okay," I finally managed, my voice thin and reedy and sounding as if it was coming from somewhere outside my body. "Leah, I'm not sure how to say this, but . . . I think I accidentally time traveled."

FROM THE SUPER EPIC ARCHIVE OF BEA TANAKA'S TOTALLY LEGENDARY HOLIDAY MOVIE LETTERS

Dear Sam and Leah,

Okay, it's time to tell y'all about a forgotten classic in the Christmas movie pantheon, a sweet little treat entitled The Christmas Locket. *The "forgotten" part really puzzles me, I gotta admit. This one has all the ingredients holiday movie enthusiasts tend to love, and unlike* Kaiju, *there is a reliable happily ever after—ya hear that, Leah?! Swoon, swoon!*

It also involves time travel, a storytelling device that is like fucking catnip to me, but from what I understand, completely reviled by the writers foolish enough to attempt including it, as it introduces a staggering number of potential plot holes, inconsistencies, and elements that require an advanced degree in physics to solve in a satisfactory manner. So who knows, maybe it was the screenwriter that wanted to forget said movie ever happening! Maybe they should send themselves back in time so they can simply not write it!

Ah, but then I would be deprived of a story I always manage to get hopelessly lost in.

The Christmas Locket *is all about a heroine named Kelly (she never gets a last name), an enterprising lass who discovers a magic locket in a charming old curio shop (yes, Sam, I know you're about to ask why there are so many old curio shops in these movies and why they are all charming instead of moldy, dusty, and stocking the occasional totally racist artifact from a different time period—I realize you may never believe in the magic of Christmas, but maybe you could start to get down with the magic of fiction?). Kelly doesn't know it's magic, of course, she's just drawn to it because it gives off an extra-shiny glow that transports her away from the drab drudgery of her daily life (there is the drab office job, the drab rotation of microwaved TV dinners eaten on a rickety fold-out tray, and the drab moments of gazing mournfully at the stray cat who keeps coming around to get fed—that's right, poor Kelly doesn't even get her own cat! Nothing in her life resembles anything remotely joy-adjacent!).*

And then! The locket LITERALLY transports her away from her life, because Kelly discovers that it makes her time travel! Holy shit, right?! See, Sam, those old curio shops contain quality items sometimes, you just have to be willing to dig for them!

Anyway, our girl Kelly immediately knows what her quest should be—she's gonna travel back to the one perfect Christmas she spent with the long-lost love of her life. She did not realize this person (a blandly handsome man named Dan) was the love of her life until he dumped her ass right after that one perfect Christmas. And she knows that the steep downturn her life took after this event is responsible for the current drab state of her existence! If only The Dumping hadn't happened, everything would be completely different. She'd be living in way sparklier style, her day-to-day wrapped in the glow of perfect love, her Christmases with boring-ass Dan stuffed to the brim with stolen moments by the tree and tipsy kisses under the mistletoe.

If Kelly can just get back to that one perfect Christmas and fix her relationship before it ends, show Dan that she IS the only one for him . . . then her life will magically undrabify itself.

But when Kelly uses the magic locket to take her back to that moment, she discovers . . . that Dan is with someone else?! During what was once Kelly's perfect Christmas with him?! Twist!! (Also, fuck off, Dan!)

Apparently Kelly's little transdimensional excursion fucked up the entire timeline, so now she has to fix both that and her life. Personally, the main issue I always have with movies involving time travel is that no one in them has ever seen A MOVIE INVOLVING TIME TRAVEL! And they never seem to realize the one overriding rule until too late: anything you do whilst time-displaced has the potential to fuck up/erase/completely change the timeline.

Remember how Marty McFly almost accidentally kept his parents from getting together and all his siblings started to disappear from the family photo? And then he messed things up so badly in the sequel that his life turned into full-on dystopia? Or when Doctor McCoy saved Edith Keeler's life, which led to the Nazis taking over the world? Mucking around with the timeline has consequences! But characters in these movies are always mucking around with wild abandon!

Anyway, Kelly's locket breaks, because of course it does, and she's trapped in the past. So she tracks down the owner of the curio shop—who we then realize is distractingly hot. Together, they decide the best way to fix both the timeline and Kelly's sad-ass life is to embark on an elaborate fake-dating scheme that will make Dan jealous and allow him and Kelly to unite in a holly-strewn happily ever after.

Naturally, things do not go as planned.

In the end, Kelly and the hot curio shop owner end up falling for each other, and Kelly decides to stay in the past and they work together to repair all the damage she's done to the timeline and have perfect Christmases together forever. Let me just say that my only problem is the bit where Kelly stays in the past—as a queer woman of color, going back in time is pretty much never an appealing prospect for me, even if it's just a few years. But I guess it works out fine for Kelly, a basic white bitch who everything always works out for, no matter how badly she's fucked up.

Perhaps this element of sheer fantasy is yet another thing that makes me love this one so much—imagine a world wherein your fuck-ups (including the ones made while freaking time traveling!) actually produce a positive result.

I'll be dreaming of the day when that's true for me, but for now I'm definitely more of a McFly or a McCoy! Although maybe if those guys had focused on time traveling to their perfect dream Christmas moments—or if they'd had a magic locket from an old curio shop!—they would've been okay.

XOXO,
McBea!

CHAPTER EIGHT

"BEBE, WHAT DO you mean 'accidentally'?!" Leah bleated in my ear. "Actually, what do you mean, period?! And don't try to tell me about that non-Hudgens time-travel movie again, you know I only recognize Christmas entertainment starring our one true mixed Asian holiday queen!"

"Valid," I squeaked, trying to shake off that woozy slow-motion sensation I couldn't seem to snap out of. "Um. So what I'm saying is, yesterday—*my* yesterday that I just experienced—was Monday, one week ago. I woke up this morning, and it was suddenly *next* Monday, and . . ."

I trailed off, images from the last few hours swirling through my brain—but still in that frustratingly hazy way, as if my own memories were reluctant to present me with the full picture.

I recounted my memories to Leah as they drifted through my mind, describing my family showing up for a trip I'd thought was happening next week, my clean apartment and fully charged devices I couldn't remember plugging in, the photo of me and Pika and the ice cream I'd promised him yesterday . . . and of course, Sam talking about a conversation I was sure we'd never had. Sam looking so downtrodden and heartbroken and convinced we'd broken up . . .

What had happened in a mere week? What had I done to make him look like that?

What kind of mess had I gotten myself into *now*?!

SARAH KUHN 93

"Have Evie and Aveda ever dealt with anything like this?" Leah asked. "God, can you imagine *Aveda* time traveling—"

"A disaster of epic proportions," I said. "And no, I don't think so. Maybe I just have some weird supernatural amnesia thing going on, although I don't remember them dealing with anything like that, either!"

I flopped forward, pressing my cheek against the rough wood of my desk. I needed to calm the frak down so I could look at the situation logically. Just like my newly mature self had gotten so used to doing.

"Do you remember anything from when you woke up this morning?" Leah pressed. I heard faint rustling on the other end of the line and just knew she was doing some kind of organizational activity to keep her hands busy—that was how Leah went into problem-solving mode. "Like, was there some kind of tell that you'd time traveled? Did you suddenly have a magic locket around your neck like that Kelly girl in your Christmas movie? Or—"

"Not a locket," I said, popping upright in my seat. "But I did have a monster headache, like I was hungover, and—oh my god!" A sudden realization hit me, another memory crystallizing. "Lee! I think this happened before. On a much smaller scale." I shook my head, trying to get the puzzle pieces to come together. "Yesterday—well, what I remember as yesterday—I sat down at my desk, and then it was suddenly the end of the workday. And I had that headache again!" I recalled Doc Kai appearing next to me with gingerbread, the sky darkening into night even though it had been morning only a few minutes earlier. "I, like, microtime-traveled!" I crowed, my heart hammering in my chest. "How is this happening?!"

"Maybe the demons are messing with you, trying to make you forget something important!" Leah exclaimed, her fidgety rustling getting more frenzied. "Like whatever you did last week is the key to saving Evie's baby from Shasta's nefarious clutches, and they can't have you remembering that!

So they sent you through time before you could do . . . um, whatever it is, and since you don't remember anything, you can't try to do it again!"

"I don't see how that could be," I said, racking my brain for what I'd been planning to do in the week ahead. Most of it was of the humdrum variety, especially given all my efforts to avoid fieldwork, tasks that took me out of the office, or anything that might put me directly in the path of anything supernatural—

"Wait!" I shrieked. "The kaiju!"

"The *what*?!" Leah demanded, as I popped up in my seat and began searching through my laptop.

"I had a possible encounter," I said, clicking to open the folder where I had taken great pains to organize all my reports in non-chaotic fashion. "Only I was pretty convinced it was a hallucination. But Past Bea promised to write up a report no matter what, soooooo . . ." I spotted the report I was looking for, right at the top of the folder. I clicked to open it and eagerly scanned through, searching for any kernel of information that might provide me with an elusive clue.

As I continued to read, my mood deflated. It was a fairly straightforward recounting of what I remembered from the night before, no extra bells or whistles. Part of my efforts to be a grown-up involved shifting away from my original style of writing reports, which had been packed to the brim with flair, color commentary, and the occasional emoji. Now it was all dry, basic sentences—just the facts, ma'am.

I saw that Past Bea had done a follow-up interview with Pika, who had repeated that he "hadn't seen nothin' except your fool ass sitting next to the garbage." Doc Kai had added some recommendations—mainly that we scan and keep an eye on the area where I may or may not have had the sighting. And also that I consider taking a few days off to rest my eyes, my brain, and any other body parts that might require some overdue relaxation.

Ugh. Nothing momentous there, and it sounded like the incident had been exactly what I'd thought it was: a hallucination courtesy of my anxiety spiral. Not a badass feat of heroics that had saved my sister's baby and prompted the Otherworld demons to send me time traveling.

"Bebe?!" Leah piped up, her voice impatient. The rustling on the other end of the line was now so frenetic, I had to strain to hear her. "Come on, explain about this kaiju, please! That sounds freaky but also kind of awesome?"

"Not awesome," I muttered. "Probably my imagination. And nothing in this report I wrote up afterward indicates that it made me time travel."

"You are always having the most outrageous adventures," Leah enthused. "Like when you started jumping into the Otherworld—true, I wasn't super into the part where you tried to sacrifice my future girlfriend to the demons, but—"

"She wasn't your girlfriend then," I retorted. "Or at least, I didn't know she was."

"Like that makes it better," Leah said, and I could just picture her sardonic eyebrow raise. "Glad we can sort of joke about this."

"I acknowledged I was totally on a misguided supervillain path. But things are different now . . ."

I trailed off, unable to ignore the pit that had reappeared in my stomach.

Because *were* they different now? Hadn't I just spent all of yesterday—well, *my* yesterday—freaking out about my emotions spilling out unbidden, about the possible changes to my power, about mind-controlling everyone in my path? Hadn't I felt that pulse of Otherworld darkness in my chest, those menacing shadows that wouldn't go away no matter how hard I tried to shove them down . . .

What if the explanation for my sudden time travel did not involve me accomplishing some feat of major heroics? What if it was the opposite?

Had this mysterious darkness pushed me to do something

that I had no memory of? Something truly evil that there was absolutely no coming back from?

Panic raged through my bloodstream, my vision going fuzzy around the edges. I forced myself to breathe deeply.

"Lee," I said slowly, my words dropping themselves between wheezy breaths. "I, um. I've been experiencing some weirdness with my power. Ever since I did that combo spell with Scott and Aveda."

"What kind of weirdness?" Leah asked.

"I . . ." I hesitated. I still couldn't bring myself to tell her about the darkness. It felt too big, too scary. "My power's, like . . . glitching," I finally settled on. "I can't control and direct it as well as I usually can—it's hard to explain. But what if this is connected to the time travel, like I'm now power-glitching on an even bigger scale and instead of only projecting my emotions, I'm projecting *my entire self* through time—"

"Bebe, *stop!*" Leah cried. I pictured her throwing an arm out, like a mom protecting a kid with no seatbelt. "That's quite a leap—bigger than an actual leap through time, even! But if you're really worried, you should talk to Evie and Aveda—"

"No!" I bellowed.

I pulled the quilt more tightly around me. That single word had torn itself from my throat with a ferocity that unnerved me.

"I've been working so hard to show Evie that she doesn't need to worry about me at all, that I'm living my best life out here." I closed my eyes and ordered my heart to quit beating so damn fast. "I can't let her worry about me anymore, okay? She's spent way too much of her life doing that already. And I don't know exactly what's going on just yet. But if something's up with my power, *I* have to be the one to handle it. I need to learn how to control it myself. That's part of being a freaking grown-up, right?"

"I suppose," Leah said, not sounding all that convinced. "But what are you going to do, Bebe? You can't just keep randomly time traveling all over the place! What if you create a *multiverse*—"

"So we've gone from time-traveling Aveda to multiple Avedas?" I said. "I can't decide which prospect is more frightening."

"No jokey deflecting!" Leah hollered.

"Sorry. But Lee . . . I need to think about what to do next. Like, what would a hero do in this situation? What's the non-villain way of proceeding? And as far as talking to Evie and Co. . . . ." I frowned, my gaze drifting to my boring report about the mini kaiju. "Isn't the first rule of time travel not to mess with the timeline? And won't me *telling* them I'm time traveling do just that?! What if I start World War III or something? Just like Dr. McCoy. He thought he was doing a good thing, saving Edith Keeler—but that single action led to him fucking over the entire world!"

"That is true," Leah conceded. "Pretty much every show or movie we've ever seen stresses that non-interference is key, and that even the smallest, most seemingly inconsequential actions can lead to catastrophic change—the whole butterfly-effect thing. But Bebe: you just told *me* about it. So haven't you already interfered?"

"Gah." My shoulders slumped. "Trust me to fuck things up immediately. Okay—so from here on out, I need to do my absolute best to *not* fuck things up. No telling anyone else. You will be my sole time-traveling confidante—my constant, if you will!"

"Not Penny's boat," Leah intoned. "All right, Bebe. But if you call me back from yet another week where you've blazed forward in time, I'm going to kill you!"

"Understood," I said, even though I currently understood very little. "I guess for now I should try to act natural? Like, be in the moment, try not to disturb the timeline, and see what I can sleuth out. Pretend like I'm in one of Lucy's British murder shows and piece together whatever happened last week."

"I don't think you and I talked last week, but there was of course texting," Leah mused. "Mostly of the inconsequential, reaction-gif variety—so your consciousness may have time traveled, but your physical body was still present, it seems like. Otherwise people would've been freaking out about you going missing."

"So maybe I do have supernatural amnesia," I said, my voice wry. "All right, Lee, I'm about to enter observation and information-gathering mode!"

"You've got this. Like you said, you just gotta stay in the moment, and even if you don't know exactly what's going on, ask yourself: WWBTD?"

"What Would Bea Tanaka Do?" I raised an eyebrow. "Not sure if that's the best idea in any circumstance, but I'll give it a go. Call ya later, Lee."

I hung up, my mind a whirl of thoughts about the space-time continuum, the possibility that my Otherworld darkness was causing my power to glitch even harder, and a multiverse of Avedas.

In the past, I would have delighted in the sheer excitement of it all, the promise of the unknown, the supernatural science experiments and unprecedented adventures I was about to have.

But now? Now I was terrified. Mostly of myself—all the things I couldn't remember, all the World War III–level fuck-ups I might be capable of. I'd have to do my best with this "be in the moment, observe, information-gather" plan. At least I'd been getting plenty of practice with the boring side of supernatural research; I'd approach this like I currently approached all my reports. I'd keep things straightforward and logical, and I'd do my absolute best not to rock the timeline boat.

Past Bea had, of course, loved nothing more than rocking as many boats as possible. Now I had to do the opposite— blend in on a whole other level.

I found myself staring at that picture of me and Pika eating ice cream, a strange artifact from a day I didn't remember. I studied every centimeter of the photo in great detail, hoping it would give me answers—or at the very least, spark a memory.

Eventually, my eyes started to droop, my brain wore itself out, and the steady drum of the rain against the roof lulled me to sleep, wrapped up in my quilt, frozen in this one moment in time.

CHAPTER NINE

WHEN I STARTED awake later, the rain had finally stopped. And I had managed not to time travel anywhere.

I checked every electronic device to be sure. And then, just to be *extra* sure, I called one of those old-school services that robotically tells you the exact date and time. I was still living through the strange future Monday that was a week later than the one I remembered. The Monday that was now my present.

I texted Evie, Aveda, and Nate, and they all confirmed that they were resting for the remainder of the evening, waiting out the storm and enjoying a Michelle Yeoh movie marathon on the hotel TV. I informed them that the forecast tomorrow (hopefully a tomorrow I'd actually wake up to) was warm and sunny and we could have the awesome beach day they'd all been looking forward to. I still had to figure out how I was going to tell Evie she couldn't put Christmas lights on palm trees, but that could wait until later.

Hmm, could my power glitch in a way that allowed me to time travel *through* that part? To a point in the future where we'd already had the conversation? Just avoid it entirely?

Maybe there were some good uses for this whole time-travel thing—

No. No. *Stop thinking like that, Bea, that is definitely at least a little supervillain-y.*

Everyone always says they're going to use time travel to kill the evil dictators of decades past (or in Christmas Locket Kelly's case, to reunite with their one true love), but most people would probably use it to avoid difficult conversations, catch up on sleep, and prank their mortal enemies.

I spent the rest of the day clicking around on my laptop, trying to piece together what had happened the week prior. It appeared that there hadn't been any other hints of supernatural activity reported on the island—nothing Doc Kai had needed to investigate beyond my mini-kaiju hallucination. And Sam and I had exchanged some texts here and there, but nothing out of the ordinary. Certainly nothing on the breakup level.

I finally gave up on my sleuthing, slipped my gardening clogs back on, and trudged home through the night, dragging my feet as much as possible. At least the rain had stopped, and my commute was as uneventful as it usually was, no mini-kaiju hallucinations in sight.

Sam was already asleep when I arrived at the bungalow, his broad form pretzeled uncomfortably into my armchair. And he'd made dinner with the meager ingredients in my fridge; a heaping portion of his savory ground beef-and-gravy concoction topped with a runny egg and served over rice was waiting for me on the dining table, obligatory bottle of sriracha perched next to it.

This was one of the dishes Sam had made for Pika while on his holiday visit—he'd jumped in to help at the restaurant during the post-Christmas rush, and had offered up a couple easy recipes when Pika ran out of his signature pancake batter. Sam made beef gravy over rice for his parents at least once a week, and explained to Pika that it was simple, tasty, filling, and could be customized to each diner's individual palate. Pika had gruffly claimed his menu didn't *need* any additions . . . but "Non-Local Boy's Beef Gravy Over Rice" had magically appeared on the menu a couple weeks later, scrawled at the bottom like a hasty addendum.

"Dammit, Sam," I muttered, shoveling delectable gravy goodness into my mouth. "If you're breaking up with me, you could at least *try* to make yourself—and your cooking— the teensiest bit less appealing."

I resisted the temptation to cross the room and curl myself into the chair with him: fitting our bodies together, feeling his skin against mine, allowing the warm glow he sparked in my heart to cradle us both.

How had everything changed *that* much in a week? To the point where doing something that had once been second nature felt like the most alien thing in the world?

I climbed into my cold, lonely bed instead, and found myself hoping I'd wake up transported back to last week—anticipating my family's visit, thinking about holiday romcoms, taking Pika to get ice cream. And still with Sam.

When light streamed in through my window the next morning, Sam was still asleep in the armchair. And even though he was only a few feet away, we felt miles apart.

"Sam," I whispered tentatively. "Are you awake?"

This was a little joke between us—whenever we spent the night together and I woke up first, I'd say "are you awake?" (and repeat it in increasingly loud stage whispers) even though I knew he wasn't. This would pretty much always cause him to wake up immediately, and then he'd break into one of his lazy grins and pull me in for a long, deep kiss, murmuring against my mouth that he was certainly awake *now*.

But this time, he didn't so much as stir.

I opened my mouth to try again, just a little bit louder, when my door was once again assaulted by the loudest knock of all time.

"*Bea!*" Aveda's commanding voice boomed through the door, and I groaned, pulling a pillow over my head. Yes, I sometimes missed the rowdy hustle and bustle of home. But the regular boundary-stomping Team Tanaka/Jupiter engaged in was better left in San Francisco. Where I was currently not.

"Beatrice!" Aveda shouted more insistently. "Come on, open up! I *must* experience those early-morning Maui waves—Scott says 7 a.m. is the absolute best time to surf out here, and I want to try some of my new moves!"

"Okay, okay," I growled in the door's general direction.

"Just . . . stop beating up my door like that, it sounds like you're about to split it in two!"

I shoved the pillow away from my head and tossed off the covers, heaving myself out of bed. Sam was somehow still fast asleep.

I padded over to the door, grumbling all the way, and felt a strange sense of relief when I saw that I hadn't plugged in any of my devices to charge. No sign of the time-traveling amnesiac zombie Bea that had cleaned and plugged everything in the day before.

"Beaaaaa!" Aveda trilled as I answered the door. "I'm so excited, I—"

"Where are Evie and Nate?" I interrupted, running a hand over my bleary eyes.

"Oh, you know our Evie, never a morning person! She's still sleeping!" Aveda sang out, brushing past me and into the bungalow. "She'll meet us at the beach later, but I *need* to see those waves! Hello Sam—why are you sleeping in a chair?"

Aveda stopped in her tracks and cocked her head at Sam. He was finally waking up, blinking away sleep, and running a hand through his mussed hair. My foolish heart fluttered at the sight. Why did he have to be so fucking hot, even when engaging in the most basic of everyday actions? Also, did he really need to take off *his entire shirt* just to sleep? He'd draped a stray quilt around his shoulders, but it didn't do much to conceal all of his . . . everything.

"He was just taking an, um, early morning nap!" I improvised, tearing my eyes away from Sam's bare chest. "'Cause y'all are adjusting to the time difference!"

"Oh." Aveda's brows drew together. "It's only three hours, and we're three hours *ahead* of San Francisco, so shouldn't he technically be waking up even *earlier*—"

"We had so much sex last night!" I blurted out, heat rising in my cheeks. "And during the day, too. We basically didn't stop until, like, now. So he's *really* tired!"

God. Given all my years of defying Evie's parenting attempts and doing everything I could to be the most rebellious teenager possible, you'd think I would have developed better lying skills.

I snuck a look at Sam. He was tilting his head at me, an amused grin tugging at the corner of his mouth. My face flushed further, and I hastily averted my eyes. At least he was wearing boxers, but . . . would it kill him to put some actual clothes on?

"That's right," Sam finally said, getting to his feet and carefully setting the quilt to the side. He crossed the room and stood beside me, lightly resting a hand on my shoulder. I was hit by warring impulses—I wanted to either lean into him or shove him away. Nothing in between. I forced myself to stand very still, doing neither.

And I studiously avoided looking anywhere near the vicinity of his chest.

"So much sex," Sam repeated. "But that, uh, nap got me all rested up, so let's get this beach day underway."

"Yessss," Aveda said, perking up. She tightened her sleek power ponytail and gave us an officious nod. "Why don't I wait outside while you two get ready? It's a bit compact in here." She glanced around at my cozy space, arching one of her perfectly groomed eyebrows. "But save any further horny fun times for later, I really want to catch those early morning waves! Ooh, maybe one of you can take some video for me? Scott says I've gotten so good, he wants me to be part of the promotional video for his surf clinic—"

"Yes, yes, we'll video you up," I said, trying not to sound impatient. I started steering her to the door as she monologued. Once Aveda got started on an Aveda-centric tangent . . . well, we'd be here all day, and we'd definitely miss those waves she was so excited about.

Could I time travel to a point after I'd finished shooting her illustrious video? Which she would probably make me shoot several thousand times before I got it just right?

I *really* needed to stop thinking like that.

"Go check out the bakery on the corner over there," I said, jerking my chin in the direction of K Okamoto. "Tell them I sent you, and Auntie Iris and her crew will hook you up with guava malasadas!"

I shut the door on her before she could respond.

"Don't say anything," I said, turning to face Sam.

He crossed his arms over his (still distractingly bare) chest, that infuriatingly charming grin pulling at the corners of his mouth again.

"You don't know what I'm going to say."

"Pretty sure I do. And can you, like . . ." I gestured in the direction of his chest. "Put a shirt on? Cover up? Something?!"

"Nothing you haven't seen before," he quipped, grabbing the quilt he'd discarded earlier and throwing it around himself. "Better?"

"Not really," I muttered. Because now I was being offered tantalizing glimpses of bare skin, and that was almost worse than *all the bare skin*.

"What do you want to happen here, Bea?" he asked, settling back into my armchair and pulling the blanket more tightly around his shoulders. I clasped my hands behind my back so they would stop twitching with the urge to *touch*. "I'm sorry, I should have figured out how to tell you this 'surprise' was happening, but I was dealing with stuff with my parents and—"

"Oh, your parents! Are they okay? Who's taking care of them—"

"Emily's in town," he said, looking at me strangely. "We talked about that last night, too?"

"I . . . sorry," I said, my eyes going to the floor.

What had happened between us? And would it disrupt the timeline if I asked him to recount our phone call from the night before in painstaking detail?

All things considered, it was probably best not to risk it. I needed to stick with my "live in the moment and sleuth it out" plan. I should proceed as I normally would in this situation, act as if it was a normal version of this day. I needed to exist in the present as best I could, at least until I figured out what was going on.

What Would Bea Tanaka Do?

Well, to start with—probably everything she could to re-assure her family that she was totally #thriving. When I'd thought about this visit before, I'd been very focused on making sure Evie would know beyond a shadow of a doubt that she didn't have to worry about me.

So if this was a normal version of this day, how would I handle the prospect of my relationship imploding in spectacular fashion right before my sister's disapproving eyes?

Probably by devising some ridiculous scheme that would sound totally bananas the minute I said it out loud.

"I know this is all weird," I said to Sam, raising my head to meet his eyes. "But, um, I kinda don't want to tell my family we're not together anymore? I'm already the resident problem child, and Evie's *finally* convinced that I'm not too much of a problem anymore, and that I totally have my life together, including my very mature committed relationship—"

"Bea." He cut me off, his expression turning serious as he stood and crossed the room to me again, quilt still draped around his shoulders. He set his hands on my shoulders, his dark eyes searching my face. I ordered myself to stay still, to not look away.

Suddenly we were back in competition with each other, mercilessly trying to win every single point, and if I looked away first . . . I just knew I'd lose. "You're not a *problem*," he said. "Why would you even think of yourself that way?"

For a moment, we stared at each other, the pure earnestness of his gaze stabbing me right in the gut. When Sam cared about someone, when Sam *loved* someone, he did it with his whole heart. That overly assured exterior hid a depth of feeling so intense, it always made me go weak in the knees. How could he look at me like that after dumping my ass? I wanted nothing more than to let myself sag against him, for him to draw me into his arms and murmur soothing nonsense words into my hair.

If I did that, I'd *really* lose.

So I shook off his grasp and took a big step back, plastering a reasonable facsimile of Aveda's trademark imperious look across my face.

"We're not together, so that's none of your business," I said, trying to make my voice cool and modulated.

"Really? Very interesting that you were about to ask me for a favor, then," he said, his earnest expression instantly replaced by that Sam Fujikawa swagger. He crossed his arms over his chest, the quilt that had been wrapped around him falling to the floor as he shifted.

Indignation sparked in my chest—he'd totally done that on purpose. He *knew* I was basically powerless in the face of that chest, those shoulders, and those ridiculous abs, hard ripples of golden-brown muscle that could only be described as "lickable."

I sternly told myself that I could *not* look away this time, no matter how enticing his goddamn abs were. He was absolutely trying to goad me into showing just how affected I was by his partial nudity. These were the kinds of games we used to play with each other all the time, always trying to tease, one-up, and get the other person to show weakness.

Sam must have forgotten just who he was playing with, though. Didn't he remember that he'd declared me the winner of every competition between us *forever*?

Apparently it was time to remind him.

"I don't think it's a major hardship for you to pretend to still be my boyfriend," I countered, turning my bravado all the way up. I crossed my own arms over my chest, then lowered them just a bit, so they were positioned right under my breasts. A frisson of electric satisfaction ran through me as I caught his eyes drifting to my plumped-up cleavage, now barely contained in the low-cut MATHLETE tank top I hadn't bothered to change out of the night before. Despite its ratty loungewear status, I knew it was one of his favorites—he always said there was nothing hotter than watching me solve complex quadratic equations. We'd played "strip math" one time, and my strategy had been to let him think he was winning early on. The more I took off, the more distracted he was, meaning I could swoop in and claim decisive victory at the very end.

I shifted, pulling the thin material of the tank even more tightly against my chest, hoping my nipples were clearly, tantalizingly outlined.

His sharp intake of breath told me they definitely were.

I told myself to *not* break into a triumphant smile.

"Well?" I demanded, shoving my chest forward again. "Are you going to answer me? Can you act like you're attracted to me for a few days? Or is it simply . . ." I raised a suggestive eyebrow. ". . . way too *hard*?"

"I-it's not hard," he managed, his breathing uneven. He shook his head, as if trying to get his thoughts under control, and finally forced himself to look away from my chest. "This is like one of those schemes in your Christmas rom-coms, right? Pretend we're dating, act like a happy couple in service of some needlessly complicated ruse . . . and then what?"

"Hijinks ensue, of course," I proclaimed, giving him jazz hands. "But nah, for real: we can very maturely break up again once you're back in the Bay. I'll explain at that point that we're both moving forward in our responsible journeys to adulthood, and said journeys ended up being separate. Or whatever." I tossed in that last bit in an offhanded way, like none of this mattered to me at all—even as tears from yesterday's cry-fest threatened to rise up again.

"Or whatever," Sam repeated softly. He stepped toward me, his gaze suddenly unreadable. He studied me intently, like he was searching for hidden meaning. I did my best to give him nothing, turning my expression into an impenetrable block of ice.

This was an extra big challenge since he was suddenly *so close*, since I was suddenly in direct proximity to all that bare skin and all those gorgeous muscles, heat rolling off his body and surrounding me like a sexy cloak.

His hand drifted to my hair, fingertips grazing strands of

blue and purple that were being overtaken by my natural dark roots.

"You changed your hair," he said nonsensically.

"Just let it grow out," I countered, trying not to think about how much he'd always loved my hair, how he'd spoken so affectionately in the past about those bright colors and how they meant he could always find me in a crowd.

Our gazes were locked now, and I didn't think I could look away even if I'd wanted to.

"We'll probably have to kiss," he finally said—and was it my imagination, or had his voice gone husky? "Just to make it really convincing."

"I'm an incredible actress." In contrast, I sounded high and breathy. "I'll make it look real."

He leaned in closer, lowering his head so his mouth was mere millimeters from my ear. A shudder ran through me, unbidden. I wasn't *that* good of an actress.

"Maybe this is our new competition," he murmured, a hint of that growl that always affected me so much creeping into his tone. "We can reset the points now that we're not together, right?"

"Definitely," I said, my voice so faint I could barely hear it.

We stayed frozen in place for a few minutes more, his breath tickling my earlobe and sending chills racing through my bloodstream. And I had to fight every instinct in my body to *not* collapse against him, drag him into bed, and declare both of us winners.

I forced myself to take a big step back from him, putting significant distance between me and all those abs.

"Why don't you get ready—go take a shower and all that?" I said, waving a queenly hand at him. "Um, a shower where I will *not* be joining you. Just so we're clear."

"Crystal," he said, flashing me a smirk and strutting toward the bathroom—yes, *strutting*. Like he wanted to make sure I noticed the way his shoulders flexed, the way those boxers were barely containing much of anything.

I managed to maintain my imperious pose until he was

safely in the bathroom. Then I collapsed against the wall, my heart beating so wildly I wondered if he could hear it over the noise of the shower.

I breathed deeply and tried to quell the sparks of excitement racing through my veins, the stimulation from our reactivated competition dancing across my skin. The competition between Sam and me had always energized all of my senses, made me feel more alive than I'd ever thought possible.

I hadn't felt that way in *months*, I realized. I could practically hear that alien darkness inside of me purring with pleasure.

And somehow I just knew all of this was very, very bad.

CHAPTER TEN

I SENT LEAH–MY constant!—a flurry of desperate texts, bringing her up to speed. I stared at my phone screen while Sam got ready, hoping she'd get back to me with some soothing Leah Kim words of wisdom. But my screen remained blank. She was probably busy seeing to Pancake's customary third breakfast.

I also reminded myself that I needed to keep this whole time-travel sleuthing thing at the forefront of my mind if I had any hopes of figuring out what was going on. And I needed to do that in addition to living in the moment, which seemed very contradictory. But my whole entire life often seemed contradictory, so what was one more thing?

I got ready myself, selecting my skimpiest bikini, a slinky silver number with flirty little ties between my breasts and at my hips. I rationalized that it was also my *favorite* bikini, but I couldn't deny that I'd mostly chosen it because I knew Sam would respond in a way that was sure to earn me a boatload of points in our reactivated competition. And hey—said competition could be an excellent mode of sleuthing, since I could goad information out of him about the week I'd skipped over.

This bikini had *tons* of Sam-goading potential.

I had to admit, the thought of said competition was still sending that zing of excitement through my nervous system. I firmly reminded myself that it was also for the greater good (hey, just like my old code! Dammit, I was probably going to have to redefine that fucking code yet again). Yes, I may have been living in the moment a little *too* hard when I'd agreed to it—the proximity of his abs made it basically impossible to do anything else. But proceeding this way was totally non-boat-rocking (and more crucially, non-timeline-rocking), as it kept up the façade of normalcy with both my family and Sam, since this was most definitely how we'd both act in the wake of a breakup. I needed to run enthusiastically toward this little game between us, guns blazing.

That's *exactly* What Bea Tanaka Would Do.

I threw an old black slip dress over my bikini and added my usual beach slippers (Keala had snort-laughed at me when I'd referred to them as "flip-flops" the first time we went to the beach together—"Slippahs or nothin', baby!" she'd proclaimed. "You're on the island now!"). At that point, we'd kinda kept Aveda waiting forever, but she didn't seem to mind. She'd purchased a gigantic bag of guava mala-sadas, which she wedged into the backseat of the rental car. As I directed her to the beach, she kept up an enthusiastic running monologue about how the bakery Aunties had been so happy to meet the one and only Aveda Jupiter, how they tried to give her the malasadas for free, but she'd insisted on paying extra.

"Evie will love these," she cooed, bopping her head to the car radio as she piloted us to our destination. "And little Galactus Tanaka-Jones should enjoy them too."

"So you finally accepted Bea's preferred baby name," Sam piped up from the backseat.

"I don't know if I'd say 'accepted,'" Aveda retorted, her brow furrowing as she bore down on the steering wheel, con-centrating on the narrow stretch of road. "'Was bludgeoned with it until I finally gave in' is more like it."

"Considering that Evie refers to you as a Forceful Blud-geon for Good, I'll take that as a compliment," I murmured, staring out the passenger-seat window. Early-morning Maui whizzed by, the sun just beginning its daily climb in the bril-liant blue sky.

"I always thought the name Galactus had a pretty heroic ring to it," Sam said, his voice tinged with amusement.

I met his eyes in the rearview mirror and he gave me one of his cocky smirks—which immediately made my blood boil *and* turned me on. Very inconveniently confusing.

"Ironic, since Galactus is a *villain*," I said, sounding out each syllable. I crossed my arms over my chest and leaned back in my seat, shooting him a challenging look in the mirror.

He just grinned and raised an index finger, then pointed to himself.

Seriously?! He was trying to award himself a point for *that*?

I shook my head vehemently and then held up my own index finger and pointed to myself. If anyone had scored a point off that last exchange, it was definitely *me*.

He shook his head and pointed to himself again. And then I pointed to myself again. And then—

"What on earth are the two of you doing?" Aveda said, giving me a puzzled sidelong look. "Is this some intimate secret language you made up? Listen, I realize you're both more brilliant than I can possibly comprehend, but please keep all your sex things private. I don't need to be part of that."

"That's not what we were . . . sorry," I muttered, sliding down in my seat like a chastised toddler.

I snuck a peek in the mirror again and saw Sam triumphantly brandishing his index finger again.

We'd just have to see about that.

So far, I was doing an excellent job of throwing myself into our competition, but I had yet to tease any useful information out of him about the past week. Thankfully, the day was still young. Surely I would find a way to triumph on every level before the sun set (unless I time traveled again before that).

We finally arrived at the beach—a semi-secret enclave for locals, particularly the folks who lived in Makawao. Doc Kai and Carmelo came here regularly and were set to join us a bit later. We parked precariously by the side of the road, joining the few early-bird cars. Like Aveda, they were probably surfers looking to catch those big, beautiful morning waves.

I grabbed the bag of malasadas while Aveda gathered all of her surf gear, and then we were descending on the expanse of soft golden sand, the gentle rumble of the tide the only sound for miles. I kicked off my slippers and let the sand seep between my toes, my eyes drifting closed as I breathed in salty ocean air tinged with fragrant hints of hibiscus and plumeria.

"This is gorgeous," Aveda said, clomping up next to me. She was already in her wetsuit, surfboard secured under one arm. "I need Scott to see this for sure." She studied the clear blue ocean in front of us. "The sea is a completely different color than it is in Northern California, hmm?"

"I think it's several different colors—like, it's so clean that you can actually see all the hues and gradients," I said. "Turquoise, aqua, royal blue. And all those bits of light filtering in make it look extra magical."

"Incredible." Aveda raised an eyebrow at me. "Are you sure it's okay for us to be here? I don't want to intrude on something that's locals only."

"This is only a semi-secret beach," I said, giving her a reassuring smile and gesturing to the other beach-goers, just a few clusters of dots scattered in the distance. "It can be cherished by respectful visitors, i.e., not the tourists who treat the island as their own personal fantasy playground—rather than a real place where real people are living their very real lives. I was so honored when Doc Kai and Carmelo brought me here after I'd been in Makawao for a couple weeks. Just don't blast out the location on social media or something."

"I would never—and anyway, you know I barely understand how to use any of those tech-y apps," Aveda said, waving a hand. A delighted gleam lit her eyes as she turned back to the waves. "Perhaps you and Sam can practice some video angles while I'm warming up, to ensure that we get the best framing for our shots."

"Oh, I don't know," Sam said. "We might be too busy playing one of our sex games—*ow!*" He threw me an injured glare, rubbing the arm I'd just delivered a monster-level pinch to. "Did you just *pinch* me?!" he growled through gritted teeth.

I bit my lip to stop the smug smile that was about to spread over my face and tried to ignore the irresistible shiver of pleasure his growl always provoked in me.

I was still getting turned on at the most inconvenient of times.

"I must confess, I do not understand the youth of today," Aveda said, her gaze going from me to Sam and back again. "Your language of intimacy is basically indecipherable to me."

"Yeah, you know us kids, we're wild and confusing, don't even try to get it," I said hastily. "Why don't you go do your warm-up? Sam and I will establish a home base here and work on our camera angles."

"Excellent!" Aveda said, already marching purposefully toward the water.

"Pinching? Really?" Sam hissed, once she was out of earshot. "Are you five?"

"Are *you*?" I shot back, doing my best to smother the thrill I felt when his warm breath tickled my ear. "'Sex games'?!"

"Hey, I was just going with the concept Aveda already set up," Sam claimed, gesturing toward the water. Aveda had arranged her board on the sand near the shoreline, and was doing a complicated-looking series of stretches, her face twisted in intense concentration. "Which is the smart way to play this whole fake-dating thing—build on whatever assumptions people are already making about your relationship. It's *strategic*."

"That is *not* strategic," I said, stomping over to the beach supplies we'd dragged from the car—and putting a little extra sway in my step. I could practically feel his gaze attaching itself to my ass. "And why are you acting like you know anything about the fake-dating trope when you're always hating on my beloved pantheon of Christmas rom-coms?"

"I'm not hating on the rom-coms, I'm hating on Christmas, aka the worst holiday that you love beyond all reason," he retorted.

"Fighting words," I hissed. That competitive spark was humming between us at full volume, making my blood pump extra furiously through my veins. Why did arguing with him always make me feel like my senses were dialed all the way up, like the world was suddenly more vibrant, like I was coming back to life after a long slumber?

And why did I enjoy it so damn much?

I pulled out a big towel and unfurled it with a more aggressive than necessary *snap*. "How am I supposed to maintain a fake relationship with you when you insist on having such obviously wrong opinions?"

"I believe the fact that we had a *real* relationship up until very recently helps," he said, grabbing the other big towel and unfurling it in a similarly aggressive manner—and making a big show of flexing his biceps while doing so.

"Our real relationship means we just need to act *natural*," I said, spreading my towel out over the sand. I bent over a little farther than necessary, and felt a vicious stab of satisfaction when he dropped the end of his towel, his eyes lingering on all the places where my slip dress was now clinging to my skin.

Just wait until I unveil my bikini. I hid yet another smug smile.

"Pretend like we're back in the beginning, back in San Francisco—easy peasy," I continued.

"If it's so easy peasy, why are you all twisted up in knots right now? And what are you doing to that towel?"

"I'm getting it all set up for our relaxing beach day," I sassed, sounding anything but relaxed. I smoothed out a particularly persistent wrinkle on the towel and set the bag of malasadas on top of the corner to anchor it in place. "See? Perfect beach spot technique!"

"No." He shook his head. "Why did you set it up vertically?"

"Because that's how *most* people would set it up—"

"Not true. If you lay the towel out horizontally . . ." He demonstrated, smoothing his own towel next to mine, our two rumpled pieces of terrycloth forming a misshapen T. "Several people can sit on it in a row and look out at the water."

"No one wants to sit on a towel like *that*," I protested, moving to shift his towel placement. "All squished together?! No, we must *lounge*—"

"*You* don't lounge," he countered, grabbing one end of his towel to protect it from my grabby hands. "You're going to be frolicking in the ocean like an excited little fish, then eating all these malasadas and making distracting food orgasm noises, then complaining about how long you have to wait before you can go back in, then—"

"These malasadas are for *Evie*," I protested, grabbing the other end of the towel. That competitive spark was positively blazing now, sending a flush through my entire body. "And when I come out of the ocean, I want to be able to lounge on my towel the correct way!"

"Well, this is *my* towel," he insisted, yanking on his end. His dark eyes flashed, making my flush intensify. "So I should be able to set it up the way I want."

"Why are you being such a *child*?" I snitted, tugging on my end.

"Why are *you*?"

"Bea! Sam!"

We both whirled around to see Evie, Nate, Doc Kai, and Carmelo strolling toward us, loaded up with their own beach gear (and yes, Christmas lights, which Nate was dutifully toting along with everything else). Evie gave us a big wave, her eyes darting around in wonder.

The end of the towel slipped from my grasp, my face on fire.

"Are you two having a tug-of-war?" Evie raised an inquisitive eyebrow as she took us in.

I flushed further, embarrassment rising in my chest. What the hell was I doing? Playing a weird and very childish game of towel tug-of-war on this beautiful semi-secret beach with my sort of estranged boyfriend who I couldn't seem to stop sexy bickering with? All while getting distracted by his stupid muscles and totally forgetting that I was supposed to be cleverly ferreting out information about everything I couldn't remember, all the days I'd missed?

My time-travel sleuthing was *so* not going well. And my attempts at showing Evie how grown-up and self-actualized I was were going *even worse*.

"Just figuring out the best towel configuration," I said hastily, my voice cracking. I cleared my throat. Out of the corner of my eye, I saw Sam very deliberately arranging the towel horizontally, smoothing out all the wrinkles. He met my eyes and drew himself up to his full height . . . then very slowly stripped his shirt off and gave me a cocky smirk, running a hand over his suddenly exposed swath of abs.

I swallowed, my mouth going dry.

Then he held up an index finger and pointed to himself. *Oh* hell *no!*

I averted my eyes and tried not to think about the fact that my face was currently doing its most convincing impression of a tomato.

"We'll add to what you've got going on here," Carmelo said, giving us a genial grin and whipping out his own pair of towels. "Man, I love any excuse for a beach day."

"You love any excuse to go for one loco moco after," Doc Kai said, shaking her head affectionately. "Since we're mere minutes from Honokowai Okazuya and Deli. Best gravy on the island."

"Don't let Pika hear you say that, yeah? And I gotta keep

carbo-loaded in order to maintain max wrestling suprem-
acy," Carmelo said, giving an exaggerated bicep flex.

"Cheeseball," Doc Kai groaned—but she couldn't stop
the smile that stretched across her face. "Bea, tell my man
to stop being such a cheeseball."

"Wouldn't dream of it," I said. "That's part of his charm."

"Shoots, Bea gets me," Carmelo enthused. "That's why I
stopped by Maui Specialty Chocolates to get her chocolate
peanut butter mochi."

"You're my favorite, Carmelo," I said, laughing a little.
"Don't tell Doc Kai—I can't upset the boss lady!"

"I do my best not to upset her either," Carmelo said, his
warm gaze going to Doc Kai. She smiled back, emotions that
required no words passing between them. "Ooh, the mochi
will go perfectly with those malasadas!" Carmelo nodded at
the bag of sweets I'd used to anchor my beach towel. "Good
lookin' out."

"So many treats," Evie said, looking dreamy. "This truly
is paradise."

I smiled back at her, the beach and the contentious towel
situation and Sam's infuriating smug grin (and lickable abs)
fading away as I took her in. She was clad in the sea-green
jumpsuit Aveda had bought for her during their vampire-
infested LA sojourn, its stretchy waistband comfortably ac-
commodating her ever-growing belly. It wasn't standard
beach wear, but it was definitely standard Evie wear—
comfortable, functional, nothing too frilly or fancy. It was
unzipped a bit so I could see that she had a swimsuit on
underneath.

Her tangle of dark brown curls had grown in the months
since I'd moved, bouncing jauntily around her shoulders.
And she was gleefully drinking in the beachscape, her smile
lighting up her whole face.

Evie had had a lot of trouble with her pregnancy early
on—in addition to Shasta trying to steal the baby, that is. My
sister had existed in a constant state of stressed, exhausted

pukiness, and she'd later confessed that she was completely terrified at the prospect of becoming a mom. I knew she and Nate had also been freaked out about the baby possibly inheriting some of their powers, since this was the first ever offspring of a superhero and a half-demon.

But now? She was legit glowing. And my heart warmed at the sight of all that joy radiating from her, the newfound zeal she seemed to have for life. My kind, generous, tender-hearted soul of a sister deserved that kind of happiness more than anything.

Which meant I really couldn't show her just how fucked up I currently was. And how at odds Sam and I were. And the fact that I was *time traveling.*

Right—keep staying in that moment, Bea! You've left most boats successfully unrocked for a whole entire morning. Although your data gathering could still use some work. Don't forget to observe! Um, observe things that are not *Sam's abs . . .*

"Damn, brah, is that your co-heroine riding the wave out there?" Carmelo piped up, gesturing toward the ocean.

We all turned to see Aveda, now confidently piloting her surfboard through the water. She was crouched low, arms set in perfect formation, ponytail flying behind her like a graceful smear of jet-black ink. She swirled around a wave just as it crested, surfboard snaking its way through the fluffy white bubble of foam.

"Holy shit, she's incredible," Doc Kai breathed. "You sure she's only been surfing a few weeks?"

"Very sure," Evie said with a laugh. "She's just awesome at everything she does. Well, except karaoke—our girl does *not* have the pipes for that."

"She mentioned something about wanting you and Sam to take videos for Scott?" Nate said.

"Right!" I yelped, scrambling to pull my phone out of my slip dress pocket. "Sam and I were just discussing all the different angles we wanted to get."

I aimed the phone toward the ocean, shifting so that

Aveda was perfectly centered in the frame. She was still riding that same wave, her board weaving in and out of the water. Hopefully she wouldn't realize I'd already missed some of her most awe-inspiring moves.

"Why are you framing her like that?" Sam's voice was suddenly in my ear, and I realized he'd moved very close to me and was peering over my shoulder, scrutinizing my work. I felt the heat rolling off his half-naked body, more intense than the blazing sun. "Putting her dead center looks . . . so . . ."

"Correct?" I snarked, hoping he didn't notice the way my voice emerged as a breathy little squeak. "Where else do you suggest I position her in the shot? Or should she even be in the shot? Would it be more *artistic* if I just took random video of the ocean, which is not at all what she asked us to do?"

"Bring her more to the side, or angle it so she's in the corner," Sam said, reaching over my shoulder to take the phone. "That looks less basic, and you can also showcase the ocean, how she's in command of such gargantuan waves."

I stubbornly tightened my grip around the phone and kept Aveda in the center.

"This is for a promotional video, Sam," I said as his fingertips wrapped around the other side of the phone, trying to get the angle he wanted. "It's supposed to be basic."

"But it doesn't have to be," he insisted, tugging the phone so Aveda was off to the side. "See? Doesn't that look better?"

"No," I said, even though it kind of did. I tugged on my side of the phone so Aveda was centered again. Our fingertips brushed, sending those electric sparks dancing over my skin. "Just . . . leave it. Let me do this."

"If you want to do it *wrong*," he said, sounding way too cocky.

"Heeeeey," Evie said, taking a step toward us. "I think all Aveda's gonna care about is how awesome she looks. And all Scott will care about is Aveda being happy. Y'all don't have to go young Scorsese here. Um, why don't we have some of this delicious-looking mochi?"

I snatched my phone back and stuffed it in my pocket, giving Sam a withering glare. He was looking a little overly flushed himself.

Everyone else took Evie's lead, settling in on the (still weirdly arranged) beach towels while Carmelo popped open a big plastic container of mochi. Normally I would've needed no further invitation to join them—the peanut butter chocolate mochi from Maui Specialty Chocolates was god tier, freshly made every day and so soft it melted in your mouth. Whenever Doc Kai bought some for the office, she always got me and Tosh our own separate containers because she knew I was the worst food sharer on the planet. Sam had expressed a little *too* much shock when he'd learned that I was willingly handing off malasada crumbs to Roger, given that I usually housed my portion of whatever delicious meal he'd made for us in three seconds flat and then sweetly cajoled him into giving me at least half of his. It was the same with the mochi—I often finished mine long before noon and then made puppy eyes at Tosh until they eventually let out a long-suffering sigh and passed me an extra piece.

And then there was the incident from the other day wherein I had possibly mind-controlled Doc Kai into fulfilling all my mochi-related fantasies . . .

I pushed that thought to the side, but even the sight of all that delectable mochi goodness wasn't enough to distract me from the antsy prickle humming through my nervous system. As my family dove for the mochi, chattering amongst themselves, I cast a sidelong look at Sam. He was still low-key preening, like a big old peacock trying to get my attention.

I'd noted earlier that time-travel sleuthing and being present in the current moment were two contradictory concepts. But I hadn't realized just *how* contradictory—it was easy for me to be in the moment with Sam because we got swept into that explosive connection that had always buzzed between us. Now I was *so* in the moment that all I wanted to do was beat him in our increasingly petty competition.

Especially since I still had no idea why he'd broken up with me.

Maybe I could at least get him to tell me that—that would be some legit time-travel sleuthing, right?

And also just *really* satisfying, since I was about to show him what he was missing out on.

That thought stoked my adrenaline, and before I knew what I was doing, I'd stripped off my slip dress and tossed it to the side, revealing my tiny bikini with its enticing little ties. Then I reached up and freed my hair from its messy topknot, oh-so-nonchalantly shaking it out so my waves cascaded over my shoulders.

Out of the corner of my eye, I saw Sam freeze in place and heard his breathing speed up.

I hid my smile, tossed my hair over my shoulder, and stretched, arching my back—so much so that the tie between my breasts nearly came undone.

"Jesus Christ," he muttered under his breath.

"We should get some videos *in* the ocean," I declared, turning back toward Aveda's graceful form cutting through the waves. "Like, get much closer to Aveda so we can capture her majesty up close and personal!"

"H-how are you going to do that?" Sam managed, still sounding like he was having difficulty breathing normally. "'Cause, uh . . . you can't swim out there and film at the same time. Unless you have some new superpowers I'm not aware of."

"I have *many* powers you aren't aware of," I said, meeting his gaze and raising an eyebrow. And okay, maybe sticking my chest out just a little bit more. "One of which is that I know this beach like the back of my hand. There's a storage shed on the far west corner that has canoes I can use to paddle out there. So that's what I'll do!"

I put my slippers back on, turned on my heel, and started marching up the beach, heading toward the shed. It did not surprise me even a little bit to hear footsteps behind me, plodding through the sand. I felt a satisfying zing of triumph.

It took everything in my power not to turn around, particularly since the shed was quite a ways away from the spot where we'd set out our towels. But I held firm until I reached my destination, a weathered old clapboard structure that looked like it had seen better days. It always appeared to be on the verge of falling apart, but according to Doc Kai, it had been here forever.

The door was never locked, so I pushed it open, taking extra care so it wouldn't fall right off its rusty hinges. Given its battered outward appearance, one might expect the shed to boast a similarly dilapidated interior. But it was always impeccably clean, the water-splotched wooden surfaces completely dust- and grime-free.

A long work table took up the far left side of the structure, a series of tiny windows casting dusty beams of light across the meticulously organized snorkel gear and life jackets piled on top of it. The canoes and paddles were stacked on the other side of the room, waiting for adventure.

"How are you going to paddle the canoe and film at the same time?" Sam piped up behind me.

I finally turned to look at him, crossing my arms over my chest and fixing him with my best *I have a mind-blowing plan you will never be able to even conceive of* look. Even though I actually had no idea how to answer his question. He met my eyes, his biceps flexing distractingly as he leaned in the doorframe.

"Like I'm going to tell you my amazing plan," I scoffed, marching toward the pile of canoes. "Watch and learn, genius."

I stopped in front of the canoes and put my hands on my hips, studying them. Okay, so step one was freeing a single canoe from this massive stack. Which was quite a bit taller than I was. And no way was I asking Sam for help.

I spied a box stuffed with excess snorkel masks hanging out near the canoe pile. Making my stride as confident as possible, I marched over and grabbed it, then emptied the masks onto the work table. Out of the corner of my eye, I saw Sam watching me.

I ignored him, dragged the box across the floor, and positioned it near the edge of the canoe pile, then turned it upside-down. Still projecting confidence with all my might, I climbed onto the box and reached for one of the pointy ends of the canoe. Maybe if I tipped it just right, I could slide it off the pile and down to the ground.

I was improvising pretty hardcore at this point, but I still tried to make my movements assured. Like I did this sort of thing every day.

Once I'd successfully freed the canoe, I could start up a casual line of conversation about our breakup—maybe I'd even pick a fight, expressing indignation and needling him until he blurted it all out. At this point, he'd gotten plenty of tantalizing eyefuls of my bikini—surely he was worked up, not thinking straight, and ready to *confess*.

"Is this how you usually dislodge a canoe from a giant pile?" Sam asked, interrupting my thoughts.

"Of course," I lied. Getting a canoe down was generally a three-person job, and I was usually lucky enough to have some combo of Doc Kai, Carmelo, Tosh, Keala, Giselle, and Pika with me on these beach jaunts. But Sam didn't need to know that. "It's a tricky maneuver, but once you've practiced enough, it comes really naturally—like your body just *learns* the movements . . ."

I was so into my speech that I didn't notice my fumblings had already managed to dislodge the top canoe from the stack. And instead of gracefully sliding to the ground the way I'd pictured, it was wobbling around in my hands, sending an unsteady tremor through the rest of the pile.

Everything seemed to slow for a moment, the canoe shaking precariously as I instinctively let go of it. Which then sent the entire pile into imminent collapse.

"Bea!" Sam yelled, as my mouth fell open in a silent scream.

Time seemed to slow further, the top canoe tumbling directly toward my face—pointy end first, of course. And I couldn't seem to move. My fight-or-flight instinct was at war with itself, my feet rooted to the box, the *clunk-clunk-clunk* of toppling canoes reverberating through my body. And then a large shape that was definitely *not* a canoe slammed into me.

I was sailing through the air before I realized it was Sam, forcefully flinging himself at me to get me out of the way of the canoe avalanche. We landed with a heavy *thud* on the dirt floor, his body shielding mine as the canoes crashed into a messy heap behind us.

For a moment, we stayed like that, our heavy breathing morphing into the loudest thing in the room while the canoe mess settled. As the shock wore off, I came back to my body, becoming aware of every sensation. The dirt floor against my back. The rapid hammering of my freaked-out heart. Sam on top of me, his hard wall of a body pressed against mine, his breathing labored as he finally pulled back and met my gaze.

"Bea," he gasped. His wild eyes scanned my face, as if searching for injuries. "What the *fuck*? Why would you fucking scare me like that—"

"Scare *you*?" I blurted out, irritation racing through my bloodstream. "You think I concocted a canoe avalanche for *your* benefit? Like I wanted you to swoop in like some cheesy-ass knight in shining armor and save me?"

"I-I don't know!" He shook his head in exasperation. "I was guessing more along the lines of: you need to prove you're right and beat me by any means necessary, so you're singlehandedly following every disastrous scheme you come up with to its equally disastrous conclusion because you're too fucking stubborn to admit you're wrong!"

"That's so freaking *offensive*!" I snarled. "I don't need 'schemes' to beat you, I . . . I . . ."

I tried to wriggle out from underneath him, but this mostly resulted in our various body parts rubbing against each other. My breasts brushed the hard muscles of his chest and immediately perked up, nipples tightening underneath the flimsy material of my bikini top. His thigh had lodged itself between my legs, so any movement only caused it to press insistently against my most sensitive spot, making my brain go hazy with lust. I shook my head, trying to clear it, but it was as if a veil had descended over all of my senses, only allowing me to perceive Sam. *All* of Sam.

I stopped wriggling as his dark eyes met mine, his lips parting slightly. His gaze was stormy, *furious,* and his breath was still escaping in ragged gasps. Pure *want* raged through me, crushing everything else.

"Bea," he growled—and oh *fuck*, it was the growl that always made me wish all my clothes would spontaneously disintegrate. "You put yourself in danger trying to prove a point—"

"Danger?! I'm a fucking superhero!" I protested, finally shoving him off me. I scrambled to my feet and stalked to the other side of the room, then whirled around and glared at him. "And why do you care, anyway? We're not together anymore, so—"

"So *what*, I shouldn't care if you get crushed to death because you couldn't admit you needed help with a fucking canoe?" He got up and crossed the room to me, a full-on glower overtaking his face. "You think I can just turn it off—everything I feel for you?"

"You broke up with me. Shouldn't be *too* hard."

"You broke up with *me*!" he insisted.

"I don't remember that!" I blurted out—and was horrified to hear my voice crack.

But seriously, what the fuck? *I'd* broken up with *him*?

My time-travel sleuthing was going even worse than I'd thought.

Frustration welled in my chest, so all-encompassing I wished the dirt floor would open up and swallow me whole.

Sam studied me, some of his anger turning to confusion. He was standing very close to me now, and I tried not to get distracted by his stupid muscles all over again, by the heat rolling off his body and making the cramped beach shack seem even tinier.

"I mean, I guess it was mutual in the end," he said slowly. "You really don't remember? I couldn't talk because I was busy with my parents and you got upset about how we *never* talk anymore, and then I pointed out that part of that is because you seem to be avoiding me lately—like you mostly just send those Christmas movie letters? That spiraled into a whole thing, and then you said maybe we shouldn't do this anymore. And, well . . . I agreed."

Tears pricked my eyes, a bizarre sort of disappointment thudding through my chest. I could envision that exchange all too well, and yet . . . if we were going to break up, shouldn't it be some kind of earth-shattering, soul-wrenching moment? Shouldn't it be over something of life-or-death importance? What he was describing was so small and sad, so *ordinary*.

"I-it hurts so much," I managed, an errant sob clogging my throat. "I . . . I don't understand how things changed so fast."

"Breaking up was the right thing, though." He met my gaze and reached out to lightly grasp my arms. "We aren't built to be long-term—we never were." Heat from his palms burned through my skin, making my brain all hazy again. His voice was gentler now—and that just made everything he was saying worse. Because he was right, I *knew* it was right, breaking up was probably the most responsible thing we could have done, considering how we both were.

Just like Thomas and Sandrine in *A Kaiju for Christmas*, we were never meant for happily ever after.

But why, then, did that warped, childish, competitive spark between us feel so *good*? Why did something so obviously wrong feel so consistently right?

"But that doesn't mean I'll ever stop caring about you," Sam continued.

"That's *exactly* what it means," I hissed, frustration bubbling through my hazy brain, combining with the lust simmering through me to make everything extra confusing.

His gaze heated, fury sparking in his eyes again.

"No, it's not—"

"You said love wasn't enough! *You* said—"

He cut me off with a kiss.

His hands tightened around my shoulders as he pulled me closer, stroking their way up my neck to tangle in my unruly hair. His mouth was rough against mine—hot, hungry, desperate. A needy moan escaping my throat as I tugged at the waistband of his shorts, pulling him flush against me. And then he growled against my mouth and I was gone.

He maneuvered me up against the wall of the beach shack, his lips never leaving mine. One of his hands slid down to my shoulder again, slipping under the strap of my bikini top to graze bare skin, sparks of electricity igniting everywhere he touched. My palms were pressed against his chest, as if I was attempting to hold on to *something*, to keep myself upright.

I closed my eyes and reveled in every sensation. The wet heat of his mouth moving down my neck and igniting my most sensitive nerve endings. The roughness of his fingers digging into my collarbone as they slid tantalizingly closer to my breasts. The sound of my ragged breathing echoing through the cramped space and syncing with my wild heartbeat.

Sam and I usually took things deliciously slow—every kiss, every touch designed to push each other to the edge. He always knew how to tease me, how to draw things out so the resulting orgasm obliterated all of my senses. But now we were unchained, ready to career headfirst over the edge because we simply could not stop *consuming* each other. The beach shack and its beautiful surroundings melted away, and I could only focus on *him*.

One of his hands moved down to grasp my hip, and he yanked me more firmly against his body, pressing between my legs so I could feel—

Oh *god*.

"You see?" he breathed. "You see how much I want you?"

"Want isn't love. And anyway—"

He cut me off with another growl. A few quick flicks of his fingers undid the flirty little ties of my bikini top and then his mouth was on me, his tongue swirling around my nipple like it was his favorite taste in the whole goddamn world.

My fingers tangled in his hair, urging him closer, and my head fell back against the wall as I drowned in the pleasure coursing through my veins and making me moan again. He moved back up and captured my mouth with his, his hands stroking my breasts. I moaned louder as our lips crashed into each other, tears springing to my eyes because this just felt *so fucking good*. Like something forbidden and inevitable that we'd both been trying our hardest to avoid—which only made me want it more.

"P-please," I sobbed. "Please touch me. I *need* you to touch me."

One of his hands slid downward, slipping under the silky material of my bikini bottoms and grazing the spot where I needed him the most. We stayed frozen that way for a moment, me practically panting with need as my eyes rolled back in my head, his fingertips barely brushing against me. He lowered his mouth to my ear, his breath whispering against my skin in a way that sent shivers down my spine.

"I love it when you beg," he growled.

I almost came right there.

"Why are you slowing down *now*?" I shot back, trying to sound indignant.

"I thought you liked slow."

"I-it just seems inconsistent at the moment. We were going at it all fast and furious, and then you just—"

He chose that moment to brush his thumb against my clit.

Any other words froze in my throat. Any other thoughts evaporated from my brain. All I wanted was *this*—us locked in this moment forever, all pleasure and nothing else.

"Is this consistent enough for you?" he breathed.

Why was he talking like he was an employee asking for a performance review instead of my ex-boyfriend sticking his entire hand down my pants? And why did that turn me on so hard?!

He repositioned his hand, stroking me lazily, his touch alternating between feather light and deliciously firm. When he finally slid a finger inside of me . . . then two . . . I was more than ready. And when his thumb brushed my clit again, a guttural scream tore itself from my throat.

He worked his way up to a relentless rhythm, burying his face in my neck. I wrapped my arms around his shoulders, just trying to hold on again. My legs were shaking, turning to Jell-O, and I knew that if I let go for even a second, I'd collapse on the spot. Pleasure washed over me and I closed my eyes, riding the wave of the orgasm that was gathering steam.

He increased his rhythm and his mouth moved downward, his teeth closing around my aching nipple. And when he started to taste me again, his tongue sweeping over that delicate flesh and making me feel like I was on fire . . . I closed my eyes and let that orgasm take me, my senses exploding into a rainbow of light that blocked out everything except me and him and how dedicated he was to making me feel so fucking good.

I screamed his name, tears streaming down my cheeks, the waves of pleasure skyrocketing through me over and over and over again. It was relentless and wonderful and it seemed like the walls were shaking all around us, an earthquake of our own making.

He stroked me down from my climax, his touch growing gentle. And then we stayed frozen in place, our rough breathing echoing through the cramped space.

After a moment, he very carefully pulled away from me, adjusting his shorts.

"Sorry," he murmured. "I . . . I don't know what that was."

"You were trying to prove you still care about me," I said, my voice very small. "So, um . . . good job."

He laughed, but there was no humor behind it. It sounded hollow, like he was a robot learning how to make basic human sounds. I awkwardly retied my bikini top, the silence between us thickening.

"So we should . . ." He made a half-hearted gesture toward the door leading back to the beach, where Aveda was probably hanging ten while Evie snacked on mochi and Nate tended to her like the devoted husband he was and Doc Kai and Carmelo snuggled up on a shared towel and whispered cute inside jokes in each other's ears.

And then there was me. The fuck-up chaos monster who just could not seem to get her life in order—and who now felt that burgeoning darkness deep in her soul. The problematic romantic who was trying to fake a relationship with the ex-boyfriend she'd sort of accidentally just fooled around with in a broke-down beach shack. The restless wanderer who was never truly happy anywhere.

I felt like I was swimming through the wreckage I'd made of my life, trying to get to my happy, well-adjusted family as they beckoned me from the shore.

"Wait!" I cried, my voice twisting into a desperate yelp. "Are we really not going to talk about what just happened?"

He stopped in his tracks. "What just happened is a perfect example of why we're not built for anything long term." He turned to face me, his eyes strained around the corners—like his skin was too tight. "This is who we are, Bea—messed up and petty and playing childish games just so we can goad each other into . . . I dunno, whatever we think is 'winning.' We can't do the stable happy thing, and we'll only make each other miserable if we try. And I need to be more stable right now, more responsible—for my parents."

"And, what? I can't understand because I don't have parents? I don't know what it means to be responsible?!" I spat out, crossing my arms over my chest. This time, I didn't try to push my cleavage up, even though it was encased in nothing but a few flimsy scraps of fabric. I was too mad.

I felt like I was swimming through wreckage again, trying to maneuver my way against rough currents, about to drown. Because hadn't I just been thinking along the same lines? I knew we shouldn't be together. I knew he was *right*.

And I fucking hated it.

"That's not what I meant—" Sam began, running an exasperated hand through his hair.

"Then what *do* you mean—"

"Wait, quiet—"

"Don't tell me to be quiet!" I roared, that rage rushing back. "Do *not*—"

"No, sorry. I meant . . ." He made a frantic sort of gesture, indicating our surroundings—and that's when I realized the beach shack was shaking.

Like, legit shaking. Not the metaphorical shaking I'd visualized when his fingers had been inside me, rendering me helpless with lust.

The tiny windows rattled violently, the walls letting out an ominous rumble that seemed to indicate imminent collapse. In the corner, the now very messy pile of canoes was shaking too, perhaps glad they'd already fallen and had nowhere else to go.

I froze in place, scanning the shack's interior. What the frak was going on? Had the storm returned? I didn't see the telltale slashes of rain pounding against the windows, couldn't find any lightning streaking the clear blue sky. In fact, the bits of sky that were visible through the window were as blue as ever.

"Let's go see what's happening," I said, attempting to shove down the worry that was percolating in my gut. "After all, it's the *responsible* thing to do."

And then I swept by him, my head held high, attempting to maintain consistent footing on the trembling ground.

I may be a fuck-up, but I'll say this for myself—in the event of a potential apocalypse, I always come up with a good comeback.

The ground kept shaking as I darted out of the beach shack. I kicked off my cumbersome slippers and raced toward the piece of shore where I'd left Evie and Co., Sam hot on my heels. My eyes scanned the wide swath of sand and sea, desperation flaring in my chest as I tried to get a handle on what was going on.

Though the sky had been blue mere seconds ago, a dark haze was reaching jagged fingers of gray across its cloudy expanse, casting an ominous dark shadow over everything. The ocean churned as if there was already a storm going, its waves erratic and choppy. I didn't see Aveda's determined little surfboard-riding speck—it appeared that everyone had abandoned the water.

In the distance, I saw all the small groups of beach-goers attempting to gather their things and flee. Evie and Co. were clustered on the towels where we'd left them, although I was too far away to see what they were doing. I noticed they'd managed to get a string of lights wrapped halfway around a palm tree, but it looked like that project had been abandoned before they could complete it.

I increased my pace, and tried to tell the panic that was now racing through my bloodstream to calm down, already. It was probably just a precursor to another storm . . . that also involved an earthquake for some reason . . .

I ran even faster.

As I got closer, I saw that everyone seemed to be clustered around a single towel. Nate was yelling something, his face twisted in fear . . . and Doc Kai looked like she was trying to reassure him . . .

And then I saw what they were all gathered around—*who* they were all gathered around.

It was Evie. She was lying on her back, hands clamped so tightly to her belly that her knuckles were white. And as I finally reached her, she threw back her head and let out an ear-shattering scream so primal, I thought it might split the earth in two.

CHAPTER ELEVEN

"EVIE!" I SHRIEKED, falling to my knees next to her.

I was vaguely aware of Sam crouching down behind me in the sand. Out of the corner of my eye, I glimpsed various random beach-goers making their hasty exits from what appeared to be a minor earthquake coupled with yet another storm. Only one person lingered, a tall woman sporting a giant sun hat and gazing out at the choppy waves. I had no idea how she was remaining so calm. Tears filled my eyes as my surroundings melted away, and all I could see was my distressed sister.

Evie released another scream, clutching her pregnant stomach and curling in on herself, tears streaming down her face.

"What happened?!" I demanded, whirling from Nate to Doc Kai and Carmelo. "What's wrong with her?"

"We don't know," Nate growled. "The ground started shaking, and suddenly she was screaming—"

Evie screamed again, as if to demonstrate. Nate laid a tentative hand on her shoulder, trying to snap her out of it.

"Baby," he said, his voice urgent. "Please, tell us what's wrong. Just *tell* us . . ."

"Is it early labor?" I blurted out, grasping for something that sounded like a fairly mundane answer. "Is the baby coming *now*?"

"We thought maybe that was it," Doc Kai said, her kind features strained with worry. "We tried calling her doctor, but we couldn't get ahold of her . . ."

"And we could get one ambulance, but I'm guessing there are no ob-gyns outside of San Francisco who will know what to do with this kind of pregnancy," Carmelo added. He held up his phone. "I called one anyway, but . . ."

Evie's screams were constant now, an ear-splitting soundtrack echoing throughout the beach. I glanced up at the sky. It had morphed to a dull slate-gray color, and the ground's shaking had stabilized to a consistent rolling rhythm beneath our feet.

This was no ordinary storm.

Out of the corner of my eye, I saw the Christmas lights half-decorating that solitary palm tree twinkling merrily away, as if trying to distract us with some twisted form of festivity. I shuddered.

As I turned back to Evie, her stomach started to shift and expand, her skin reshaping itself like a blob of Play-Doh, ridiculously malleable.

And then it transformed into something long and pointed, her belly funneling itself into a blade-like point that tore through the middle of her jumpsuit. As if Little Galactus Tanaka-Jones was trying to free themselves from her body by any means necessary.

She looked like a character in the *Alien* movies, right when the chest-burster decides to make an appearance. The Christmas lights seemed to twinkle even more furiously, as if acknowledging that this was a thoroughly bizarre moment.

"That is *not* early labor," Nate said, his voice hoarse with panic. He gripped Evie's shoulder, but she continued to scream, like she'd been transported to a whole other reality that was nothing but pain. Like she didn't see or hear any of us at all. "This is my mother—Shasta's doing this."

His face crumpled, and I could practically feel the unspeakable terror overwhelming him. Shasta was trying to literally rip Evie's baby from her body—while we all hovered around, freaked out and helpless.

And those fucking Christmas lights just kept on twinkling.

"Where's Aveda?" I asked, grasping around for something, anything. Some kind of solid course of action.

"She's still out there," Carmelo said, jerking his chin toward the water. "Although . . ." He frowned, his usual jovial expression grim. "I don't see her."

"How is Shasta getting to Evie?" Sam interjected. "She's failed at everything she's tried before—"

"And that just means she's gonna keep trying until she gets it right," I muttered.

"Bea." Nate had gathered Evie's thrashing form in his arms and was trying to stroke her hair, to soothe her. "Can you make contact with Scott? If he can do his power combo spell, maybe you two can . . ."

"Can *what*?" I spat out. Fear gathered in my chest, a dark cloud to rival the one currently overtaking the sky.

"I don't know!" he shot back, cradling Evie closer. She thrashed harder, her limbs shooting out in all different directions as her belly continue to morph into those bizarre alien shapes. "But we have to try *something*, or . . ."

"Let me find Aveda," I managed, willing my voice to stop trembling. I threw on my discarded slip dress and scrambled to my feet, wobbling around on the still-rumbling earth. "Just . . . Nate. Don't let her die. Please." That last word came out as a strangled sob, and I hastily swiped a hand over my eyes, ordering myself to stay calm.

He didn't look up, his dark gaze locked on Evie. "I'll give my life before that happens."

I gave him a tight nod and turned back to face the ocean. I just had to maneuver myself toward the shoreline. I'd done pretty okay with the running before, so I tried that again, focusing on the determined *slap-slap-slap* of my feet as they beat the sand into submission. I kept my eyes trained on the choppy expanse of sea, silently telling myself to *not* turn around, to not dwell on the fact that my sister, one of the most precious people to me, might be about to die in the arms of the sweet man she deserved to live happily ever after with.

I would *not* think about that.

I finally reached the shoreline and frantically scanned the waves, whipping my head back and forth, trying to get more ocean in my eyeline. The water lapped at my toes, a shock jolting through my system as I realized it was ice cold. I instinctively jumped back. The ocean in Maui was pretty much *never* cold. It usually had the soothing feel of slipping into a perfectly warm bath, the sun glittering off its surface like a scatter of stars.

I sternly told myself not to get distracted and trained my gaze on the waves once more, trying to locate Aveda.

But there was no one out there. Not a single soul. The ocean crashed against a tall, craggy rock formation in the distance, like it was trying to do battle against the earth itself.

It was an eerie sight, this totally abandoned ocean. Even on the roughest weather days, there were still a few colorful specks out there, determined surfers who weren't about to let some big waves get in the way of their favorite sport. In fact, the extra challenge made it all the more enticing.

A chill ran through me that had nothing to do with the freezing water still tickling the tips of my toes.

I realized then that the ground had stopped shaking.

I chanced a glance over my shoulder, locating my little cluster of family gathered around Evie on the beach. I couldn't make out all the details, but it looked like Nate was still cradling her close.

I took a deep breath and released it slowly, trying to figure out what the fuck to do. I'd barely completed my exhale when an all-new ominous rumble crept into my eardrums—and this one seemed to be coming directly from the sea.

I whirled back around just in time to see the freakiest fucking monster I'd ever witnessed bursting out of the ocean.

My eyes widened, my jaw dropped, and terror blazed through me. The freezing cold ocean was now swirling around my feet, submerging my ankles, but I barely felt it.

Because what. The. Actual. *Fuck!*

Team Tanaka/Jupiter had battled ghosts, vampires, and demons of all stripes. This was something else entirely.

I squinted at the thing as it rose from the ocean, sending water cascading over its spiky back. And that's when I realized I *had* seen something like this. Only in miniature form.

It was a gigantic version of the mini kaiju I'd witnessed the night before. Or I guess . . . a week ago? An encounter I'd nearly forgotten about amidst all the time-travel madness.

It was as tall as a skyscraper and looked like a mash-up of Godzilla and a dragon and a gargoyle, its body like a bulbous Tyrannosaurus rex covered in a series of sharp spikes. Monstrous wings exploded from its back, flapping through the water and setting off another series of violent waves. Its eyes glowed with malevolent golden light, and as it opened its mouth to release a mighty roar, it revealed a series of teeth as sharp and dangerous-looking as the spikes lining its iridescent, rainbow-hued hide. It snapped its lobster-like claws in the air.

This all would have been really cool if I wasn't positive this gigantic kaiju monster was about to destroy us all.

It roared again, a horrible sound that seemed to come from deep within its belly—and the ground shook once more.

I tried to plant myself firmly, rooting my feet in the sand even as icy water swirled around my legs. And I stared up at the kaiju, wondering what the hell I could do to stop it. All I'd done with the mini kaiju was shut up and cower and it had vanished.

Had that been real after all?! I'd been so convinced I was hallucinating, but . . .

The kaiju turned toward me, its glowing eyes scanning the shore, its massive body setting off a near tsunami of a wave as it took a step, laboriously moving forward in the water. What could it be thinking? Was it capable of that? Was it guided by savage instinct? Or puppeted by Shasta, its only mission to destroy?

And was I really spending this moment trying to figure out the specific ins and outs of kaiju psychology?

Except . . . *wait*. I could use that.

I could *so* use that.

Thoughts, feelings, impulses: these were all key to my superpower, weren't they? So didn't it follow that I could totally—

No. You can't.

Because I had a new code, a commitment to never use my power, to be extra careful about letting my emotions out, to *blend the fuck in . . .*

The monster roared again and slapped the ocean with one of its giant claws, sending a whole new tsunami of waves rolling my way. In the distance, Evie let out a particularly wrenching howl.

I focused on the kaiju, its golden eyes meeting mine.

And suddenly, I knew what I had to do.

Yes, I'd been on the more heroic path, the "don't make a scene, always choose the morally pure way, be the boring background Christmas tree you want to see in the world" journey.

But that was before my sister was being tortured to death so demons could steal her baby. Before a gigantic monster rose up and threatened my family and my wonderful new friends and the precious island that had become a second home to me. I felt a pang of regret, thinking of Doc Kai's idealistic dream of friendly sea monsters that was never meant to be.

I had to lean all the way into my evil-adjacent power. I had to fully embrace everything I'd been avoiding, all of those overflowing feelings I'd been so terrified of recently.

I had to take *control*.

The darkness inside of me thrummed with pleasure, letting me know it was ready to rise up just as the kaiju had. I focused on the monster, which was now attempting another lumbering step through the water.

I'd keep my Canary Cry in my back pocket, ready to deploy. If I let loose with it now . . . well, I wasn't sure how this creature worked. It was probably reasonable to assume it was connected to the Otherworld, but it was so *big*. What if my scream made it explode or something, all its huge, spiky, monster-y bits flinging themselves at the natural beauty of Maui, the people on the shore, anyone who might still be in the water? Like Aveda, if she was out there.

That seemed like a disaster in the making.

No, I would have to start with my OG power. I'd emotionally project onto this monster. I'd dial the mind control all the way up, no guardrails in place. I'd make it feel the way I wanted it to feel. Do what I wanted it to do.

I'd finally embrace my supervillain side.

And then I'd make the monster destroy itself.

My darkness thrummed again, practically purring with glee. I would need to call on that darkness however I could, I realized—hopefully its supernatural origin would bolster my power in that special freaky way and help me exert control over something so big, beastly, and Otherworld-enhanced.

And in the back of my mind, I just knew . . . once I made that turn, once I stepped over that line . . . well, that was it, wasn't it? I'd *never* be able to refuse my power's siren song again. I knew myself well enough to know that, down to my bones.

There was a strange sense of relief in accepting the inevitability of this. Right now, I could revert back to thinking like Past Bea—that flighty, irresponsible, commitment-phobe I'd described to Roger. I would let go of stressing over consequences and just do what felt good in the moment.

What Would Bea Tanaka Do?

Exactly what she was always meant to, motherfucker.

I took a deep breath and closed my eyes, and the world seemed to still around me, even as the ground kept shaking underneath my feet. I gathered up every emotion I was feeling. Rage and terror and the strange exhilaration that came with letting go of the struggle I'd wrestled with ever since the power combo spell—the struggle to do the right thing.

I felt that Otherworld darkness inside of me rise up, pulsating through my soul and hissing that yes, *this* was the right thing for me. I added that to my big ball of feelings, encasing my projection in that weird magic I kept trying to resist.

I steeled myself, preparing to project with all my might—
NO NO HURT HELP HELP HURT PLEASE HELP

I gasped and jumped back, the icy water sloshing against my bare legs. Somehow I knew that was the kaiju, just as I had the other day. The big kaiju's thoughts reverberated through my head, its distressed emotions smacking me in the chest. It felt just like it had with the mini kaiju, only dialed way, way up. I projected back at the monster, trying to overwhelm it with my own feeling so I could control it. How did these kaiju keep projecting their emotions and thoughts onto *me*?! That was supposed to be my gig! Although my own mood didn't seem to be affected by their thoughts, so it wasn't quite emotional projection. More like messed-up telepathy? Or a Vulcan mind-meld gone wrong?

And why was the kaiju, currently the scariest thing on the whole beach, crying out for help? Maybe it felt the threat of my mental hold already, and it just knew that was going to keep it from stealing Evie's baby and killing her in the process.

I brushed the thought aside and focused on my projection, stringing together everything I wanted the monster to feel . . . to *do* . . .

I could sense the Otherworld darkness inside of me luxuriating in the monster's thoughts. Yeah, the darkness was *so* loving all of this.

Embrace it! I reminded myself. *You* want *the darkness to feel good—we're going all in!*

I focused on the kaiju with all my might.

You want me, I thought at the monster. *Not my sister's annoying baby. All babies do is cry and shit and siphon energy off their caretakers. You're an attractive young kaiju with lots of life left to live! You still have so many years of carefree adventures ahead of you, adventures that definitely do not involve 3 a.m. feedings or being forced to memorize the oeuvre of Peppa Pig.*

The kaiju stopped in its tracks and cocked its head to the side, like it was listening to something.

That's right, motherfucker—you're listening to me. You are controlled by me. *I am the kaiju now!*

And I swore I saw it nod.

I dialed up all the thoughts and feelings I was projecting at the kaiju, urging it closer. It started to move again, its glowing eyes trained on me. I met its gaze and did my best not to flinch.

Come closer, I ordered the kaiju. *Don't even look at anyone else. It's just you and me.*

I started wading into the freezing water. I needed to walk out as far as I could—no need to bring this beast *too* close to land, where it could do a lot of accidental damage. The cold bit into my bare skin, needles of ice stabbing at my thighs. The kaiju kept moving closer to me, every step setting off another massive roiling wave.

That's it, that's it—almost there, I thought at it. My darkness sang with pleasure, a giddy pulse through my veins.

I planted my feet in the wet sand below the ocean. I was up to my chest now, my teeth chattering as goosebumps pimpled my exposed skin. A strangely peaceful feeling settled in my chest, everything else melting away as the monster approached.

This would be my last battle, my last stand against evil—because I was about to *become* evil, and I didn't know exactly what would happen to me after that. It was all for the best. My family would survive, hopefully thrive, Evie would finally get her happy ending . . . and Sam would find someone else. Someone he could be all *responsible* with.

I focused extra hard on the kaiju, drawing it to me, thrilling at every lumbering step it took, reveling in the darkness—

And then something pushed back *hard* against my mind.

I drew a sharp inhale, flailing around in the freezing water. The kaiju stopped in its tracks again, its golden gaze leaving mine and becoming unfocused. It turned to the sky, as if it had just heard something.

I looked around frantically, trying to figure out what was going on . . . and then I felt my projection slip, an invisible wall slamming down between my brain and the kaiju's. I could no longer sense its thoughts, couldn't feel it at all. I tried to gather all my feelings again, to send out my projection again, I *had* been controlling it, I'd been so close—

Before I could get a handle on what was happening, a tiny black speck burst out of a gigantic wave and aimed itself directly at the kaiju's roaring mouth.

What the . . .

I squinted up at the speck, my concentration thoroughly broken. And I realized it was none other than Aveda Jupiter, perched on her surfboard. She was trying to *surf* her way to the kaiju's face.

I couldn't see her super well, but her power ponytail flew triumphantly behind her, and her body was crouched in perfect formation, one of her hands curling to form a mighty fist.

"Aveda!" I screamed. But of course she couldn't hear me.

Dammit, she needed to get out of the monster's way. She needed to let *me* handle it.

I thrashed around in the water, trying to move farther in. The cold hit me right in the chest and it felt like my heart was freezing over. As numbness spread throughout my body, I saw something sparkly dancing across my vision: the string of Christmas lights that had been twinkling around that palm tree. The lights twisted their way through the air and out over the ocean, swooping toward the monster—I couldn't tell if they were attacking the kaiju or Aveda or . . . maybe she was guiding them using her telekinesis? If I could just get a little closer . . .

I screamed Aveda's name over and over again, tried to reestablish my connection with the monster—but it was too late, I couldn't get it back, that invisible mental wall was holding firm.

Aveda was almost to the kaiju's mouth now. It opened its

jaws wide, about to swallow her alive, and I was frozen in place, I couldn't do anything, I couldn't—

And then a wave rolled over me and I went under, choking on saltwater and my own tears.

And everything went black.

FROM THE SUPER EPIC ARCHIVE OF BEA TANAKA'S TOTALLY LEGENDARY HOLIDAY MOVIE LETTERS

Dear Sam and Leah,

I'm pretty sure both of you are all too aware that one of my greatest passions in life is none other than TROPES! Fake dating, there's only one bed, second-chance romance, enemies to lovers, friends to lovers, friends to enemies to lovers (or any permutation of these elements, as long as it ends with lovers) . . . I adore them all.

So today I'm going to go into great detail about one of the most trope-tastic holiday movies of all time, Princess Christmas! (The official title includes the exclamation point, obviously.)

Princess Christmas! is all about a small-town Christmas pageant wherein one lucky soul is crowned Christmas Queen of the quaint, charming, totally made-up burg known as Comet Gulch. Our scrappy twentysomething heroine, Mari, has just returned to Comet Gulch after attending college abroad and then working for a few years in some glamorously vague European country in an equally glamorously vague job that seems to be related to fashion.

Mari's parents died when she was young, and she was raised by her doting grandmother, who has now ALSO died (god, poor Mari, she's an orphan several times over—truly a hard-knock life for her!). After getting fired from her glamorously vague job, Mari goes home to lick her wounds and hermit up for Christmas in her dead grandma's house that she has just conveniently inherited.

But because no one in Comet Gulch has seen Mari since she was a scrawny, mousy teen . . . no one recognizes her (yeah, I guess they don't use social media in Comet Gulch either?!). Through a series of all-too-convenient mix-ups, Mari is mistaken for an AC-TUAL princess hailing from the vaguely glamorous European country she has just flown in from!

You can probably guess where this is going. (Sam, stop rolling your eyes! Yes, the tropes in my beloved Christmas movies can be predictable sometimes, but the beauty is in seeing how swoonily they're executed! Back me up, Lee, I know you get it!) Mari decides being a princess sounds way, way better than being her jobless, directionless orphan self, so she just goes with it. Enthralls the whole town with stories about castles and ballgowns and what it means to be royalty! And they drink that shit up like it's hot buttered rum! (btw have y'all tried this with whipped cream on top? Truly next level! Sam, I bet your chef's brain could come up with even more twists on this classic wintertime beverage!)

Things take a turn when Mari is pressured into participating in the Comet Gulch Christmas Queen pageant. The pageant's popularity has decreased in recent years, which is an issue for Comet Gulch, because apparently said pageant generates so much tourist revenue, the town is usually set for the rest of the year. Now they need a new community center, but that will only be possible if the pageant is the smash-hit success it's been in the past! So what better way to drum up interest than to feature a real! Live! Princess!!!

Mari goes along with it and in the beginning, she's trying to just keep her head down—to present the perfect image of a polished royal and not let on that she's actually a big fucking mess. But as she reconnects to the awkward Comet Gulch teen she once was, she remembers how much fun she and her grandma used to have together. How their relationship was so special and lovely because they were both kind of outlandish and unpredictable, causing delightful chaos wherever they went. (And hey, you have to be just a little bit chaotic to go along with the mistaken assumption that you're a princess!)

Mari ends up rediscovering her own brand of delightful chaos, which leads to her attempting to juggle three different holiday suitors at once and trying to keep all of them from finding out about each other. There's the formerly nerdy high-school BFF who is now an extremely hot-high school football coach, the suspicious reporter who has a hunch and sets out to expose Mari's fake identity, and the fellow pageant contestant with a heart of gold who starts out as Mari's rival before they have a total bonding moment over wearing old sneakers under their long, beautiful ballgowns.

So in one single movie, you've got friends to lovers AND enemies to lovers AND enemies to friends to lovers. Comet Gulch is one horny, trope-y little town!

Anyway, major hijinks ensue and Mari rediscovers her sense of self and her love of her small hometown, finding that she can build a beautiful community there even if she's not a princess. Of course, her multiple ruses eventually crumble, and she gives a tearful speech during the Christmas Queen crowning ceremony wherein she finally lets that perfect princess façade slip away for good and reveals herself in all her messy, chaotic glory. And of course, Comet Gulch embraces her for who she is. (And also magically raises enough money for that dang community center.)

I suppose it's obvious to y'all, the two people who know me best, why I love this one—in addition to all the tropes, I mean. Mari's situation is exactly the kind of mess I seem to get myself into all the time! I've always been impressed with her ability to turn it all around and use that chaos power for good.

And as for which of her promising suitors she chooses . . . you know what, I think y'all should watch the movie to find out! Because what's Christmas without a little small-town royal mistaken-identity mystery! (That's another trope—several for the price of one, in fact.)

XOXO,

Princess Bea, aka the Real Christmas Queen (yes, I can be both at once, shut up)

Chapter Twelve

MY EYES CREAKED open, slivers of light filtering into my vision.

Wait. This wasn't right.

My heavy limbs should be pushing against the freezing cold tide, my lungs fighting for air. I was sinking to the bottom of the ocean, waiting to be claimed by its murky depths . . .

I jerked into a sitting position, gulping in greedy mouthfuls of air, my hand flying to my chest.

My very dry, not-at-all-submerged chest. Which was currently clad in a silky red slip of a nightgown with garish green lace trim. I blinked a few times, trying to wake up, and my surroundings slowly came into focus. The soft bed beneath me, the fairy lights strung around the room, the window to my right with its curtains slightly open, revealing a few rays of morning light.

The headache I was becoming all too accustomed to hit me like a big-ass truck blazing down the highway at full speed, pain stabbing me in the temple.

Heart hammering in my chest, I threw myself out of bed and padded over to the window, wincing as the headache spread, as if trying to take over my skull. I threw the curtains open in appropriately dramatic fashion, revealing the colorful old Victorians and sloping streets of the lower Haight.

I was back in San Francisco. This was my trusty old bedroom in HQ, fairy lights still flickering after I'd abandoned them so many months ago.

I turned away from the window, reflexively pinching my

arm. Was I dreaming? Was this the afterlife? Were the fairy lights perhaps a representation of the Christmas lights I'd just seen dancing over the ocean . . .

No, come on, Bea, you know what this is—the headache is the tell! You've gone time traveling again. But to when, *exactly?*

I'd just been in the middle of a very important battle. And now I seemed to be wearing some sort of Christmas-themed nightgown? I ran my hands over the silky material, my gaze wandering the rest of the room. I saw popcorn garlands strung next to the fairy lights (though not so close that they'd catch on fire). Pillows embroidered with adorable ginger-bread people in ugly holiday sweaters dotted my bed. And there was mistletoe affixed to the headboard.

Okay, so it was presumably the holiday season. But what *year* was it? Was this before or after my big battle against the kaiju? And if it was after, how the hell had I survived long enough to make it to this Hallmark-worthy atmosphere?!

Before I could spiral any further, the door flew open and Aveda Jupiter marched into my room.

"Good morning!" she sang out, waving a cluster of jingle bells she had clutched in her fist. I recoiled as the dissonant jangling assaulted my eardrums, and the pain in my temple turned itself all the way up.

"M-morning," I managed, my foggy brain helpfully re-minding me not to say anything that might reveal what was going on. I had to remain vigilant in my mission to not fuck with the timeline, even if I didn't know where I currently was in said timeline. "Um." I looked Aveda up and down. "What are you wearing?"

"Is it too much?" She put a hand on her hip and struck a sassy pose so I could fully take in her outfit. She was clad in what could only be described as a sexy Santa costume: red velvet dress with a strapless bustier top and short flared skirt, trimmed in festive winter white; black over-the-knee boots; and a classic Santa hat.

"I feel like you're about to serenade me with an

inappropriately sultry version of 'Jingle Bell Rock,'" I said. "Inappropriate not because there's anything wrong with being a slutty Santa, but due to our close familial relationship."

"I will do no such thing," she declared, dropping out of her pose and crossing her arms over her chest. "Evie always tells me I have a terrible singing voice. But for your event today, going all out was a *must*."

"Event . . ." I murmured under my breath, still scrabbling around for clues. I needed to call Leah—my constant. Maybe she could help me fill in the blanks. Unless this was a *past* Christmas, in which case . . . Past Leah wouldn't remember our conversation, since it hadn't happened yet. I mean, right? Should I even risk asking her about it, or would that fuck up the timeline even more?

Ugh. Time travel was so confusing.

"Did I hear my name? Are y'all ready to go yet?" Suddenly Evie was shuffling into the room, clad in jeans and a sweatshirt emblazoned with cartoon mochi, all sporting cute little faces and their very own Santa hats.

And in her arms . . .

I gasped and felt all the blood drain from my face.

Because she was holding the tiniest, most precious baby. *Her* baby.

"Little Galactus Tanaka-Jones," I breathed, tears springing to my eyes.

"Enough with that nickname!" Aveda groaned. "She likes Vivi." She turned to the baby, pitching her voice into cutesy chipmunk territory. "Don't you like Vivi, little baby? Sounds kind of like Aveda, right? Because Auntie Aveda loves you *the most*."

"Short for *Vivian*," Evie retorted good-naturedly, stroking the baby's unruly cap of black hair. The baby made a restless cooing sound, her squashy, dimpled face rearranging itself. "And we've discussed how there isn't, like, an Auntie Olympics. No one to compete with here, Annie."

"Vivian . . . you named her after Mom?" I blurted out, my tears spilling over. "Oh, of course you did. And both of you are here and beautiful and so *alive* . . ."

"God, Bea, Christmas really does make you more sentimental!" Aveda said, arching an eyebrow at me.

"Are you okay?" Evie asked, her forehead crinkling. She shifted tiny Vivian to one arm and reached out to pat my shoulder. "Are you nervous about the event today? You and Leah put so much work in, I'm sure it's going to be absolutely perfect."

I barely heard anything she'd said. I was still focused on that sweet baby clutched in her arms. She had Nate's dark, brooding eyes, and she was using them to stare at me in that curious way babies have, like they're not sure what reality consists of just yet.

Vivian Tanaka-Jones. *Wow.*

So that meant this was the Christmas *after* the battle. And we'd all survived. Evie was okay and Vivi must've been about six months old and Aveda had surfed her way to kaiju-defying victory. Maybe she'd punched the monster in the face and taken it down? Or strangled it with the Christmas lights?

But how had I not drowned?

I gnawed on my lower lip, a confusing mix of emotions washing over me. I wanted to know absolutely everything, but I had no idea where to begin or how to ask without revealing too much. For once in my life, I was truly at a loss for words.

I felt like I was holding very, very still in a room full of delicate glass sculptures or precious porcelain figurines. One wrong move and the whole thing would shatter.

Evie stepped back and surveyed Aveda and me. "Am I way underdressed? This is a whole lotta festive right here." She gestured to both of us, Aveda in her Slutty Santa wear and me in my red and green nightgown.

"These are my pajamas," I said nonsensically.

She cocked her head at me. "Right. Soooooo . . ."

"I have to change! Um. Remind me about the, er, dress code for this event again?"

"Weird of you to ask since you had such a big hand in organizing it," Aveda said, brushing lint from the furry white trim on her skirt. "I think all the invite said was 'festive.'"

"Festive," I repeated, still trying to get my bearings. "I can do that."

"I should think so, given how fanatical you are about Christmas," Aveda sniffed. "Come on, Evie, let's give this one some space—because while it would be very on brand for her to be late to her own event, I presume she wishes to be punctual!"

"Sure," Evie said, studying me like she was trying to work something out. Vivi let out a little whine, and she bounced the baby against her chest. She started to follow Aveda out of the room and I pasted a smile on my face and breathed deeply, just trying to get through the moment.

Evie was almost to the door when she turned and shot me a worried look. "Hey Bea," she said. "Please tell me you broke up with both of them already. Because otherwise to-day's gonna be *really* awkward."

Damn. Shit. Fuck a fucking partridge in a pear tree.

I was drowning again, flailing my limbs through a strange experience I didn't understand.

I'd given Evie bland confirmation that I'd "broken up with" whoever she was talking about. A quick scan through my phone revealed absolutely nothing—I'd been trying to nip my digital hoarder ways in the bud, so I'd set my phone up to auto-delete all texts after a certain period of time. And whaddya know, it had done just that. Email also yielded no further information. I couldn't even find anything about this big event I'd supposedly planned with Leah.

The only thing I'd managed to confirm was that it was

definitely mid-December, about nine months after my fateful battle on the beach. When I glanced in the mirror, I saw that I'd continued to let my mermaid hair grow out. Blue and purple danced around the tips, but my head had gone almost completely brunette. Another strange marker of the months I couldn't remember.

I texted Leah an SOS, asking if we could talk. I kept it vague since I still had very little information about what was going on, and putting time travel–related freakouts in written communication seemed like something I shouldn't do. Also, what if I'd unwittingly disrupted the timeline *already* and Leah didn't know what was going on after all? And wait a second, wasn't Leah supposed to be on a road trip, wearing the winter-appropriate puffy coat she'd been so into? Wasn't my family supposed to be scattered, leaving only Evie and Nate in the Victorian?

Wasn't I supposed to still be in Maui, hiding from everything and everyone?

What had happened? What had *changed*?

The possibilities were truly endless. At least I didn't appear to have created a major McFly/McCoy-level global disaster. Yet.

I stared at my screen for a few minutes, but heard nothing back from Leah—I guessed she was preparing for whatever this big event was. I'd have to find an unobtrusive way to pull her aside and talk to her there.

I also impulsively tried to call Sam, my pathetic ears desperate to hear his voice. But the number had been disconnected, and his contact had been erased from my phone.

So whatever had happened in the last few months, however we'd managed to escape that battle on the beach with Evie and baby Vivi and kaiju-surfin' Aveda intact . . . well, it looked like he and I had stayed broken up. He wasn't one of the mysterious suitors Evie had asked me about.

But who were they?! How had I managed to find two whole people willing to date my disaster self in such a compressed

time period? And how long had I been back in San Francisco?

I attempted to calm myself as I carefully selected my festive outfit. I needed to get back into Observe, Sleuth, and
Blend In mode. Back to being in the moment, sussing out
clues that would help me fill in all the blanks, and trying to
figure out why my power was glitching so hard it had started
sending me through time. Back to asking, *What Would Bea
Tanaka Do?*

Although, if my previous attempt at this sort of thing was
any indication, the answer was, "Get totally distracted by
her hot ex-boyfriend, start obsessing about his abs when
she's supposed to be doing all that awesome observing/
sleuthing, and then fight it out with a massive sea kaiju, all
while gathering absolutely no helpful information about her
power glitch, time travel, or pretty much anything else."

I refocused on my mission. At least there was a silver lining to the breakup—fewer chances for me to get distracted
by abs, fewer opportunities for me to get sucked into petty
competitions wherein I kept forgetting about everything I
was supposed to be doing.

All right, Future Bea, let's do this! I thought to myself,
trying to get determination to take root. *First things first—
put your armor on.*

I changed out of my silky slip of a nightgown and into
festive daywear: a red scoop-neck bodysuit topped with a
tiered green skirt made of fluttery tulle, black tights, and
little black ankle boots. The holidays were the only time I
broke from my magical goth girl aesthetic, though I still
slathered on enough eyeliner to make a raccoon blush. It
might not have quite been a "blend in" outfit, but at least it
went with the seasonal theme.

It turned out that this mysterious event was taking place at
It's Lit, the heavenly romance-focused bookstore Leah managed (and was apparently trying to become the owner of)—
my former place of work. Leah's girlfriend Nicole had taken

over my job after I'd left for Maui. Leah and I had been brought together thanks to the store, after I'd seen a copy of one of my absolute favorite books of all time in the front window. We'd bonded instantly over our shared biracial experience and our shared love of books featuring hot, kickass dragon-shifter ladies, and it was hard to believe there'd been such a long period of my life when I hadn't known her.

It's Lit had also played host to my climactic battle with Mom-Demon, not to mention my awesome going-away party a month later. It was safe to say I couldn't really imagine my life without this very important location, either.

I dutifully followed my family as Aveda led our messy procession up the street and toward the store. She was still in that Slutty Santa getup, and Scott had dressed to match, donning his own Santa garb with no shirt underneath. My heart warmed watching Aveda walk purposefully in front of us, Scott's arm slung around her waist. He kept whispering in her ear and I knew he was very sweetly telling her that she could probably stand to slow down. Lucy and her wife Rose were right behind them, holding hands, Lucy keeping up a running monologue about what did and did not qualify as a Christmas song, at least when it came to karaoke.

And I brought up the rear alongside Evie and Nate, Nate pushing their tiny daughter in one of those tricked-out strollers that resembles a military-grade tank. Evie had convinced him to wear a mochi holiday sweatshirt that matched hers—possibly the most un-Nate-like garment I could imagine. If it lit up in any way, I was pretty sure I'd pass out on the spot.

"She's smiling again," Nate declared, peering into Vivi's stroller. "Look—this is different from the smile she had two days ago, do you see? The left side of her mouth is curling up slightly more than the right side, whereas two days ago, the right side was curling up more than the left side!" A look of wonder lit his eyes as he beamed down at his baby daughter. "Littlest, is this a new smile from you? I'll have to record this data later, but I am fairly certain she is quite far ahead of many of her peers in terms of producing multiple kinds of smiles!"

"Does he have a spreadsheet for that?" I murmured to Evie.

"You know he does," she said, reaching over to squeeze my hand. She smiled affectionately at her husband as he wheeled the stroller further ahead of us, still muttering to himself about Vivi's precocious nature. "It's pretty adorable. He's delighted by literally everything she does."

"And the bit about 'Littlest'?"

"He calls her that because she's the Littlest Tanaka," Evie said. "I was wondering when you were going to finally ask about that nickname—you've held out for months!"

"Um, just wanted to see if I could figure it out on my own," I improvised, returning her hand-squeeze. I couldn't even express how happy it made me to see her and Nate and their sweet little family, such a contrast to the last time I'd seen them. His face twisted as he cradled her close, her unable to feel anything except excruciating pain . . .

"Hey . . . Bea." Evie stopped and faced me, her hand still clasping mine. "I'm glad you're here. I know everyone canceled their holiday plans and stayed in the city because they were worried about me and Vivi. I know that's why *you* came back over the summer—"

"After the battle on the beach," I said, trying to rapidly do the math. "Summer" indicated it had been at least a few months after we'd fought the kaiju. Had I returned for Vivi's birth, maybe? My heart twisted at the idea that I'd missed such a big moment. I'd probably missed *a lot* of moments.

"I . . . yes, I guess it was after that," Evie said, looking at me curiously. "But what I meant was, I know y'all are worried about how I'm handling the fact that my birth experience was . . ." A shadow passed over her face. "Less than ideal. I sometimes wonder if I'll ever have a normal milestone moment. I told Nate I loved him when I was about to die, I was possessed by demonic forces on my wedding day, and then when I had Vivi . . ." Her gaze darkened further. "I

know we're lucky that Shasta never made another baby-
stealing attempt after that day on the beach. And I know
everything we've been through has made all of us stronger,
but I guess I just wish . . ." One side of her mouth lifted in an
attempt at a smile. But her eyes looked haunted. "I wish that
particular moment hadn't been quite *so* hard. Sometimes I
look at her . . ." She cast her gaze toward Nate, pushing Vivi
ahead in her stroller. "And all I can see is everything that
could possibly go wrong. I still worry about her inheriting
our powers—or whatever other supernatural effects you get
when you combine superheroine and demon DNA."

"So you've transferred all your worrywarting from me to
your actual child." I smiled, trying to make my tone light.
"Seems right."

She laughed, but her face held that haunted look. "I suppose so. But my point is, I don't want *you* to worry about *me*.
I'm so happy you're here, especially for the holidays. And I
love that everyone's here for Vivi's first Christmas, but you
don't have to stay for me—I know Kai keeps asking when
you're coming back."

"Oh, uh, sure," I said, trying to process everything she'd
just told me. "Of course. I know that, but—"

"No buts," Evie said. "I'm okay."

But I could see it in her eyes—she wasn't. Whatever had
happened during the birth had stayed with her all these
months. And in true Evie fashion, her greatest concern was
worrying about everyone else while trying to make sure no
one worried about her.

I studied her, taking in her shaky smile and anxious gaze.
And I wished like hell there was something I could do to
make it better. I mean, technically there *was* something I
could do to change her feelings—turn up the mind-control
mojo and have at it.

I'd actually developed my original "your power is only for
the greater good" code after I'd spent the lead-up to Evie's
wedding using my emotional projection to relax her nerves
and soothe her into a calm state of mind. (I would also just

like to note that this was *Aveda's* idea, though there can be no argument that I'd run with it, gleeful at the thought of testing out my newly discovered abilities.) I would never manipulate my sister that way again. It was one of the first instances where I'd truly realized that my power could very easily be used for taking away someone's free will, making them do things they didn't want to.

"Big Sis," I said slowly. "You know I'm always here if you need to talk about anything—"

"Oh . . . no." She waved a hand and forced out a small laugh. "I think I'm all talked out at this point. But thank you." She turned back to the unwieldy parade of our family that had now marched a couple blocks ahead of us, Aveda still leading the way. "Let's go catch up with them. Don't want you to be late."

She squeezed my hand once more, then started marching in that direction, putting on a brave face.

I studied her retreating back, overwhelmed by everything she'd told me.

The only thing I knew for certain was this: if I could have done anything *not* evil to take away the pain that was very clearly still on her mind, I would have done it in a heartbeat.

CHAPTER THIRTEEN

WHEN WE FINALLY reached the colorful façade of It's Lit, I plastered on my best game face. At least I was about to find out what this mysterious event was all about.

I really needed to start writing down the stuff I'd learned so far. I was finally, maybe getting somewhere with the whole time-travel sleuthing thing. But only if I could actually remember the crucial scraps of info I'd been able to attain.

I cataloged those bits in my head for later:

1. After an unsuccessful attempt at baby-snatching back on that Maui beach, Shasta hadn't tried anything again. (Good.)

2. I had returned to San Francisco during the summer because I was worried about Evie. (Maybe good?)

3. This was because Evie had a very traumatic experience with childbirth. (*Not* good!)

4. In the time I'd been back, I had somehow acquired two mysterious suitors who I was supposed to break up with—but knowing me, there was no way to be sure that I'd actually followed through. (*Probably* not good, but also kinda small potatoes in the grand scheme of things.)

Perhaps I could really up my sleuthing game during this event—there was bound to be tons of small talk, right? Surely I could take advantage of that. I made a mental note to catalog all of my observations in a very grown-up, mature way (no emojis, fun pen colors, or wordy tangents).

"Here we are!" Aveda sang out as she threw open the

bookstore door, gesturing grandly to our processional that had formed behind her.

As soon as I set foot inside, glorious scents washed over me, cranberry and peppermint and of course gingerbread. I closed my eyes and inhaled deeply, basking in the holiday cheer as the familiar melodies of Christmas carols tinkled in my ears. There was a crowd milling about the store, though I still didn't know what they were here for. For now, I just allowed myself to luxuriate in all that gingerbread.

My little moment was immediately interrupted by the sound of raucous barking.

And my eyes flew open just in time to see a tiny ball of brown and white fur launching itself directly at my ankles.

"Pancake!" I shrieked, falling to my knees so I could catch the little dog in my arms. I scooped him up and cuddled him to my chest, struggling to hold on to his flailing body as he enthusiastically licked my face, his tail wagging so hard it made him flop around like a distressed fish. "Hey, buddy," I whispered, unexpected tears filling my eyes. "I've missed you so much."

"What, since yesterday?" a familiar voice said.

My head jerked up to see Leah standing over me, eyebrow raised, her mane of black curls listing to the side.

"Lee!" I screamed, leaping to my feet—as carefully as possible, so as not to dislodge Pancake. "It's so amazing to see you!" One of my tears slipped down my cheek as I moved in to give her an awkward one-armed hug, shifting Pancake to my other side. He gave an indignant little whuffle and shot me an annoyed stare with his one eye, clearly irritated to no longer be the center of attention.

"And again: since yesterday?" Leah asked, dutifully returning my hug. "Oh right, Aveda always says you get way more sentimental around Christmas—"

"Hope there's some of that sugar left for me," a new voice purred in my ear.

I pulled back from Leah—prompting another indignant

whuffle from Pancake—and turned to see a drop-dead gorgeous girl. She looked about my age and had coppery-bronze skin, soft brown eyes, and a lush, curvy body contained in a floaty silk dress in shimmering shades of red. She was mischievously holding a bit of mistletoe over her head and giving me what I could only describe as a come-hither look, batting her impossibly long lashes, her painted red lips curving into a seductive smile.

"Um" was all I could say. Right before she swooped in and pressed her lips to mine.

She smelled like strawberries and fresh cream and everything good, and for a confused few seconds, I sank into the kiss, her teeth gently teasing my lips open to stroke my tongue with hers.

Then Pancake let out an extremely aggrieved bark and we split apart.

"Um," I said again, my head spinning.

"Aw, babe, you're so cute when you're flustered," the incredibly hot stranger cooed, her hand idly stroking my back. "And this one . . ." She stuck her tongue out at Pancake. ". . . is a champion buzzkill."

She shot me an exuberant grin, her smile as dazzling as one might expect from a being so effortlessly gorgeous.

"The event is spectacular! Not that I'd expect anything less from two holiday-lovin' geniuses." She gave Leah and me a broad wink. "Bea, babe, I'm gonna go get us some punch—the cranberry concoction Nikki came up with is divine! None for the buzzkill, though." She gave Pancake a reproving look and sashayed off through the crowd.

"So you didn't break up with her," Leah said, as the hot stranger moved out of hearing range. "Bebe! You were supposed to take care of this before our ginormous event!" She gestured to the store, and my gaze followed her arm, finally taking in the full scene.

It's Lit was always a paradise, an airy space stuffed with books and accented with bold decorating choices like the pink velvet couch that graced the middle of the room and a fleet of porcelain unicorns from Charlotte's massive collection (I'd had a traumatic run-in with those unicorns when Otherworld magic had caused them to come to life and inflate to monstrous sizes, wreaking havoc on the bookstore. I'd given them a fairly judgy side-eye ever since). A big garage-style door opened into the café area, where baristas slung book-themed drinks and pastries.

Today, everything was Christmas-themed—to the extreme. Holly and wreaths were crammed into every available nook, cute plush gingerbread people posed around the register, and cotton-spun drifts of "snow" were strewn on the floor. Craning my neck a bit, I could see a table laden with holiday treats and a gigantic punch bowl decorating the café area. Nicole stood behind the table, wearing a headband with mini reindeer antlers and cheerily serving up punch for the eager crowd.

"Bebe!" Leah tugged insistently on my sleeve, snapping me out of my reverie. "Answer meeeee!"

"Sorry." I met her gaze and absently stroked Pancake's fur. He'd settled in my arms like they were his own personal throne, head lolling lazily over my elbow as he assessed every passerby like they were his loyal subjects. Which, honestly, they probably were. "I, um . . ." I glanced around furtively.

Shit. We were trapped in the middle of a crowd, I couldn't make with the time-travel talk just yet. I needed to get Leah somewhere private so we could really dive in. And I could tell by the tension in her spine that she was stressed about this event we'd apparently planned together, so now probably wasn't the time. I'd have to wait until the party died down.

"Sorry," I repeated. "This is going to sound absolutely bananas, but who is that hotter-than-fire girl who just made out with me?"

"Stop trying to make me laugh," Leah protested, swatting me on the arm. "You really don't recognize Olivia? Your supposed-to-be-ex-girlfriend? That you told me you would definitely break up with before our event?"

"Mmm, apologies for that," I said, playing along. "It's just, I mean, she's *so* hot. I guess I couldn't do it. You know how I am: flighty, impulsive Bea! Always acting like I'm made of pure id!"

"Awesome." Leah rolled her eyes. "Does that mean you didn't break up with Terrence, either?" She jerked her chin at a burly man across the way with tousled blond hair and a very square jaw. He looked a bit like an off-brand Hemsworth, and was wearing what was probably supposed to be an ugly Christmas sweater—but it stretched across his broad chest and hugged his considerable biceps in such a way that any supposed ugliness was rendered moot. He was sipping punch and chatting with a guy who was blatantly looking him up and down, noting every place the Christmas sweater was just a little too tight.

"I'm dating him, too?!" I blurted out, clutching Pancake to my chest. He wriggled around and let out a crabby whine. I shot Leah an accusing look. "I told you not to let me date white guys!"

"I *tried*," she shot back, giving me an indignant look nearly as potent as Pancake's. "You were like, 'I know, Lee, but I gotta climb at least one pseudo-Hemsworth like a tree before I die.' And then you did. And *then* you got bored with him immediately, just like you always do, and since you were also bored of Olivia at that point, you promised to dump them *before* our event so they wouldn't find out about each other and set off a drama bomb!"

"Wait a minute, I'm exclusive with both of them?!" I yelped. "I managed to sneak around and keep them from each other like some kind of hokey sitcom character?"

"Oh, Bebe." Leah shook her head at me. "You are acting so weird. Tell me the truth: did you engineer this whole scenario just so you could take center stage in some kind of twisted version of all of our favorite holiday rom-coms?

'Cause normally I'd be into that sort of thing, but . . ." Her eyes narrowed. ". . . not at an event we spent four freaking months planning! This is supposed to be my audition for Charlotte, remember? If I pull it off, she said she'd actually consider letting me buy her out of the store!"

"Um, of course I remember!" I exclaimed, guilt bubbling through my chest. First, I'd had no idea about my best friend's dream. Now I was on a course to completely destroy it? Pancake shot me what I could only describe as an accusing look. "I . . . I'll handle it! Don't worry, Lee! Now, can you tell me . . ."

I frowned, scanning the space again. What *was* this event we'd apparently put so much time and effort into? This event that was so crucial to Leah accomplishing the next step of her quest?

If I asked her that, I'd look even more foolish and thoughtless than I already did. Luckily, the cavalry arrived in the form of Nicole Yamamoto, who was careening our way with a huge smile on her face, mini antlers bobbing atop her head.

"Hey Bea!" she enthused, beaming at me. I smiled back mechanically. Nicole and I had a tortured history that began with us being best friends as kids. In middle school, after my mom died, I'd pushed her away, and she had then convinced everyone that I was an outcast weirdo. When I'd started working at the bookstore, she'd been a stressed law student who'd come in for endless cups of coffee, and we'd renewed our contentious relationship—culminating in that now infamous incident where I'd tried to drag her ass to the Otherworld. And then she and Leah had fallen for each other and she and I had realized we'd both evolved, and maybe it was better to work toward friendship again.

I hadn't spent much time with her since then, as I'd moved to Maui right after we'd reconciled. But she looked very happy to see me, so Future Bea must be doing okay in that area. That made me feel a little bit better.

"Oh, you forgot your antlers!" Nicole exclaimed. She reached into the giant bag marked SANTA'S TOYS that she was dragging along behind her. "Good thing I have extras!" She handed me a reindeer headband that matched hers.

"Thanks," I said, popping the antlers on my head. "So how is everything . . . going?"

"Fantastic!" Nicole cried, wrapping an arm around Leah's waist and giving her a peck on the cheek. "You two did such an awesome job with this whole Bookish Holidays theme. The rec table is slammed." She nodded toward the Paranormal Romance section in the back of the store, where a large table piled high with books was surrounded with eager customers. "And the Secret Admirer Santa basket already has some takers!"

"Ooh, that sounds cool!" I blurted out, my gaze following her pointy finger to an oversized basket strewn with tinsel. A couple of wrapped, book-shaped packages had been tossed inside.

"It should, since it was your idea," Leah said, giving me another weird look.

"And an awesome one at that!" Nicole crowed. "Folks at the party pick out a book that they believe communicates who they are, down to their soul! Then they address it to someone they're interested in here." She gestured to the crowd again. "We wrap it up for them—and at the end of the party, you can go see if anyone's left a book for you!"

"Yeah, you wanted to help people feel like they might actually be able to get a date for New Year's," Leah said. "And as I recall, you were hoping to land a few dates yourself. But since you didn't break up with either of your current dates—"

"Oh no," Nicole exclaimed, her dark eyes widening. "Is this a classic Beatrice Tanaka *Situation*? Because I haven't been part of one of those in years!"

"Ah yes, I did it just for you!" I vamped, flashing her a winning grin. "Merry Christmas!"

"Yaaaaaaargh," Leah moaned. "Just keep the drama from drama-ing too hard, Bebe. Shake those cute little antlers of yours and distract your suitors. Make sure they don't find out

168 HOLIDAY HEROINE

about each other! This event needs to be a disaster-free zone or Charlotte will never see me as the strong, capable business owner I could be!"

"I got you," I said, shimmying around so that my cute little antlers did indeed shake. "Don't worry, Lee, this party's going to be a massive success! It's Lit is as good as yours!"

I gave her a broad wink and tried to infuse my step with bravado, walking purposefully toward the Almost Hemsworth. Pancake, who was still resting in my arms, raised his head and let out an inquiring whine.

"Yeah, buddy," I whispered. "I'm also questioning many of the decisions of Past Bea. Or Middle Bea? The Bea of the last few months who did all the shit I'm still learning about. And I'm gonna grill your mom on the time-travel tip later, but right now, we've gotta help her out. She's my best friend in the whole world, she deserves her dreams more than anyone I know, and I have to be there for her in true ride-or-die fashion—even if I have no idea what I'm doing."

I pasted yet another big smile on my face and wiggled my reindeer antlers in what I hoped was an enticing manner as I strutted up to the Almost Hemsworth.

"Lambie!" he greeted me, breaking into a blinding white smile. Perfect teeth, up and down. Of course. "You look *smokin'*."

I kept my smile firmly plastered across my face as he swept me (and Pancake) into a bear hug.

Lambie?!

Smokin'?!?!

Oh, Past Bea . . . what the fuck were you thinking?

The darkness inside of me rumbled, but I couldn't tell if it agreed with my assessment.

"You and Leah-san did such a monumental job on this celebration," Almost Hemsworth beamed, finally releasing me from the hug. "But before you fill up on Westernized treats, I want to give you one of your solstice gifts."

"I . . ." Any words died in my throat. He'd just said a lot

of stuff I'd normally have a ton of questions about. But to be honest, I was still stuck on "Lambie."

Almost Hemsworth reached into his stylish canvas sling-pack and produced a small brown box tied up with plain twine. I accepted it, opened it, and was confronted by four misshapen blobs of . . . something. I stared at the gift, willing the blobs to tell me what they were so I wouldn't have to spend any time playing guessing games with this guy.

"It's mochi!" Almost Hemsworth screeched, clapping his big hands together in delight. "I made it myself! I used all the most authentic techniques. Try it!"

Oh *hell* no.

Not only had Leah let me date a white guy, she'd let me date a *faux-woke Asianphile white guy*. The worst fucking kind.

I swallowed a scream and reminded myself that Past Bea was more to blame here. After all, she—*I*—had apparently gone for it.

Almost Hemsworth must be really good at sex.

"Lambie-chan?" Almost Hemsworth regarded me with big puppy eyes, his voice plaintive. "Don't you want to try some?"

Lambie-*chan*?! Past Bea let this guy get away with using Japanese suffixes?

Pancake lifted his head and unleashed a small growl in Almost Hemsworth's direction. I set him down on the floor and he scampered off. I could not help but agree with his assessment.

I pushed aside my rage and tried to refocus on the tragic mochi in front of me. No, I was not putting that in my mouth. And no, I could not throw it in his handsome face, which would make a scene and possibly tank both the event and Leah's dreams. As soon as I was able to get her alone, I was going to have a lot of questions.

But for now, I needed to do the one thing she'd asked of me.

Time to *not* make a scene.

"It looks so, um, delicious that I want to save it for a later!" I chirped, stuffing the box in my skirt pocket. "Everything's so hectic in here, I can't really savor, you know?"

"Mmm, totally." Not Hemsworth brightened and took my hand. "Why don't we take a stroll down the Candy Cane Lane Leah set up in the café and spend some quality time under the mistletoe?" He waggled his eyebrows at me.

"Oh, um . . ." My gaze went to the café area, where Olivia was lingering by the punch bowl. She'd struck up a conversation with a few customers I recognized as It's Lit regulars, and was laughing appreciatively at something one of them had said, her mane of raven hair swishing back and forth.

"We don't need to go to the café for that!" I blurted out, grabbing Almost Hemsworth's arm and turning him toward me. "We can kiss right here!"

And then, before I could think too hard about it, I threw my arms around his neck and planted my mouth on his. He responded immediately, his hands going to my waist to pull me closer as his eyes fluttered shut.

I kept mine open, trying to fix my gaze on Olivia and the café.

Almost Hemsworth was a terrible kisser. There was somehow both too much and not enough saliva, and the fact that I was thinking about saliva had to mean other aspects of the kiss weren't so great, either.

"Mmm, Lambie-chan," he said, his eyes still closed tight. "I love it when you make a scene."

Aw, shit. That's what I was trying my damndest *not* to do.

I took a deep breath, trying to calm myself even as panic seized my chest. The darkness inside of me rumbled again, but I had no idea what it wanted me to do, how I could squelch it.

Did it, like, *approve* of this whole situation? Or find it as panic-inducing as I did?

I risked pulling my gaze from the café for a moment . . . and saw that people were indeed looking our way, murmuring in a vaguely scandalized manner. I saw Lucy, giggling and whispering something to Rose. Evie, looking mildly exasperated as she rocked Vivi against her chest. Pancake near Evie's feet, his impressive side-eye on display. And next to Pancake was a colorful, spiky blob that looked just like—

Oh *no*.

I tore away from the heinous kiss, my gaze now laser focused on the mini kaiju that had invaded my festive-as-fuck bookstore.

Chapter Fourteen

"LAMBIE?"

Almost Hemsworth's wounded voice echoed in my ear, but I barely registered it. The mini kaiju locked eyes with me and gave me a terrified look, then darted behind Pancake and out of sight.

"Goddammit," I muttered under my breath.

I needed to go after it. And continue to keep Almost Hemsworth and Olivia apart. And not make a scene.

Sure, fine. Totally easy.

I found myself waiting for my darkness to make some noise again, but it was totally silent. Wait, why the hell was I seeking out some kind of reaction from the darkness now? Was I starting to care about its opinion or something?!

Some of the partygoers were still staring and tittering over my makeout session with my apparent boyfriend. My gaze pinged back over to the café area, where Olivia was craning her neck, trying to see what all the fuss was about. The world seemed to move in slow motion as she set her punch down and started walking toward us, still trying to see around the crowd.

"Sorry, Alm—Terrence," I said, my voice pitched way too high. Thank god I remembered his real name. "I have to pee!"

I darted away from him before he could respond, the box of his unwanted mochi smacking against my hip. I zigzagged through the crowd until I got Olivia in sight, her brow furrowed as she headed in Terrence's direction. Crap. I wondered if she'd seen anything.

"There you are, um, lover!" I screeched, planting myself in front of her. "I've been looking for youuuuuu!"

"Ooooh, are we doing cute nicknames now?" she queried, her velvet brown eyes shining. "Babe, I thought the day would never come!"

"Yeah, *babe*!" I yelped, putting way too much emphasis on that word. I sounded truly bananas. "Should we go have some of that punch you were talking about earlier?"

"Sure, and . . ." Olivia frowned at something over my shoulder. "Is that douchey-looking guy bothering you? It looks like he's trying to get your attention?"

I whipped around to see Terrence heading in our direction, one beefy hand raised in an eager wave.

"Oh yeah, he wanted personalized book recommendations!" I improvised, grabbing Olivia's elbow and steering her in the opposite direction.

"Isn't there a whole station for that?" she asked, gesturing toward the rec table.

"Yeah, he just knows I'm one of the most knowledgeable people around! He was a regular customer back when I worked here and we have the same, um, taste. In books."

"Really?" Olivia's voice was skeptical. She glanced over her shoulder again, assessing the Almost Hemsworth. "He doesn't look like someone you would have much in common with."

"Appearances can be deceiving! Anyway, how about some of that punch—"

I stopped in my tracks, my heartbeat ratcheting upward. The kaiju was flitting along the floor, darting in between people's feet. I *had* to go after it.

"Babe . . . ?" Olivia said.

"Lambie-chan!"

I turned and saw Terrence bearing down on us, still waving his arms around like a fool. Then I turned back and saw the mini kaiju skittering into the It's Lit bathroom.

I made a game-time decision, yanked Olivia into the bathroom with me, and slammed the door behind us.

"Babe?" she repeated, as I flicked on the light. "Are you okay?"

"O-of course!" I exclaimed, reinstating my big smile. "Just wanted to show you one of my favorite spots in the store!"

While this may have sounded completely weird, it was also true: the It's Lit bathroom was a marvel, a warm and welcoming space bathed in soft light—the better to reflect the scribbly collage of words and art projects patrons had affixed to the walls over the years. It was a nice mix of book recommendations, affirmations, and people's deepest, darkest secrets. This very wall had actually provided a major clue during my whole Mom-Demon adventure, and I saw that the message I'd written right before I'd left for Maui was still intact.

I don't know exactly what I'm doing. I don't know exactly what I'll be. But I do know this.

I choose joy.

I choose love.

I choose hope.

And I can be anything I want.

Yeah, how's that working out for you, Future Bea?

"Babe, I'm well aware this is one of your favorite spots," Olivia said, crossing her arms over her bountiful chest. "It's also been *our* spot a few times. Is that why you pulled me in here?"

Her red lips curved into a sultry smile as she took a step toward me, hips swaying hypnotically. She closed the space between us and brushed an unruly lock of hair out of my eyes, then ran her fingertips down my cheek. I flushed, all the air leaving my lungs. Unlike Almost Hemsworth, I could definitely see why Past Bea had been into Olivia. She leaned in closer and I inhaled her irresistible strawberries-and-cream scent, my brain going fuzzy.

What was I supposed to be doing in here, again? Besides keeping Olivia and Terrence from running into each other?

Oh, right—the mini kaiju!

My gaze swept the floor, frantically trying to get that pesky little blob in sight. But it was nowhere to be found. It must have discovered a really excellent hiding place. Or maybe it had disappeared. Or maybe I'd straight-up imagined it, since—

Olivia kissed me and my brain fuzzed again as her tongue expertly swept my lips apart and stroked against mine. Her hands grazed my sides, her thumbs lightly brushing my nipples through the thin fabric of my bodysuit, then moved upward to toy with the low neckline. A needy moan escaped from my throat, and I couldn't help but lean into her touch.

"Babe . . ." she breathed, then pulled back, her brow creasing. "Are you okay? Feeling all right?" She put a hand on my forehead. "You're a little warm."

"Wh-what?" I squeaked, still overcome with lust.

"Maybe we should take you home, fix you up with some hot tea!" Olivia said, her demeanor shifting from sultry to efficient. "I'll smash you up some raw garlic and tuck you into bed."

"Um . . ."

Holy shit, Past Bea.

I was starting to piece together what had happened to me—at least in a dating sense—during the months I'd missed. I'd clearly been devastated by my breakup with Sam, so I'd resorted to some of my old dating foibles. Keep busy with as many people as possible, so you don't have to sit with yourself, thinking about all the reasons that you're sad and hopeless and will never be truly loved. Don't be with anyone who could actually know you, because that's fucking scary. And definitely choose suitors who fit into some of your preferred types: himbos who are physically impressive but otherwise repulsive, meaning you can have tons of sex but never get emotionally attached, and ridiculously hot women who want to take care of you, thereby satisfying your not-so-latent mommy issues.

I'd thought I'd grown past all that. Clearly Past Bea was doing some heavy regressing.

"And if none of that works, we'll go to that herb shop on Church and get them to mix you up something good." Olivia was still going on about how we were going to cure my mystery illness.

"I'm totally fine, babe!" I insisted. "Why don't you try kissing me again, that was working pretty well—"

BANG BANG BANG

Someone was knocking very enthusiastically on the bathroom door.

"We'll be out in a minute!" Olivia yelled.

"Lambie!" a voice bleated from the other side.

"Why," I whimpered, wondering if it was possible for me to melt into the bathroom wall, becoming one with all the affirming messages.

"Is that the douchey guy who was trying to find you?" Olivia queried, jerking her head at the door. "The one who wanted book recommendations? He was yelling for 'Lambie.'"

"Lambie-chan!" the voice screamed more insistently. "I'm worried about you!"

"Lambie is the, um, nickname he gave Pancake," I improvised, my heart hammering so loudly in my chest, I could practically feel it slamming against my breastbone. "He's always concerned about that tiny dog getting stepped on when there are a lot of people in the store. But we don't have to worry about that." I stroked her arm, trying to get her attention back on me. "Let's just be really quiet; maybe he'll go away."

"Lambie—*Beatrice!*"

"Seems like he wants *you*," Olivia said.

"He probably thinks I know where Pancake is!" I yelped, acutely aware of how frantic I sounded. "You know what, let me just . . ."

I had no idea what I was doing at this point, I was operating on desperation-fueled instinct. I was also possibly having some kind of out-of-body experience—like some other force was lifting my legs as I trudged toward the bathroom door, reminding me that I still needed to figure out where that pesky kaiju was . . .

I flung the door open and blocked the entrance with my body, my synapses firing like mad.

"Terrence," I said. "What do you need? I can meet you over in the café area for those, uh, recommendations. But—"

"Who's that?" Terrence asked, his brow crinkling as he stared over my shoulder.

"I'm Olivia," Olivia said, stepping forward and laying a proprietary hand on my shoulder. "Her girlfriend."

"Gal pals, I gotcha!" Terrence exclaimed, giving us finger guns. "Are you all doing girl stuff in here?"

"You could say that," Olivia replied, her voice laced with amusement.

"I'm all for it," he said, giving her a weird little salute. "I always make sure m'lady here has a range of menstrual products when the time comes. I was actually the one who introduced her to period panties—"

"Anyway!" I interjected as loudly as possible—loudly enough for Olivia to gloss right over that "m'lady here," hopefully. "We support all people who have periods! Yay for us! Now if you'll excuse me, Terrence, I'll be with you in just one minute."

"All right," he said, fixing me with a smarmy look that made me want to vomit.

At least it looked like I was on the precipice of escaping this situation without either of them realizing I was dating them both. Or making a scene. My shoulders relaxed the tiniest bit.

"I'll be waiting for you," Terrence continued, locking our eyes extra meaningfully.

"Don't wait too long," Olivia said, squeezing my shoulder. She pulled me a little closer and nuzzled my neck. "Us gal pals have a lot of palling around to do."

Oh god.

The Almost Hemsworth might not have been the sharpest tool in the box, but even he managed to pick up on that.

"Lambie?" he said, his voice very soft. He looked from me to Olivia and back again. "What's going on?"

"And why is he calling you Lambie?" Olivia demanded, her dark eyes flashing. "I thought you said that was his nickname for Pancake!"

"Pancake?" Terrence frowned. "The dog? I mean, I don't do *this* with the dog!"

And before I knew what was happening, he was pulling me in for another deeply terrible kiss.

"What the fuck, Bea!" Olivia shrieked.

"Are you with *her*?" Terrence blustered, breaking our kiss.

"Are you with *him*?" Olivia echoed, looking like she was about to explode.

"Oh, for . . ." I disentangled myself from Terrence, then grabbed his hand and pulled him inside the bathroom, slamming the door behind him.

I planted my hands on my hips and turned to face them.

"So if you must know: yes, I'm dating both of you, I tried to keep it a secret, and now it's totally blown up in my face. Which means you should both dump me immediately and get out of here, but in a way that causes no disruptions whatsoever and definitely does *not* make a scene. I'm admitting full wrongdoing, I acted like an asshole, and you can both leave with the satisfaction that you have the moral high ground and this is all my fault. Also, you're both hot to a degree that is truly disturbing, which means neither of you will have any problem finding more people you want to date, fuck, or give cutesy nicknames to. Okay?"

I sagged against the bathroom wall, winded. This scenario had *not* unfolded the way so many Christmas rom-coms had promised me it would. And it would probably be a hilarious story to tell later, but . . .

My heart twisted. Because the person I wanted to tell this

story to, the person who I knew would laugh his ass off and make me repeat the most embarrassing parts . . . was Sam. I could already picture his sly grin, his dark eyes sparkling with amusement.

"Wow, Lambie," Terrence said, studying me.

"Yeah," Olivia murmured. "Wow."

They both stared at me for an excruciatingly long moment. Then Olivia batted her long lashes.

"I have *never* been more attracted to you, babe. The level of chaos? *Incredible.*"

"Agreed," Terrence said, nodding fervently. "And you know, Lambie, we never said we were exclusive." He gave Olivia an inquisitive sidelong look. "Maybe we could all—"

"Not a chance," she said flatly. "But Bea . . ." She stepped forward and brushed my hair off my face, giving me that luscious red-lipped smile again. "I'd still be into finishing what we started. And I don't mind an audience." She smiled at Terrence, who looked like he was about to witness a Christmas miracle.

"I'm, uh, good," I managed, putting a little space between us.

My gaze swept the bathroom again, and then I turned back to Olivia and Terrence.

"But if you two really would like to help me with something—want to participate in an extensive bathroom search for a mini kaiju?"

CHAPTER FIFTEEN

"WOW, BEBE." LEAH giggled so hard, she had to flop forward onto the It's Lit front counter. The upper half of her body shook with mirth, sending the reindeer antlers she was still wearing into a series of adorable twitches. "I can't believe you lived out a whole Christmas rom-com scenario in the *bathroom*."

"Excuse me, but you're welcome," I snarked at her, fiddling with my own antlers. They'd gotten kind of droopy during the chaos of the party. "I managed to live out a whole Christmas rom-com scenario in the bathroom without making a scene."

"True, true, and I am ever grateful," Leah said, straightening back up and clapping a hand over her heart. "The party was an undeniable success! I think I more than proved I can handle running the store. We'll see what Charlotte says!"

It was evening now, the foggy San Francisco sky already almost pitch-black, and the party was over. Everyone had finally cleared out of It's Lit, leaving Leah and me to clean up the detritus—crumpled punch cups, teetering stacks of abandoned books, lonely gingerbread mittens, and errant bits of tinsel. No mini kaiju, though—I'd combed the entire store three times. Maybe I'd imagined it? Hallucinated it out of nothing? The big kaiju had definitely been real—the other people on the beach had seen it, reacted to it, run from it in terror. But nobody else had witnessed either mini kaiju I thought I'd seen. Perhaps extreme hallucinations were also part of this whole time-travel deal?

Nicole had lingered around for a while, and had only just left. I'd spent an hour trying to subtly shove her out the door so I could *finally* talk to Leah.

"I know I told you to keep things drama-free, but I'm kinda disappointed you didn't have holiday-party sex," Leah continued, sweeping bits of red and green confetti off the counter. "Rumor has it that Aveda and Scott hooked up in the back room—I can't blame either of them, those Slutty Santa costumes were really something."

"No holiday-party sex for me," I confirmed, frowning at my screen. "But now both Terrence and Olivia are blowing up my phone! I guess my attempt to dump them made me even more irresistible." I shook my head, scrolling through. If Terrence and Olivia had one thing in common—besides me—it was a passion for expressive strings of increasingly dirty emojis.

"Only you, Bebe," Leah said affectionately.

Pancake, who was situated on his favorite pink pillow atop the counter, gave a whuffle of agreement.

"Anyway!" I exclaimed, stuffing the phone back in my pocket and trying to stay focused. "Now that we're alone: I really, *really* need to talk to you."

"Shoot!" she called over her shoulder as she strolled toward the now-ravaged Secret Admirer Santa basket. It had gotten knocked over during the party, and was teetering on the floor in exceptionally forlorn fashion.

"So remember a few months ago, when I told you I thought I'd accidentally time traveled to the day of my family's visit—"

"*What!*" Leah stopped in her tracks, her eyes going wide.

My brow crinkled. "So I didn't tell you? Man, how badly have I fucked up the timeline—"

"No, you *did* tell me," she clarified, shaking her mane of curls. "But after that day, I thought it never happened again? You were waiting and waiting—"

"So I think it *did* happen again," I interjected, eager to get to the meat of the issue. "Leah, the last thing I remember before I woke up today is fighting a gigantic kaiju on a Maui beach nine months ago!"

"Holy shit!" she gasped. "Bebe, I remember hearing bits and pieces about that battle, it sounded bananas—"

"What did I tell you?" I cut in, my heartbeat speeding up. "Because most of what I remember involves almost drowning."

"Honestly, not much," she said. "I just know that everyone got out of it okay, and you came back to the Bay three months later, after Evie gave birth. You never want to talk about it, you always dodge the subject. And when you don't want to talk about something, Bebe, it's like trying to pry bacon directly out of Pancake's mouth—an impossibly challenging endeavor!"

"Okay, so you at least know there was a gigantic kaiju," I said, trying to keep us on track. "And I felt a certain connection to it, like I could hear its thoughts, feel what it was feeling . . ." I leaned against the counter, reaching out to idly stroke Pancake's fur while the events from the beach played through my head. "I was going to control it, Lee. I was going to save everyone by going full dark side. And then . . ." I frowned into space. "Then it fought back against me? Like, slammed a wall down between our brains so my projection wasn't getting to it anymore. I thought I was drowning and everything went black, and suddenly I'm waking up in my bed this morning and Aveda's dressed as a Slutty Santa, and I'm juggling two suitors and have a whole-ass baby *niece*—"

"You time traveled nine months!" Leah exclaimed. "That's longer than before, right?"

"If I only talked to you the one time about time travel, then yes," I confirmed, my words spilling out. "That was only a week. And the time before was just a few hours. And . . ." My brow furrowed. "I think *that* was the first time, the day of Doc Kai's unexpected gingerbreading. Unless I've been time traveling so freaking much that there are instances I don't remember, which means I've probably messed with the timeline somewhere, despite all my efforts to be in the moment and not disrupt anything or rock any boats—"

"Bebe!" Leah stomped her foot and held up a hand to get my attention. "Rewind. What did you mean about going full dark side—during the kaiju battle?"

"I . . ." I hesitated, gnawing on my lower lip. "I'd been trying so hard to do the right thing, to keep myself and my power under control. But in that moment, facing off against that big-ass kaiju, I had to decide between saving my family and avoiding mind-controlly supervillain status, and . . . well. I guess for some people that would have been an impossible choice, just like the one Thomas has to deal with in *A Kaiju for Christmas*. But for me . . ." I flashed back to the full-body fear I'd felt in that moment. "I knew that was how it had to be. Even in *Kaiju*, either side of the impossible choice means sacrifice."

"So why do *you* have to be the sacrifice?" Leah protested. "And why are you so sure using your power in that way means you've totally gone to the dark side?"

Leah knelt down to fix the fallen Secret Admirer Santa basket so it was upright once more, then began rifling through the few book presents that remained inside. People who would never know about their crush's feelings and were probably doomed to a dateless New Year's. I knew this meant she was turning all the information over in her brain, trying to piece it together, her mind stimulated once again when she was engaged in organizational-type tasks.

I wasn't sure how to answer her. I shifted uncomfortably from foot to foot and stroked Pancake's fur again, just to have something to do. He'd started to drift off to doggy sleep, his breath turning into snores. His front paws twitched, and I wondered if he was chasing his own mini kaiju in his sleep.

"When we talked after your initial time-travel jaunts, you

theorized that your power was glitching," Leah said slowly, organizing the leftover book packages into neat stacks. "That instead of merely projecting your emotions, you were now projecting yourself through time. And you also said . . ." She looked up and tilted her head at me. I squirmed under the directness of her gaze and kept stroking Pancake's fur. ". . . that you'd been noticing some issues with your power since the combo spell with Scott and Aveda. But you kind of glossed over what that meant. What's going on?"

I froze, my blood going cold, and broke her gaze so she wouldn't see the visceral fear in my eyes. I was still stroking Pancake's fur, his snores reverberating through my hand like a steady heartbeat. It was strangely meditative. Comforting. It grounded me in the moment enough for my panic to ease, and I felt the familiar atmosphere of the bookstore envelop me like a cozy blanket. This place had been my haven so many times in the past, my escape from fights with Evie and the disappointed judgment of the rest of the team and whatever mess I'd managed to make of my life in any given week.

And Leah . . . she'd *always* been there for me. There was a reason she was my constant.

"Lee," I blurted out before I could stop myself, "I have to tell you something."

"As we've discussed extensively, that phrase never precedes anything good. And I'm guessing there are no endless ice-cream buffets in sight here." She was trying to sound breezy, but I heard the concern brewing underneath her light tone.

I made myself face her. She paused in her industrious book stacking and gave me an expectant look.

"Why can't it ever be an endless ice-cream buffet," I lamented, trying to match her attempt at lightness. "So. I mentioned that I haven't been able to control my power as well since the whole combo spell with Scott and Aveda—"

"The spell to stop the vampires," Leah confirmed. "Well,

the terrible white woman who was creating all the vampires. Or actually, Shasta, who was collaborating with the terrible white woman to create a freaking vampire army—"

"Correct," I said, laughing a little in spite of myself. "And damn, does Team Tanaka/Jupiter never do things the easy way. Anyway, Scott does the power combo spell the same way he does all of his spells—he accesses and manipulates bits of Otherworld magic. I felt that magic flowing through me the whole time, and . . . look, I don't know if it then fused with the Otherworld magic we pulled out of the terrible white woman, but . . ." I stopped petting Pancake and started pacing, my limbs jittery and unsettled. "This might sound bananas, Lee, but I'm pretty sure a piece of that Otherworld magic stayed inside of me. Like, it took up residence and started to fuse with my power and now it's like . . . this dark weirdness. I envision it as spiky shadows, these bizarre alien things that I know don't belong, but there's something about them that's so *compelling*."

I paused in front of the Paranormal Romance section, winded from my latest bout of motormouthing. The cheery rainbow of book spines was another thing that always soothed me. As if on cue, I felt the darkness pulse, reminding me not to get too comfortable.

"It's similar to the feeling I got when I kept jumping into the Otherworld," I continued, determined to get everything out.

"During your Mom-Demon phase," Leah clarified, crossing back to the counter with her stacks of books.

"Yes. Every time I went to the Otherworld, my power morphed—like, the contact with Otherworld magic made it so much stronger, so much more dangerous. And it felt so *good*, even though it was all wrong."

I forced myself to turn and face her again. She'd set her books down and picked Pancake up, cradling him to her chest as he snored away, completely unbothered by the fraught nature of our conversation.

Leah met my gaze, her eyes kind, not judging me at all. That only made me feel worse.

"I think this new darkness is messing with my power—making it erratic, unpredictable, and *way* more dangerous," I barreled on. "I've felt my emotions spilling onto other people sometimes, affecting their moods. Maybe even controlling them and getting them to do things, like gift me an entire store's worth of mochi. And I've tried so hard to get it under control, to figure it out, but now . . ." Dread bubbled up in my chest. "Now I think my souped-up dark power is sending me *through time*."

"Bebe." Leah set Pancake down, and started fiddling with the left-behind Secret Admirer Santa packages again. "Given all of this, why don't you try experimenting? You always get so excited about doing all the science things like that! I mean, during your stint of Mom-Demon Otherworld jumping, you got *so* into testing your new abilities, pushing them to their limits. You tried to convince Evie and Nate and the rest of the team to let you go all out with your experimentation, even though they were so against it—"

"Leah!" I hustled back over to the counter. "Okay, so first of all—no reaction to my confession that I very possibly have dark Otherworld magic just living inside of me right now?!"

She studied me, a slight smile playing across her lips. "To be honest, Bebe, that doesn't sound any wilder than the stuff you've been through before. Which is another reason I'm surprised you haven't tried any time-travel experiments to figure out how everything works. You *love* figuring out how things work!"

"I-I do," I said, gobsmacked. I'd expected her expression to change as soon as I told her everything, to see disgust and revulsion in her eyes.

I'd expected her to look at me like I was a monster.

But . . . no. Same Leah Kim. Kind and bubbly and my constant, forevermore. I couldn't help but mist over, a lump rising in my throat.

"I haven't tried anything because I still don't want to disrupt anything!" I sputtered. "I don't want to accidentally start World War III, remember?!" I flashed back to earlier that morning, me feeling like I was standing very still in a room full of precious breakables. "And Lee, do you really not remember what happened while I was doing all that Otherworld-related experimenting? I couldn't stop giving in to temptation, like it was the biggest, shiniest thing I'd ever seen! I mind-controlled Sam's siblings, and I went there with barely a second thought! I tried to turn your girlfriend into a human sacrifice, for fuck's sake—"

"You wouldn't do that again!" Leah insisted stubbornly. "You were spiraling, Bebe, in a super dark place—you were still working through your grief over your mom, and you and Evie were fighting constantly, and everything happening around you was making you feel so . . . so *small*—"

"And who's to say I won't spiral again!" I slumped over the countertop and stroked Pancake's fur, trying to breathe my way back to calm. "Clearly I can't be trusted with this amount of chaotic power!" The darkness shifted inside of me, but I couldn't tell if it was agreeing or attempting to convince me I was wrong and should totally let myself fall into a megalomaniacal abyss.

"You should talk to Evie and the rest of your family," Leah insisted. "Maybe Nate would have some ideas? You two always love coming up with a good hypothesis together!"

"I *can't*," I groaned, burying my face in my hands and shoving the darkness to the side. "It's back to that whole timeline-disruption thing. I really don't want to mess things up any more than I already have."

My voice cracked on that last word, my sentence petering out to nothing.

"Hey." I felt Leah's arm around my shoulders, squeezing me close. I peeked out from behind my fingers and saw Pancake's paw reaching out as well, brushing against my elbow.

Damn, was this tiny terror of a dog trying to comfort me, too?

Then his paw started twitching again. He was fast asleep. Probably back to dreaming about chasing kaiju.

"Bebe." Leah's voice was very gentle. "It's *okay.* We'll figure it out. Your power glitch, your new darkness—all of it. I take my duties as constant very seriously. And I'm your family too, right?"

"Of course," I whispered, tears thick in my throat.

"Let's keep thinking on it," Leah said, giving me a final squeeze. "Or maybe we should try *not* to think on it—like, you know how sometimes the perfect solution just falls into your brain when you're not focusing on the problem at all! Maybe you're in the shower, or drifting off to sleep during a movie . . ."

She went back to arranging her pile of unclaimed Secret Admirer Santa packages into an even more precise stack, every book perfectly aligned.

I sighed, brushing the last few tears from my eyes. Leah was the best friend I'd ever had, and when she said something, I tended to believe it. But all of this felt way too big and scary—even for the combined minds of Tanaka and Kim.

"Bebe . . ." Leah snapped me out of my reverie, plucking a cheerily wrapped package from her stack. "I think this one's for you."

"Really?" I took the present from her, relieved to have something else to fixate on. "Why do you think that?"

"Read the label," she said, amusement lacing her voice.

I looked down at the label, where the Admirer was supposed to describe their Admiree in flattering-yet-easily-recognizable terms.

For the girl with blue and purple hair, it read.

"That could literally be so many people," I scoffed. "And anyway, my hair is mostly back to its natural state—"

"Flip it over," Leah said wryly.

I did as I was told. And saw that there was a part two to the descriptor.

. . . who may already have two whole suitors after her, but

thought I'd shoot my shot. If interested, meet me at Cake My Day's gingerbread house extravaganza tomorrow at 1!

"Okay, still not *totally* convinced," I mumbled.

I ripped off the snowman-festooned wrapping paper and flipped the book over to reveal a very familiar cover. The jewel-toned painting depicted a handsome man clutching the spiky hand of a rainbow-hued kaiju wearing a Santa hat. The kaiju roared menacingly while the man gazed at its monstrous form in adoring fashion.

"Oh, shit!" I squealed. "This is the novel tie-in edition of *A Kaiju for Christmas*! Do you know how rare this is? I've never actually seen a copy in person!"

I hugged the book to my chest, my heart filling with a warm glow.

Because there was only one person who could have given this to me. Only one possible Secret Admirer Santa who knew what it would mean to me, and how romantic a gesture it was.

"So who's it from?" Leah prompted.

"*Sam!*" I shrieked, barely able to contain myself. "It has to be from Sam."

Tears sprang to my eyes and I hugged the book tighter. No, I had no idea what was happening with the Otherworld darkness that now lived inside of me, or what to do about its apparent effects on my power. But this book, coming from Sam . . . it was the kind of gesture both of us loved. It could only mean that he wanted to be with me again, that we were about to reunite under the most romantic of circumstances.

Hmm. Maybe—*just maybe?!*—it was a blessing in disguise that I'd skipped over all those months between the big kaiju battle and now. I'd missed all those weeks of heartbreak and tears and regressing back into disposable hookups with inappropriate people that would never mean anything more—

"Bebe." Leah tugged insistently on my sleeve, pulling me out of my runaway train of thought.

"What?"

She looked at me, her eyes full of confusion. Pancake gazed at me the same way, as if I'd grown another head.

Leah leaned in, her puzzled frown deepening.

"Who's Sam?"

CHAPTER SIXTEEN

I TRIED TO explain. I frantically searched my phone for photos—but of course there were none. I attempted to pull up Sam's contact listing—and was promptly reminded that it hadn't been in my phone when I'd checked earlier. I resorted to Google, countless social media apps, and even searched out the Bay Area Hunky Hot Hotties calendar Sam had posed for a while back.

Nothing, nada, zilch.

Sam Fujikawa did not exist in this timeline. Sam Fujikawa had disappeared from this timeline. Sam Fujikawa was no longer a person, his sly smiles and secretly tender heart fully eradicated from the planet.

The more I tried to explain, the more unhinged I sounded.

Leah believed me, but didn't know how to fix it or how to console me, especially since I worked myself into a frenzy the more I tried to talk about Sam. I finally told her I'd explain more coherently later, gave up, and trudged home. I plodded through streets lit up with holiday dazzle, wreaths adorning lampposts and coffee shops advertising hot cocoa laced with peppermint and cinnamon. With every thudding step, I felt my heart break a little bit more.

And when I got home and spirited myself up to my bedroom, I allowed myself to collapse: heaving sobs wracking my body, an endless flood of tears making my eyes red and puffy.

This had to be my fault. Despite all my best efforts, I had

definitely fucked up the timeline. So much so that a whole person had disappeared.

And not just any person. The person I loved with my entire heart. I flashed back to me trying to convince Sam that love was the most important thing, enough to conquer all.

I'd been so wrong.

Even when he'd rebuffed me, even when we weren't technically together . . . I'd never wished for him to just not be here. A world without Sam Fujikawa was less vibrant, less interesting. Even when he drove me absolutely bananas, even when he worked me into an incandescent rage . . . I still wanted him to be here.

And now he wasn't.

I should have started theorizing immediately, should've scoured my memories for possible clues or engaged in further sleuthing or tried to track my way through everything that had happened today, to see if I could pick up on any other anomalies in the current timeline.

But I couldn't do any of that. I was completely broken.

I buried my face in my pillow and cried myself to sleep.

🔥

My eyes cracked open to daylight streaming in through the window, casting a soft glow over the popcorn garlands and smiling gingerbread people decorating my room. Usually the effect would have been magical.

Right now, I found it creepy.

I groaned and rolled over, pulling a pillow over my head. My eyes felt crusty and swollen, as if they were permanently coated with tears. My chest was tight, my heart clenched like a fist.

Night had fallen and day had dawned and Sam Fujikawa still didn't exist in the world.

I could simply not be conscious for that, so I pulled the pillow more tightly over my head and squeezed my aching eyeballs shut, determined to go back to sleep.

"grawr . . ."

My eyes flew open. That had sounded awfully like a tiny roar.

But, nah. Any sleep I'd gotten was definitely not quality, and my overtaxed brain was probably playing tricks on itself. I shut my eyes again.

"Graaaaaaaawrrrrrr!"

The roar returned, this time louder and more insistent. And then something spiky brushed against my fingertips.

I bolted upright in bed, throwing the pillow to the side, my gaze landing on the source of the noise.

And yup, it was a mini kaiju. This one had spikes and fangs and those glowing eyes, but it wasn't staring at me or trying to attack me or disappearing into a bookstore bathroom.

No, it was simply . . . rolling? Like, rolling back and forth next to my pillow? Its tiny spikes brushed my hand again as it tried to turn itself over.

I had no earthly idea what to do next, so I studied it. It opened its little mouth and let out another *graaawr!*, this one sounding extra plaintive. And when it blinked its glowing eyes, bits of water drifted down its face. Oh—not just water. *Tears.*

This mini kaiju was crying.

Now I *really* had no idea what to do. How did one deal with an inconsolable monster?

The kaiju finally noticed me staring and jumped to its feet, angrily brushing its tears away.

"Um, yes?" I said, feeling ridiculous.

I tried reaching out with my mind, trying to connect to the kaiju's emotions as I'd done with the others.

Complete devastation roared back at me. I gasped at the strength of it; it was like being walloped in the chest by a two-by-four.

sad sad sad can't go on so sad

The mini kaiju stamped its foot impatiently, then jumped down from the bed and zipped into the bathroom.

"Oh . . . no," I muttered groggily. "Why do y'all keep

escaping into bathrooms? What is in there that is so darn fascinating?"

I forced myself out of bed and trudged to the bathroom, valiantly trying to blink the crust out of my eyes.

"Let me guess," I said, scrabbling around for the light switch. "I'm gonna turn this on only to dramatically reveal a whole lot of nothing—just like yesterday, when I scoured every inch of the It's Lit bathroom. I may have learned enough to become a legit plumber . . ."

My fingertips finally found the light switch and I flicked it on with as much drama as I could muster (which honestly wasn't much since I was barely awake).

And then I clapped a hand over my mouth to keep from screaming.

My bathroom was *not* empty—quite the opposite.

It was *swarming* with mini kaiju.

You know that scene in *Ratatouille* where all the cartoon rats come pouring out of the kitchen? Like that.

They were varied in shape and color, a rainbow of tiny bundles of energy covering my floor, bouncing on the toilet seat, peeking out from behind my shower door. I spotted the one who had been crying next to my pillow perched on the edge of my sink.

As soon as they saw me, they all started crying and wailing and rolling around. And that feeling of complete devastation hit me square in the chest again, knocking the wind out of me.

sad sad sad sad sad saaaaaaaaaadddddddd

I fell to my knees, gasping for air.

"St-stop," I managed. But my voice was barely a whisper. That only made them wail louder.

I clapped my hands over my ears and doubled over, curling myself into a fetal position. Covering my ears was a useless instinct. The noise wasn't the problem—it was all the soul-gutting emotions they were projecting.

Panic raged through me, a bright knife slicing through all my exhaustion and denial and sadness. I clamped my lips shut and curled myself even tighter, making my body as small as possible.

I breathed deeply, and after a moment or two, I realized that I wasn't hearing all that mini-kaiju wailing anymore. Still sprawled on the ground, I directed my gaze back to the bathroom.

The mini kaiju were gone.

My bathroom was clean, pristine, empty.

My hand fluttered to my chest as my brain scrambled around, trying to figure out what had just happened. Had my grief caused me to have another massive hallucination? Was any of this real?

But my lungs still hurt from holding my breath, and my eyes were still crusty, and overwhelming grief was still stabbing relentlessly at my heart.

Maybe I had imagined the swarm of mini kaiju—but that grief was *definitely* real.

🔥

After I was done with my morning hallucination, I went through something like a routine on autopilot. Getting back into bed suddenly didn't seem appealing, so I brushed my teeth, showered, and threw on one of my slip dresses, woolly tights, and a long cardigan. I applied makeup like I usually did, finger-combed my waves, and then stood in the middle of my bedroom, wondering what to do next.

I realized this flurry of activity was distracting me from thinking too much about Sam—maybe if I could keep the flurry going, I'd be able to figure out my next move.

My gaze darted around my room, flitting over every Christmas decoration in turn, until it finally landed on the book I'd hastily tossed atop my nightstand next to my phone.

A Kaiju for Christmas.

I crossed the room and picked up the book, turning it over in my hands.

Sam couldn't have sent me the book, since he currently didn't exist. But who *had* sent it? Who else would want to convey their admiration and/or secret crush using a story that held such a specific, special place in my heart?

I pulled the crumpled wrapping paper off the book, my brain spinning as I re-read the message my admirer had written.

If interested, meet me at Cake My Day's gingerbread house extravaganza tomorrow at 1!

Hmm. I closed my eyes and forced myself to think logically. Well, the Bea Tanaka version of logically.

There had to be a way to restore Sam to the timeline. And the more clues I could gather about my missing memories, the better my chances were of figuring out what to do. This person wasn't Sam, but given the fact that they'd given me such a Sam present . . . well, maybe it was worth it to at least solve the mystery of their identity and see if anything they had to say might help with my time-travel sleuthing.

I hugged the book to my chest, terrified to hope.

While I had nothing resembling a solid Bring Sam Back! plan, I at least had some kind of forward momentum, and I used that to catapult myself into another flurry of activity. There were still a few hours until the gingerbread-house rendezvous with my Secret Admirer Santa, so I threw myself into other tasks with gusto. I texted Leah and asked her to join me as backup—if my meeting with the mystery admirer ended up being a dead-end bust, at least she and I could do some more time-travel theorizing.

I returned to internet sleuthing, and determined that the rest of Sam's family still existed—this wasn't like an MCU Thanos snap situation, where a bunch of the population up and vanished. It was literally one person.

Sam's parents still lived where they always had, his uncle still owned a curry joint in Japantown, and his older siblings were still off in their own worlds and totally insufferable. I came across a fifty-seven-tweet thread from Emily blathering

on and on about the Asian Girl Hair Streak "stereotype"—
something I had schooled her on when she'd tried to call out
my hair streaks. But since Sam didn't exist, Emily and I had
no reason to ever meet, which meant she'd never heard my
infuriated monologue about how I, a *Real* Asian Girl with
many delightful traits and intriguing qualities beyond my
beautiful hair streaks, am not a stereotype. Oh, and also that
I loved my hair streaks and was not planning on getting rid
of them just because some blabbermouths on Twitter wanted
to show off all the big words they learned in grad school.

I could not help but wonder, just for a second, what Emily
would think of my current, more mature hair situation, those
tiny bits of Technicolor flitting around the ends of my natural dark brown waves.

My stomach started growling, so I marched down to the
kitchen and was pleased to find a variety of holiday treats
peppering the fridge and countertops. The perfect breakfast,
really. Well, after Pika's kālua pig plate lunch—oh! Pika! I
flashed back to Evie's mention of Doc Kai the day before and
took my phone out to text the Maui crew. But I didn't see any
texts to or from them over the past week, and everything
prior to that had auto-deleted.

I paused, gnawing on my lower lip. I wondered if I'd pulled
back on contacting them, just like I had with Sam and Leah
when I'd started freaking out about my power changing. It
was certainly possible. And therefore probably best to keep
not contacting them, since they might find it weird, inadvertently setting off more ripples in the timeline. I'd already
made one person completely disappear, I didn't need to be
disrupting things any further.

I put my phone away and turned back to the kitchen
counter's cornucopia of holiday treats. I made myself a nu-
tritious breakfast plate of cookies and mochi and that three-
flavor popcorn that always comes in a gigantic bucket.

The Victorian was weirdly quiet. It was still early, so maybe
everyone was sleeping? Even the baby? Though, from my

limited understanding, I thought babies were *most* ready to party when their parents were trying to sleep.

"Morning, Bea—I see you're fortifying yourself for the day," I turned to see Aveda sauntering into the kitchen, yawning as she tightened a silky red robe around her waist.

"You're up late, no?" I said. "I thought you'd trained your body to wake up at 6 a.m. every day—you're always going on and on about how you don't need an alarm clock!"

"Mmm." She shuffled over to the coffee maker and began to prepare her morning cup. "After my LA adventure with the vampires, I started to understand that I need to dedicate more time to restorative sleep. I was so burned out I couldn't see how severely lacking my life was in terms of self-care— and I don't mean like the white-woman brand of 'let's go buy candles and take extravagant spa trips because our fragility has gotten the best of us and we simply cannot handle the blowback from all the microaggressions we indulge in every day' self-care."

"Specific yet true," I said, adding more tri-flavor popcorn to my plate.

"In any case, I managed to deprogram myself from the whole body-alarm thing." Aveda gave a satisfied nod. "Scott helps by making staying in bed an extremely appealing prospect."

"Generous of him," I said, stuffing a piece of mochi into my mouth. The texture was utterly perfect, unlike the monstrosities the Almost Hemsworth had tried to present me with the day before. "Well, Aveda, if anyone deserves extra sleeping in time, it's you—you and Evie have been through so damn much in your superheroing careers. I'd probably need to sleep for at least a full year to make up for all that."

"I . . . yes. Well." She turned back to face me as the coffee maker burbled, a shadow passing over her face.

"Sorry, did I say something . . . are you okay?" I asked, trying to puzzle out the meaning behind the sudden slump in her shoulders, the contemplative look in her eyes.

"Are you reading my mind?!" she blurted, her spine straightening. "No creeping around my private thoughts, Beatrice!"

"I'm not! That's not even within the scope of my powers!"

Except possibly when it came to all the kaiju I'd been hanging out with recently? I seemed to be able to read *their* minds just fine. But I left that part unsaid.

"The only time I actually 'read your mind' was during the power combo spell," I said. "And as you may recall, I tried *not* to do that, since you had some spicy thoughts about Scott and he's like a brother to me—"

"Right—yes, of course," she said, huffing her way over to the kitchen cabinet that held all the mugs. "Sorry, I suppose my face is just *very* expressive. And by the way, are you and Scott going to do any more experimenting with the power combo? He says you don't seem enthusiastic about the topic as of late, which is confusing since you were *so* into it—he actually asked me if you were mad at him."

"Of course not," I said, guilt flashing through me. "Sorry, I'll let him know that . . . that it's not him. Scott is so sweet, I don't think he even knows *how* to make people mad."

"It's true," Aveda said, smiling slightly. "You'd be pressed to find a soul more wholesome." She turned and snagged a mug, then faced me again. "In any case—what you likely picked up thanks to my very expressive face is that I've been a bit worried about our Evie. She's been getting a little . . ." Aveda waved her mug around in a vague gesture. "Hmm, I guess . . . stuck? Her birth experience was not exactly ideal. I know she hasn't spoken to you much about it, but . . ." She trailed off.

"Can you tell me more?" I said, jumping at the chance to fill in some blanks. "I know it was hard, but she hasn't given me many details."

Aveda crossed back to the coffee maker and began fussing with the machine and her cup. She finally got her first dose of morning caffeine to her liking and turned back to me,

looking like she was a million miles away. "It was . . . well."
That shadow crossed her face again. "You may know some
of the basic facts of the situation already, but she went into
labor during our battle against the french-fry puppy demons
at The Gutter—"

"Not fries!" I yelped. "Evie *loves* fries! That's like being
forced to fight one of your greatest passions!"

"Her true love turned into her enemy!" Aveda agreed, her
eyes narrowing dramatically. "And we'd gone to The Gutter
to *celebrate*. We'd just decided to give all of our young
charges—Pippa, Shelby, Julie, and Tess—promotions on
Team Tanaka/Jupiter! Everyone was over the moon and
ready to go all in on some bad junk food and even worse
karaoke."

I nodded along, absorbing these details. Pippa and her
friends were enterprising college students Evie and Aveda
had taken under their superheroing wing during their adventure at Evie's alma mater, Morgan College. Pippa also had
some lingering vampire characteristics from Aveda's run-in
with the LA vamp squad, and Shelby was a ghost girl. They
fit in perfectly with the team, and Aveda was always talking
about how empowering it was to mentor the next generation
of superheroes. It was unsurprising that they'd gone to The
Gutter to celebrate this milestone—the dank, seedy karaoke
bar was a beloved hangout for Team Tanaka/Jupiter, despite
the rather alarming amount of supernatural hijinks that had
gone down within its crumbling walls. The place was pre-
sided over by the fabulous-yet-eternally-grouchy Kevin,
whose favorite pastimes were wearing tees with sassy slo-
gans and insulting Evie and Aveda.

"You know how it is these days, Bea, we've been dealing
with a lot of random Otherworld bullshit thanks to the walls
between worlds growing thin—and in this case, we got demonic french fries." Aveda shuddered and took a long sip of
her coffee. "We did what we usually do, cleared all the civilians out and got down to business. But then . . . Evie went
into labor. Loud, painful, extremely dramatic labor."

She paused with the mug halfway to her mouth, her eyes getting the same haunted look I'd seen in Evie's the day before. I stayed quiet, both wanting and not wanting to hear the rest of the story.

"The demonic french fries . . ." Aveda's brow furrowed as she called up the memory. "Our young charges managed to chase them outside, but they formed a barrier around The Gutter. Like, not just physically, there was some clear force-field shit going on. So Evie and I were trapped inside by ourselves, the girls were fighting the french-fry demons outside . . ." She shook her head. "It was an absolute mess. But that baby was coming, so Aveda Jupiter stepped up to the plate."

"Of course she did," I said, smiling as Aveda drew herself up tall, some of her bravado restored.

"I-I delivered the baby," Aveda said, her authoritative voice shaking a bit. "I used telekinesis and what I could remember from YouTube videos, and all of this was happening while our girls were still fighting off french-fry demons outside the bar. And everything turned out okay, but . . ."

"But what?" I prompted softly.

"I wish I could have been there for her—beyond the mechanics of the delivery. I had to concentrate *so* hard, and I was terrified something was going to go wrong, and she kept screaming . . ." She swallowed, the beginnings of tears gathering in the corners of her eyes. "I think she felt so alone, Bea. She was in all this pain and obviously even more scared than I was, and I couldn't *do* anything. There were times when I thought I was going to lose them both . . ." She took a long drag of her boiling-hot coffee, as if trying to burn the memory away.

"But everything's okay now, right?" I urged, even as Evie's haunted look from the day before rose up in my mind. "She and Nate are so in love with Vivi, and Vivi is just *perfect*, and—"

"Yes, I think overall, she's happy." A slight smile crossed Aveda's lips. "But I can see her flashing back to that birth moment constantly. I can see her turning it over in her mind, reliving it all, and wishing it was just a little bit different— that her first association with her adorable daughter wasn't total pain and trauma."

"But she survived," I said. "You all did! You all made it out okay. That's what our family does, right? We survive all that shit and get stronger. More resilient. We can't get to that happily ever after without enduring some kind of pain, be- cause that's just how life is, in all its messy glory."

"Well . . . sure," Aveda said. She slugged back her final gulp of coffee and set the mug on the counter. "But you know, Bea, I don't know that that's always how it *should* be. People talk about traumatic experiences being character-building, but I feel like I've been through enough to have *plenty* of character, hmm? And I don't see why women of color are constantly *expected* to be resilient. It's like, what? We're not worthy unless we've spent most of our lives suffering?"

She frowned into space for a moment, then shook it off, picking up her mug and toting it to the sink.

"I don't regret that experience, and I don't think Evie does, either," she said. "It happened the way the universe wanted it to, and now we have Vivi. But sometimes when I see Evie wrestling with that memory . . ." She paused, setting the mug in the sink. "I wish I could go back in time and fig- ure out how to make it just a little bit better."

She flashed me a smile, and snagged her own handful of tri-flavor popcorn.

"Can you imagine Aveda Jupiter time traveling, though? What a disaster that would be!"

"You have no idea," I muttered, not knowing what else to say as she bustled out of the kitchen.

CHAPTER SEVENTEEN

I WANDERED FROM the empty kitchen, heading toward the nook of a room that Evie and Aveda had converted into a makeshift den/rec area, Aveda's words heavy on my mind. My heart broke, thinking of Evie enduring all that while I was thousands of miles away. No wonder I'd returned home and stayed for so long.

I tried to brush away the lingering image of Evie in horrific pain as I entered the den. After all, there was nothing I could do about that now—except be there for her, and try my best to fix this janky Sam-less timeline.

The Tanaka/Jupiter den was a cozy room dominated by the gigantic TV and a pair of comfy couches. The wall near the entrance was the designated photo area, displaying a gallery of family pictures: Lucy and Rose singing karaoke to each other at their wedding, Aveda throwing back her head and laughing with Scott on a sunny LA beach, me and Evie stuffing our faces with so much mochi that our cheeks were puffed out like chipmunks trying to store nuts for the winter.

I saw a few new additions: Evie and Aveda standing back to back as the iconic Hollywood sign loomed over them in the distance, Lucy and Evie high-fiving at Evie's baby shower, Nate holding teeny baby Vivi for what must have been the first time, his face lit with a proud dad smile. And right next to a snap of Pancake dressed as a grumpy elf, there was an adorable family photo of Evie, Nate, and Vivi. It looked like they were up in Topanga Canyon, surrounded by the area's golden glow and blooming greenery, and Nate was holding Vivi up like she was baby Simba in *The Lion King*. They all looked so joyful. My heart warmed—as Aveda had said, Evie was happy overall. She'd eventually process her way through the painful birth memory.

The den appeared to have developed a bit of a playroom vibe during my missing months and was now littered with soft toys and one of those bouncy seat thingies that's supposed to keep your baby mildly entertained for a few precious seconds.

I turned and nearly yelped out loud, clapping a hand over my mouth just in time.

Nate was slouched on one of the comfy couches, so quiet and still I hadn't seen him at first. He was like a chameleon, the black of his clothes melding with the black of the couch and concealing his massive frame. I stepped further into the room and saw that Vivi was cradled against his broad chest, totally passed out. A movie played across the TV—the volume turned all the way down, the subtitles flashing across the screen.

Seeing this big, scowly man go to such great lengths in order to not wake a tiny little baby warmed my heart all over again.

"Hey," I whispered, doing my best to creep over to the couch as noiselessly as possible.

"Morning, Beatrice," he whispered back, his face breaking into a smile. "Is that breakfast?"

"Are you gonna lecture me about it?" I retorted teasingly, plopping myself next to him on the couch as I crammed a handful of tri-flavor popcorn in my mouth. There was just something about the way the cloying sweet of caramel rubbed up against the dusty plastic taste of fake cheese—it shouldn't work, but it did.

"Not at all," he said, without missing a beat. "I believe Evie ate the same breakfast yesterday. And over the years, I have come to appreciate some of her more eccentric food preferences. Can I trouble you for some popcorn?"

I deposited all three flavors into his free hand and we munched in companionable silence as the movie flickered silently onscreen.

"Ahhh, *The Knight Before Christmas*," I murmured, keeping my voice down so as not to wake Vivi. "The sole Vanessa Hudgens holiday classic wherein there is only *one* Vanessa Hudgens." I cast a sidelong look at Nate as I shoved more popcorn into my mouth. "You're watching this voluntarily? Or does Vivi have your appendages so totally trapped, you can't get the remote?"

"I chose this movie, yes," he said, amusement softening his harsh features.

"Damn." I shook my head. "All those years, I forced you to do a Holiday Hudgens-a-thon with me while we strung popcorn garlands, and *every time*, you wouldn't shut up about how multiple identical Vanessa Hudgenses existing is a statistical improbability and how the time travel in *Knight* defies all laws of physics!"

"Repeat exposure made these movies . . . appealing to me," Nate said, giving me a rueful half-smile. "I watch them year-round now."

"What?!" I yelped, then clapped a hand over my mouth, casting a nervous eye toward Vivi. She was still totally conked out. "Nathaniel Jones, did I turn you into a rom-com stan? Because if so, I need to claim that as my true superpower."

"I enjoy them," he said, gently rocking Vivi against him. "Especially if I have already seen them before. Given how unpredictable our lives tend to be, it is comforting to watch something knowing exactly how it ends—and still feeling the same happiness every time it does."

"You're kinda swooning over there. It really is a sight to see."

"I also think . . ." He paused and rocked Vivi a little more, his eyes trained on the screen. Vanessa was about to get kissed by her handsome knight. "Watching these movies always reminds me of you, Beatrice. I can practically hear your voice in my ear, explaining why it is, in fact, plausible for many identical versions of Ms. Hudgens to exist in our world." A slight smile played across his lips. "And even if I am not quite convinced of that, when you are in Maui, watching these movies makes me feel as though you are not so far away." He turned and met my eyes, his smile widening. "Perhaps this is something that makes me miss you just a little bit less."

"You miss me?" I asked, my mouth full of popcorn.

"Of course." He gave me a puzzled look. "We all do."

"Oh." I turned back to the TV, gnawing on my popcorn. I wasn't sure why that surprised me so much. I'd been missing my family so fiercely, but since I was the one who'd decided to move, I supposed I always pictured them going about their business as usual. I imagined that their collective daily life had simply reformed around the new normal, that they were all so busy anyway with ghosts and vampires and Evie's pregnancy . . . that they didn't have time to miss me, really.

"Evie might murder me for telling you this," Nate said, "so please keep it between us." He paused, cuddling Vivi closer. She adjusted herself in his arms, making cute little snorty sounds. "The night you left for Maui, she took a blanket you'd left behind on your bed, wrapped herself up in it, and fell asleep that way. The two of you had never really been apart, not for as long as you've been alive. She wanted you to go because she knew it was what *you* wanted, what was best for the next chapter of your life. But she also didn't quite know how to live without you."

I poked at my remaining popcorn, tears pricking my eyes. Oh, Evie. She wanted me to think she was also #thriving. How was it that I'd only been gone from the Bay for . . . well, now it would be over a year. But thanks to my time traveling, I'd missed months of that.

"We were all glad you decided to come home early for the holidays," Nate continued. "I'm sure Kai and all your friends out there are missing you, but it has been pleasing to have you back with us."

My gaze returned to the screen, where Vanessa and her knight were engaging in further Christmassy hijinks.

"Nate," I said slowly. "Can I ask you something odd? It, um, has to do with a hypothesis I'm working on. Just go with it?"

"Of course," he said, his eyes sparking with interest. Nothing got Nate going like brainstorming new scientific theories.

"When you and Evie and Aveda and . . . um, just Aveda," I amended clumsily, remembering that Sam didn't exist. "When you all came to visit me in Makawao, what do you remember about the big beach battle? With the kaiju?"

A shadow passed through his eyes, and he clutched Vivi closer.

"Most of what I remember is from the sidelines," he said. "I was with Evie, just trying to . . ." He trailed off, the color leaching from his face. My breath caught, remembering how desperate he'd looked while Evie screamed, how he'd said he'd give his life before he let anything happen to her. I couldn't even imagine what he must have felt like when she'd actually given birth—I could picture him trying to fight his way through the demonic french fries and their force field, desperate to get to her. He must have been scared out of his mind.

"What did you see me doing during the battle?" I said. "Was I still in view when I went to the edge of the water?"

"From a distance. I remember you saying you wanted to find Aveda, so you ran down there. And then the monster appeared."

"The kaiju," I murmured, shuddering as a vision of its giant spikes and glowing eyes rose up in my brain.

"Kai started screaming for you to come back," Nate continued. "Carmelo convinced her not to run down there herself—that you are a superhero, after all, and that there was nothing she could do to protect you."

"Doc Kai treats all of us like her kids," I said, thinking of how maternal she always was to me and Tosh and Keala and Giselle—even Pika, who had a few decades on her. "She's kind of the best."

"Agreed," Nate said, a soft smile touching his lips. "You started waving your arms around. You were yelling something, but none of us could make out the words. You waded into the water until you were almost up to your neck—we could barely see you at that point, you were bobbing in and out of view. And then the monster started to move closer to you."

"Yes," I breathed, my heartbeat speeding up. It was weird to be hanging on every word of a story that had actually happened to me in real life. But I didn't remember what had come next.

"And then all of a sudden . . ." Something like amusement passed through his eyes. "Aveda burst out of the water, riding a big wave on her surfboard. And—"

"And she tried to *surf* into the creature's face?" I finished, a bit of glee bubbling over my anticipation. "Wow. How Aveda was that?"

"So Aveda," Nate said, grinning at me. "I understand that she also used her telekinesis on the Christmas lights we'd used to decorate one of the palm trees, and I vaguely remember them flying through the air. But just as she got right next to the monster's giant, fanged mouth . . . it disappeared. The entire kaiju vanished into thin air."

"Mmm," I said, my heartbeat speeding up again. "And where was I when this happened?"

"You bobbed out of sight, and we were worried you'd drowned in all the excessively large waves the creature was causing," Nate said. "But then your head popped back into view and you and Aveda were able to get out of the water and back to us. As soon as the creature disappeared, Evie's early labor stopped and she was no longer in pain. It was like everything reset in that moment. And . . ." He frowned, his gaze darkening as he cocked his head to the side, like he was trying to hear something just out of range.

"What is it?" I pressed.

"I . . ." His frown deepened. "I feel as though something else happened in that moment, something crucial. As if there's a shadow lurking around the edges of my memory, but I cannot get it to come into focus." He turned and met my gaze. "Was there someone else there? Did my mother make an appearance?" He held Vivi close, his face going pale again.

"No!" I reassured him. "Part of why I'm asking you this is I feel like there's something important I can't remember, either."

But my brain had seized on this bit about the shadow, turning it over and trying to get it to make sense. Did Nate have a latent memory of Sam? Was there a way to get it to return without simply telling him everything?

And if I could get people to remember Sam, was *that* what would bring him back?

"I suppose the important part is that the monster was vanquished," Nate said, relaxing his hold on Vivi a bit. "And we haven't heard anything from Mother or the Otherworld since. Your reports from Maui indicate things have been similarly mundane out there."

"Yeah, totally mundane," I mumbled, wishing I could remember literally anything about the reports I'd sent. Maybe I could look for them on my computer later. I turned back to the TV and let the movie wash over me. On the surface, this really was an ideal holiday situation—me eating tri-flavor popcorn and enjoying the beginning of a Hudgens-a-thon while my usually gruff brother-in-law made goo-goo faces at his precious baby daughter.

Except Sam didn't exist, so how was I supposed to enjoy any of it?

I cast a sidelong look at Nate. Should I prod him about Sam? Or just tell him what was going on with me? He'd always been my favorite person to theorize with—well, until I'd met Doc Kai. Now I'd put them on equal footing in the Awesome to Brainstorm Science Stuff With game. Nate had always encouraged my wild tangents instead of immediately shutting them down the way Evie tended to. And he'd seen something in me almost no else had—including myself. He'd always thought I could be a great demonologist, scientist-adventurer, or whatever I set my mind to. According to him, my brain's chaotic state of being helped me see things in a different way and come up with the most creative solutions. He'd been ecstatic when I'd accepted the job with Doc Kai, saying our meeting of the minds was going to be something truly special.

Maybe if we talked like we always did, he could help me devise some new theories—perhaps we could figure out how to bring Sam back, how to stop my power from glitching, and how to deal with the kaiju that kept appearing out of no-where in my very messy life.

I frowned down at my popcorn, a stew of conflicting emotions brewing in my chest. I was *still* terrified of messing up the timeline more than I already had.

Maybe if I positioned things in firmly hypothetical territory, we could talk it out?

"Hey, Nate," I said, jerking my head at the screen. "Remember when we hypothesized about time travel, after watching a whole boatload of these movies? I know you think it's impossible or whatever, but—"

"I'm not sure I think anything is impossible anymore," he countered. "Not after everything we've seen over the years."

"Point. But anyway, I seem to recall that the one constant in all our hypothesizing was that anything the time traveler does has the potential to fuck up the timeline—including telling people they're time travelers."

Nate turned and met my eyes, his dark gaze probing. "Yes. That seems to be a common element in fictional representations of time travel. But Beatrice . . ." He studied me intently. "Are you all right?"

I held his gaze for a moment, sweat beading my brow and my mouth going dry. Had he figured it out?

Although Nate hated socializing and sometimes felt like

he didn't say things exactly right, he knew how to read people, and he could be incredibly perceptive. (In fact, that was part of his own superpower: he was able to observe things on a deeper level, like a special sixth sense.)

Before I could figure out how to answer him, Vivi opened her mouth and screamed with such force, I swore I felt the windows rattle.

"Holy . . ." I dropped my plate of Holiday Treat Breakfast and clapped my hands over my ears, wincing as her distressed shrieks pierced my skull.

"Shhhh." Nate immediately went into Papa Bear mode, pulling her against his chest with her little head propped on his shoulder. He stroked her back, murmuring in her ear. "It's all right, Littlest. You'll be all right, we'll feed you soon and then you can take another nap and you'll be all better. Remember how we're trying to let Mama sleep in . . ."

Despite the truly impressive sounds that were still emanating from that tiny little body, I softened. He was so *tender* with her. Nate had been just as freaked out as Evie during their pregnancy. Given that none of us had the best parental role models, I could certainly understand that. And given that their baby was the first superhero-demon hybrid in existence . . . well, I could double understand it.

But look at them now. Him all sweet and attentive, doing everything in his power to prevent his daughter from experiencing a single moment of discomfort and addressing her with cutesy nicknames. And Evie yesterday, running her family like a boss, trying to take care of everyone like she always did. She'd work through the trauma of her birth moment, and then they'd be living their best happy ending.

I could *not* disrupt that. I had just affirmed the hypothesis that anything a time traveler did could affect our existing reality. If I told him I actually *was* time traveling . . . well, who knew what might happen. What if he disappeared, too?

Then again, if I figured out how to bring Sam back, would that fuck up the current reality even *more*?

But . . . no, Sam was *supposed* to be here. Something had

happened on that beach, something that had caused him to wink out of existence while leaving everything else the same. I needed to get to the bottom of this. And the only tangible step I had in front of me was meeting with my Secret Admirer Santa.

I slipped my phone out of my pocket and glanced at the screen. The gingerbread house–making extravaganza was only an hour away.

"I should go freshen up," I said, brushing crumbs off my lap. "Got some hot holiday joy planned for the afternoon."

"Just remember to be back here by seven," Nate said, bouncing Vivi against his chest. She'd settled and gazed up at him adoringly, cooing in her sweet baby voice. He beamed back at her, his harsh features softening into teddy-bear territory.

Good lord, this child was going to be so spoiled.

"Evie and Aveda want to make sure everything's prepared for the party tonight," Nate continued.

"Party?!" I exclaimed, jumping to my feet. "Evie actually agreed to have a holiday party?!"

"I believe you talked her into it, did you not?" Nate asked, amusement lighting his eyes.

"Oh, um, of course I did," I said hastily. "I can't wait."

"And Beatrice . . ."

"Yes?"

Nate grinned at me and pointed to the TV screen. "Don't you want to watch the ending?"

I returned his grin and sat down on the couch again, watching Vanessa and her knight fall into each other's arms.

Nate let out what I could only describe as a dreamy sigh.

"This is my favorite part," he said.

Tears brimmed in my eyes once more. "Mine too."

CHAPTER EIGHTEEN

AFTER NATE AND I had successfully witnessed Vanessa Hudgens find the holiday love she so richly deserved, I did my freshening up and prepared to set out on my gingerbread-making mission.

Once my phone charged back up, it immediately pinged with an avalanche of text notifications. I groaned as I scrolled through them—all the messages were from Terrence and Olivia, most of them spiraling into territory that was downright pornographic. Don't get me wrong, I'm usually all for such things, but in this case, I needed both of them to chill out, leave me alone, and get on with their lives. I understood that me rejecting them had apparently been the hottest thing either of them had ever experienced, but I also didn't need to complicate the timeline any further by attracting my very own stalkers.

I sent them a firm "see ya never!" type message, and blocked both of their numbers. Then I jetted over to Cake My Day.

"Hey Bebe!" Leah chirped as I jogged up to meet her at the entrance.

All my text triaging had made me late. Pancake was strapped to Leah's chest in what I can only describe as a baby carrier for dogs. He gave me an imperious look and lowered his head for scritches. The little pup was bundled in a fluffy white onesie that was supposed to make him look like a snowman, topped off with a scarf and matching booties.

"I can't believe you carry him around like that in the winter," I said. "Who exactly is training who?"

"He refuses to walk on cold ground, and he's got *all* of us trained," Leah retorted. "Even you." She looked pointedly at my hand, which was obediently scratching Pancake behind the ears.

"Guilty." I ruffled Pancake's fur. "He is our tiny king and we are lucky to exist in his realm."

"So we're your backup," Leah declared, putting her hands on her hips and striking a power pose. Pancake straightened in his carrier, his ears perking. "What do you want us to do? I know you're dealing with some very important—and sounds like traumatic?—time-travel stuff right now, but I gotta say, I'm looking forward to seeing you annihilate the competition in all things gingerbread."

"You can observe me and the mystery Secret Admirer Santa from afar while constructing your own gingerbread house," I said, narrowing my eyes at Cake My Day's pastel exterior. "If I need assistance or a quick escape, I'll say some code phrase really loud. Like, um . . ." I scoured my brain for situationally appropriate phrases.

"How about 'needs more buttercream'?" Leah piped up, stabbing an index finger through the air.

"You're a genius!" I enthused, patting her shoulder. "And we can talk about time travel and my trauma after we unmask my Secret Admirer Santa. Oh! And Charlotte should be here, right? Maybe you can speak to her about buying the store? I'll be happy to provide many glowing testimonials about how amazing you are and what a smashing success the event was!"

"Yessss!" Leah exclaimed, pumping her fist in the air. "Oh man, Bebe, I love when we multitask!"

And with that, we headed into the bakery.

We were only a few minutes late, but people were already setting up their stations. The Cake My Day Gingerbread House Extravaganza was a venerated yearly tradition I was already familiar with, so at least I wouldn't spend the first bit of it playing catch-up. Every holiday season, pastry enthusiasts gathered on one fine December afternoon to build their best cookie-based structures out of ingredients provided by the bakery. Cake My Day was owned by Charlotte, the same successful entrepreneur who owned It's Lit, and the interior was a sugar-laden wonderland boasting rainbow swirls of frosting, decadent pillowy cakes, and more porcelain unicorns. Charlotte usually developed a new gingerbread variety every year to add flavor (heh) to the proceedings. The year before I'd left home, it was citrus-infused, tart top notes contrasting perfectly with the rich spice of the cookie. Last Christmas, it had involved a hefty extra scoop of molasses, making for a richer taste. Leah sent me some in a Christmas care package.

I wondered what it would be this time.

I breathed in the heady scents of sugar, spice, and everything absolutely fucking delicious and scanned the space for the person who could be my Secret Admirer Santa. I assumed they knew what I looked like, since they'd been admiring me and all, but I'd brought my copy of *A Kaiju for Christmas* anyway. I hugged the book to my chest like a shield.

The place looked like it usually did for this event. Tables were spaced out on the floor, each one big enough to contain two people. Various craft supplies and decorating tools were neatly arranged on top of each table. And at the front of the room, all that beautiful sugar was laid out on a long counter: sparkly gumdrops and candy canes and piping bags plump with icing. And of course, stacks and stacks of square gingerbread pieces, perfect for building miniature houses. I couldn't help but smile at the sight of it all.

Most of the tables were already claimed, people settling in and eagerly discussing their future creations. I saw that Leah had managed to snag a table, setting Pancake up in the second chair. He was looking at her inquisitively as he sniffed the air.

My stomach dropped as I realized there was definitely nobody here who looked anything like Sam. Deep down, I'd probably been holding out hope that he'd magically appear and everything would be okay—a true Christmas miracle.

In fact, there was no one here I recognized at all. I tried to display the book more prominently in front of me, a Bat Signal awaiting its answering hero.

"Hey, um . . . Bea! It's Bea, right?" I whipped around to see a tiny slip of a girl waving at me, a tentative smile spreading over her face.

"Yes, that's me," I responded, crossing the room and sitting down next to her. I studied her, searching for potential clues.

She looked like she was about my age, her small frame swimming in a bulky sweater emblazoned with a glittery Christmas tree. She wore this over black leggings, candy-cane earrings peeking out from her short brown bob. Her clear blue eyes were big and saucer-like, a Keane painting come to life. And she projected a certain whimsical quality I usually associated with twee indie musicians, like I fully expected her to have a popular TikTok account wherein she sang mournful covers of pop songs and accompanied herself on the ukulele.

"I'm Dahlia!" she chirped, leaning forward eagerly. She gazed at me through long lashes, looking shy. "I'm so happy you came."

"I . . . yes," I sputtered, unsure of what to think of this situation. Could it be that this very innocent-looking girl actually was a secret admirer, nothing more? That she'd simply seen me across the way at the store and thought I was hot and . . .

I shook my head. Yes, this might count as a meet-cute, but I'd seen enough holiday rom-coms to know that there was *always* another twist.

I remembered the book and set it on the table.

"So," I said, feeling it out, "*A Kaiju for Christmas*. The novelization. That's a pretty deep-cut holiday tome to give to someone."

"Oh, I knooooow," Dahlia said, letting out a delicate, musical laugh. "But I also knew *that* was the way to get your attention. Because let's face it, Bea—"

"Hello, everyone. Welcome to Cake My Day's annual Gingerbread House Extravaganza."

We swiveled to face front as a bored monotone cut through the crowd noise. Charlotte was now taking her place at the front of the room next to the long table of ingredients. She stared back at us, her expression as bland as ever. Charlotte always seemed like she was truly going through it, her demeanor aggressively morose. It was fascinating to me that she'd managed to start and nurture two successful businesses dedicated to such joyous things as books and sweets.

"This year's special gingerbread flavor is infused with a pinch of cocoa powder," Charlotte continued, half-heartedly holding up a hand, index finger and thumb held a millimeter apart. "It's meant to capture the taste of cookies and hot chocolate, all in one handy concoction." She paused as everyone *ooh*-ed and *aah*-ed. I snuck a look at Leah, who was raising a questioning brow in my direction. I offered a one-shoulder shrug in return. I'd barely gotten a chance to converse with Dahlia and I still wasn't sure what her deal was.

"I've also decided to add a special twist to this year's Extravaganza," Charlotte droned on. "Given the popularity of such shows as *The Great British Bake-Off*, I thought it would be fun to do a competitive version."

"Has she ever had fun, though?" Dahlia muttered. "Like, in her life?"

I giggled. Maybe Dahlia would end up being sassier than her twee-white-girl exterior indicated.

"So," Charlotte continued, waving a limp finger in the air, "first you have to get your materials." She gestured to the counter of goodies. "You will have thirty seconds to do so. After that, you will all have two hours to construct the house of your dreams. And then . . . I'll judge you." Her lips arranged themselves into something resembling a reluctant smile. Sounded like that last bit was the only part of the competition she found enjoyable.

"Oh, dear," Dahlia said, her bow-shaped mouth pursing into a perfect little moue. "I wasn't prepared for a *contest*. Do you think people will be . . ." She leaned in, her eyes widening in alarm. "Like, *violent*?"

"Count on it," I said, noting that everyone around me was already tensing up, squaring their shoulders, preparing to rush the ingredient table. "But don't worry, I know how to throw elbows. Just follow my lead!"

"On the count of three," Charlotte droned. "One . . . two . . . *three*!"

All the gingerbread enthusiasts sprang into action, swarming the table and shoving each other out of the way. I, however, did not shove—I moved gracefully, dodging the flailing limbs of others, slipping through the spaces they clumsily created in their attempts to get to the table. I'd like to think I looked downright balletic, or like one of the jaw-droppingly acrobatic heroines in Evie and Aveda's favorite action movie, *The Heroic Trio*. I swept sheets of gingerbread, gumdrops, candy canes, and other materials into my arms, swiftly passing some to a bewildered Dahlia as I went.

When Charlotte called out a five-second warning, I didn't dilly-dally—I knew I had everything I needed. I sailed back to my table and carefully set everything down, then glanced around at my competition. Everyone else was flushed, gasping for breath, and trying to piece together whatever random shit they'd managed to grab. It looked like a lot of gingerbread had gotten broken or just straight-up crumbled into dust during the fracas.

I gazed down at my own neat pile of perfect gingerbread and yeah, okay—I gloated. Just a little bit.

I snuck a glance at Leah, who was puzzling over her own broken gingerbread scraps. Pancake sniffed suspiciously at a gumdrop that had gotten stuck to her sleeve. She caught sight of my impeccable pile of ingredients and flashed me a grin, then mouthed "the GOAT!" I gave her a surreptitious thumbs-up.

"Wow," Dahlia gasped, returning to our table. She set down the pile of ingredients I'd passed to her, careful not to disturb my pristine cookies. "Have you been on *The Great British Bake-Off*? Or some other cooking competition show? Or, like, *Supermarket Sweep*? Because that was god tier."

"I know my way around gingerbread," I said, striking a confident pose. "Not so much baking it, but assembling it? Yes. My boyf—"

I cut myself off, my face getting hot. I'd almost started blabbering about my boyfriend, Sam, the one who was actually good at cooking and baking things. The one who didn't exist anymore. I forced myself to shove that thought aside, even as grief rose in my chest and tears pricked my eyes.

Dahlia stared at me with an uncertain smile, making no effort to fill in the awkward silence.

"Um, anyway!" I sang out, hastily swiping a hand over my eyes. "We've only got two hours, so let's get to work!"

"Do you have an idea?" Dahlia asked, her big blue eyes going to the piles of ingredients collected on our table. "Like, a *vision*?"

"Hmm." I stared at the gingerbread and gumdrops, visualizing what their sugary forms could become. Then my gaze moved to the book sitting next to them.

Ah, yes—I needed to get her talking about why she'd picked that book.

"What if we use *this* as inspiration?" I suggested, scooping up *A Kaiju for Christmas* and brandishing it in front of me. "We could craft tiny kaiju out of the gingerbread, give them gumdrop spikes and dots of icing for eyes." Even though the grief and confusion over Sam's disappearance was still humming through me, even though I was trying to remain focused on my clue-gathering mission . . . I felt a little spark as my vision took shape.

Damn, I love Christmas. And all its accoutrements.

"And our house could be sort of deconstructed, like the

kaiju's attacking it?" I continued. "That also gives us an easy way of covering up any mistakes!"

"Love it," Dahlia enthused, grabbing a piece of gingerbread.

"Why don't you start on the kaiju?" I said, passing her the book. "Use this as a model, but feel free to improvise as you see fit. I'll get to work on the basic structure of the house . . ." My brain was already buzzing, hooking into our project. Nothing focused me like a good project.

"Roger that," Dahlia said, settling back into her seat. She started breaking the gingerbread into smaller pieces, her forehead crinkling in concentration.

I sat down and carefully smoothed out the piece of butcher paper we'd been given over the tabletop. We'd also been given a ruler, so I started measuring the gingerbread pieces, figuring out the best way to go about creating our deconstructed house.

I worked up a series of questions about the book to ask Dahlia as I erected the first wall of our house, and was about to launch into my low-key interrogation when she tugged at my sleeve.

"Hey, Bea?" she said, her voice tentative.

I turned to see her brandishing a first attempt at a gingerbread kaiju. She'd ended up crumbling the cookie and smooshing it into a blobby shape with the icing as a binding agent. Gumdrops marched down its back, a reasonable facsimile of spikes. And two tiny dots of icing served as eyes.

It wasn't perfect—the icing made things a little *too* blobby, so the kaiju looked like he was melting, his gumdrop eyes ready to ooze right off his face. But it got the job done, and we were still about to be the most unique entry here.

"I love it!" I exclaimed, clapping my hands together. "I can totally see this baby kaiju going 'grawr'!"

She nodded thoughtfully, scrutinizing her creation. "It's a bit . . . lumpy, though, isn't it? Not very realistic."

A slow smile stretched across Dahlia's face as she brandished the pastry kaiju. That smile transformed her entire demeanor, making her blue eyes glitter with something that could only be described as malice. She met my gaze, and unease slid through my gut, dark and insidious.

Why did she suddenly seem so . . . *familiar* . . .

"Certainly not as realistic as the one I brought to the beach," she said, her musical voice filled with hate. "Don't you think, Bea?"

CHAPTER NINETEEN

"WHO ARE YOU?" I hissed. I made my voice firm, trying not to betray the fear building in my chest, the shock rattling through my bones. "And what are you trying to do?"

I glanced around, but everyone else was fully focused on building their own gingerbread houses. No one seemed to notice that we'd stopped working and were now engaged in hushed, tense conversation.

"God, you are all so *stupid*." Dahlia set the pastry kaiju down on the table. Its gumdrop eyes stared at me blankly. "You know, I'd like to think I make this shit pretty obvious, but apparently I need to start dropping clue anvils left and right!"

"I . . ." I shook my head, my brain working frantically to put the pieces together. Dahlia's musical voice had taken on a sharp, condescending tone—and as I replayed her words, horrified recognition pinged through me.

"*Shasta?*" I whispered, my eyes widening in disbelief.

"Very good," she smarmed, gifting me with a delicate golf clap. "Got it in one."

"How are you *here*? I thought your bumbling ass was trapped in the Otherworld!"

"My physical ass, yes," she preened, twirling a bit of Dahlia's wispy brown hair. "But something happened during that adorable power combo spell you did with Aveda Jupiter and her consort. I suppose I should tell you all about it, since it will answer many of your questions."

"I am just fucking delighted to listen to another one of

your long-winded supervillain monologues," I snarked back. "But first—are you about to destroy this bakery or any of these people with some demon shit? Because in that case, we might have to battle it out first."

"Oh, Beatrice." Dahlia-Shasta gave me a disappointed look. "Of course I mean you no harm. I merely want to talk."

"What do you mean *of course*?!" I exploded. A few heads turned our way. I tamped down my rage and pasted a smile on my face. "Sorry!" I called out to the other contestants. "Just having a slight disagreement about our artistic direction!"

"Don't you remember?" Shasta purred without missing a beat. "You and I were almost partners, back during my unfortunate battle with Evie and my useless son and the rest of their annoying *entourage*. You came to me, Beatrice. You were so lost and alone and I was going to make you a powerful demon hybrid! We could have ruled both of our dimensions together, but alas . . ." She pouted. "Your disgusting human instincts won out. Those ugly *feelings* of yours ruin things every time."

I squirmed in my seat, humiliation flooding through me. That incident still filled me with visceral shame. I'd almost burned down my entire life, my *family's* life, because I'd been pissed at Evie.

Yes, I'd been an impressionable teenager with a ton of unprocessed trauma. I'd also almost become a full-on supervillain because of a dopey fight with my sister.

"Not exactly my proudest moment." I crossed my arms over my chest, trying to keep my bravado intact. "Now *talk*."

"Let's keep building this quaint little art project while we chat," Shasta simpered, plucking another piece of gingerbread from the stack. "Wouldn't want to make a scene—even though that *is* your specialty."

I gritted my teeth and went back to work on my gingerbread wall, motioning for her to keep going.

"So," Shasta said, primly crushing her piece of gingerbread with our tiny craft mallet. "The power combo spell. Scott gave you access to Otherworld magic. And then the dark energy Aveda pulled out of my human minion—Mercedes—gave that magic an extra boost. As you may have surmised, Otherworld magic seems to connect to your power in a very special way, Beatrice."

The darkness inside of me purred with satisfaction, like it was super excited to be recognized in this manner. I shifted uneasily.

"So when your projection power and that souped-up Otherworld magic touched and intermingled . . ." Shasta laced her hands together to demonstrate. "It made for some interesting effects. Way more interesting than when you were jumping into the Otherworld with your so-called 'Mom-Demon'—from what I understand, the effects you experienced back then faded with time and none of that magic took up residence inside of you. But *this* . . ." She gave me that unnerving smile again. "This is so much more intriguing!"

"How? What are all these 'interesting effects,' exactly?"

"I am not entirely sure," Shasta said, "since these sorts of things never happened before I connected with the filthy human realm—"

"You mean when you *invaded* the filthy human realm?" I retorted, unable to resist ribbing her a little. "Which, as I seem to recall, you did very badly."

"In any case," Shasta said, pulverizing a piece of gingerbread way too enthusiastically with the craft mallet, "I am guessing you—the only *somewhat* clever member of Team Tanaka/Jupiter—have already deduced some things. Like that you seem to be able to use your emotional projection in new, exciting ways—projecting yourself through time, for example!"

"Correct." I gave her a grudging nod. That was basically what I'd hypothesized with Leah. Except I wasn't really *using* my power to do that, it just kept . . . happening.

"Incredible," she breathed, smashing the gingerbread even more vigorously. She set the mallet to the side and grabbed the piping bag of icing. "So here's what I experienced during that battle with your power combo spell—to back up a bit, I'd found I was able to inhabit Mercedes' body alongside her consciousness, which is how I spied on Aveda when she was having her LA adventures with all the vampires."

"I remember," I said, watching as she squeezed a blob of icing onto a pile of crumbs and started to squish it into a mini kaiju shape. I'd basically given up on any semblance of gingerbreading; I was focused on committing everything she said to memory.

"When the power combo spell ejected my consciousness and all traces of Otherworld energy from Mercedes, I suppose you all hypothesized that my consciousness was bounced back to the Otherworld and reunited with my own body," Shasta said, flashing a toothy grin.

I shuddered. It was so weird to hear her gloaty words coming out of Dahlia's sweet bow of a mouth.

"We did," I managed.

"But that's not what happened!" she crowed. "Instead, my consciousness was free floating around the earthly realm— and I soon realized that just as I could share Mercedes' body with her . . . well, I could do it with other humans as well!"

"Is 'sharing' really a fair characterization of what's happening?" I interjected. I looked her up and down. "I don't know the real Dahlia, but I'm not sensing a lot of her here. I'm actually not sensing anyone other than you."

"So clever again!" Shasta exclaimed. "I realized that with just a bit more force, I could fully possess a human body. It is such a beautiful thing!"

"Gross," I muttered, feeling bad for poor Dahlia. Even twee, ukulele-playing white girls didn't deserve this fate.

"But Bea, I think this new ability of mine also has something to do with your power merging with Otherworld magic!" Shasta said, widening Dahlia's blue eyes dramatically. "Because this happened after our battle, and what I'm doing here is concentrating on *projecting* my consciousness over Dahlia's—so that's yet another form of projection, isn't it?"

"What . . ." I set my gingerbread wall to the side, queasiness turning my stomach. All this fucked-up shit was happening because of me, my chaotic power mixing with dark Otherworld magic and causing all sorts of unprecedented disasters. "So was it you menacing us—well, mostly me—with all these kaiju? Including the big-ass motherfucker on the beach? Were the little ones—"

Were the little ones real or products of my overactive imagination?

I swallowed, not sure which scenario terrified me more.

"They were all crafted by yours truly, of course!" Shasta beamed, popping gumdrop eyes onto her new gingerbread kaiju. "I've been trying to get your attention with the little ones! As your team has theorized in the past, I've figured out how to manipulate lingering emotional energy to create demonically powered versions of the fictional creatures you weak humans fear so much. First ghosts, then vampires. And now I've chosen monsters that are the most fantastical and fearsome yet! Absolutely genius, if I do say so myself. And I do."

She let out a tinkling laugh and inclined her head at me, as if waiting for me to agree.

I wasn't about to give her that.

"So what happened to Sam?" I demanded. "Why isn't he here anymore—if you know so much, if you've made so much of this happen . . ." I trailed off, the beginnings of tears clogging my throat. "Then I'm guessing you made that happen too."

"Mmmm." Her eyes glittered. She was clearly delighted to have me at her mercy. "Actually, dearest, *you're* the one responsible for that. But you know what, why don't I simply show you . . ."

She held her hand out to me, palm facing up.

"Take my hand," she commanded. "I've discovered I'm able to store and share my memories from when I inhabit human bodies. Such a handy parlor trick!"

I grudgingly slipped my hand into hers, recoiling as her

ice-cold fingers tangled with mine. I closed my eyes, breathed deeply . . .

And suddenly I was on the beach again.

Only I was in a different spot, standing further down the shore and watching my family from a distance. I felt a curious weight on my head, reached up, and realized I was wearing a massive sun hat.

A scrap of memory flashed through my brain—the tall woman I'd seen from afar that day, the one with the big sun hat, the one who wasn't fleeing the beach with all the other civilians.

Shasta must have possessed that beach-goer's body, I realized. She'd been there the whole time, hanging out in plain sight.

I craned my neck, trying to find my family at the other end of the beach.

I saw Evie screaming, Nate desperately trying to contain her flailing body. I saw myself running for the water, my mostly brown hair bobbing frantically as I whipped my head around, scanning the ocean for Aveda.

I saw the kaiju rise up and roar . . . myself wading closer . . . the kaiju lumbering closer to *me* . . .

I saw the Christmas lights flinging themselves through the air, a cruel parody of merriment.

I saw Aveda surfing toward the kaiju's gaping mouth, her fist poised.

The kaiju batted her out of the way with one of its massive claws and she flew back into the ocean.

"Aveda!!" I screamed helplessly from my vantage point in this stranger's body. But the voice wasn't mine, and she couldn't hear me anyway.

And then the kaiju lurched toward me once more—the me flailing around in the ocean, the one who thought she was in control. I saw my tiny form wade out just a little too far, her head barely bobbing above water. She went under, then popped up again . . .

And this time, I saw what I hadn't before.

It was Sam—running down the beach, throwing himself into the ocean, and shoving me out of the way just as the kaiju reached down to sweep me up . . .

Its claw caught Sam instead, and then the kaiju was popping him into its giant mouth and he was *gone*.

"No!" I screamed in that stranger's voice.

I knew there was nothing I could actually *do*—all of this had already happened, I was merely reliving Shasta's memory. But I still wanted to run toward the ocean, to launch myself at the kaiju, to save Sam . . .

The scene in front of me started to disintegrate, fading and turning patchy. The kaiju disappeared, winking out of existence and leaving nothing but that beautiful beach vista in its wake—all calm now, the water smooth and unbothered. I watched my head pop out of the ocean again, shaking water from my ears, looking around like I was lost . . .

And then the scene crumbled before my eyes and I was back in Cake My Day, clapping a hand over my mouth before I screamed for real.

"Now you know," Shasta said, her lips curving into a calculating smile. "Sam sacrificed himself to save you."

I shook my head at her, even though I knew it was the truth. Tears pooled in my eyes and my breathing turned stuttery. I felt like I was drowning again, air rushing from my lungs as I was towed underwater.

Why had he done that? *Why* . . .

"What happened to him—and to the kaiju?" I wheezed, struggling to breathe normally. "Why did it just disappear like that?"

"Ah." Shasta leaned back in her seat and regarded me with narrowed eyes. "And now my story truly begins, Beatrice."

I stifled a groan. Shasta could supervillain monologue like no other.

"The kaiju are part of a new experiment of mine," she continued. "I'm still able to communicate with the great scientific minds of the Otherworld while I'm floating around on

Earth, and we deduced that if I could create a large enough creature, I could also make it into a portal back to my home dimension—and I do wish to return home eventually! The big creature in the sea was my first attempt at such a massive monster. There was ever so much wonderful lingering emotional energy on that beach for me to manipulate." She let out a happy sigh.

"A portal . . ." I murmured. "Does that mean Sam got booted to the Otherworld when the kaiju gobbled him up? Is he still alive, just . . ." The tiniest bit of hope sparked in my chest. "I don't know, trapped? Like the humans who were trapped in a prison dimension by my Mom-Demon—"

"I'm afraid not," Shasta said, extinguishing my hope with a faux-regretful head tilt. "Because it wasn't supposed to be Sam who was taken by the kaiju portal. It was supposed to be—"

"Vivi," I breathed. "You were trying to rip Evie's baby from her, so . . . what? You've been after that baby for months now. What is your actual plan? Because you don't seem like the doting grandma type."

"I can be doting," Shasta protested, a distressed hand flying to her chest. "I can dote with the best of them! But since you've asked so nicely, I'll give you even more of the story. Back in the Otherworld, there's an ancient prophecy passed down through demonic royalty that reads: 'The child born of two worlds will wield unique power and heal all wounds—but only once the destroyer has been fed and fulfilled, after which this evil shall vanish.' I've consulted with my fellow demon royals and we all agree: that child of two worlds *has* to be Vivi."

"Sounds like the kind of bullshit people say to biracial folks all the time," I muttered. "Like we're supposed to heal everything while also getting hate from a delightful cornucopia of sources and being told we don't actually belong anywhere. Vivi isn't here to be your symbol."

"She's so much more than that," Shasta insisted, her eyes flashing. "If I'm able to take her back to the Otherworld—"

"You can create a permanent bridge between your dimension and ours, thereby making it way easy for your to conquer Earth?" I glowered at her. "Because I'm pretty sure that's what your minions have claimed is the ultimate goal."

"Oh my, no!" Shasta shot me a reproving look and returned to sculpting more gingerbread kaiju. "Well, all right ... perhaps that's what I was thinking during the initial stages of my experiments. But after so much trial and error, and further consultation with the scientific minds of the Otherworld, I've figured out my goal is the opposite." She placed two gingerbread kaiju on opposite ends of our butcher paper, as if to demonstrate. "Through studying the prophecy, we've deduced that as soon as Vivi passes through the portal, it will seal and disappear—and so will any other portal that still exists in your human dimension."

"Is that the second part of the prophecy?" I asked, trying to follow the thread. "Like the big kaiju portal is the 'destroyer' and you're 'feeding' it with Vivi, which then makes it vanish?"

"Exactly!" Shasta exclaimed, grinning at me like I was a student who'd just answered correctly. "I'd been attempting to follow your family around for quite a while after I was ejected from Mercedes' body, hoping for an opportunity to take Vivi—and when I found out about the planned trip to Maui, well! It was just perfect, wasn't it? I created my big kaiju portal on the beach, and then tried doing a spell to pull Vivi from Evie's body and take her with me—"

"Hold on," I said, my brain working to follow her logic. "If you can possess human bodies now, why haven't you tried to possess anyone on Team Tanaka/Jupiter and take Vivi that way? Uh, not that I want to give you any super evil ideas—*shit* . . ."

"Not to worry, that one won't work anyway," Shasta said, popping gumdrop eyes onto another gingerbread kaiju. "I thought about it, but . . ." Her nose wrinkled, like she'd just smelled something bad. "Something always goes wrong whenever I get too close to those fools—and my ability to possess human bodies for long periods of time has proved to be rather erratic. I simply can't risk it."

"Okay," I said, still trying to follow the thread. Shasta's threads were always so freaking *tangled*. "So back to fulfilling this prophecy and closing up all the portals—why do you want that? What made you change your plan from full-on invasion?"

Shasta regarded me sagely, toying with a candy-cane shard. "Vivi *is* a child of two worlds, just as the prophecy says," she said. "She has some of the Otherworld in her, thanks to my useless son. And further analysis of the prophecy revealed to me that once she's back where she belongs, this unique heritage of hers will fuse with my dimension's magic, ushering in a new era of greatness. I'll have no use for this horrible human dimension, because the Otherworld will thrive—and since I'm the one who shepherded Vivi, I'll finally be recognized as the revered queen I deserve to be instead of the mere princess I am now. And anyway . . ." She made a repulsed face and tossed the candy-cane shard to the side. "My encounters and entanglements with humanity over the years have really shown me that this dimension is never going to be anything more than a cesspool of mediocrity. Vivi is the only thing I need from Earth."

She brandished one of her gingerbread kaiju at me again, making it do a macabre little dance. God, this was all just too weird.

"Beatrice, don't you see!" Shasta-Dahlia's smile widened, and she landed the gingerbread kaiju in a finishing pose, like *ta-da!* "This will end the strife we've been dealing with for all these years. That connection from so long ago, the one that never should have happened . . ." She laced her fingers together and then pulled them apart. "Once all the portals seal and disappear, it will be over. Vivi will sever that connection forever. You can live peacefully in your dimension, I'll be back in mine, and Evie and Aveda will never have to deal with demonic interference ever again. A perfect happy ending!"

"Except Vivi will now be trapped in the Otherworld with you, no?" I snapped. "That's definitely *not* a happy ending for Evie or Nate. Or Vivi, probably."

"But I can make it that way!" she insisted, leaning forward emphatically. "The kaiju portal . . . during my experimentations, I discovered that it completely erases the human that 'feeds' it. And once the prophecy is fulfilled and the kaiju disappears, that's it. That's why no one recalls your Sam—he was completely eliminated from the timeline, no traces left behind."

She grinned to herself and I had to sit on my hands so I wouldn't punch her in the face.

"If it had been Vivi, like it was supposed to be, I believe no one would remember her either," Shasta continued. "And because my portal was calibrated for her unique heritage, she would have survived—thrived, in fact, as she was meant to! But then your Sam just had to go and ruin my perfect plan!"

"I don't think it's all that perfect if it's so easy to mess up," I protested. "I mean, the kaiju was maybe trying to eat me too? What if Sam hadn't shoved me out of the way? Would I have disappeared like he did, or would I be in the Otherworld right now?"

"I will confess I am not entirely sure." Shasta crossed her arms over her chest and sized me up. "As I said, your power's mingling with Otherworld magic has caused all kinds of intriguing oddities. You are certainly an unexpected variable I hadn't accounted for in my grand plan. You may have noticed that you can hear the thoughts and feelings of these kaiju I've been creating, yes? As if they are projecting at *you*! You were able to control the large kaiju portal up to a point with your own emotional projections—until it figured out what you were doing and fought back. And then of course, the time travel . . ." She smiled slightly. "I believe that's why *you* remember Sam—you are not currently existing on the same linear plane as the rest of humanity. And incidentally, neither am I, since my consciousness is so free-floating in your realm—though I cannot travel through time as you can. So I'm not sure what would have happened to you—perhaps something truly magical, given these new abilities of yours!"

I hesitated, studying her. Was it my imagination, or did she sound . . . admiring? Like she thought these chaotic new enhancements to my power were *cool* or something?

Shasta picked up the craft mallet again and met my eyes.

"I've figured it out, Beatrice. These upgrades to your power are essential to carrying out the prophecy and saving both our worlds. We can *use* your time traveling to fix everything! Together, you and I can guarantee everyone's happily ever afters!"

"Do I even want to know?" I grumbled, glaring resentfully at the row of blobby kaiju Shasta had constructed.

"As I said—you are the only member of Team Tanaka/ Jupiter with true *vision*, the one who can see the bigger picture. And now with your potentially incredible power enhancements . . . well, you are the key. The only one who can help me fulfill the prophecy." She arched an eyebrow at me and smashed another piece of gingerbread, hitting the cookie in just the right spot to get it to crumble.

"You have to use your time travel to return to that moment on the beach," she continued. "That's where everything went wrong, in so many ways. But this time, you'll know what to do. You can help me get Vivi safely to the portal—just find me in my sun hat–sporting form, bring me over to your family, and make sure they stay nice and docile while I extract the baby from Evie. You can mentally project onto them if they attempt to fight me. Once Vivi passes through the portal with me, she'll be erased from everyone's memories. Evie won't remember that she was ever pregnant in the first place. And you'll have your Sam back."

She set the craft mallet down and turned back to her blobby gingerbread kaiju, idly tapping each one on its head.

"You'll be the hero you've always longed to be—you'll have saved your disgusting human realm! You alone will have eradicated the demon threat that's plagued your species for over a decade—you alone can do that!" One corner of her mouth tipped upward. "Pretty amazing, right? You're like the Chosen One!"

I looked down at my lap, where my hands were curling into fists. My mind was a jumble of way too many disparate thoughts. Nothing made sense. "Look, not that I want to give you more evil-type ideas, but . . . why does time travel need to be involved? Why can't you create your big-ass portal now and take Vivi?"

Shasta's brows drew together, her gaze darkening. "Because after six months of life, she is much too *human*. I need her before she has memories, experiences. Before she has been tainted by this horrible world!"

"Sure," I said, trying not to sound irritated. "Next question: why would I ever do that? Like, work with you? And why would I sacrifice my sweet baby niece—"

"Because you know it's the right thing," Shasta cut in. "It's for the greater good. Vivi is the only one who can close all the portals and finally bring peace to both our realms." She appraised me, Dahlia's saucer-blue eyes glittering shrewdly. "I know you're probably trying to come up with some 'clever' alternate plan right now, something that you believe will allow you to have it all—your whole family intact and Sam by your side and an exciting life as a dazzling superheroine. And you want all that to just be handed to you, no sacrifice required. You want to find some kind of loophole or clever trickery—you want to *cheat*." Shasta leaned forward, a shrewd glint in her eyes. "But you know, deep down, that it will never work out that way. Happy endings only come *after* you've worked your way through pain and suffering and made the hard choices. Happily ever after *always* requires sacrifice."

She flashed me a smile, but there was little humor in it. "And you know that better than anyone, Beatrice. Isn't that a major feature of so many of your beloved Christmas movies? Like this one . . ." She tapped the cover of *A Kaiju for Christmas*. "Thomas faces an impossible choice, yes? And in the end, he does what's necessary. He makes that sacrifice."

I studied her for a long moment. I didn't even know where to begin.

"Say I agree with you," I said slowly. "How am I supposed to accomplish all this? That day at the beach has already happened, I can't just—"

"But you *can*," Shasta said, her eyes glittering. "You can utilize your brilliant new power and project yourself back to that fateful moment. And then you can change everything. It's your only chance to save Sam—and the world."

"Well, here's the thing, I don't actually know *how* to time travel," I countered. "Like, with purpose. All the times that have happened so far have been total accidents."

Shasta laughed softly, her index finger tracing swirly patterns in the gingerbread crumbs.

"You'll figure it out," she said. "I have faith in you, Bea Tanaka."

Then she picked up the icing tube and squirted a few blobs throughout her field of gingerbread crumbs. I stared down at our creation, which had strayed pretty far from its original idea.

And I was only sure of one thing in that moment: our broke-down gingerbread house was about to come in dead last.

CHAPTER TWENTY

YEAH, SO WE came in dead last. I understand there was a lot of way more important shit to worry about, but that just seemed like an extra insulting cherry on top of the big ol' shit sundae.

Shasta-Dahlia vanished during the chaos of judging, and I was left trying to explain to Leah and Pancake that my new quest involved sacrificing my adorable baby niece to a giant kaiju portal created by her evil demon grandma.

"Wow, Bebe!" Leah goggled at me as we marched back to HQ. "Is this like your impossible choice, a la what Thomas faces in *Kaiju*—you can save Sam or Vivi, but not both?!"

"And don't forget: if I give up Vivi, all the portals will close and rid Earth of demons for good," I muttered, stomping down the street a little more aggressively. My limbs were restless and twitchy, and I couldn't seem to get my mind to focus. "And that's supposedly what Team Tanaka/Jupiter has been fighting for since the beginning."

"Can you do that, though?" Leah asked, casting a sidelong glance my way. Pancake did the same, his single eye narrowing in judgment. "Give up Vivi? To *Shasta*?"

"I don't know!" I yelped, throwing my hands up in frustration. "It's truly wild that *I'm* the member of the team being entrusted with this impossible choice. Literally *anyone else* would've been a better option!" I stopped in my tracks and leaned against the whimsically painted wall of a neighborhood coffee shop, trying to even out my wheezy breathing. "I could also just . . . stay here."

Leah leaned against the wall next to me. Pancake looked up at her, his ears flicking back and forth. "What do you mean?"

"What if I just chill in the current timeline?" I said, trying to work it out. "Everyone in my family seems pretty dang close to their happily ever afters. Christmas is Christmassing. The demon threat is *there*, but not unmanageable. And no one remembers Sam except me." I steadied the tremor that was trying to work its way through my voice.

"Is that what you think is best, Bebe?" Leah asked, her voice very gentle.

I bit my lip, my chest constricting as it tried to contain my roiling stew of emotions. Yes, my family was mostly happy (aside from the haunted look Evie got whenever she thought about Vivi's birth). Yes, teaming up with an *actual* supervillain like Shasta seemed like not the best idea, even if what she was proposing was for the greater good. And yes, chilling out in the current timeline and making a concentrated effort not to rock any boats seemed more in line with my whole "blend in and don't make trouble" initiative.

But . . .

My chest constricted again. I couldn't deny how *wrong* the world felt right now. How there was a big Sam-shaped hole— a hole I'd at least partially caused. And everything felt off because of that.

"I don't know what's best," I finally answered. "I don't know if I can sacrifice Vivi or Sam or . . ." I shook my head, my tangle of feelings threatening to overwhelm me again. "Like I said, why would anyone trust *me* to make the best choice? And I still don't trust Shasta, even if a lot of what she said seems to line up with what I've been experiencing and what I saw on the beach. But . . ."

I pushed off from the wall, straightened my spine, and looked up at the sky—focusing on a murky patch of cloud cover that refused to burn off, its wispy tendrils blocking the sun. My thoughts started to organize themselves a little better, the relevant headlines making themselves known. My fingertips twitched, eager to get started on *some* kind of plan.

"I don't know a lot right now," I said. "But I know I need to get back to that day at the beach. So at least one thing is clear to me: I have to learn how to time travel. Like, on purpose."

🔥

"You're gonna wear a groove in the floor." Leah nodded at me as I paced back and forth in my bedroom, my feet slapping purposefully against the hardwood surface.

HQ was empty when we got back, everyone on the team out picking things up for tonight's holiday party. So Leah, Pancake, and I had spirited ourselves up to my room, where I was now trying to brainstorm time-travel ideas.

I wasn't getting very far, hence the pacing.

"Here's the thing," I said. "I'm trying to think of what all these instances of accidental time travel have in common— but so far, nothing I've thought of is the actual trigger. I get a massive headache each time, but it's always *after*. So if I tried to, like, give myself a headache on purpose, I don't think it would work. And even if I figure out a trigger, I also don't know how to aim myself. I've gone forward a few hours, then a week, then several months. Oh, and that's another thing!" I stopped in my tracks and faced Leah and Pancake, who were both lounging on the bed. Pancake inclined his head at me, his ears perking. "Every time, I've traveled *forward*. How do I go *back* in time?! *Gah!*"

I threw up my hands and started pacing again.

"Bebe!" Leah waved her arms around, trying to get my attention. "You usually love this stuff—hypothesizing, experimenting, taking things apart and putting them back together again. But don't you have a method for getting your brain going?"

"I . . ." I shook my head, like that would make my thoughts assemble themselves in an orderly fashion.

I used to make my infamous, glitter-encrusted poster-boards for that sort of thing, my brain spilling itself onto a large canvas until it made sense to me. Seeing all my gathered information and theories spread out yet contained within the borders of the posterboard—and so pleasingly decorated!—spurred my mind to start making connections, drawing lines from one sparkly bit of flair to the next.

But ever since I'd started working so hard to be more mature, I'd stopped with that mode of work. I mean, work was supposed to be *work*, right? And I was supposed to be growing up. That's why I'd started writing my reports in a more basic, serious, professional manner. What if I wanted to follow in Doc Kai's footsteps and pursue advanced degrees in academia? Fancy professors of demonology probably wouldn't be too keen on my glittery posterboards.

"The posterboards, right?" Leah encouraged, waving one of Pancake's paws—like he was cheering me on. He gave her a disdainful look.

"I, um . . ." I chewed on my lower lip, my gaze going to the stack of blank posterboards in cheery colors that were tucked next to my tinkering work table—neon yellow, petal pink, eye-searing orange. Right where I'd left them when I'd departed for Maui and my new job. "It's not . . . I mean, I don't really do that anymore, I don't work like that—"

"But why?" Leah pressed. "It always helps you put your best theories together, right?"

I frowned at the posterboards, which seemed to be flashing their bright colors with wild abandon, calling to me.

Well, why not? Nothing else was working. And it wasn't like this was actual scientific research I was going to present to Doc Kai.

I grabbed the neon yellow posterboard and my bucket of craft supplies and spread everything out on the floor, then motioned for Leah and Pancake to join me.

"What are we doing here, Bebe?" Leah asked, her eyes narrowing shrewdly as she surveyed the vast expanse of blank posterboard. "How can Pancake and I be your best research assistants?"

"I'm going to start by visualizing the strongest sense memories I have from each time-travel instance," I said, uncapping one of my markers. "Hopefully that will help me find connections. And while I'm doing that, maybe we can talk through some more time-travel theories."

"Right," Leah said, nodding emphatically. "That will free your creative mind up—and you'll get the most natural versions of your experiences onto the posterboard. You won't be thinking about them too hard, so they can flow more organically."

I nodded and focused on the posterboard, holding my marker aloft—poised to strike. I took a deep breath and thought back to my first known instance of time travel—that day with Doc Kai and the gingerbread. I began sketching out cute little gingerbread people, each one with a different whimsical outfit.

The moment my marker brushed the posterboard, my shoulders relaxed, my brain going into a meditative state as I drew. Making these posterboards had always calmed me, because I felt like I could finally *see* the cavalcade of disparate thoughts that tended to pile up in my brain. All those things felt less overwhelming when contained within the bounds of a big, colorful rectangle.

"So," I said, sketching a whimsical bow tie on one of my gingerbread people, "what are some other common elements of time travel we've gotten from different pop culture things— you know, like the 'don't disturb the timeline' bit. I know it might seem odd to go to fictional examples for our theorizing, but given that I'm the only known human with the projecting superpower . . ." I shrugged, scrutinizing my gingerbread person's bow tie. It definitely needed polka dots. "We don't have 'real life' data to work with. And Nate's always told me that there are no wrong places to start when it comes to developing scientific theories based in the supernatural."

"You're trying to home in on a trigger, right?" Leah said, helpfully sprinkling glitter onto my gingerbread-person posse. "How do people figure that shit out in the movies?"

"Hmm." I finished with the gingerbread people and moved on to visualizing my next bout of time traveling—right before my family had arrived for their ill-fated visit. What had I been doing right before? Oh, right! I'd fallen asleep watching *A Kaiju for Christmas*. I started to sketch Sandrine in her glorious monster form. "I actually just re-watched *The Knight Before Christmas* with Nate this morning," I continued. "In that case, it's like . . . a witch casts a spell, but she also has this enchanted medallion?"

"Isn't there also an enchanted medallion in *Kaiju*?" Leah asked. "Which I still maintain is not a true rom-com and also there's no time travel involved, but seriously, what's up with all the medallions?"

"Magical objects make the Christmas movieverse go round," I said, batting Pancake's paw away from a gluey spot on the posterboard. He gave me an aggrieved look. "Look at our girl Kelly in *The Christmas Locket*—her magical object is the actual title, even!" I paused and switched markers, going with a deep purple to shade in Sandrine's claws. "What about when time travel is mechanical rather than magical—like in *Back to the Future*, it's all scientific, Doc Brown builds the flux capacitor and—"

"And it's still contained in a special object, though!" Leah cried, enthusiastically dumping a little too much glitter onto Sandrine's iridescent hide. "He puts the capacitor in what is basically a magic DeLorean, right? We all recognize that car as the *thing* that makes time travel happen."

"True." I paused my sketching, closing my eyes and picturing enchanted medallions and magic lockets and souped-up DeLoreans. "Maybe I need a talisman. Some kind of important object that can help trigger the time travel? Maybe if I hold said object and focus really hard, it will activate my projection power in that special way?" I opened my eyes and met Leah's gaze. "This all sounds ridiculous, doesn't it?"

"Not any more so than all the other adventures you've had with Team Tanaka/Jupiter!" Leah chirped, grinning at me. "Y'all have faced down vampires who made up a whole-ass TV show to lure Aveda into their clutches, ghosts who forced Evie to confront her past trauma by reliving her tortured grad school days, and I haven't even gotten to the demonic cupcakes, literal bridezillas, or actually cursed karaoke!"

"Well, when you put it *that* way . . ." I laughed, putting the finishing touches on my final drawing. "So that's at least a place to start with experimenting—we can try some different potential talismans and see if they work."

"How are we going to figure out which special objects to try?" Leah asked. "Should we go to a weird curio shop and purchase all their rusty old lockets? Troll the retirement communities until we find an elderly witch with an enchanted medallion collection? Attempt to build a flux capacitor?!"

"Wow, would I *love* that," I said dreamily, instantly fantasizing about my very own Doc Brown–style tinkering workshop. "But . . . no." I set aside my marker and grabbed a handful of festive pom-pom balls—the perfect final flourish. I always dug the cheery three-dimensional aesthetic of a good pom-pom ball. "Because here is where Nate would remind me that the first step of any supernatural experiment should contain as few variables as possible. So I should start with simple, basic objects—and if that doesn't work, we start adding in the variables, like maybe I can figure out how to get Scott to 'enchant' something for me without arousing his suspicion."

"Okay," Leah said, her eyes eagerly scanning the posterboard. "What objects do you want to try, Bebe?"

"Let's go back to thinking about all three instances of time travel—which is what we're trying to do with this posterboard," I said, glancing over my work. I sat back on my heels, taking in everything I'd just drawn and decorated. My brain was buzzing now, all synapses firing as it attempted to make connections.

My first drawing was that collection of eclectic gingerbread people, all smiling gamely at me in their glitter-festooned outfits. One of them danced over to the second drawing, which depicted Sandrine as that amazing kaiju, rising out of the ocean and sporting a tiny Santa hat. Her massive claw was kicking up a big, bedazzled wave that stretched into the final drawing—my most recent instance of time travel, when I'd fallen into the sea and woken up at HQ.

For this one, I'd drawn myself in the festive red and green outfit I'd worn to the It's Lit event. I'd then added a bunch of cartoony elements floating around my head—mistletoe and cups of overflowing holiday punch and cute little reindeer ears. I looked very confused, despite the pleasing pom-pom ball flourishes I'd added everywhere. I noticed Pancake had managed to add some flourishes of his own in the form of gluey paw prints.

"Wow," Leah said, still studying the posterboard intently. "This actually looks like a legit poster for one of your holiday movies, Bebe! And you're the heroine who moves back to her small hometown and starts an artisanal candle business and decides to rename herself something extra whimsical, like Clove."

"*Clove?*" I spat out. "I think not. But . . ." My eyes narrowed as they surveyed the posterboard yet again, a frisson of excitement running through me. "Lee, you're a genius. That's it!"

"What's it?" Leah asked, clutching Pancake to her chest. He let out an indignant whuffle. "I mean, yay me! But also . . . um, what's it?"

"It's *Christmas!*" I exclaimed, gesturing grandly to the posterboard. "That's the connective tissue for all of these incidents. For that first bit of time travel, my strongest sense memory is Doc Kai's gingerbread. For the second, I remember falling asleep to *A Kaiju for Christmas*. And for the third . . ." I tapped my confused cartoon face. "I traveled *to*

HOLIDAY HEROINE

Christmas. After sort of celebrating fake Christmas with my family." I flashed back to Evie's merry lights twirling around the palm tree. "Whatever I'm doing here is connected to the holidays. So maybe the talisman is, too!"

I leapt to my feet, hope blazing through me. My synapses were firing so fast, I could barely keep up, and my fingers twitched again, eager to experiment and find my talisman.

This was always the moment I loved during a bout of hypothesizing—that *a-ha!* bit, where maybe you haven't solved everything or arrived at your ultimate solution, but you've connected enough dots for a mini breakthrough. I smiled at my posterboard, its glitter sparkling in the late afternoon light streaming through the window.

"I'm gonna go gather a bunch of Christmas shit!" I crowed, clapping my hands together. "Which shouldn't be too hard since it's literally all over the house right now. And if my talisman isn't here, we'll keep looking—we can try some stuff at It's Lit, we can clean out the holiday aisle at Target. And hey, maybe we *will* go to an old curio shop, they've always got a whole-ass Christmas section—"

"Yessss, Bebe!" Leah jumped up to stand next to me, Pancake still clutched to her chest. He was gazing haughtily at both of us. "Look at you, reclaiming your essential Bebeness!"

"What are you talking about?" I giggled and reached over to ruffle Pancake's fur, which only made his haughty look increase about a thousand fold. "I'm still me, time travel notwithstanding."

"Of course you are," Leah said. "It's just . . ." She studied me, her dark eyes narrowing. "You've been missing a little of your spark lately. I'm not sure how to describe it. You've just seemed . . ." She shook her head. "I don't know, like you're holding back? Or scared to be fully yourself? Like you're an echo of the most essential *you*, in a way."

"I'm not exactly sure what I've been up to the past few months, given that I skipped over them," I said lightly. "But maybe what you're feeling is that sense of the timeline being wrong, with Sam missing and all."

"I'm talking about way earlier than that," Leah pressed. "After you moved to Maui." She hesitated, assessing me again. I tried not to squirm under the intensity of her gaze. "When you told me about what happened to you during the power combo spell, it kinda clicked for me. *That* was when you stopped texting and calling as often. When you started communicating with me mostly through those letters about your favorite Christmas movies. I thought maybe with your cool new grown-up life, you were drifting away from me—"

"Never," I insisted fervently. "But god, Leah, I'm so sorry I made you feel that way. I feel like the worst friend in the world. I can't believe I didn't know anything about your plan to buy the bookstore—oh! What happened with Charlotte, did you get to talk to her today?"

"No," Leah said. "The chaos at that competition was a little too busy . . . you know, chaos-ing. But back to you, Bebe. I can see it now—I think you stopped trusting yourself after that spell. You seem to think this new darkness you're feeling means you're two seconds away from going full bad guy at any given moment."

"That makes sense, doesn't it?" I retorted. "If I can't figure out how to control it and all. Look what happened before, when I got just a little taste of the darkness—do I need to remind you yet again that I almost trapped your girlfriend in a demonic prison dimension? I didn't even think that hard about it, it was my *instinct*—"

"You wouldn't do that now," Leah cut in. Pancake let out another whuffle, but I couldn't tell if he agreed with her or not. "You've learned so much about your power, Bebe—and about yourself, too. You're working out your shit—"

"I'm still *me*," I said, trying to sound jokey and self-deprecating. "Chaos personified and a little too interested in my own pleasure above all else. I'm trying to grow up now, to do things the mature way—"

"And I don't know why you keep describing yourself like you're some kind of cartoon character!" Leah exploded. "Yeah, okay, you've made some crappy decisions—so have we all! Pancake still hasn't forgiven me for that time I tried to dye the tips of his ears pink!" Pancake grunted and gave her the stink-eye, apparently holding a grudge. "But you *have* grown, Bebe. You don't have to change everything about yourself and become some kind of blah, blending-in automaton to be a good person—you already *are* a good person! I am your constant, and that means I *know* you. I can see how freaking lit up you are right now, and it's because you're getting shit done *your* way instead of trying to put all of this . . ." She gestured to the bright, explosive colors of my posterboard. ". . . into some kind of boring-ass report!"

"Leah . . ." I pulled her into an impulsive hug. Pancake started squirming around, displeased at being squished. I didn't know what to say. A wave of love for my best friend surged through me—how could she believe in me so much when I barely knew what I was doing? I'd erased my whole boyfriend from the timeline and gotten pulled into a demonic scheme that involved a sacrificial baby, and she still thought I could fix everything somehow.

I couldn't deny that she was right about the posterboard, though. I felt more inspired than I had in months, that zing of possible scientific discovery goosing all of my senses and sending my mind spinning in all different directions—

Wait. Wasn't it bad when my mind spun in all different directions? Like, didn't that lead very naturally down the rabbit hole of terrible decisions?

I couldn't worry too much about that right now. I had to focus on finding my talisman. And my brain acting all sparky seemed to be leading me in that direction.

"You *are* my constant," I said to Leah, pulling back from the hug. I gave her what I hoped was a reassuring smile. "Thank you for believing in me so hard." *Even though I don't quite believe in myself.* "And, um . . . I'm sorry I pulled away. I was so scared to talk to you about the whole power combo spell thing, but talking to you always makes me feel better. Like maybe the problem isn't quite as scary as I thought it was."

"And I feel the same way about you," Leah said. "Please don't not talk to me ever again? I love your Christmas movie commentary, but I need *you*. You're my constant, too."

"Deal," I said, squeezing her hand.

"And please consider that this darkness is something you don't have to be totally scared of!" she added. "I know you can figure it out, Bebe—"

"Whoa, whoa!" I held up my hands, laughing a little. "Let's figure out one of the other five thousand things we're dealing with first. We need to get you your store and find me my talisman." I gave Pancake a conciliatory pat on the head, as if to reassure him that the squishening was finished. "I'm gonna run downstairs and grab every Christmas-looking thing I can find. Then I'll bring that bounty up here and we can try them all out! And then we'll brainstorm ideas for you talking to Charlotte—ooh, we can start a whole new poster-board for that!" Another frisson of anticipation ran through me. Experiment time! My absolute favorite!

"Hurry up!" Leah called after me as I hustled out the door. "I think Pancake's getting hungry—I might need to feed him his third lunch once we're done with all this experimenting!"

I headed downstairs, a sense of purpose flowing through my veins. No, I still didn't know what I'd actually do once I made it back to that day at the beach. Could I really sacrifice Vivi? Or Sam? Would I fuck up the timeline all over again?

But . . . the fact that maybe I could figure out *how* to get back there made me feel better. Perhaps once I accomplished this bit of intentional time travel, the rest of my path would become clear.

I started my search in the main living room, where a massive Christmas tree had been erected, its intoxicating scent of pine wafting through the space. My heart warmed at the very sight of it—in the past, I'd been the lone voice advocating for a real Christmas tree, and I hadn't been able to get anyone else on Team Tanaka/Jupiter to join my quest. I surveyed the eclectic assortment of ornaments dotting its branches: glittering silver orbs, cute animals wearing Santa hats. And then I saw it.

Right there in the middle of the tree was an ornament I'd acquired when I was a mere tween, shortly after Mom died and Dad left. It was shaped like . . . well, I'd always thought it was a dragon, but it was so blobby that I wasn't entirely sure of the artist's intent. It looked like someone had gotten really high and tried to invent their own mythical creature that didn't quite work out. It was wearing a scarf and a Santa hat—and for some reason, it was painted metallic pink.

I'd discovered it in a dumpster, perched on top of all the other trash and calling to me like a very tacky beacon. It was objectively ugly, but my little twelve-year-old magpie self thought it was one of the most beautiful things she'd ever seen.

It called to me again now, its bright surface glittering amidst the gentle green of the tree.

I reached out, my fingertips brushing its scratched-up surface. Was this my talisman? It wasn't enchanted, but hey—it had certainly enchanted *me* the first time I'd laid eyes on it. I plucked it from the tree, my heartbeat speeding up as my fingers closed around the hard plastic.

Yes. This felt right.

It was an object that was special to me, an object most definitely tied to Christmas. And I couldn't deny that holding it in my hand gave me the same tingly fated feeling Kelly the whimsical holiday time traveler had described when she discovered her magic locket.

What had Kelly done once she had the locket? I tried to remember. I could practically see the movie unspooling in my mind, taking me to the moment when Kelly first finds the locket and clasps it in her hand. It reminds her so much of the love she's lost that she starts envisioning all the Christmas sights and smells and sounds . . .

I held the ornament tighter, the garish plastic warming as my palm grew sweaty. If Christmas united all my time-travel incidents, if it was part of the trigger . . . maybe I should follow Kelly's lead?

I closed my eyes, breathing in the scent of pine and picturing the wreaths I'd seen attached to lampposts the night before, the decadent smell of gingerbread, the Candy Cane Lane from our It's Lit party . . .

I held my breath, waiting for something to happen.

Nothing did.

I opened my eyes, hoping maybe I was wrong and I was about to encounter the sight of the sea, the scent of the surf.

Nope. It was still the cozy Victorian and a twinkling holiday tableau I normally would have been completely into.

I blew out an exasperated breath and stared at the ornament, its pink surface taunting me. It had felt so *right* . . . and yet it hadn't worked. If something I'd felt such a fated call to wasn't my talisman, then what on earth *was*?

I realized then that I'd completely abandoned my original plan. I'd meant to gather all the Christmas objects, then go back upstairs so Leah and I could work on this experiment together. (Another thing Nate was always reminding me of: when it came to hardcore supernatural experimentation, safety dictated that you should always use the buddy system. Especially if you were the guinea pig—and I always seemed to make myself the guinea pig.)

And yet, as soon as I'd felt the call of something shiny, I'd given in to my impulses and forged ahead.

How was I expected to save the timeline, the world, and possibly Sam if I couldn't even do this part right?!

I stared at the offending ornament, glaring at the dragon's misshapen wings. I felt the urge to chuck the ornament across the room, maybe knock down the tree, really give in to all those destructive instincts. A scream bubbled up in my throat and I wanted to let it out so badly, to vocalize all my rage and impotence and the fact that I couldn't even do a simple bit of experimentation correctly . . .

CRASH!

I turned, my fist closing around the ornament. And I saw the now-unmistakable flash of a mini kaiju, darting behind our holly-strewn coffee table. A candle shaped like a candy cane had been knocked to the ground, and the mini kaiju was skittering out of the way.

I opened my mouth to scream, even as the living room started to go fuzzy around the edges, even as I felt the plastic of my garish dragon ornament press more firmly into my hand, even as I started to figure out what was happening, except it was already happening, it was . . .

And then I felt myself falling, the scream evaporating in my throat as everything went black.

CHAPTER TWENTY-ONE

WHEN MY EYES popped open this time, the first thing that entered my consciousness was the smell of gravy. Rich and savory and laden with mouthwatering notes of herbs and spices. I sat up slowly, drinking in my surroundings. I was cocooned in a faded old quilt, buttery soft from an infinite number of trips through the washing machine. And I seemed to be lying on some kind of couch . . .

Oh!

The rest of my senses started to come online as I realized where I was—this was the designated "napping couch" in Doc Kai's study, the coziest room in the homey bungalow she shared with Carmelo.

I was back in Makawao. And someone was making gravy.

Both of these seemed like pleasing conditions on the surface of it all, but *when* was I? That was the real question. I hadn't returned to that day on the beach, but had I managed to aim myself in the correct general vicinity? Was I maybe just a few days out from that?

The headache hit me then, that now-familiar lance of pain stabbing me in the temple.

I needed to call Leah, my constant. I looked around for my phone, then realized something was clutched in my sweaty hand. I uncurled my fingers to reveal a blobby lump of iridescent pink plastic—the dragon ornament! Giddiness surged through me, making my headache fade. My talisman had worked! My *whole experiment* had worked! Though I still needed to solve the *when* of it all—

"Beeeeeeaaaaa!"

I jerked around to see Keala barging into the study, her expression a bit put out. She stopped in front of the couch and clamped her hands on her hips.

"Huff!" she snorted. "How long are you gonna sleep? We gotta start round two of the grand holiday feasting, and Carmelo's gravy is apparently best served exactly ten minutes after it hits the boiling point, otherwise—"

"Holiday feasting?!" I blurted out. "Is it . . . Christmas . . ."

"How deep were you sleeping?" Keala asked, her face turning amused. "Yeah, still Christmas. And the first course of Kai and Carmelo's epic feast is all pau, but if you can't remember it . . . ." She shook her head in mock disapproval. "That's one holiday tragedy."

"I . . ." I rubbed my thumb against the shiny surface of the ornament, trying to get my brain to unfog. "I'm sure it will all come back to me. Was there musubi? Kālua pig, perhaps?"

"Pika's finest," Keala affirmed. "Next up is Carmelo's Filipino loco moco, surrounded by one bunch of other heavenly-sounding grinds." She beamed at me. "Love you for wrangling me an invite to this most excellent day of eating. Neither Giselle nor I can cook, so Christmas is usually frozen lasagna and one MTV *Challenge* marathon, yeah? But *this* . . ." She inhaled deeply, her eyes fluttering closed as she took in the gravy once more. "This is highly superior."

"No problem," I said faintly, my fingers wrapping more tightly around the ornament. My foggy brain was slowly starting to put the pieces together—the way Keala was talking, this had to be my very first Christmas in Maui, after I'd only been out here for a couple months.

So that meant I'd successfully traveled *back* in time. But not to the right spot.

And say, this was also the Christmas Sam had come to visit me. Could that mean . . .

My heartbeat intensified, my fingers wrapping so tightly

around the ornament that the blobby dragon's plastic wings dug into my skin.

"Let's go see about that gravy," I said, leaping to my feet. I stuffed the ornament into my pocket and followed Keala out into the dining room, where a long table was threatening to collapse under the weight of several metric tons of food. I saw piles of musubi, a half-full platter of kālua pig, and heaping bowls of fluffy rice and mac salad. I saw a few take-out containers from some of the gang's favorite spots: there were overflowing tubs of saimin from Sam Sato's, trays of mouthwatering katsu from Restaurant Matsu, and a pile of the scrumptious, condiment-laden dollar hot dogs from Fukushima Store. I saw Carmelo proudly placing a massive serving dish of his special loco moco in the center of the table as Doc Kai clapped her hands in delight and Tosh leaned over to examine the full glory of the gravy. I saw Giselle taking a seat next to Pika, who looked as cantankerous as ever.

And I saw two empty seats waiting for me and Keala. But no Sam.

My heart sank—now I was in a whole other part of this timeline where Sam didn't exist.

I reached in my pocket again to find my phone . . . then realized there was no way I could call Leah. Because all of this was *before* I'd told her anything about the time travel. She likely wouldn't know what I was talking about, and that was yet another chance to fuck up the timeline. I mean, even more than I already had.

So now I was stuck in the wrong moment in the past, at a point when absolutely no one had any clue about what was going on with me.

Awesome.

"There ya are!" Doc Kai exclaimed, grinning at me. "C'mon, Bea, you gotta get in here for part two of our all-day holiday feast! It's the tradition around here, and I know you're gonna love Carmelo's special twist on the loco moco, yeah?"

"Shoots!" Carmelo exclaimed, then gestured to his creation with genial glee. "My pride and joy, and if you add a little plop of sriracha . . ." His smile widened, and he rubbed his belly. "So 'ono."

I plastered a smile on my face and took the empty seat next to Pika, a confusing mess of feelings raging through me. My memories were starting to cohere, and I could practically see how this scene had unfolded the first time I'd lived it. I remembered the warmth that had washed over me as I took a seat at Doc Kai's table, all the gratitude I'd felt toward this wonderful group of people who'd readily accepted me into the fold, treating me like I'd always been part of their various circles. That had made me a little less homesick, a little less sad to be away from Evie and the rest of my family on Christmas.

And of course Sam had been there, too.

"Hey, did I mention the possibility of, like . . . bringing anyone? To this awesome shindig?" I blurted out, grasping at straws.

"You brought Keala and Giselle!" Doc Kai said, eagerly passing the loco moco platter to Giselle. "And we love having one big ol' crowd for Christmas. Or any time, really."

"I still can't believe we lived so close to Kai and Carmelo, but had never met before," Giselle said, her slight French accent giving her words a lilting cast. "Keala and I are usually on our own for the holidays, so this is lovely."

"Sounds like the quintessential Bea Tanaka extreme social butterfly charm at work!" Tosh piped up. "I swear, Bea, you met more locals your first week in Makawao than I have . . . maybe ever."

"That's because you always claim you don't like people— just in general," Doc Kai teased. "Thank god we got Bea out here now, she's making you expand your friendship horizons!"

"Hmph," Tosh said, pretending to be offended. "Maybe she can also help me expand my dating horizons. It's hard to find someone to kiss when you don't like most people." They arched an eyebrow at me and placed a dramatic hand over their chest. "What do you say, Bea, can you help the world's most unromantic person in matters of the heart?"

"Stop it!" Doc Kai laughed, reaching over to swat Tosh on the arm. "We still gotta find Bea her soulmate so she can enjoy the kine holiday rom-com life she was clearly meant for!"

Everyone laughed, and I plastered a smile across my face—even though it felt like my heart was shattering. I remembered a different version of this moment, where Sam had been here with me—and Doc Kai had cheerfully commented that we already seemed to be living the holiday rom-com life, what with his sweet surprise visit to me and all.

It felt strangely cruel to live out what had been such a beautiful, happy memory among friends with the harsh knowledge that it had been so horribly altered, twisted into something that just wasn't right. Tears pricked my eyes and I blinked them back.

Enough dwelling, I told myself firmly. *You accomplished at least part of your mission, yeah? And you have a talisman now! You just have to figure out how to aim yourself directly at that day on the beach. That's the key . . .*

I slipped my hand into my pocket and squeezed the dragon ornament, hoping it would give me strength. Or at least focus my brain so I could figure out a next step.

I needed to try the intentional time travel again, using my talisman. But how was I going to figure out how to travel to a specific moment? What was I missing? I gnawed on my lower lip and looked down at my plate as Carmelo's loco moco platter continued its trek around the table.

Maybe I could gather more data before my next attempt— if I tried to time travel again right now, in the middle of all this important holiday feasting, it might deposit me in yet another random moment from my life. I needed to figure out what to do differently—what variables I could add to my experiment.

If anything about this extremely disconcerting scene could be considered a positive (besides all the amazing food), it was the fact that I was currently sitting at a table with someone I considered one of the world's leading (and coolest) supernatural scientists. Surely I could figure out a way to work with that.

I eyed Doc Kai as she enthusiastically piled bits of loco moco onto her fork, crafting the perfect bite.

What else had we done on this day? I remembered all the feasting. I remembered spiriting myself away for a nap after the first round, leaving Sam chattering away with Pika about old cars. I cast a sidelong glance at Pika, who had remained so quiet, I'd nearly forgotten that he was sitting next to me. He was frowning down at his plate, poking at the gravy with his chopsticks. Perhaps he was comparing it unfavorably to one of his own concoctions.

What had we done next, once everyone was stuffed to bursting and about to fall into a collective food coma? We'd gone to the living room, plopped ourselves on various couches and cushions, and then—

"*Back to the Future!*" I blurted out.

Everyone swiveled to look at me, and I clapped a hand over my mouth. Goddammit. My lack of impulse control really made me one of the worst time travelers ever.

"Um, sorry," I said, pasting on another smile. "I was just, um, remembering that Doc Kai said we were going to watch that movie after the second round of holiday feasting."

"That's right, Bea!" Doc Kai beamed at me. "We always need at least a two-hour break between the second feasting course and the dessert course. And ever since you gave me my super cool nickname, I've been thinking about that movie nonstop!"

"A classic!" Carmelo exclaimed, stabbing his chopsticks in the air. "Damn, I remember small-kid times, wishing more than anything that I had one flux capacitor."

"Me too," I said, grinning at him. "But y'know, Doc Kai,

it's always interesting to see how pop culture of the distant past portrayed stuff that still hasn't been invented yet—like time travel. Do you think we'll ever be able to accomplish such a feat?"

"Oh, yeah!" Doc Kai nodded, her eyes getting that mad-scientist gleam—I loved watching her big brain open up in real time, loved feeling it sparking with mine, all sorts of new theories exploding as we riffed back and forth. "Look at all the outrageous, unprecedented things that have happened in our world, yeah? Stuff no scientist would've ever predicted. Demons and superpowers and out-of-this-world dimensions existing alongside ours! Time travel can't be far behind!"

"What do you think it will look like?" I asked, attempting to sound like I was casually walking it out, the way we usually did. "Like, is it gonna be *Back to the Future*-style, plutonium and lightning storms and souped-up cars?" I glanced over at Pika when I mentioned the cars, since that was usually something that would spark his interest. But he was still poking at his gravy, the furrows in his brow deepening.

"Mmm," Doc Kai said, setting down her fork for a moment, her face turning contemplative. "I dunno, I feel like it will occur in a way that's more . . . unexpected? There was a lot of intentionality from Doc Brown there, he was avidly pursuing the goal of time travel! Whereas in our current world, we're mostly wrapped up in studying the Otherworld and how demons and superpowers work. The exploration of time travel feels like one tangent—not exactly related to all that."

"But what if you *could* go back in time, Doc?" Keala asked. "Would you eliminate the demon threat before it even had a chance to take root?"

"Like, what, head off the original invasion attempt?" Tosh asked, going in for a second helping of loco moco. "Make it so we never learned about the demon threat at all?"

"Ahh, now we are in the hypothetical land, non?" Giselle exclaimed, her green eyes intrigued. "But it is, how do you say . . . ironic? Because if demons never came to this world, what would have happened to all of you who have made the demonology such a big part of your lives?"

"Aisus, that's one pickle!" Carmelo guffawed, slapping his knee. "This crew loves talkin' demons. Nothing more fascinating, y'know."

I couldn't help but grin—I always enjoyed Carmelo's predilection for expansive gestures coupled with his explosive, braying laugh. It was another thing that had made me instantly at home with him and Doc Kai. I felt a little pang, realizing how much I'd missed all of them during my recent time-travel sojourn to the Bay Area.

Carmelo turned to Doc Kai, covering her hand with his. "If there were no demons, we mighta never met, Doc! Remember, ya interviewed me about one of those possible demon encounters way back when. And you were super impressed with my muscles." He flexed to demonstrate as Doc Kai blushed and rolled her eyes, pretending to be embarrassed.

"Cheeseball," she murmured—but there was nothing but love in her voice. "You know, I think about these kinds of hypotheticals all the time—what if you could go back in time and fix something you thought was wrong or bad or just didn't happen the way you wanted it to?" She smiled and gave a helpless sort of shrug. "We make a thousand choices every day, yeah? What we're gonna wear, what we're gonna eat. We're writing our own futures, bit by bit. So say I made the choice to travel back and try to change something. That's now part of my path, an undeniable piece of my story—a culmination of all the choices I've made, big and small, that brought me to that moment."

"But it's a different kind of choice, isn't it?" I couldn't help but ask. "Because you'd be changing what was already meant to be, right? You'd be messing up the timeline, altering the existence of everyone's lives, which could have catastrophic consequences—"

I cut myself off abruptly, my face flushing hot as my heart

hammered in my chest. Pika had stopped picking at his gravy and was staring at me, his eyes blank and unreadable.

"We change each other's lives all the time, simply by being in them," Doc Kai said, meeting my gaze. One corner of her mouth lifted into a slight smile. "There's no 'what was supposed to be,' only what *is*. If you think about it, all of us are altering the timeline every single day. I don't think that's catastrophic—I think it's beautiful."

I couldn't help but smile back. Trust Doc Kai to see things in such a positive light—big-brained, big-hearted, unfailingly optimistic Doc Kai, the woman who still believed friendly demonic sea monsters were going to rise out of the ocean.

"But what about the times when all of our lives and our choices and . . . well, everything, crash into each other in a bad way?" I persisted. "Humans are really good at catastrophe! Remember how firm Doc Brown is when Marty tries to tell him literally anything about the future—it's 'cause he doesn't want to fuck it up!"

"Ah, but remember the *end* of the movie!" Doc Kai crowed. "Doc reads Marty's letter after all and straps on a bulletproof vest—and so he gets to live instead of being gunned down during the birth of his greatest scientific discovery. Marty changed the timeline for the *better*. Not every choice is the wrong one, yeah?"

"I . . . I guess that's true," I mumbled, turning that over in my mind. In all my theorizing with Leah, I hadn't actually thought about how so many of these fictional scenarios concluded. But I supposed the key word there was *fictional*—it wasn't like a feel-good comedy like *Back to the Future* was going to end by killing off its most beloved character.

"Sigh! Forget about the sequels, though," Keala piped up. "That lolo dystopian alternate timeline was *not* it."

"Not to mention the egregious sidelining of Crispin Glover," Tosh added.

"Aw, c'mon, that time-traveling train in the third one was cool!" Carmelo protested. "Plus it was a Western, which is pretty tight."

"This is why I love our meeting of the minds, though, Bea," Doc Kai said, her grin widening. "You always make me think about things in a way that's so completely unexpected. That big, wild brain of yours jumped off the page as soon as I read one of your reports." She snagged another musubi, chuckling to herself. "Your insights, your perspective . . . they were so vibrant, so *alive*. It was like no other scientific report I'd read before. And then when I saw those posterboards you do . . ." She raised her hand and unfurled her fingers, miming her brain exploding. "*Whoa*. It gave me chicken skin, it was like I could *see* all these phenomena you'd encountered, could really visualize these sequences of extraordinary events."

"That's why I love the posterboards," I murmured.

"And I couldn't believe that you were working with Nate, of all people," Doc Kai continued. "Stuffy Nathaniel Jones, the most drop-dead serious demonology student I've ever encountered." She shook her head, her grin getting even wider. "But he thought you were brilliant, too. Even if he did edit out some of your emojis. All in all, I'd say you altered the course of both of our lives in the most incredible of ways!"

I looked down at my plate, flushing again. There was that lovely and infinite Doc Kai positivity again. The woman had never encountered anything she couldn't spin into a glass-half-full situation, and I loved her for it. And that sheer, un-bridled enthusiasm in her voice was making me remember how I'd felt those first couple of heady months I'd been in Maui, when the possibilities had stretched out in front of me like the shiniest of rainbows, when I'd been so excited about my new job, my new friends, and the constantly stimulating meeting of the minds I'd had with my cool new boss. Past Bea Tanaka had possessed plenty of that wide-eyed optimism herself, and I felt a rush of sadness for what was about to become of her.

I opened my mouth to offer a bland thank-you of sorts, in as few words as possible so as not to let on what I was really feeling, when I felt a sudden tug on my sleeve.

"Gravy. *I need the gravy.*"

"Pika?" I turned to him as he yanked my sleeve again, his gaze agitated. "What's wrong?" I looked down at his plate. "You've got plenty of gravy, still."

"No." He shook his head emphatically. "I need that simple one, you know—beef gravy over rice."

"I can rustle up some more gravy for ya!" Carmelo declared, popping up from his seat. "And beef, too—hold that thought, brah." He gave Pika a hearty clap on the back as he hustled toward the kitchen, whistling what sounded like an off-key version of "Rudolph the Red-Nosed Reindeer."

"Shoots, let's keep the gravy flowin'!" Doc Kai cried, digging back into her loco moco with gusto. "That's the Christmas spirit!"

"Okay, but I'm reconsidering my stance, eh? Can we watch all the *Back to the Future*s, even that weird dystopian one?" Keala said. "Giselle's never seen any of them!"

"Oui, I know nothing of the Marty McFly," Giselle agreed.

"Sacrilege!" bellowed Doc Kai, pounding on the tabletop.

The table devolved into random chatter, a plethora of overlapping conversations bubbling up all at once.

I stared down at my plate, trying not to freak out about Pika's urgent gravy request. But his hand was still on my sleeve, tugging insistently.

"Pika," I whispered. "What is it? What's wrong? Carmelo's getting you the gravy—"

"Don't want none of that," he retorted, shaking his head. He leaned in close, his voice so low I had to strain to hear him. "Bea," he said, his tone growing urgent. "Where's your non-local boy? That one who made beef gravy over rice?"

CHAPTER TWENTY-TWO

PIKA REMEMBERS SAM.

That thought played itself on a loop in my brain, an unbroken chain of three little words that simply would not stop. How was that possible? Shasta had said that once you disappeared from the timeline, there was no trace left behind. I remembered him because of all of the time traveling, but no one else was supposed to.

And yet . . . here was Pika. Nattering on about my nonlocal boy. Somehow, he remembered too.

As our second round of holiday feasting devolved into the expected food comas and sleepy small talk, I dragged Pika over to one of the plush couches in the living room while the rest of the gang lingered around the table and Doc Kai bustled into the kitchen to prep the dessert course. I'd acted like I simply wanted to give him the present I'd gotten for him—a first edition of the *Columbo* novel *A Christmas Killing*, which was notable in that it had never actually been made into an episode of the TV show. This was the present I'd given him when I'd first experienced this particular Christmas.

"Bea." Pika's wizened face lit up as he tore off the wrapping. "Extra-special bonus episode, yeah? Never made it to TV!"

"That's right!" I agreed, studying him intently. He seemed to have snapped back to his usual self once Carmelo had presented him with a plate of beef gravy over rice. I didn't want to get him all distressed again, but I *really* needed to ask him about Sam. "Ah, Pika . . . was that gravy okay? Satisfied your cravings?"

"All fine," he said, waving a hand. "Not as good as the first time I had it, though." He eyed me shrewdly. "Non-local boy makes it best."

"And who is the non-local boy?"

"You know who he is," Pika said, nodding sagely. "You gonna find him and we gonna go hang out with the Car Uncles. Good time for everyone."

"How?" I pressed. "How am I going to find him?"

"You just are," he said, as if this was the most obvious thing in the world. His gaze drifted over to the neat stack of DVDs Doc Kai had pulled out—Doc Kai and Carmelo adored old-school tech and owned two DVD players, three VCRs, and one sweet VCR/TV combo Doc Kai had carted all the way to the mainland and back when she'd gone to college and grad school. Thus, the three *Back to the Future* movies were always at her disposal.

Pika grabbed the DVD of the first movie, a faint smile passing over his face as he studied the photo of Marty in his iconic orange vest. He tapped the image of the infamous car/time machine, its tires skidding into flames.

"We just get one of these," he said. "Car Uncles gonna fix it up real good. Your non-local boy will love that, eh?"

"The Car Uncles got *a DeLorean*?!" I blurted out. "How . . . you know what, I'm not even gonna ask."

"Usually better with the Car Uncles if you don't," Pika agreed.

I gazed at the DVD cover, the door of that DeLorean rising majestically into the night sky, beckoning Marty inside.

I was starting to get what was probably a terrible idea—the kind of chaotic, thoroughly ridiculous idea Past Bea was so known for.

But hey—technically I *was* Past Bea right now. So wouldn't it make sense if I did exactly what she would? Hadn't *What Would Bea Tanaka Do?* been my mantra (that I had since totally forgotten about)?

Also, had Leah and I ever clarified *which* Bea Tanaka we were referring to? Because being in this piece of the timeline kept reminding me of how excited, fearless, and absolutely *not blending in* Past Bea had been.

Who was I trying to be right now?

"Hey Pika," I said impulsively. "Wanna sneak out?"

🔥

Pika and the Car Uncles had parked the DeLorean on a patch of Makawao farmland, the green and golden glow of the countryside disrupted only by a narrow gravel road slithering through the grass like a snake.

It wasn't too far from Doc Kai and Carmelo's place, so Pika had been happy to walk me over after we'd slipped out. Pika seemed to have reverted fully to his grouchy-yet-genial self, and nattered on as we approached the car, explaining how one of the Car Uncles had found it abandoned in the misty backwoods of a nature preserve near one of Maui's gorgeous waterfalls.

"No sign of where it come from, no clue of where it been," Pika said, shaking his head in wonder. "This car just appear like magic, eh? Was clearly one burnt-out husk of itself."

He reached up to grasp the weatherproof protective covering the Car Uncles had carefully draped over the car and gave it a tug, revealing the car with a flourish.

"We restored her paint," Pika said, lovingly patting the DeLorean's shiny silver surface. "Got the rust off her metal bits. Now working on the engine—almost there, but she still accelerating too hard. A beauty, right?"

"She is," I murmured. The car did look a lot like the De-Lorean in *Back to the Future*, all glimmering silver surfaces and those blunt, boxy angles that had been so hip in the '80s.

Pika reached down and lifted the handle, and that winged door rose into the air with a dramatic *whoosh*.

Goosebumps pricked my forearms. Why did my most bananas ideas give me a certain special, fated feeling? That feeling of rightness, of *this is the way!*

Like, had I really asked Pika to show me the DeLorean because I'd thought, hey! What if I drove the DeLorean really, really fast—just like Marty McFly!—while clutching my talisman and thinking about Christmas . . . and that's what will send me back in time? And since my current issue seemed to be about aiming myself correctly, I'd drive in the direction of the beach! So my souped-up projection power would know where to go.

I was mixing in way more variables now, and Nate would probably tell me that my approach was verging toward instinctual rather than logical. But I couldn't help but think of a mode of experimentation *I'd* introduced *him* to: there are no theories too weird, no ideas too wild!

I'd explained to him that once you've gone through a couple standard theories and standard experiments, it can't hurt to open up your mind and attempt the most bananas thing that comes to you. That thing you were afraid to say because it was just *too weird*.

Our world is weird. Science is weird. Your theory might, in fact, be the ultimate answer!

I'd been surprised when Nate had agreed with me—and had even gotten all intrigued, going on and on about how not even his fanciest professors had ever thought to pitch such a thing.

I thought of what Doc Kai had said, about how both she and Nate thought I was so brilliant. They seemed to think so highly of Past Bea, and they were two of the smartest people I knew. Why was she—why was *I*—always dismissing that?

"Hey, Bea!" Pika's voice snapped me out of my reverie. He gestured to the car. "You want see what it's like to sit inside?"

"I do," I said, striding forward through the unwieldy grass. I reached the car and ran my hand over the shiny paint. It was warm from the midday sun and its reflective surface gave off an unearthly glow—another thing that seemed to beckon to me in a fated sort of way. "I actually want to do even more than sit in the front seat." I gave Pika my most winning grin. "I want to drive it!"

"Wha . . ." Pika threw back his head and let out a hearty laugh. "No way, Bea! The engine, she's not done yet. Accelerates way too fast, goes at top speed too long."

"That sounds perfect," I muttered—then realized I'd said that out loud. "I mean, um . . . I've driven through the most hellishly hilly parts of San Francisco, I'm pretty sure I can handle it."

"Car Uncles don't let nobody else drive their finds," Pika said, his mouth going flat. "We got a code with each other. Only one we broke it for was . . ." His brow furrowed and his eyes rolled skyward, like he was trying to remember something dancing around the edges of his consciousness.

"The non-local boy," I whispered. But he still heard me.

"Yes." Pika's eyes widened. "Bea. I don't quite know what I know, but . . . he's supposed to be here, yeah?"

"Yeah," I said, swallowing the lump in my throat. "I think he is. And I think driving this thing . . ." I gestured to the DeLorean. ". . . might help him come back?"

"Then we gotta do it!" Pika exclaimed. He kneeled down and snagged something from under the car's floor mat—the ignition key. He stood and brandished it, eyes flickering with eagerness. "But I drive, okay?"

"What . . . no!" I shook my head vehemently. "Pika, you can't! You're not the, ah, safest driver? To begin with? And anyway, what if . . ." I bit back the rest of the sentence, but I was trying to work out the mechanics of my time travel. It seemed that my consciousness traveled, but not my physical body. So if I time traveled straight out of the DeLorean, Past Bea would presumably still be here with Pika. But would she be totally (and correctly) confused as to how she'd ended up barreling down a dirt road in a DeLorean piloted by her favorite *Columbo* fan?

Or would that even happen if I managed to successfully correct the timeline? Wouldn't the past right itself as well?

I gnawed on my lower lip, staring at the key Pika was waving in front of me. I supposed it would be better if he drove—that way, if I time traveled, no one would be losing control of the car and driving over a cliff, *Thelma & Louise*–style.

Though one could never say for certain with Pika at the wheel.

"All right," I finally said, nodding at him. "You drive. But you have to do exactly what I tell you. If I suddenly get all weird and seem confused, I'm sorry. I think that's what's supposed to happen."

"You got it," he said, giving me a staunch nod.

I scurried over to the passenger side of the car, grabbing the handle and watching in awe as the door lifted to the sky. Damn, that was truly majestic—just like in the movie.

Pika and I slid inside, adjusting our seats before hitting the switch that closed the doors. I strapped on my seatbelt, feeling like a space explorer readying for a mission to Mars.

"Tell me when," Pika said, waving the key around. "But after this, Bea, you owe me—we gonna go back and you have to read me that *Columbo* book. With all the voices."

"All the voices," I agreed, a surprise lump appearing in my throat. "Pika . . ." I swiped a hasty hand over my eyes. "Thank you for doing this with me. For me. You're kinda the best."

"I know," he said gruffly.

I bowed my head so he wouldn't witness the tears that kept wanting to slide down my cheeks. After a moment thick with silence, I saw his hand passing over the gearshift to cover mine.

"Bea," he said, his voice even gruffer. "I never have kids. But if I had, I know they'd be like you. Know why?"

"Why?" I asked, laughing a little through my tears.

"You got one bright light. Just like me." He grinned and

preened a bit, as if expecting applause. "People love us, huh? 'Cause we just that fun to be around!"

"Well, yeah," I said, laughing even harder. "Yeah, we are!"

"And we gotta work to keep that light on," Pika said, his demeanor turning solemn. "Protect it. Believe we got it at all times. Not let nobody tell us to turn it off. Always get four scoops of Guri-Guri."

"These rules are getting very specific—"

"This non-local boy I can't stop remembering," he interrupted. "I can tell he special, too. You gotta go find him. But just so we're clear . . ." He gave me a shrewd look. "I'd help you with anything. Our bright lights—they came together for a reason."

"Oh . . . Pika." I couldn't stop the tears from spilling down my cheeks now. "I . . . "

"What?" he said, his tone dropping back to gruff. "I not taking anyone's place, eh? Your fool daddy out there acting like he never had kids."

"H-he is," I managed, warmth flooding my chest. I'd never felt a connection to my father in Hawai'i, even though he'd grown up not far from here. And maybe deep down, I'd still held out hope that I would feel that at some point, an undeniable surge of recognition that would help me finally make sense of myself. But I had found something much better—a connection that felt like it had always been in my life, something that was meant to be. A bright light contained in this cantankerous senior car enthusiast who always made time to fix me dinner and talk story after a long day of work.

Like Doc Kai said, we change each other's lives simply by being in them.

"My dad's both out there and a fool," I continued. "And I just want to say . . . thank you. I feel the same." I squeezed his hand. "I'm glad my light found yours."

"Hmph, no need to get all sentimental," Pika scoffed, pulling away from my grasp—but not before squeezing my hand one more time. "Let's get this show on the road!"

He stuck the key in the ignition and the car revved to life.

Anticipation bubbled through my veins, a glittery thread of hope. I was practically bouncing up and down in my seat.

"Where to?" Pika queried.

"Turn right onto the gravel road," I said, gesturing to the spot. "Then gun it as fast as you can and keep going. Um. We aren't in danger of going off a cliff, right?"

"Not for at least sixty miles," Pika said, a little too breezily. "And also we won't run into anyone—no one on this road during Christmas."

"Okay, then," I said, nerves mingling with my anticipation and making all my senses stand at attention. What was about to happen? And was I more excited or terrified? Hard to say.

I pulled the lumpy dragon ornament from my dress pocket and clasped it in my hand as Pika maneuvered the DeLorean out of the grass and onto the narrow strip of gravel road. Should I think about Christmas again? Or was that another variable to change up, since I wasn't trying to land anywhere in the timeline during an actual Christmas? That's where my last two jumps had sent me, after all.

For some reason Doc Kai's voice popped into my head, enthusing about my posterboards.

It was like I could see *all these phenomena you'd encountered, could really visualize these sequences of extraordinary events.*

Hmm. If I was truly leaning into the Past Bea way of doing things, maybe *that* was the variable I could add—I'd picture the spot in the timeline I wanted to go, visualize it like it was one of my posterboards.

"Ready?" Pika asked, settling the car on the road.

I gazed out at the strip of gravel stretching in front of us, bisecting the green and gold of the fields. The sky was as blue and open as always, as if beckoning us to another world.

My heartbeat sped up, my palm growing sweaty around the ornament. This was it.

"Let's go," I said.

And then Pika gunned the engine and it felt like we were flying, careening down that road and spitting gravel in our wake, the sky endless above us. I closed my eyes and clutched the ornament, picturing the beach, the kaiju, and Evie's terrified screams in the background . . .

thud thud THUD

We hit a bump in the road and my eyes flew open, my heart leaping into my throat, what was happening, were we about to go over a cliff, had I just killed Pika, oh god oh god oh

god

My eyes snapped shut as terror consumed me, sending me hurtling into the great unknown.

CHAPTER TWENTY-THREE

I COULD STILL hear Evie screaming. That was my first thought when my eyes popped open again, that full-body terror still consuming me. Only . . . I cocked my head, attempting to listen more carefully. These were actual screams, not part of a memory I was trying to conjure in order to aim myself correctly on the timeline. My sister sounded like she was being ripped apart.

I sat up shakily, trying to clear my foggy mind, trying to breathe through the terror and the now all-too-familiar headache blossoming around my temples.

Screaming . . . that's good, *though, right? That means maybe I made it back to the right point in time . . .*

And yet, everything else was *wrong*.

I wasn't sprawled in the sand of a beautiful beach or flailing around in the clear blue ocean. I seemed to be stuck inside a cramped, stuffy, dimly lit room . . .

I forced myself to stand, wincing as another wave of headache pain hit me like a boulder slamming directly into my brain. One of my hands scrabbled against the wall for support and was met with a papery sort of feeling. I squinted intently at the wall, which appeared to be covered top to bottom with a crumbling array of old business cards . . .

Oh.

I was in The Gutter, that dank hole-in-the-wall of a karaoke bar. I scanned my surroundings as my eyes adjusted to the dim lighting, clocking the toilet and sink. Yeah, I'd somehow time traveled to the freaking *bathroom*?

What point in time was this? I'd been to The Gutter plenty of times in the past—trying to sneak in and score a few forbidden sips of alcohol had been one of my favorite Evie-antagonizing activities as a wayward teen. And I was guessing I'd return plenty of times in the future, but—

My thoughts were cut off by another ear-piercing scream. Yeah, that was *definitely* my sister.

Instinct kicked in, adrenaline blazing through my bloodstream. I kicked the bathroom door open and sprinted down the hall, running toward that horrifying sound. I emerged in the bar area, my head whipping back and forth as I tried to find Evie amidst the usual array of sticky floors and tables festooned with patchy red velvet tablecloths. The karaoke stage loomed in the center of the space like a specter, a single mic illuminated by a half-hearted spotlight.

"Evelyn! I need you to stay with me—*please*. I know this is hard, but—"

I found them just as Evie let out another blood-curdling roar of pain. She was lying on top of a jumble of velvet tablecloths that had been hastily arranged on the floor right next to the stage. Another tablecloth had been draped over her lower half, and her feet were planted on the floor, knees bent. Aveda was peering under the tablecloth, her brow furrowed in intense concentration.

"I'm just trying to find this video I watched before on YouTube," Aveda continued, brandishing her phone. "But I can't get any reception, I think—"

"*YouTube?!*" Evie shrieked. "Are you fucking serious right now?"

I realized, with dawning horror, what I was looking at.

My sister was giving birth. It was the exact scenario Aveda had described to me, the one that had been so traumatic, the memory that had given Evie that haunted look so many months later.

But why was *I* here? I hadn't been around for this, even in the altered, Sam-less version of the timeline. And previously, I'd only time traveled to moments where I'd actually been physically present. Did that mean my whole physical body had projected itself, leaving Pika all alone in his about-to-crash DeLorean?

And why had I landed at *this* moment in particular?

I needed to get out of here. Before they—

"Bea!"

As if on cue, Aveda's head swiveled toward me, her eyes widening in shock.

"What are you doing here?" she demanded. *"How* did you get here?!"

"Bea . . ." Evie's gaze caught mine, her eyes cloudy with pain.

"Come help me!" Aveda barked, gesturing with her phone.

"But—" I squeaked out.

"No buts!" Aveda snarled. "This baby's coming *now*, and we need you!"

"How did you get in?" Evie managed, her words labored and wheezy. "I thought there was a . . . force . . . field . . ." She grimaced, then threw back her head and screamed again.

That scream was like some kind of magnet drawing me to her, my instinct to protect her and take away her pain overriding everything else. I scurried over to her and Aveda, pinpricks of anxiety racing over my skin.

"Our young charges led the french-fry demons outside," Aveda said briskly, as if I already knew what was going on. Thanks to our conversation that had taken place several months in the future, I supposed I did. "And there's some kind of force field situation happening. But I have to trust them to take care of it, because . . ."

She trailed off. Her face had gone pale, her forehead pinched with worry.

"Because like you said, this baby's coming *now*," I finished. "What can I do?"

"See if you can find a better way to support her head, her back," Aveda said, jerking her chin at Evie. "And try to calm her down while I figure out the mechanics. I know that's a tall order, but—"

"Calm?!" Evie choked out, her breathing rapid and uneven. "You really expect me to be *calm*?!" Her last few words emerged as a broken sob.

"Go," Aveda hissed at me, fumbling around with her phone.

I scrambled up to where Evie's head was positioned, taking note of Aveda's hasty birthing setup. It looked like she'd managed to get a decent mass of velvet tablecloths underneath Evie's body, but the crumpled bundle of napkins she'd shoved under her neck was definitely not doing the trick.

"I'm lifting your head, Sis," I said, only to be answered with a pathetic whimper.

I swallowed down my own fear as I gently maneuvered her, getting rid of the janky napkin bundle and positioning my body behind hers. I very carefully moved her into a semi-sitting position and pulled her against me so that I was supporting the top half of her body, her back pressing against my front as I attempted to cradle her. Her head lolled against my shoulder.

"Hey, this is just like the Matterhorn bobsleds at Disneyland," I said, gesturing to our semi-spooning forms. "Or at least, this is what I imagine the Matterhorn bobsleds are like, given that we've never gotten to actually go to Disneyland—"

"Beatrice Constance Tanaka!" Aveda shot me an exasperated look. "I will take you to Disneyland after all this if you calm her down!"

"On it," I murmured, then winced as Evie screamed again. Now that she was pressing back against me, those screams reverberated through my entire body. "Hey. Big Sis." I grabbed one of her hands and squeezed. "You got this, okay? I *know* you've got this. You're the strongest person I know—"

Evie responded with a moan-sob combo so soul-shattering, tears sprang to my eyes. Her grip on my hand tightened painfully, squeezing so hard it felt like she was cutting off my circulation.

"I . . . I can't," she whimpered, twisting her head around

to look at me. Her sweet hazel eyes were muddy with tears, her mouth pinched around the edges. And her skin had turned an alarming shade of gray. "This isn't how this was supposed to be. This isn't how she was supposed to . . . get here . . ."

Her eyes drifted closed, tears spilling down her cheeks. And I swore I felt her skin go cold—

"Check her heartbeat!" Aveda snapped.

I obediently pressed my fingers to Evie's wrist, the faintest of flutters pulsing against her skin. Like a gentle brush of butterfly wings, getting slower . . . slower . . .

"It's there. But she's losing consciousness—"

"*Evelyn!*" Aveda gripped Evie's knees through the velvet tablecloth covering, her dark eyes flashing with terror. "Stay with me. I mean it. I know this is far from an ideal situation, but I will never forgive you if you die dramatically in childbirth like some kind of tragic, Dickensian heroine—and you know I'll figure out a way to get all up in your business even if you're dead, so you have to *stay the fuck with me!*"

I took Evie's hand again and squeezed, willing her clammy skin to warm up, her heartbeat to return strong and sure.

"Evie," I murmured, using my other hand to brush her sweaty curls off her forehead. "Please listen to Aveda. We'll get through this . . ."

Tears filled my eyes as her head drooped, eyelashes fluttering. I held her hand more firmly, unwilling to let any piece of her slip away.

"Bea . . ." she croaked, her voice so faint I had to lean in to hear it. Her eyes opened more fully and she gave me a look of utter exhaustion. "I . . . this is all wrong," she whimpered again. "Nate's not here. Mom's not here. I wish Mom was . . . here . . ." Her voice broke and she started crying again, her sobs so helpless and inconsolable, I felt my heart crumble.

Evie almost never wished out loud for our mother. I'd been the walking open wound when she'd died, I'd been the one to devolve into unrelenting sobs over something as inconsequential as a jar of peanut butter, a reminder of a sandwich Mom and I had loved making together. I'd been the grieving child, the one whose endless pain had overwhelmed both of us. And she'd stepped up and been my parent, the one who could never cry because she had to be there for me.

My hand tightened around hers again.

"Bea!" Aveda hissed.

My head snapped up and I met her gaze. She was positioned between Evie's legs, her eyes projecting grim determination. Her power ponytail was bedraggled, flyaway strands twisting themselves loose from their moorings—but it was still there, still standing. Aveda looked like she was all but commanding it to stay in place.

"She's going to have to push soon," Aveda said. "And I'm going to deliver this baby using a mix of telekinesis and everything I learned on YouTube when I was trying to prepare myself for this moment. I've tried calling Dr. Goo, but the force field's blocking me." Her gaze drifted to Evie's pale, tear-streaked face. "You *have* to calm her down. I need to concentrate on the basic mechanics. But if her muscles get all tense from stress or she gives up and can't push . . ." Aveda shook her head, unwilling to finish that thought.

"I-I'm trying!" I yelped. "B-but I'm not exactly known for being a calming sort of person in any conceivable way—"

"You might need to try something more . . . potent," Aveda said, her mouth flattening into a grim line.

I realized, in an instant, what she was suggesting.

"No!" I gasped, a shudder of fear running through me. "I *can't* do that—"

"Bea." Evie finally squeezed my hand back. Her face was stained with tears. But I could feel her trying to even out her breathing, trying to hold on, trying to stay with us. "Please. I-it's okay. I know you'll do it the right way this time. I *know* that." She gripped my hand even tighter, a flash of that fight sparking in her eyes. "I trust you."

I took a deep, shuddering breath, unable to look away

from her. She was here. She was *fighting*. And this time, instead of collapsing on the floor and sobbing while she comforted me . . . I was going to fight, too.

"Okay," I whispered, taking another breath. "Okay."

I closed my eyes and gathered everything I wanted her to feel in my chest.

Calm. Serenity. Hope. The promise of a future too beautiful for her to even imagine. The happily ever after that I knew was waiting for her on the other side of this. I inhaled again and sent all of those feelings spinning her way—I tried to take care to send them *gently*, to lean into my whole aromatherapy candle thing. I wasn't trying to overwhelm her. I wasn't going to control her.

I was just going to make this moment a little bit better.

The Otherworld darkness inside of me pulsed, and I could feel it expanding outward, enveloping my projection until it was a shadowy force threatening to devour my mind

I shook my head, my instinct to repress that darkness as hard as I could rising up.

But then it pulsed again . . . I frowned, trying to home in on it. The darkness didn't feel like it was trying to overtake me. It wasn't smothering my brain or attempting to convince me to do something evil.

No, it was *gentler* than that. As if it was floating around my projection in those jagged shadows, waiting for its marching orders. As if it was waiting for *me* to tell it what to do.

I paused and just *felt* the darkness for a moment. There was a strange softness to it, an amorphous quality—once I stopped trying to shove it away or bury it down deep, it didn't feel like this big scary force. Instead, it felt like it was enhancing my projection in a way that gave it more layers, more wrinkles of nuance. I could see each feeling I was sending toward Evie in multi-hued glory, a prism reflecting the complexity of every single emotion. And . . . hmm. It felt like my entire brain plane was expanding, all of the emotions enveloped by a large protective space.

In visual terms, I'd previously perceived my mind as a

dinky studio apartment with no windows. Now it was more akin to that vast field of green and gold where Pika and I had tested out his DeLorean.

I drew in a deep breath and carefully sent those feelings spinning toward Evie again, and . . . *damn.* I really could sense every single color of every single emotion. It was as if I'd developed a shiny new sixth sense.

I opened my eyes and saw my projection hit, felt her shoulders relax the tiniest millimeter as some of the tension around her eyes evaporated.

"That's it," I murmured, smoothing her hair. "Relax. Aveda's got this. And we're gonna bring a freakin' baby into this world."

"That's good, Bea," Aveda said, giving me a brisk nod. She inhaled deeply as she activated her telekinesis, getting to work.

Evie's hold on my hand morphed into a death grip again and I squelched a yelp of pain.

"It hurts so goddamn bad," Evie growled through gritted teeth. "And I'm so . . . scared . . ."

Tears filled her eyes again, but her muscles felt more slack against me, and her breathing was steady.

"I know," I said. "I mean . . . I don't actually know since I don't have any firsthand experience in birthing a whole human being, but I can tell this is so fucking hard, and I'm sorry." I gnawed on my lower lip, scanning her face. "Do you feel . . . um, like you're still you? Nothing too mind-controlly?"

"I'm me," she said, managing to give me a sardonic eyebrow raise. "I feel . . ." She paused, considering. "Like everything I'm feeling is still there, but there's more, like . . . space for it?" She closed her eyes, trying to find the words. Or maybe just steeling herself against another wave of pain. "This sounds so dorky, but it's like all my feelings have room to breathe . . ."

"This is all lovely," Aveda interjected. "But I need you to use that space to gather up all your badassery, Evelyn, because it's almost time to push. Little Galactus Tanaka-Jones is ready to punch her way out of here."

"Oh god," Evie blurted, her eyes widening in panic. I felt her body tense up again, her shoulders going rigid. "No, I don't think I can do that, I . . . *no* . . ."

"Listen to me," I said, rubbing her shoulders. "I'm going to project that soothing wave onto you again—hopefully you'll feel that sense of space, that freedom to, like, feel all your feelings. And then . . ." I adjusted my position so I was supporting her back more firmly. "You're gonna have to summon all your strength and push, Evie. I'll be right here with you—"

"I can't!" she wailed. "I'm t-too scared!"

"She's tightening up again," Aveda hissed at me. "I've got a telekinetic hold on the baby, but I can't just yank it out of her! That could be very bad for both of them—"

"*What?!*" Evie cried, picking up on Aveda's whispering despite her distressed state. Her shoulders went rigid.

"Evie . . ." Helplessness blossomed in my chest. What else could I do?

The darkness nudged at my mind, and I saw that gold and green field again, felt that sense of *space* again . . . all of my feelings free to expand to the biggest, brightest versions of themselves . . .

"I-I'm trying to be strong," Evie sobbed. "I'm trying to hold all this pain in, bear down and get through it and . . . and be fucking brave like the superheroine I supposedly am, but I just . . . I *can't* . . ."

"Don't do that," I blurted out—then winced as Aveda shot me a death glare.

Trust me, I mouthed at her.

"Big Sis," I said, turning back to Evie, "don't hold the pain in. Let it *out*."

"What?" She shook her head at me, her eyes wild.

"I know it's hard," I said, my voice growing steady, more confident. "And I know so much for you has been hard. I-I'm sorry Mom's not here. But . . ." Tears sprang to my eyes and the darkness seemed to swirl around my hurt, allowing the feeling to flow through me unencumbered. "Evie, I meant it when I said you're the strongest person I know. You take care of everyone and you protect your family with everything you have and you would go to the ends of the earth for the people you love. And you had to . . ." My throat thickened as one of the tears drifted down my cheek. "You had to work really fucking hard to get there. You had to learn how to feel things without shame. To be who you are, fully."

"That's you," Evie murmured, her voice barely a whisper. "You've always been . . . exactly who you are . . ."

"I got to do that because you took care of me," I said, stroking her damp hair. "And I'm telling you: you don't have to be brave right now. Because I'll be brave enough for both of us."

And then I reached deep inside of me and gathered up every bit of that visceral, bone-deep, endlessly complicated love I had for her. I thought about the rush of warmth I'd felt when I'd seen her holding her baby daughter. I remembered what Nate had told me about her wrapping herself in my sad little blanket because she couldn't stand to be apart from me. I cycled through every fight we'd ever had, every petty misunderstanding and earth-shattering blowout. I recalled the moment she'd told me she was pregnant, how she was so scared—and how I'd never doubted her for a second. I visualized her flopping down on the floor with me while I cried over peanut butter all those years ago, her gentle presence making me feel protected even as I fell apart.

I thought about my heart crying out for hers across an entire ocean.

I put all those feelings together—and I felt my darkness bolstering them, giving them room to breathe, making them more powerful . . .

I sent all of that spinning toward her.

"Let those feelings out, Big Sis," I urged. "I'm here—and you're safe. I promise."

She met my gaze, her eyes wide with wonder.

"Bea," she murmured. "Oh, Bea . . ."

I readjusted my position to support her more firmly—and felt something hard brush against my hip. I reached in my pocket and pulled out the blobby dragon ornament. My talisman.

"Here," I said, impulsively pressing the ornament into her hand. "Squeeze this while you push and let out all those feelings. Like a really weird-looking stress ball!"

"Wow," she croaked, taking it from me. "I remember this—you brought it home one Christmas and tried to cheer me up . . ."

"Hold on to it," I said, squeezing her hand. "Now *push*."

She stared at me for a moment more, so much love in her eyes. Then she managed to give me a small nod and squeezed back, the ornament firmly clutched in her other hand.

And before I knew what was happening, she was throwing her head back to let out the most all-consuming, full-body scream I'd ever heard.

But this time? She didn't sound scared. She sounded like she was exorcising every bit of terror and uncertainty from her soul. Like she was determined not to let any of that beat her. Ever.

"That's it!" Aveda crowed, nodding vigorously. "Keep it up, both of you!"

"Again," I whispered to Evie.

She screamed again. And again. And then so many times, I lost track. The force of it rattled my bones, my teeth clacking together. But I never let go of her hand.

"She's coming!" Aveda bellowed, her eyes widening with delirious glee. "I've almost got her . . . I've . . . oh god. This is *gross*. Why are there so many fluids?!"

"Weren't there fluids in all those YouTube videos you watched?" Evie shot back, actually sounding a bit like her snarky self.

"Not like this!" Aveda exclaimed, making a face. "Just one more push . . . okay . . . *yes*!!!"

Things started to happen so fast, I could barely absorb each moment. I felt Evie relax against me—but at last, it was from relief. I saw Aveda brandishing the blood-and-slime-soaked bundle that was Vivi, I heard that tiny baby's ear-shattering cry pierce the air . . .

And then Aveda was carefully placing Vivi in Evie's arms, and my sister's face lit up with pure joy.

"Oh," she whispered, gazing down at her baby daughter for the first time.

Tears streamed down my cheeks and my soul felt like it was about to burst, overwhelmed with so much love.

And then, the dank environs of The Gutter started to go blurry around the edges.

"What . . . *no*!" I gasped. "I'm not even holding my talisman, I'm not visualizing anything, I want to stay *right here*!"

But no one heard me because the room was already dissolving around me and my vision was clouding over and I could feel myself falling through time.

CHAPTER TWENTY-FOUR

AT THIS POINT, the whole time-travel drill was all too familiar.

Eyes flying open in a disoriented alarm—check.

All-new locale that is not at all what you're expecting—check.

And of course, the monster headache that feels like it's crushing your brains out of your head—yeah, extra double check there!

I sat up slowly, and realized I was lying on my bed back at HQ. My room was still all done up with Christmas décor, and . . .

I looked down, clocking my outfit.

I was clad in a short velvet dress the color of deep red wine. It had a smocked bodice, a full skirt, and sleeves that puffed out at the shoulders before flowing into something more fitted on the arms.

Before I could contemplate my ensemble any further, Leah burst into the room, an aggrieved-looking Pancake clutched in her arms.

"Bebe!" she bellowed. "You should get down there, the party's in full swing, and I know you don't want to miss out on the special gingerbread treats!" She gave me a quick once-over. "Wow, great ensemble! Very festive."

"Ummmm . . ." I swallowed, adrenaline from my most recent escapade still coursing through me.

"Wait!" She held up a hand. "That look!" She circled an

index finger at my face while Pancake gave me his usual side-eye. "I think I know that look! Did you just go time travel-ing?"

"Yes!" I shrieked, jumping off the bed. "I was back in Makawao during last Christmas and I couldn't even call you because I was in the *past*, and then Pika had a DeLorean and he wouldn't let me drive it, but I used my talisman while *he* was driving it, and then I ended up at Evie's birth moment, which I'm still really confused by because I wasn't there for that in the first place, and then I helped my sister deliver her baby, and—oh! The baby!" The adrenaline that was still flow-ing through my veins spiked. "Is everything okay with my sister and Vivi?! Or did me being there fuck everything up? What was the last interaction you had with me? What day is it?!"

"One question at a time!" Leah cried, shutting the bed-room door behind her. "Let me see. It's the day of the gin-gerbread house competition, the same day we made our inspirational posterboard. You went downstairs to find your talisman, but came back up to your room just a little later and said you'd tried something and it hadn't worked—"

"Did I say what I'd tried?"

"No," Leah said. "I asked, but you seemed a bit . . ." She waved a hand around. "Unclear on that front. And *really* frustrated, so I didn't push too hard. Then you said you were going to lie down before the holiday party and see if letting your mind relax would unleash some new theories." She glanced at my outfit. "It looks like you managed to change for the party, too. And now . . . the party's happening!" She gestured toward the door—I could hear faint bustling sounds wafting up from downstairs, signs that there were more peo-ple in the house than usual. "And Evie and Vivi are totally fine, as far as I can tell. Though I have heard the tale of Bebe the Amazing Birthing Coach quite a few times now."

"Have you heard anything about how I suddenly appeared at The Gutter when I was supposed to be in Maui?"

"There was a story about how you wanted to surprise Evie with a visit or something?" Leah said, her head tilting to the side. "And then afterward, you stayed in the Bay. You haven't been back to Maui since."

"Okay . . ." I blew out a long breath, unable to process the mass of information cycling through my brain. "So let me explain everything that happened from my perspective. Um, in a way that is hopefully more coherent than what I just word vomited all over you." I launched into an epic recap of what had transpired after I'd gone downstairs and found my blobby dragon ornament. It must have been pretty compelling—even Pancake managed to stay silent during my dramatic tale.

"Damn, Bebe!" Leah shrieked, once I'd finished. "So your talisman actually worked, which is awesome! And it seems like your idea to visualize where you wanted to go sort of worked? But you went to the wrong spot again?"

"And it was a moment I wasn't even present for the first time it happened!" I reiterated. "So does that mean my whole physical body time traveled this time, leaving Pika all alone in his out-of-control car—fuck!" I cut myself off abruptly and yanked my phone from my dress pocket, fumbling with sweaty fingers as I frantically tapped Pika's name in my contacts.

"What?" he answered.

"Pika?" I said, my voice twisting up at the end. "Are you okay?"

"Why wouldn't I be?" he huffed. "And why you interrupting my *Columbo* time?"

"I, um, just wanted to say hi," I said, my shoulders relaxing a smidge. "Hey, this is going to be a weird question, but do you remember us taking a joyride last Christmas in the Car Uncles' DeLorean?"

"'Course," he grumbled. "How could I forget? You wanna ride in that car so bad, then suddenly you start screaming and acting like you don't know how you got there!"

"I see," I said, turning that bit of info over in my mind. "But we both got out of that situation, ah, unscathed?"

"Sure. DeLorean still not working quite right, though." He paused for a long moment—so long I thought maybe he'd hung up on me. "Hey Bea," he finally said. "I'm remembering more about that day. You find your non-local boy?"

"I don't think so. Go back to your *Columbo*, Pika, I'll talk to you later."

Pika, as usual, hung up without saying good-bye.

"He's okay?" Leah asked.

"As okay as he ever is," I said, tucking the phone back into my pocket. "So it seems my physical body stayed in the car with him—which means it was either my consciousness somehow taking me to a moment I wasn't previously part of, or maybe I split into two different physical bodies—"

I shook my head. I was already confusing myself.

"Oh my god," Leah breathed. "Maybe you *did* create a multiverse! Instead of all the Avedas, it's a squad of time-traveling Bebes—"

"Noooooooo!" I wailed. "Man, I hope not. Oh, but Lee, Pika reminded me of something else—he remembers Sam! That's why he was so willing to help me out with the DeLorean. What do you think it means? Um, I'm assuming Sam still doesn't exist here?"

"No." Leah pulled a regretful face. "But Bebe . . ." She cocked her head at me, considering. Pancake mimicked the gesture. "Didn't Shasta say there was absolutely no trace of him left behind? That you only remember because you're not currently existing on the same temporal plane?"

"Something like that," I growled, shaking my head. "Maybe Sam left some kind of imprint on the timeline after all. Or maybe Pika's also existing on some other temporal plane. Or . . ." I sat back down on my bed, my mind spinning with possibilities.

"So your experiments didn't immediately take you back to that battle on the beach like you wanted," Leah said thoughtfully, scritching behind Pancake's ears. He snuggled against her, settling in for a nap. "But you gained some new data, right?"

"Data I'm not sure how to make sense of." I frowned at the fairy lights that were still sparkling away above my bed. "The talisman and the visualizing seemed to work as far as triggering time travel, but I still can't aim myself correctly. And now I'm traveling to random spots where I'm not supposed to be."

"You theorized before that your power might be morphing due to that Otherworld darkness you felt—you thought maybe it was glitching and sending you time traveling in the first place," Leah prompted. "Maybe now it's morphing even further? Like a Pokémon on its next evolution!"

"Awesome," I muttered. "I'm about to become Raichu or some shit."

I stared at the twinkle lights for a long moment, trying to get everything crashing through my consciousness to come together and make sense. The darkness inside of me rumbled, as if to remind me of its presence. I flashed back to how much I'd felt it while Evie was in labor, how it had seemed to swirl around my power and fully meld with it . . .

At the time, that had felt cool—and weirdly natural. But now that I wasn't plopped in the middle of a super stressful life-or-death situation and had a moment to think about what that kind of melding could mean . . .

I shuddered.

"I-I think it is morphing further," I stuttered. "Or to be more precise: I think the Otherworld darkness is becoming way more enmeshed with my power. I felt that while I was projecting onto Evie. And that seems . . . very bad."

I tried to breathe deeply, to squelch the massive wave of panic threatening to overwhelm me.

"But you *helped* Evie," Leah insisted. "And Past You hasn't wanted to talk about the experience very much, but you did tell me that using your power in that moment actually felt . . . good?"

"Using my power *always* feels good!" I countered,

throwing up my hands. "That's the problem—it feels really fucking good, and it's only later, when I realize what I've done . . ." I trailed off. "I have to fix this, Lee. I *have* to get back to that day on the beach. I erased Sam and now I forever altered Evie's birth moment in ways that may have damaged the timeline further, and my power is possibly going full evil without even asking me, and then once I actually get back to that battle I still have to figure out if I can make some kind of impossible choice . . ." I gasped for breath, my motormouthing sucking up all available oxygen.

"Do you want to try aiming yourself again?" Leah asked, her voice soft. Pancake startled awake from his nap and whuffled out something that sounded like agreement.

"Yes." I nodded emphatically, seizing on a course of action. "I need my talisman, and . . ." I frowned, my gaze sweeping the room. "Wait. Where's my talisman?" I stuffed my hands into my dress pockets, but there was nothing. "Dammit. When I time traveled to the Christmas in Makawao, it stayed in my hand. But now it's just . . . not here?"

"We'll find it," Leah said, giving me an encouraging nod. "Maybe it ended up back on the tree or something, since that's where it was previously?"

"Maybe," I said, scrambling to my feet and trying to work out a plan. "I'm going to go down there and look for it—and maybe I can also find Nate and try to talk through some time-travel theories with him. In a hypothetical sense, of course. I started to do that . . . well, I guess technically it was just this morning! But I didn't get very far because Vivi needed tending to."

"What should Pancake and I do?" Leah asked. "We can be your wingpeople again!"

"For now, just mingle. And let's talk again once I've found the talisman. And—oh! What's the status of your quest to own It's Lit? Did you talk to Charlotte?"

"Yeah," Leah said, her shoulders slumping. "It's still a no. I don't know what I have to do!"

"We'll figure it out. Think of what posterboard you want to use for that, okay? I'll meet you downstairs, I just need a moment to gather myself."

"You got it." Leah clutched Pancake more tightly to her chest and marched toward the door. "Time-travel warriors—away!" Pancake squirmed around in her arms, as if protesting this notion.

Once they'd left, I pawed through my jewelry and added a matching choker to my ensemble. I swept my hair into a messy-on-purpose up-do, then stepped in front of my full-length mirror for a style check.

Hmm, not bad. My stressed-out state had gifted me with a paler-than-usual complexion and dark circles under my eyes, but the overall effect made me look kind of like a haunted Victorian doll. The deep wine color of the dress elevated that to *festive* haunted Victorian doll.

I'd take it.

"You look freaking hot!"

I whipped around, my eyes going to my bedroom window. The voice had come from outside—at least, I thought it had. Maybe someone downstairs was just feeling super complimentary.

"We can't see you!" another voice yelled. "We just *know* you're hot!"

Okay, that was weird. Dual catcallers? Who couldn't even see the person they were trying to catcall?

"You're always fire hot, Bea Tanaka!" the first voice yelled. "Please! Just listen to me!"

"Listen to *us*!" the second voice said, sounding whiny. "Remember, we agreed this was a team effort!"

"I didn't agree to that!" the first voice protested. "*I* had a plan that *you* glommed on to!"

I crossed the room and threw open the window, already certain of what I was about to see. Because even though I'd just spent a considerable amount of time in, well . . . completely different parts of the timeline, I could still remember plenty of the disasters that were happening right now. (Was "right now" even a concept I understood at the moment? Hard to say.)

Two figures had parked themselves outside the Victorian and were jumping up and down, trying to get my attention. And even though darkness was falling, rendering the street a web of shadows, I could still tell who they were.

Really, there were only two possibilities.

"Olivia!" I yelled. "Terrence! Are y'all stalking me now?! I blocked you both on everything, that should've sent a clear message! And actually, my whole entire speech wherein I *broke up with both of you* should have also sent that message!" I fluttered my fingers at them, like I was shooing flies. "Get out of here! Go find some other awesome holiday party where your hotness will be celebrated by more appreciative souls!"

"But Beaaaaaaaa," Olivia wailed. "We only want you! And we don't have to be exclusive, we're willing to share! Not that way," she said hastily, as Terrence started to open his mouth.

"*I* don't want that, though!" I protested. "And I kinda feel like my opinion matters, here. And—oh, holy fuck, do y'all have a *boom box*?!"

"I told you the boom box was a mistake," Terrence hissed, snatching it from Olivia and trying to hide it behind his back. "Fuckin' cheesy."

"*Leave!*" I bellowed, flapping my hand at them more vigorously. "Seriously. I'm really not that great, and you both have better things to do—things that do *not* involve creepily hanging out in the cold with outdated tech. Good-bye!"

I made my wave extra dramatic as I slammed the window shut.

Then I aimed myself at the door again. Time to find my talisman and do some much-needed theorizing with Nate.

I was doing a pretty good job of hustling down the hall, keeping an eye out for my wayward dragon ornament while also making sure to not get distracted . . . when a wail of pure anguish pierced the air.

I froze in my tracks. At this point, I knew that wail all too well.

That was my sister. And she was clearly in danger again.

CHAPTER TWENTY-FIVE

I DIDN'T HESITATE. I switched course immediately, following the source of the wail to Evie and Nate's bedroom and catapulting myself inside.

"Evie!" I cried, looking around frantically. "What's happening? What . . ."

I trailed off, heart hammering in my chest, and took stock of the scene. Evie was sprawled on her bed, surrounded by a sea of garments. It looked like her entire closet had vomited its contents all over her.

"Did you fall?" I demanded. "Or hurt yourself? Or are you somehow giving birth again, because . . ."

"Nooooooo!" she wailed, sitting up in bed. Her eyes were red-rimmed and puffy and she was wearing a ratty, hole-riddled yellow sweatsuit—an ensemble that was not exactly holiday-party material. "I . . . this is so stupid, but . . ."

Her lower lip quivered and I held my breath, terrified of whatever she was about to say.

"I can't figure out what to weaaaaaar!" she exploded.

Wait, *what*?

Was my sister, who I'd just witnessed going through one of the most painful, gut-wrenching, life-threatening experiences she'd ever had . . . dealing with a problem that was utterly and undeniably *mundane*?

Did I even know how to deal with normal-type problems anymore?

"Oh . . . kay," I said, trying to get my thoughts in order. I eased myself onto the edge of the bed, pushing aside a filmy silver dress. "Sis, I know you're not the fancy outfit type, but I don't think it matters. Wear whatever you feel comfortable in." I held up the silver dress and waved it around, like a desperate mom trying to entertain her kid with a shiny toy. "This is super nice!"

That only set her lip quivering again. "It doesn't fit! My body . . . like, obviously it changed during pregnancy, but it's still changing and I don't know if it's going back or forward or in a complete different direction, and this . . . area . . ." She gestured to her chest. "I mean, look at them. They're freaking *huge*!"

"All right, all right," I said, trying to make my voice as soothing as possible. I scooched closer to her on the bed and wrapped my arms around her. "It's gonna be okay, I promise. Remember when we made you that toilet-paper dress during your bachelorette party? In a pinch, me and Aveda and Lucy can whip up something like that again. Although I don't know if you want us to do that since said bachelorette party ended with an all-out brawl against a squad of literal bridezillas. I'm just saying: our last-minute fashion-design skills are unmatched."

"Th-they are," Evie managed, a hiccup punctuating her snorty giggle. "And I'm pretty sure whatever you make for me won't be haunted, possessed, or otherwise demonified, so major bonus points there." She leaned her head against my shoulder, tears drifting down her cheeks. "I'm sorry. I feel silly, but . . . I'm so happy that we're all together to celebrate, especially for Vivi's first Christmas. And I love that her Auntie Bea made it home just in time to welcome her into the world." She threaded her fingers through mine, squeezing my hand. "I guess I just want to look nice for this fun party we're having for all our friends—this is really the first time we've done something like this, you know? I wanted to feel festive and pretty and not like I look exhausted and covered in spit-up, wearing clothes that don't fit my suddenly weird body with its gigantic inflated melons *that also leak sometimes*!" Her voice caught, and she scraped a hand over her eyes.

I rubbed her back and let her cry. Why was all of this strangely comforting to me, my sister in distress and sobbing her eyes out?

I supposed it had to do with what I'd observed before: this was such an aggressively *normal* problem. And she was reacting to it in a pretty normal way. I didn't see that haunted look in her eyes, that strange sadness I'd witnessed before whenever she talked about giving birth. She was upset because she couldn't figure out what to wear to a party, but this wasn't something that was going to eat away at her very soul.

It was, like . . . refreshingly low stakes.

"It'll be okay," I said. "Are you, um. Feeling okay otherwise? Anything else going on?"

"I'm fine," Evie managed, swiping a hand over her eyes. "I know I'm extra hormonal, and I guess I'm still trying to work through all the trauma from Vivi's birth." She gave me a watery smile. "I know I've said it a million times, but I don't know what I would've done if you hadn't been there, Bea. You really helped me get through it. Every time I start reliving it, getting stuck in that moment . . . I remember your face, how you told me to stop trying to be brave and let everything out. And I feel a little bit better."

"I'm glad," I murmured, still marveling at the fact that I didn't see that haunted shadow descending over her. She'd still been through an undeniable trauma, but she seemed to be processing it instead of holding everything inside and letting it consume her.

"Look, I still have it!" Evie exclaimed, reaching over to snatch something off the dresser.

My eyes widened as she brandished the shiny, garish object at me—it was my blobby dragon ornament. My talisman.

"I remember when you brought this home—back when you were twelve?" Evie continued, smiling faintly at the ornament. "We'd just moved into that shitty apartment after Dad took off. You wanted me to join you in your full-on

Christmas fandom—and everything from that time period is such a blur, but I'm sure I rained all over your parade because I didn't understand why you wanted us to display some messed-up sculpture you'd found in the trash."

"You actually did smile for a minute when I showed it to you," I murmured. "It was the first time in . . . forever."

"Ah." Her smile widened. "Well, now I totally see the majesty of the questionable neon-pink dragon. I've been keeping it by my bed. Just looking at it reminds me of how much you were there for me when Vivi arrived."

She set the ornament back down on the dresser, giving it a little pat on the head.

Well, shit. How could I reclaim my talisman when it had come to mean so much to my sister? Like, I couldn't exactly snatch it right now. Maybe I could sneak back in once she got dressed and went downstairs? But what if the dragon fell through time when I did—would she freak out if it vanished from her bedside table?

I guess that was a problem for Future Bea. Present Bea needed to get on with her mission.

Present Bea also couldn't help but feel the smallest flash of pride. I'd assumed me time traveling to a moment where I didn't belong meant I'd managed to irrevocably mess things up—and during one of the most important experiences of my sister's life.

But it seemed like I'd actually made that one little moment . . . *better*? Was that possible?

I guessed I'd have to wait and see—perhaps there were big consequences to the timeline that would become apparent later. Like maybe I'd made someone else disappear—

Ugh. Okay, Present Bea—let's not go down that spiral.

"Sis, I'm glad you finally understand why my blobby pink dragon is awesome," I said, slipping my phone from my pocket and tapping out a text. "But listen, we need to get you ready for that party! So let's fix your wardrobe catastrophe— I'm calling in an expert."

Seconds later, Aveda barged into the room.

"Fashion SOS!" she proclaimed, surveying the mess of clothes on the bed. "Luckily, Aveda Jupiter is *prepared*." She marched over to Evie's closet and flung it open. "Mmm. I require reinforcements."

"I'm texting Shruti," I said, referring to one of our fabulous friends who also had a superpower, the ability to grow her hair out at will and grab on to stuff with it—though really, her most incredible power was an extensive knowledge of vintage fashion and how to wear it. She owned several lovely boutiques in the Bay Area, and was always swooping in to save us from sartorial disasters. "I assume she is in attendance at this shindig, and I think we need custom tailoring." I cocked an eyebrow at Evie. "For the, um, melons."

"Bea!" she shrieked, snatching a pillow and smacking it against my arm. "Not funny!"

"Sorry, I thought it kind of was?" I jumped off the bed to avoid her pillow attack. "Let me get out of the fashion squad's way, though. My work here is done."

I scurried out of the bedroom just as Evie threw the pillow at my head. And couldn't resist grinning to myself a little bit. She really did seem . . . okay? Or on the path to being okay, melon-related emergencies notwithstanding.

I knew Aveda, the queen of never half-assing anything, was probably going to take a while. Which meant I wouldn't be able to snag my little dragon friend right away. But I could make progress on the other part of my mission—theorizing with Nate about time travel. I should do that first anyway. Perhaps it would give me some key grist for the mill once I had a chance to try the talisman again.

I hustled downstairs and surveyed the scene. The party was in full swing. I saw Lucy and Rose fiddling with a massive karaoke setup, passing out a stack of songbooks to eager Mariahs in the making. The junior members of the team— Pippa, Shelby, Tess, and Julie—were clustered around the massive Christmas tree, admiring the decorations.

Scott was helping Lucy's singer friend Celine arrange

cookies on a tray—though his "helping" mostly seemed to consist of shoving cookies in his mouth when she wasn't looking. I caught his eye and mimed zipping my lips, indicating I'd never tell. He grinned and gave me a thumbs-up.

My gaze swept over the rest of the crowd—friends and colleagues and a few folks I didn't recognize. I found Nate standing next to the punch bowl, cradling Vivi in his arms. I was amused to see that he was wearing his usual black t-shirt and jeans, but had made concessions to the holiday spirit by plopping a Santa hat on top of his head. Vivi, meanwhile, was dressed as a cute little elf. I wondered if Evie had gotten her an entire wardrobe of adorable holiday outfits.

Or actually, maybe *I* had. That seemed like a very Auntie Bea thing to do.

I zeroed in on Nate, trying to get my hectic thoughts in order. Maybe I could feel things out by talking to him like I had earlier—using time-travel hypotheticals I could apply to my current situation. Luckily, he was all by himself, no one trying to hit him up for small talk. Nate avoided small talk like the freakin' plague.

I crossed the room and patted him on the arm.

"Hey, big brother," I said genially. "Love the hat."

"Trying to get in the spirit," he said, smiling down at Vivi. "If the Littlest is getting dressed up, I feel that I should at least make an effort—as I did with that strange novelty sweatshirt Evie liked so much. And give me your best assessment..." He held Vivi up in front of me, her chubby fingers reaching for mine. "This looks like another new smile to me. It has characteristics of the smile she displayed yesterday, but there are subtle differences I need to catalog. Do you think she's developing a holiday-specific set of pleased expressions?"

"I think you're the cutest science dad I've ever seen," I said, holding up my hand so Vivi could wrap her little fist around my index finger. "I am also developing a hypothesis that she wants Auntie Bea to hold her."

"Hypothesis accepted," he said, an amused glint lighting

his eyes. He carefully passed Vivi to me and she let out a soft coo, her grip tightening on my finger. I felt a visceral flash of protectiveness, that connection of family. She was definitely a Tanaka. I couldn't really explain why. I could just *feel* it.

"Speaking of hypotheses," I said, bouncing Vivi against my chest, "I was wondering if I could run some time-travel shit by you again. I'm trying to, um . . . come up with some discussion points. For my Christmas rom-com online discussion group. To *discuss*."

"Of course," Nate said, his expression growing intrigued. "That sounds fascinating."

"Say you've figured out you have the ability to time travel, but no way to control it," I began, feeling it out. "And you need to travel to a very specific point in time. How would you go about figuring out the trigger?"

"A good question," Nate said, not missing a beat. "I'd probably start by thinking about all the times I've time traveled—if I can remember them, that is. What was I doing at the time? What was I thinking about? Was I visualizing anything in particular, or remembering something of great significance? Because in these movies, there is usually a logic to how the time travel is happening, yes? It's never truly random."

"Never," I agreed, making a funny face at Vivi. She giggled in appreciation. "Although a lot of times in these movies, the time travel is triggered by an external device, not necessarily something the traveler is doing—a talisman."

"Like the medallion wielded by the old witch in *The Knight Before Christmas*," Nate said, his brow furrowing. "Yes, I see."

"So say you're exploring these paths, trying to come up with different variables," I continued. "Say you're thinking about *how* to best come up with new variables . . . Nate? You still with me?"

He'd gotten a glazed look in his eyes, his attention drifting away from me and Vivi. I followed his gaze and saw . . . oh.

It was Evie. Descending down the staircase. And Aveda and Shruti had definitely accomplished all their glam squad goals.

She was clad in what looked like a refashioned version of Aveda's Slutty Santa outfit—Shruti had worked her expert tailoring magic to fit the dress to Evie's curvier frame, and the results were stunning.

The dress was still red velvet with white fur trim, and the skirt was still short and flared. But the top part now had sleeves and was cut in an off-the-shoulders style that plunged to a deep vee, enhancing and framing her impressive cleavage. And speaking of that cleavage, Aveda had clearly gotten her into some wizard-level undergarments, because the "melons" she'd been so self-conscious about were pushed up, supported, and displayed to their best possible advantage. The glam squad had also given Evie dramatic makeup, a seductive smoky eye paired with an impeccable red lip.

There was no other way to say it—my sister looked fucking hot.

I shifted my gaze to Nate, who was clearly taking notice—his pupils dilated, his breath going shallow. He swallowed hard, his Adam's apple bobbing as he reached over to grip the end of the punch table.

"I'm only saying this because you can't understand words yet," I cooed to Vivi. "I think your dad's mad horny."

"What?" Nate blurted, shaking his head—and still unable to tear his eyes away from Evie. "Sorry, you . . . *we* were talking about . . . time travel?"

"Yeah," I said. "We were talking about external triggers—like the witch and the medallion—versus the traveler themselves being the trigger. If I can walk out both of those scenarios—"

"Scenarios," Nate repeated, like it was a word he'd never heard of before.

"Scenarios," I agreed, trying to make my voice forceful enough to snap him out of his intense visual exploration of

Evie's breasts. "But what variables would you consider adding? Because I'm thinking . . ."

I trailed off, as I could tell he was not hearing a single
word out of my mouth. Across the room, Evie, Aveda, and
Shruti had clustered up around a tray of elaborately frosted
cupcakes someone had set on an end table. They all plucked
a cupcake from the tray and clinked them together like
champagne flutes, laughing merrily. A blob of frosting jos-
tled free from Evie's cupcake, landing on the exposed slope
of her left breast. She laughed again and swiped the frosting
with her index finger, then lifted that finger to her lips, lick-
ing it off.

I glanced down at Nate's hand, still gripping the table. His
knuckles turned white.

"Oh, for . . ." I muttered under my breath.

I was all for my beloved sister and brother-in-law keeping
the flame alive. But did they really have to do so when I
needed his big old brain for important theorizing that could
very possibly help me save the timeline from my chaotic
fuckery?

I glanced back over at Evie. She was taking her sweet time
sucking all that frosting off her finger, her tongue darting
between her bright red lips. And Nate was looking at her like
a starving man who'd just been presented with an infinity-
course meal.

He was definitely not thinking with the head I needed
right now.

"Big brother," I said, even though he still wasn't looking
at me, "I'm going to ask this as delicately as possible: have
you and Evie not had a lot of, um, alone time recently?"

"What?" he said, like he'd forgotten there was someone
standing next to him. "Oh. I suppose . . . not really. Vivi's kept
us very busy."

"Good thing Auntie Bea's here, then!" I trilled, bouncing
Vivi against me. She gave an appreciative gurgle. "Nate, listen to me—I know you don't want to let the Littlest out of

your sight, and given everything that's happened to this family over the last decade, I completely understand. But you also need some couple-y reconnecting time. So go wait in the coat closet—the one in the foyer."

"What?!" That was enough to finally get him to tear his attention from Evie, meeting my gaze with a look of disbelief.

"You heard me." I made a shooing motion in his direction. "I'll watch Vivi, and I'll tell Evie to meet you there."

"In the closet? While we're supposed to be hosting a party?" He looked vaguely scandalized.

"Yes, yes," I said, my shooing motion intensifying. "Don't act all innocent with me, Evie's a blabbermouth when she's sauced, and I've heard *all about* how much the two of you enjoy enclosed spaces during big, bustling events. Didn't you sneak off to the Gutter closet during your own wedding reception?"

"I . . . that is . . ." His eyes shifted back and forth, his cheeks flushing.

"Mmm-hmm. Go. The karaoke's loud, the party's hoppin'. No one will notice if you take a moment or two. I'll take care of Vivi, I promise."

His eyes drifted back to Evie, who had finally stopped deep-throating her frosting-coated finger and was laughing about something with Aveda and Shruti, face flushed and eyes shining.

"I . . . thank you," he said.

Then he kissed the top of Vivi's head and took off for the foyer, moving so fast he nearly tripped over the karaoke setup. With that part of my task accomplished, I tightened my hold on Vivi and aimed myself toward Evie and the cupcake tray.

"Damn," I murmured to Vivi. "I can't believe I have to do a whole pre-mission just to accomplish my *actual* mission. And that the pre-mission involves getting your parents to bone."

She gurgled in agreement, her tiny hand reaching out to clutch a lock of hair that had freed itself from my up-do. I felt that surge of protectiveness again.

"Heeeey, Sis!" I sang out, sidling up next to Evie.

"Oh, there's my girl!" she exclaimed, reaching her arms out for Vivi. "Bea, thank you so much for the fashion intervention. Look at this! Shruti made it fit like a glove. And Annie wrestled my giant boobs into submission."

"They look magnificent," I said, nodding in approval. "In fact, they are such marvels of nature that I had to send your husband to horny jail. Which is the foyer coat closet. Why don't you go meet him there?"

"What?" Evie squawked, flushing bright red.

"Oh, stop," Aveda said, examining her nails. "We all know about this combo, Evelyn."

"You, Nate, an enclosed space, and a party," Shruti chirped in agreement. "It's a tradition!"

"I already said I would watch Vivi," I said, holding the baby out of her reach. "So go meet your husband and let him appreciate those melons in a way that would be massively weird and inappropriate coming from anyone else!"

"I should never have called them 'melons' in front of you," Evie lamented. She leaned in to kiss Vivi, a sheepish grin spreading over her face. "But thank you."

Then she took off, nearly tripping over the karaoke setup the same way Nate had.

"Hmph, that man is about to destroy all of my intricate corsetry work," Aveda huffed.

"I think it's more like he's about to very deeply admire your intricate corsetry work," Shruti corrected, giving her a playful tap on the shoulder. "That's a job well done. Do you think he'll keep the Santa hat on, though?"

"Whoa, commotion alert at the entrance!" a new voice piped up. We all turned to see Pippa skipping up to us, her swoop of platinum hair bobbing jauntily. "I think someone's trying to crash the party! Those Eveda superfans are insatiable, eh?"

"Now, now, nothing wrong with an adoring public," Aveda said, smoothing her mane of raven hair. "Perhaps I should go investigate."

"No way, they could be full-on stalkers!" Pippa exclaimed. "What if they kidnap you or possess you or try to turn you into a big, gross pile of demonic goo—"

"Pretty sure all of those things have happened already," I murmured.

"And I handled it every time," Aveda proclaimed, straightening her spine and giving us her best imperious look.

"True," Pippa said. "But—"

"*Beaaaaaaaaaaaa!*"

The voice cut through the party noise, stopping the latest round of karaoke carols dead in their tracks.

"Oh no," I muttered, recognizing that whiny tone instantly. "Let *me* go investigate this, actually."

I turned on my heel before they could respond, hurrying through the party and bouncing Vivi against my chest. I zipped into the foyer and found Scott standing in the doorway, hands held up as he placated the person on the other side.

People on the other side.

"We're *definitely* on the list!" Olivia insisted.

"Yes, please check again," Terrence chimed in. "Is there a manager I can speak to?"

"I live here?" Scott said, sounding mildly confused.

"I've got this, Scott," I said, sidling up to him. "Oh, and um . . . by the way. I'm not mad at you."

"Okay?" he said, his confusion increasing.

"Aveda told me you thought that—I don't think I've ever been mad at you in my entire life. I . . . I do want to try out stuff with the power combo spell again," I yammered on. "I've just been busy and I've got a lot of weird shit going on. I appreciate you always being awesome and supportive of everything I want to do, even when it's super out there."

"Any time, Bug—I'll be ready whenever you are," he said, giving me his easy grin. "I'm always here for you."

"And so are weeee!" Olivia cried from the porch.

I took a long, deep breath, trying not to let full-body irritation overtake me. Terrence and Olivia were standing on the front steps of the Victorian, jostling against each other so they both occupied equal real estate in the doorframe.

"Babe, you sent me an invite, what gives?" Olivia continued, her full lips reshaping themselves into a pout.

"I . . . probably did," I acquiesced, silently cursing Past Bea yet again. "But given that I dumped both of you yesterday, all invites were rescinded, and I don't understand why y'all would want to come to the party of a girl who just broke up with you?"

"Not a breakup, just a break," Terrence said, giving me a sage nod.

"The same thing in this case," I fired back.

"Bug . . . ?" Scott said next to me, his voice uncertain.

"Sorry, take Vivi," I said, passing the cooing baby over to him. "Go back to the party, and I'll take care of this."

"You got it," he said, cradling Vivi against his chest. "Oh, also—there are some weird sounds coming from the foyer closet, should I—"

"I'll take care of that, too," I said hastily.

At least Evie and Nate were having fun.

"Both of you need to listen to me," I began, turning back to Terrence and Olivia—but my two would-be suitors were apparently planning on doing anything but.

"No, listen to *us*," Olivia insisted. "We know you didn't like the boom box, but luckily we have something else planned."

"Something that pays homage to one of your most favorite things—the holiday rom-com," Terrence intoned, trying to sound like he was on *Masterpiece Theater*.

"So without further ado . . . ." Olivia said with a wink.

It was then that I realized they'd both been holding something behind their backs. And when they each produced a stack of gigantic notecards, I almost screamed.

"At Christmas, you tell the truth," Terrence said solemnly,

brandishing his first notecard—which just happened to be emblazoned with those very words.

"No!" I yelled, slicing my arm through the air with a forceful chopping motion. "Absolutely fucking not."

I paused, trying to center myself. They were both gaping at me, notecards still clutched to their chests, as if frozen in time.

If only I *could* freeze time.

"Listen," I said, pinching the bridge of my nose, "I'm sorry if I gave either of you the wrong impression at any point, but I do think I was pretty clear yesterday. I don't want to date either of you. I barely know either of you. And this stunt just proves it, because if either of you had bothered to get to know *me*, you'd know that the holiday movie you're referencing so hard is the only one I hate with a passion so great, it rivals any number of dying suns. I refuse to call it a rom-com, because it's not. And what you're doing right now—showing up at my house, harassing me and my family, stalking me until I give in . . . none of that's romantic. It's *creepy*. So please. *Stop*."

I slammed the door in their shocked faces, then slumped back against the wall.

Seriously, all I wanted to do was talk to my brother-in-law about time-travel theories cleverly disguised as movie-based hypotheticals so I could figure out how to save everyone from a gigantic kaiju and rescue my time-displaced boyfriend.

Why did that have to be *hard*?

I eyed the foyer closet and heard faint sounds emanating from it, which I did my best to immediately block out. I wondered how much longer Evie and Nate were going to be enjoying themselves. Hopefully Nate would emerge with a clear head, no longer addled by lust, and I could—

knock knock knock

I startled, pushing off from the wall, and threw open the front door again.

"Olivia and Terrence, I *swear*—"

My words died in my throat as I realized our newest guests were not Olivia and Terrence.

"Mr. and Mrs. Fujikawa," I breathed, taking in the sight of Sam's parents on my doorstep.

Warmth surged through me as I clocked their familiar presence. Sam's mom barely cleared five feet, but was one of those Aunties who seemed dedicated to taking up as much space as possible—her clothes were always a cacophony of patterns and colors, and her hair flew out in all directions, a half-permed mane liberally streaked with silver. In contrast, Sam's dad was stoic and straight-spined—with his tiny, wire-rimmed spectacles and ever-present plaid golf cap, he looked like what you'd get if you looked up "mild-mannered accountant" on Wikipedia.

"Bea Tanaka," Sam's mom said, her eyes narrowing shrewdly.

"That's me," I said, at a complete loss for anything else. "Um, come in. And also, refresh my memory—have we met before?"

"No," Mrs. Fujikawa said, shaking her silver-streaked mane back and forth. "But I saw your name mentioned in a recent *Bay Bridge Kiss* blog posting, and I had a funny feeling—I am a little bit psychic, ne?" She raised a bushy eyebrow at me, then grabbed my sleeve, her expression growing urgent. "You know where my son is."

My blood ran cold.

"Ahh, Sa-chan, we've talked about this," Mr. Fujikawa said gently. "Alex does not live here anymore. He will be back to visit someday."

"No." Mrs. Fujikawa shook her head again. "My *other* son."

"We don't have another son," Mr. Fujikawa said. "Miss Bea, I am very sorry for my wife, she insisted on coming over here—"

"You *know*," Mrs. Fujikawa insisted, her grip tightening on my sleeve.

"I . . ." My mouth had gone very dry and my vision was narrowing, pinholing in on a single point of light.

"Please," Mrs. Fujikawa was saying. But now my brain was whirling, my breathing coming too fast, like I was about to pass out. She suddenly sounded like she was far away, trying to call for me from the top of a distant mountain. "I do not know how or why, but I know I am supposed to give you this."

She pressed a small, rubbery object into my hand as I continued to replay her words in my mind, over and over and over—

CRASH

"Holy shit!"

"What the fuck *are* those?!"

"Where's Evie? Fuck, we need to contain these things—"

I swiveled toward the sudden commotion, which was coming from the living room. My fist was still curled around the object Mrs. Fujikawa had just pressed into my hand, but I moved instinctively toward the ruckus. I felt like I was floating outside of my body, moving through a dream-like scene that just kept spiraling further and further into ridiculousness . . .

And that didn't stop when I entered the living room.

Which was now positively swarming with mini kaiju.

They skittered across the floor, threw themselves gleefully into the punch bowl, surged up into the Christmas tree . . .

I heard screams, glass shattering. My vision fragmented, giving me hazy snapshots of what was happening. I saw Lucy attempting to herd everyone out of the kaiju army's path, Aveda trying to move mobs of kaiju with her telekinesis, Shruti catching them with her hair . . .

I shook my head, trying to get a more coherent handle on the situation—and what I should do next.

"Bea Tanaka." I swiveled to see Mrs. Fujikawa tugging insistently on my sleeve. "Please. *Remember.*"

Her hand moved to my wrist and she gave it a little shake, reminding me of the rubbery object that was still enclosed in my sweaty fist.

I opened my hand.

And there, right in the center of my palm, was a cheesy trophy-shaped eraser with a big #1 emblazoned on it.

"Sam . . ." I whispered.

All the air drained from my lungs and my stomach dropped to my feet. And then my vision was narrowing again into that tiny pinhole of light, and I felt my body start to fall and everything went black.

CHAPTER TWENTY-SIX

"BEA . . . BEA!"

My eyes snapped open, my surroundings nothing more than bleary shapes and colors. I blinked rapidly, trying to get them to come into focus.

I felt strong hands gripping my shoulders, a hard dirt floor against my back . . . had I passed out in the midst of my family's holiday party just as it devolved into a mini-kaiju battle?

Why did I always miss all the fun?

And why did I hear the ocean in the distance . . .

"Bea!" the voice yelled again.

And then his face swam into view and I didn't care about anything else—not even the monster headache that was already stabbing me in the temples.

"Sam!" I screamed, throwing my arms around him. I buried my face in his neck, my tears coming fast and furious, my body shaking with sobs. I inhaled his irresistible spicy, woodsy scent, feeling as if life itself was rushing back into my lungs. I never wanted to let him go. Not ever again.

"Hey, it's okay," he said, his voice soft and confused. He stroked a tentative hand down my back as I shuddered against him, my breathing escaping in a staccato series of gasps. "I think you fainted. I'm sorry we were arguing, I just—"

"What?" I pulled back from him, swiping tears from my face. And then I realized where we were.

The canoes were in a jumble in the corner and the sounds

of waves I'd thought I'd heard were the actual sea and I was wearing my flimsy silver bikini, the ties clumsily re-done after fooling around with Sam.

Sam.

God. He was actually *here.*

And I'd done it. I'd finally traveled back to the correct spot in the timeline—right before the battle on the beach.

But . . . how? I hadn't been actively trying to time travel. I hadn't even had a chance to talk to Nate or attempt using my dragon talisman again. And what was with that freaking army of mini kaiju? Why was Shasta sending more kaiju after me?! She'd gotten my attention, she knew I was trying to get back here. I was doing exactly what she wanted.

I realized then that my hand was balled into a fist, clenched around something. I uncurled my fingers and saw that cheesy #1 eraser—the one Sam's mom had pressed into my hand right before I'd fallen through time.

Was *that* my talisman? Er, second talisman? How many time-travel talismans did one person need?

"Bea?" Sam murmured, rubbing my arm. "Are you okay?"

Before I could answer him or ruminate on my current state any further, the earth began to shake.

"I-I have to go," I said, meeting his eyes—those eyes I thought I'd never see again. I could fucking drown in them right now. "I can't explain everything, and I'm sorry. But please, listen: I'm going to go out there and I need you to stay in the beach shack. Don't move until someone comes to get you."

"What?!" He shook his head, exasperation tensing his shoulders. "You really expect me to let you charge out there while I do nothing? Because that's—"

"I'm a superhero!" I retorted, jumping to my feet. "I have skills that are relevant to any battle! And also, lots of supernatural-type wisdom that I need you to pay attention to! The best thing you can do right now is stay here and stay *safe.*"

I darted for the door, but he was already leaping to his feet, more protests on the tip of his tongue.

"*Hey.*" He grabbed me by the shoulders and spun me around, his expression anguished. "Why can't you tell me—"

"Sam, *please.*" My voice cracked, tears springing to my eyes. "If you ever loved me, can you please listen? Just this once?"

"If I ever . . ." He released his grip on me, his frown deepening. "Of course I love you. I *still* love you. I—"

"Good to know!" I blurted, even as an ecstatic glow sparked in my heart. "Okay, bye!"

I whirled around and flung myself out of the beach shack, wishing like hell that there was a way I could just lock him in. I would *not* lose him again.

I raced through the sand, heart hammering as sweat streaked my hair. I'd finally made it back to the beach. And I had no idea what I was going to do.

I'd thought maybe once I was here, the obvious solution would present itself. Like I'd be hit with the same feeling of fated *rightness* I'd gotten when I'd spied Pika's DeLorean. I'd know that sacrificing Vivi to Shasta was the only way, maybe—I'd feel that greater good pulsing through my veins, telling me that this was how it had to be.

I scanned the beach, spotting the tall, sun hat–wearing woman in the distance—the one I now knew to be Shasta. And then I saw Evie, writhing and screaming in pain just as she'd done the last time I'd been here. Nate's face was pale with terror as he pulled her against him, trying to figure out what was wrong.

My chest constricted and all the air left my lungs. I stopped in my tracks and doubled over, wheezing as those little pinpricks of anxiety raced over my skin. My eraser was still gripped in my sweaty fist, and I squeezed it extra hard.

No.

I couldn't sacrifice Vivi. Even if Shasta closed all the portals, even if it was for the greater good, even if I didn't currently have a better alternative. Somewhere deep inside me, I'd probably always known that to be true—that when it came down to it, I just wouldn't be able to make that impossible choice.

I forced myself to straighten back up, finding Evie and Nate again in the distance. I watched them for a moment, struggling and fighting so hard. I remembered Evie during labor, how she'd thought she would never get through it—and how she'd lit up the first time Vivi was placed in her arms. I thought about Nate cradling Vivi on the couch, gazing at her like she was pure magic and cataloging all of her smiles.

I thought of Vivi reaching that little hand out to grasp my finger. And how I'd felt something visceral, a deep *knowing* that she was already part of the family, regardless of whatever timeline we were existing in.

When Evie had been in labor, I'd told her I knew she would go to the ends of the earth to protect the people she loved.

Turns out, I was exactly the same.

I pivoted and headed straight for the ocean. I still wasn't sure of what I was going to do, but there had to be another way. And I'd find it—even if it took everything I had, I'd fucking find it.

When my feet hit the water, I was prepared for the cold, even as it sent a full-body shiver through my bloodstream. I started wading in immediately, forging ahead with purpose. If nothing else, I'd be *ready* for the kaiju this time. I couldn't try to control it as I'd done before. That would likely draw Sam out, and we'd end up in the timeline I'd been trying to prevent. (I also didn't trust him to actually stay put—because hell, I wouldn't. And he and I were just a little too much alike.)

But what could I do differently? If I reached out with my mind for the kaiju again . . . hmm, maybe I could reason with it instead of trying to control it? I thought back to Evie's birth moment, how I'd been able to gently soothe her. Perhaps I could try something similar with the kaiju? It had seemed distressed the last time we'd faced off, beaming out fearful thoughts. But what did it have to be distressed about? It was the biggest, meanest motherfucker on this beach.

Maybe it had been confused, having just appeared in a totally disorienting situation. Maybe it was mad that freaking Shasta was the one who created it. Maybe—

My ruminations were interrupted by the kaiju itself exploding from the ocean. I tuned out the feverish screams of all the beach-goers, and tried not to get too freaked when the monster unhinged its jaw and revealed its massive fangs, shimmering like shards of broken mirror in the morning light.

My brain scrabbled around, trying to remember the plan I'd only just started to hastily assemble.

Think, Bea—come on, think! *How did you manage to calm Evie so well?! Let's see, you started by telling Aveda you're actually one of the least calming people around—*

The darkness inside of me rumbled, and I reflexively tried to tune that out, too. But it rumbled more insistently, like it was trying to get me to pay attention to something . . .

Wait. *That's right!* During Evie's birth moment, I *hadn't* shoved it down! I'd done the exact opposite: made space for it, let it swirl around my power, felt them melding together . . .

The idea of my power becoming so entwined with the darkness still seemed like a very bad thing, but hey—in true Bea Tanaka fashion, I was improvising. Leaning into the chaos and flying by the seat of my pants. I squeezed the cheesy eraser that was still clutched in my hand, calling on my talisman for strength.

Then I closed my eyes and felt the darkness rise up and mingle with all the feelings that were gathering in my chest.

I'd send out peace. Calm. Gentle empathy, letting the creature know I totally felt everything it was going through. Maybe I could help it come to terms with its most monstrous self?

I inhaled deeply and sensed my mind strengthen, my power and the darkness bolstering all those feelings and giving them space to breathe.

Yes. I could do this.

I took one more long inhale and sent my projection spinning—I swore I could see it flying across the ocean, streaks of magic as glittery and rainbow-hued as what I'd felt during the power combo spell. And that errant string of Christmas lights twirled around it all, illuminating the entire sky in an unconventional display of fireworks.

That's it, that's it . . . it's gonna be okay, Big Kaiju, I promise. I can help you. I can—

NO NO HURT HELP HELP HURT PLEASE HELP

Its thoughts and emotions came right at me, just as they had before. I gasped at the sheer force of them—this kaiju's pain was so raw. It felt like I was being relentlessly pummeled in the brain by its panic, its desperation.

I turned my own projection up. I called on the darkness to make that space, just as it had done with Evie. I didn't want to control the kaiju, I wanted to communicate with it.

Hey, I thought. *It's really okay, I promise.*

NO, the kaiju thought plaintively. *No . . .*

I took another deep breath and kept my projection going, feeling the darkness open up space for the kaiju. It had paused its stomp through the water and locked its golden eyes with mine, looking at me in a way that was almost . . . contemplative?

What's wrong? I asked impulsively, feeling ridiculous. Was I about to give this gigantic sea monster therapy? *You seem really cool and powerful! Why are you so upset and, like, throwing a full-on oceanic tantrum?*

We must stop, the kaiju thought. Its mental state seemed to be evening out, morphing into something that could almost be described as mellow. And . . . I inclined my head to the side, exploring my brain space. It felt like we weren't merely projecting at each other—I swore I could sense the kaiju's entire consciousness now, as if our minds were linked, a tenuous thread of connection pulsing between us.

Stop, the kaiju repeated.

Stop what? I pressed, keeping my tone gentle.

It held itself in that weirdly thoughtful pose, eyes locked with mine. For a moment, we both stayed very still and I felt the kaiju inhale deeply, as if matching my breath. I sensed its mood mellowing further, the spikes on its iridescent hide drooping a little. As if less prepared to strike.

The prophecy, it finally thought at me.

You have to stop the prophecy? I queried. *The one about the child born of two worlds and the destroyer—*

No! The kaiju shook its massive head, sending tsunami-level waves toward the shore again. I bobbed through them, laser focused on maintaining our mental link. *Not stop the prophecy*, the kaiju clarified. *Prophecy says we must be fed. To end suffering. To keep . . . safe. But . . .*

It stilled again. I turned up my projection, trying to keep those soothing feelings going.

You are safe, I thought at it, my sentiment sincere. *I'll do everything I can to help you feel that way.*

It seemed to let out a very long exhale, its spikes drooping further, its golden eyes softening. Perhaps I *was* therapizing this gigantic sea creature.

We have to . . . look. Look at prophecy . . . differently . . .

What? I frowned, confused. *I'm sorry, what do you mean?*

We . . . The big kaiju tilted its head to the side, as if hearing something in the distance.

Stay with me, I thought at it, fear tingling up my spine. *What are you trying to tell me about the prophecy? What—*

Suddenly, I felt a massive mental shove.

NO!!! a new voice screamed in my head.

My eyes flew open, my mind abruptly breaking my link with the monster. I felt a wall slam down around my consciousness, blocking me from the kaiju. That was . . . what was it?! Was the kaiju really trying to attack now, after we'd been conversing so well? Had I accidentally scared it, or . . .

I shook my head, searching for my darkness—I could sense it struggling too, trying to bust through that invisible wall.

Stop!!! that new voice repeated in my brain. *You're about to fuck it all up! Just like you* always *do. Just like you can't seem to stop doing!*

I stumbled backward, my eyes filling with tears. That invisible force was pushing hard against my mind now, blocking me from gathering my projection—and putting weird, intrusive thoughts in my head. I felt my darkness resisting with all its might, trying to break free of this alien force.

I shook myself, desperately wanting to liberate my brain from the sudden mental hold. My head whipped around as if of its own volition, and my gaze landed on a lone figure in the distance.

The woman in the sun hat. *Shasta.*

Who was now staring directly at me, her arms hanging slack at her sides.

Give up. Now.

And then I felt an even harder push against my mind, those invisible walls closing in, as if my brain was being overtaken, *devoured* . . .

I fell to my knees on the ocean floor, clapping a palm over one ear, my eraser still stubbornly clutched in my other hand. I viciously shoved down the scream that wanted to spill out of my body.

In the distance, I heard the kaiju roar and thrash in the water, sending tidal waves toward shore. I flopped helplessly in the ocean, tasting salt and feeling my limbs grow heavy.

My brain was flailing and all I could do was shove everything down, tell myself not to feel, tell the darkness to go away, *just stop, we have to stop, we have to*—

And then I felt something hard smack me in the shoulder and the ocean absorbed my body, the waves towing me under. I choked as my lungs clogged, my arms pushing fruitlessly against the weight of water. My mind fought hard, mentally punching whatever it could even though it didn't know what it was fighting against.

And then I didn't feel anything at all.

CHAPTER TWENTY-SEVEN

WHEN I STARTLED awake this time, I was enveloped in darkness. And for a moment, I thought I was truly dead.

But then the familiar shapes of my bedroom back at Tanaka/Jupiter HQ coalesced into something solid, and I could make out the popcorn garlands I'd put up, the pillows embroidered with gingerbread people, the mistletoe still attached to the headboard.

And my tiny #1 eraser was still improbably clutched in my fist.

I bolted upright and felt around on my nightstand for my phone. No, I had not plugged it in, but it still boasted a whopping fifteen percent. I glanced at the date. December 24. I checked the year. Yes, okay—it was still the holiday season I'd just departed, the one that was nine months after the battle on the beach. And I'd traveled all the way forward to Christmas Eve.

My fumbling fingers managed to pull up Leah's contact info, and I punched the call button with more force than necessary. She answered on the second ring.

"Bebe?" she slurred, sounding half asleep. "It's 5 a.m. Is something wrong?"

"Sorry, Lee, I did a little light time traveling again. I'll call back when you're more awake, but I really need this one bit of information." I closed my eyes, took a deep breath, and allowed the tiniest bit of hope to spark in my heart. "Do you know a Sam Fujikawa?"

There was a long pause on the other end, and panic galloped through my chest as I wondered what she would say.

"Bebe, are you sure you're all right?" Leah finally said, sounding a bit more alert. "You mean Sam as in *Sam*? Our friend, your ex-boyfriend, Pancake's preferred bacon chef, all of those things?"

"Yes!" I hollered, punching the air in triumph. "So he exists? He . . . he's alive?"

"Of course," Leah said, her voice puzzled. In the background, I heard Pancake give a yelp of protest. "I know you haven't seen him in a while, he moved in full-time with his parents, and I thought y'all decided a clean break was best. But that doesn't mean he stopped existing?"

"Right, okay," I said, my heartbeat speeding up as giddiness overtook my fear. "Um, one more question—what about Vivi?"

"The baby?" Now Leah sounded even more confused. "Yeah, she exists too? Bebe, what is this about—"

"Never mind, go back to sleep! Sorry again, Lee, I'll call you later!"

I could practically hear her snoring as I hung up.

I hugged my phone to my chest, tears streaming freely down my cheeks.

I'd done it. I'd saved Sam. I'd saved Vivi. And I'd ended up back here—and seemingly unscathed.

So did that mean my spontaneous, seat-of-the-pants plan had actually *worked*? Even though I hadn't been able to stick around for the whole thing? But what about that sudden shove against my mind, the mental wall that had slammed down around my consciousness, my brain feeling like it was being consumed . . .

And Shasta, staring at me from across the shore.

I'd been getting somewhere with the kaiju, I had felt that— we seemed to have some sort of bizarre connection. Perhaps Shasta had realized what I was up to, had been pissed I'd managed to connect with her creature and wasn't about to go along with her "Let's kidnap Vivi and take her to the Otherworld" plan. And she'd tried to literally get in my head somehow . . .

I flopped back against my pillow, working it out. I'd time traveled without even trying again, but had the Bea back on the beach managed to finish the job? Maybe I . . . she . . . Past Bea? Had figured it out. She must have figured out *something*, since Sam and Vivi were still here.

I glanced around my room again. Soft early-morning light was beginning to filter in through my window, illuminating the cavalcade of Christmas decorations.

Hmm. Maybe all of the hows and whys didn't matter.

Sam and Vivi both existed in the world and now it was Christmas and the timeline was set right at last.

I threw off my covers and wrapped a fluffy robe around my silky red-and-green nightgown. Maybe someone else in the house was awake, and I could pump them for info. Evie and Nate were probably up at all hours with Vivi, and Nate had night-owl tendencies anyway. I stuffed my feet into slippers with big rainbow unicorn heads and padded down the hall.

The house was dark, silent. I almost never experienced HQ being totally silent, so this made the whole enterprise extra eerie. I slowed my steps, looking around carefully—as if expecting something to leap out at me from behind a particularly shadowy corner.

It was also cold. I pulled my robe more tightly around me to ward off the chill, frowning as I shivered my way to the staircase. Due to Aveda's obsession with perfect temperature regulation, the Victorian was *never* cold. Our surroundings were cozy and toasty in the winter, breezy and balmy in the summer.

But now my teeth were chattering, freezing air seeping through my robe and into my bones.

I hurried down the staircase as quickly as possible, aiming myself at the den/rec room. Maybe I'd find Nate in there just as I had last time, watching *The Knight Before Christmas* and cuddling Vivi. The very thought put a huge smile on my face.

Then I hit the bottom of the stairs and saw the living room . . . and my smile faded away.

It was empty. Well, not totally. The basic furniture was still there. But there was no glorious Christmas tree emitting its fragrant pine scent, no holly accents, no candy-cane candles for wayward kaiju to knock over. It was bare, sterile. Like a showroom at IKEA.

Still frowning, I continued on to the den. Like the rest of the house, it was dark and quiet, no Nate or Vivi to be found. I switched on the light, feeling like I was doing something vaguely illicit.

Momentary relief rushed through me when I saw Vivi's toys and bouncy seat scattered across the floor. While there were still no Christmas decorations, this room looked pretty much the same. And this was some reassuring further confirmation of Vivi's existence.

I wandered over to the photo wall, still trying to fend off the shivers running through me. Why was it so damn *cold*?

I scanned the jumble of photos, smiling at the pictures I'd noticed before—Lucy and Rose singing to each other at their wedding, Aveda laughing with Scott on the beach, Nate holding Vivi for the first time, smiling his proud dad smile . . .

Except . . .

I frowned, leaning forward so I could scrutinize the photo further. And I realized Nate wasn't actually smiling. No, he was looking at Vivi with trepidation, his dark eyes conflicted. Like he didn't quite understand why she was there. My gaze swept over the wall, looking for the photo of Nate and Evie and Vivi together. Maybe I was remembering the Nate/Vivi photo incorrectly, but the pure sweetness of their family portrait was seared into my brain. I finally located the photo, right next to that familiar picture of Pancake dressed like a grumpy elf.

And I did a double take. Because this photo wasn't the same, either.

It had the same background, the soft golden glow of Topanga Canyon. The same setup, Nate holding Vivi up like
she was little Simba in *The Lion King*. But right next to him,
where Evie should be . . . there was nothing. No one. Just
more golden glow from Topanga, and a big empty space that
had once contained a whole other human.

My heartbeat sped up and my blood ran even colder as I
scanned the wall more frantically, going to the images I
knew like the back of my hand.

There was Aveda, standing in front of the iconic Hollywood sign, posing as if she was back to back with someone—
only she was all by herself, one half of a clear whole. There
was Lucy, high-fiving open air. And there was me, huge grin
in place as I stuffed my face with mochi. Sitting all alone,
another conspicuous swath of blank space next to me.

I stumbled backward, blood pounding in my ears. I
slumped onto the couch as my heart thrummed faster, trying
to alert me to the fact that something was desperately wrong.

With shaking hands, I managed to free my phone from my
robe pocket and dialed Leah once more.

"Hey, Lee," I blurted before she could even get so much
as a *hello* in. "I've got another weird question: do I have a
sister?"

CHAPTER TWENTY-EIGHT

THE ANSWER WAS, of course, a resounding *no*.

So to recap: I'd saved Sam and Vivi . . . but somehow managed to erase a whole entire sister in the process?

Awesome.

Leah had seemed confused by my query, but had slowly explained that no? I was a pretty obvious only child?!

"But Aveda's parents and your parents were super tight," she'd said. "I guess she took you under her wing when you were younger? Did this not happen in whatever timeline you just flew in from?"

"Not exactly." I leaned back against the couch and squeezed my eyes shut, as if willing my current reality to disappear. "Another question, and I really will explain later, but: Nate has a baby, right?"

"The demonology guy? Yeah. That situation's a little weird, I guess he just showed up with her one day. No one knows who the mom is, and actually, even he seems confused if you ask. I thought maybe it was part of his demon magic or something?"

"Argh," I muttered. "One more thing—did Aveda develop an affinity for, like, super cold temperatures recently? Because the Victorian is fucking freezing, and that is definitely not how I left it."

"Pretty sure the heat's not on because no one else is there," Leah said, puzzled. "They all had other holiday plans? And actually, I thought you were going to stay in Maui, but you came home at the last minute. Something about needing to wallow in the vast, unending sea of your own misery?"

"Sounds about right." I let out a long, gusty sigh. "Thanks, Lee. I'll call you later."

I hung up and dug the heels of my hands into my eyes until I saw stars. What the hell was I going to do? If Evie had been erased from the timeline, was there someone else who might remember her? Like Mrs. Fujikawa and Pika had remembered Sam? My eyes went back to the photo wall, Nate looking sad and confused as he cradled Vivi. If her memory was going to linger with anyone, it would be him.

I pulled out my phone again, searching through for Nate's contact info. But it wasn't there. He wasn't in my phone at all. I remembered the curious way Leah had referred to him—"the demonology guy." Maybe in this timeline, he and I weren't even friends. Maybe we barely knew each other.

Well, that probably wasn't a great avenue of investigation anyway, considering that both Pika and Mrs. Fujikawa had seemed so confused—their wispy remembrances of Sam had mostly served to reinforce that he was supposed to exist in the world.

I shook my head stubbornly, determined to keep sadness from washing over me. I could fix this. I knew I could.

I mean, I'd figured out how to time travel with purpose, I'd gotten back to the beach and saved both Sam and Vivi, and I'd managed to take a detour to help my sister deliver her baby. I'd even made that moment just a little bit better for her. Surely I could handle yet another fucked-up time-line?

I wrapped my arms around myself, trying to stave off the chill again, trying to *think*. My brain replayed the events on the beach, attempting to pinpoint where I'd lost Evie. I cycled through waking up to Sam, racing outside, realizing I couldn't sacrifice Vivi . . . I remembered calling on the darkness, connecting to the kaiju, feeling like it was calming down and we were actually starting to communicate . . . then that weird shove against my mind, the voice demanding I stop what I was doing, saying that I'd fuck things up like I always do, that sensation of my brain being overtaken, and then—

Shasta. Staring at me with that malevolent glint in her eyes.

Rage bloomed in my chest. *She'd* done this. She'd made Evie disappear.

My rage spread like wildfire. My darkness sang with joy, carving out space for the anger that was pounding through my bloodstream. I had to find Shasta. Even if it was just to give her a very large, very loud piece of my mind.

Was this the most logical, meticulously thought-out course of action? Probably not.

But it was definitely the most *Bea Tanaka* course of action. So that's what I was going to do.

🔥

I followed a wisp of a hunch—and TikTok.

I opened the app and plunged myself down an unending spiral of twee white girls playing ukuleles, probably messing up my algorithm forever. I was just about to give up (and possibly throw my phone into the sea) when I found her.

Dahlia. Her hair done up in cute barrettes shaped like butterflies, her blue eyes wide and winsome. Singing a ditty as she strummed away, a cavalcade of "likes" and admiring comments scattering over her like confetti.

TikTok did not offer any actual contact information for Ms. Dahlia. Luckily, my internet sleuthing skills didn't fail me this time. After many keyword searches and tumbling down a rabbit hole of interconnected social media accounts, I finally got a lead. Dahlia played a regular set every Saturday morning at a local music store, and today she was performing a medley of "reimagined holiday classics." Despite my best efforts, I couldn't tell if the woman I was now cyber stalking was plain old Dahlia or a Shasta-possessed Dahlia. But as this was my only solid lead thus far, I decided to follow it.

The music store, Picks 'n' Slides, was your typical teeny-yet-charming Bay Area business, its cozy walls lined with mad jumbles of guitars and flutes and tambourines. Unruly stacks of crumbling sheet music were piled high on most countertops, nearly tall enough to obscure the current main attraction—that would be Dahlia herself, perched on a stool facing the counter. She was clad in a prim red and green floral dress with lacy accents at the high neckline and long sleeves. Her pixie cut was fluffed and teased out, and her only makeup was a thick, winged layer of shiny black liner curving over each eye. Her audience today wasn't huge, just a handful of curious shoppers milling about the store. It would have been very difficult to hide.

And you know what? I wasn't planning on it.

Fuck this "blending in" bullshit.

I parked myself right up front, watching as Dahlia cycled through wistful versions of "Deck the Halls" and "I'll Be Home for Christmas" and even "Jingle Bells" (I'm still not sure how she managed to make freaking "Jingle Bells" sound melancholy).

As she hit the last mournful note of her set, Dahlia looked right at me, her limpid blue eyes meeting mine. Then her lips curved into a knowing smile, her gaze sparking with malice.

So that was definitely Shasta, then.

I hung back as "Dahlia" greeted her adoring public, posing for photos with the few shoppers who'd stuck around for her whole show. As soon as the final music enthusiast bid her good-bye, I pounced.

"You're *you*, aren't you?" I hissed, sidling up to her as she packed her ukulele into its carrying case. "Well, actually *not* you, the person whose face you're currently wearing, but what I meant was—"

"I got it, Beatrice," Shasta-Dahlia trilled, breaking into a toothy grin.

I suppressed a shudder. It was still super weird to hear Shasta speak in this poor woman's voice, her poisonous words expressing themselves in such sweet, musical tones.

Shasta-Dahlia turned to face me and planted her hands on her hips.

"So. Now that we're here, what the fuck was that back on the beach?" she spat. "I thought I made my instructions very clear."

"Where's Evie?" I demanded, refusing to answer her. "What did you do to her?"

"Ah." Shasta's eyes flashed. "It wasn't me, Beatrice—once again, this is all your fault. Let me show you."

She extended her hand, just as she had back at the bakery. I reluctantly took it.

And suddenly I was back on the beach again, the dusty atmosphere of the music shop melting away. I was in the Shasta-beach-goer's body, watching from afar as my tiny self walked deeper into the ocean. I saw Evie screaming, Nate cradling her close . . . and then something in the ocean caught my sister's eye. She was still obviously in pain, her stomach distorting into those jagged shapes. But she wrenched away from Nate and pitched herself forward, landing on all fours as she screamed into the distance.

And then I realized she was screaming my name.

Goddammit.

Evie had spotted me marching into the ocean like a fool. She didn't know what I was doing, but she sensed I was in danger and knew she needed to protect me. Just like she always did.

I watched helplessly as the kaiju began to lurch toward shore, as I bobbed lower and lower, submerged by waves. Evie was trying to crawl forward and Nate was trying to get her to stop and before I could even process what was happening, a massive blast of flames exploded from Evie's palm and careened toward the kaiju.

The kaiju unhinged its jaw, consuming the fire like it was a tasty afternoon snack. It sucked the flames into its gaping maw, absorbing them into its body. And then it just kept going, eagerly sucking up the fire, turning itself into a tractor beam for the blaze. The force of this was so powerful, it pulled Evie right off the beach—she flew through the air, her flailing body sailing over the ocean and directly into the creature's mouth.

I screamed even though no one could hear me.

Then the beach crumbled, and I was standing in front of Shasta-Dahlia once more, wishing I could smack the satisfied smirk off of her face.

"So once again," Shasta said, carefully rearranging Dahlia's jumbled stack of sheet music, "a misguided soul tried to save your sorry ass and ended up getting eaten by the kaiju instead. And because I was in the midst of my spell to pull Vivi from Evie's body before being so rudely interrupted by your sister's attempt at heroics, Vivi stayed in your dimension—though my useless son remembers nothing of how she came into the world." Shasta sniffed. "How many times must we repeat this scenario before you get it right?"

She *tsk*-ed at me as she shoved the sheet music into Dahlia's public radio–branded canvas tote bag. "This seems to be your way—chaos, constant disasters, and an unparalleled ability to destroy the lives of everyone around you. The fact that you've now made two people disappear, two people you claim to love . . ." She *tsk*-ed again. "Fucking up seems to be your one true superpower."

"What about what you were trying to do to me?" I shot back. "That shove against my mind, that sudden voice in my head—that was you, right?!"

"Only because you refused to follow instructions," Shasta said, examining her nails. Each one had a tiny candy cane painted on it—I was guessing that was Dahlia's stylistic choice. "Just trying to give you a gentle reminder about what you were supposed to be doing."

"It was more than that!" I insisted. "It was like you were trying to . . . to *take over*! Consume my brain and . . . wait a second . . ." The realization hit me square in the chest. "Were you trying to *possess* me? Pass your free-floating consciousness from beach-goer lady's body to mine, assert your will, and force me to do your bidding like a little puppet?!"

"Like you haven't done the same in the past!" Shasta scoffed. She was trying to look imperious, but I saw a flash of raw nerves surface in her eyes.

Hmm. Maybe I wasn't supposed to have guessed that part? *Interesting*.

"Wasn't that your whole thing for a bit, Beatrice? Turning people into *your* puppets?" Shasta continued, her eyes shifting back and forth. "Since you weren't getting the job done, I thought I could take over and take Vivi that way—make the noble, responsible sacrifice you were too selfish to even try, the one that could save both our dimensions! But it was too late." She looked down her nose at me, attempting to reclaim her smug sense of bravado. "That Otherworld darkness has made your power even more unpredictable and freakish than ever before. Otherwise I could have—" She cut herself off abruptly, pinching her lips together.

"Could have what?" I pressed.

Those raw nerves surfaced in her eyes again. "N-nothing. Just, by the time I figured out what was happening with your meddling sister, it was too late for me to deploy my possession effectively. You were quite the sight. All your disgusting human emotions had you flailing around in the surf, and that darkness made your projections at the kaiju so unhinged, so *erratic*—just like those big, messy feelings you're always having. My poor kaiju was ever so distressed and confused, and that made it even more prone to violence! You could have killed so many innocent bystanders!" She glowered at me. "You ruined everything. And Evie paid the ultimate price."

I flinched, soul-wrenching sadness disrupting my rage. Not just Evie. Nate, with that haunted look in his eyes. Vivi, who would grow up without a mother. Aveda . . . tears pricked my eyes. Evie had said before that she and Aveda were basically part of each other's DNA. How could one survive without the other?

"Beatrice." Shasta gave me what was probably supposed to be a sympathetic look. She was very bad at it, even when deploying Dahlia's big blue eyes. "I'm sorry, but it's like I said before—happily ever after always requires sacrifice. And not just in your Christmas movies. Look at the people you love! Think of everything Evie had to go through, all the things she had to give up—she never got to be young. She's spent the majority of her life terrified of burning everything down around her, worrying about whether *you* were going to be okay. And even as a superheroine, she's had so many traumatic challenges."

Evie's pale, pinched face floated through my mind. I pictured her as I'd just seen her in the beach vision, struggling to send a blaze of fire at the kaiju. Trying to save me when it seemed impossible. Even now, she couldn't seem to stop sacrificing everything for her wayward little sister.

"You were so happy for her—remember?" Shasta continued. "You loved seeing her living out her beautiful fairy-tale ending with the man she loves and a fulfilling life packed with heroics and dear friends. But she'll only get there if you return to that moment on the beach and do what you're supposed to. Make that impossible choice—that sacrifice."

I studied her, guilt and panic and everything in between churning through me. The darkness rumbled, adding to the mix, and I instinctively tried to shove it down . . . but it only rumbled more insistently. Just as it had when I'd tried to brush it off while attempting to communicate with the kaiju.

I paused, homing in on the darkness. It felt more . . . substantial? As if it had grown so much brighter. And as I took stock of everything swirling around inside of me, I realized that the darkness seemed to have merged more fully with my projection power. I perceived the two as one now, a single column of sparkling rainbow light. And that column seemed to be trying to wrap itself around my panic, to get me to breathe deeply and remember . . . what?

Something was niggling at the back of my brain. Actually, several somethings, but I couldn't get them to cohere into a totally clear picture.

My darkness was trying to tell me something important.

And I was surprised to find that I really, really wanted to listen.

"Shasta," I blurted out, trying to piece together those scraps of thoughts and remembrances that were bugging me so much. "Um. What did that prophecy say again? The one about Vivi?"

"The child born of two worlds will wield unique power and heal all wounds," Shasta intoned dramatically. "But only once the destroyer—"

"—has been fed and fulfilled, after which this evil shall vanish," I murmured.

"That's correct," Shasta confirmed.

"Right," I said, turning that over in my mind. My newly formed sparkly rainbow column of darkness pulsed, as if encouraging me to see something I hadn't been able to before.

I was starting to see it. Or the beginning of whatever "it" was.

And now I was devising a truly bananas idea on the spot— a chaotic, unpredictable, thoroughly Bea Tanaka type of plan. Even though I hadn't figured out every single step, my darkness clearly wanted me to go with it.

And you know what? That's totally what I was going to do. I couldn't quite explain it and I didn't have all the pieces yet, but I was getting that fated feeling of *rightness* again. I could envision that epic DeLorean door, lifting majestically into the sky.

Let's *do this*, sparkly rainbow darkness!

"Once Vivi passes through the portal, everything will happen like you said it would," I continued, tentatively feeling out a hunch. "The portals will close, the links between our worlds will be severed forever, and everyone will forget Vivi existed in the first place."

"Indeed," Shasta beamed—and was it my imagination, or did she look *relieved*? Those raw nerves I'd seen before were still simmering around the edges of her expression, but she was doing a better job of hiding them now.

I screwed up my face, pretending to think it over. My darkness pulsed again, as if to compliment me on my amazing acting skills.

"All right," I finally said. "I'll do it. You were right the first time—this is for the greater good. It's the impossible choice that needs to be made."

"Lovely," Shasta smarmed, clapping her hands together. "I knew you'd see the light, Beatrice. When it comes down to it, you and I are very much the same. We recognize what needs to be done, even if it seems unpleasant. And we're always willing to do it."

"Yup, that's us—peas in a pod," I said, giving her a big, toothy grin.

She mirrored my grin, totally unaware that I'd just lied to her fucking face.

CHAPTER TWENTY-NINE

"I CAN BEAT Shasta."

"Well, hello to you too!" Leah sang out, looking up from her perch behind the front counter at It's Lit. Pancake raised his head too, his expression unimpressed as usual. "I must say, Bebe, I'm very into this confident superheroine swagger you've got going on!"

"Thank you!" I bustled up to the counter. "Wait. How much do you remember about my time-traveling adventures so far? Because it seems like whenever the timeline changes or gets reset, you sort of get reset with it? Like, you still don't recall Sam being missing, correct?"

"No," she said, her eyebrows drawing together. "But I remember us talking about time travel, me becoming your constant, you experimenting with aiming yourself, the talismans . . ." She shook her head, as if trying to clear the cobwebs. "It's weird, Bebe, it's all a little fuzzy? And the harder I try to remember, the fuzzier it gets. But of course I remember evil-ass Shasta and the gingerbread-house competition and how she was trying to get you to sacrifice . . ." Her brow furrowed further. "Vivi? The baby? Why does Shasta want some random baby?"

"Because she's not a random baby," I said. "But listen, this current timeline's not right either, Lee—someone else important is missing, and I have to fix it. And I think I've sort of figured out how. Well, pieces of it, anyway."

I studied her for a moment, trying to commit everything

about her to memory. Those expressive dark eyes, the easy smile that lit up her whole face. That sweet, open way she had of accepting people immediately and making them feel like they'd known her forever. And of course her loyal puppy sidekick and his disgruntled visage, a constant contrast to her sunny demeanor.

After today, I might never see Leah—or Pancake—again. But I wasn't going to tell her that part.

No, I was simply going to talk through some of the other puzzle pieces that seemed to be coming together in my mind, get her very necessary take on my most recent theorizing. Through all of this, Leah had been my constant—and hopefully my final parting gift would show her how much I appreciated her. I'd made a very special stop on the way to It's Lit to ensure that everything was squared away.

"Bebe, are you okay?" Leah queried, scrunching her nose up. "You look a little misty. I know you always get sentimental around the holidays—"

"I really do," I laughed, swiping a hand over my teary eyes. "Sorry, just having a lot of feelings—from multiple timelines. Let me get to the supernatural hypothesizing bit."

I paused, trying to mentally organize what I wanted to say. I thought back to my conversation with Shasta-Dahlia, how certain things she'd said had stuck out to me and pinned themselves to my very own mental posterboard—I could see connections forming in my mind, glittery pieces of information sparking together.

And my darkness had pushed me to *really* see it.

"Here's the main thing," I began. "I'm pretty sure that asshole Shasta flat-out lied to me about a shit-ton of stuff. And I don't know why I just believed her, except that I guess I've gotten a little *too* good at thinking I'm a natural destroyer of everything and everyone around me—the forever problem child."

"Oh, Bebe," Leah murmured. "I wish you could see yourself the way I do."

"That's the thing, Lee!" I exclaimed. "I think maybe I finally *do* see myself that way. Shasta kept saying all this stuff to me that I've always said about *myself*—that I'm irresponsible and disaster-prone and fucking up is my real superpower. And this time . . ." I shook my head in wonder. "This time, I just couldn't believe any of it. All these words were spewing out of her smug little mouth, and for once, I *knew* they weren't true!"

"So you had a momentous and triumphant revelation about your existential crisis while conversing with a supervillain?!" Leah shrieked. "Of course you did—only you, Bebe."

Pancake nudged my hand, as if encouraging me to continue my epic monologue—but really, he was annoyed I'd been standing here for several minutes without petting him. I obliged, scritching him behind the ears.

"During our first little chat about all this—the one at the gingerbread contest—Shasta kept talking rapturously about my power and all these cool, fascinating, thoroughly unpredictable elements the Otherworld darkness was adding to it," I mused. "She called me the freaking Chosen One! But then today, she said my power was 'erratic' and 'unhinged' and seemed to imply that it was part of what makes me such a hapless fuck-up. And she got all, like, fumbly about it. I could see in her eyes that she was trying to cover something up. She wanted me to think less of my power, when actually, it's becoming so much more!"

"Ah, classic manipulator and abuser technique," Leah hissed. "Love bomb, then undermine."

"And when it's a supervillain doing the love-bombing, there's an extra element to the manipulation. Like, if it's a supervillain calling me the Chosen One, well—that's not exactly going to make me feel good about myself. It only confirms all the bad shit I already believe."

"Which was that you were on the villain path as well," Leah murmured.

"And maybe that made me more inclined to believe everything else she said. Or to just, like . . . accept it."

"She made you feel bad so she could control you!" Leah cried, her eyes narrowing in indignation.

"And she has been trying to control me," I said, scritching Pancake's ears more aggressively. He leaned into it. "She admitted she tried to possess me the way she has other humans during this most recent battle on the beach—well, she admitted it after I totally guessed what was going on. But here's the thing: I think she's actually tried to possess me before. I know I've felt that exact same mental shove sensation, that invisible wall slamming down in my brain! It happened the very first time I faced the big kaiju—I thought it *was* the kaiju, trying to fight me. And Shasta didn't get very far because I went time traveling."

"Whoa, so is this another layer of her evil plan?!" Leah said.

"It's a layer she can't get to work," I said, my brain hooking into the hypothesis. "Because think about it: if she could successfully mind-control me, couldn't she just take over my brain and use me to steal Vivi on the beach? She wouldn't need me to agree or be part of her plan. But she can't get in here." I tapped my temple. "And I think at least some of that is because of that new darkness merging with my power. She got *extra* fumbly when she was talking about that!"

"She's scared of what you can do," Leah said, nodding emphatically. "And she wants you to feel bad and wrong about your power so you won't use it—so *you'll* be scared of it, too!"

"Exactly!" I shrieked, pumping my fist. Pancake shot me a disapproving look—probably because fist-pumping meant I wasn't petting him anymore. "And listen, that's a great, extra evil manipulation tactic to use with me, because like I said, that *is* how I've felt in the past. But when she was going on and on about how destructive I supposedly am . . . ." A small smile played around the corners of my mouth. "I couldn't help but think about all the things I've done on these time-travel adventures, and all the things people I love so much have said to me along the way. Like Doc Kai telling me how much she loves the way I science. Or how Pika told me we both have these bright lights, and we can't let anyone take that away from us. Or Nate saying how much he and the whole team miss me—oh, Lee, in the correct version of the timeline, Nate's my brother-in-law and he's married to Evie, my older sister. Evie's the person who's missing!"

"Holy shit, Bebe!" Leah gasped. "Missing a whole sister?! I'm so sorry!"

"I'll get her back—I know I will," I said fiercely. Pancake let out a little whine of agreement.

"I have no doubt. And y'know, Bebe, I'd just like to point out that ever since the whole Mom-Demon drama, you haven't even used your power in a mundane sort of way to get what you want, when it would in fact be very easy for you to do so."

"What do you mean?"

"Like . . ." Leah scrunched up her nose again, thinking it through. "Remember when you and Sam broke up and you wanted to get back together? You could have just mind-controlled him into being with you. Or with Terrence and Olivia—"

"Oh god, I still dated them?!" I lamented.

"I think you were trying to make Sammy jealous," Leah said. "But in any case, you could have also just supernaturally compelled them to go away, and you didn't—even though they were really fucking annoying!"

"So annoying. But . . . wow. I guess you're right." I leaned against the counter, turning that over in my mind. "Shasta and I currently have similar elements to our powers," I said slowly. "Because she's totally mind-controlling people with this whole possession thing. And she talked about how alike we are. We're not, are we?"

"Not even a little bit," Leah said. "Remember Ms.

Marvel: 'Good is not a thing you are. It's a thing you *do*.' And y'know what? Same thing with evil." She looked at me intently, her gaze going super serious. "Your power isn't inherently evil, Bebe—it never has been. It's all about how you use it."

"Well, now I'm gonna try to use it for the most heroic good that I can!" I declared, drawing myself up tall. My darkness pulsed in agreement. "I need to get back to that battle on the beach again, Lee. Because here's another thing Shasta lied to me about—my connection with her kaiju. From the start, I've been able to sense their emotions, hear their thoughts. And when I connected to the big kaiju this last time, I felt like we were really starting to communicate! There was an extra bit of connection, beyond us simply projecting at each other. There were things it wanted to tell me, and the kaiju seemed grateful to link up—it was starting to calm down and mellow out, even. But Shasta said the opposite, that my projection made the kaiju more violent and angry. I *know* what I felt. And I know that's not true."

"I'm liking where this is going," Leah said, nodding thoughtfully. Pancake lifted his head and studied me in an equally thoughtful way. "Do you know how to get back to the beach for sure? Did you ever figure out how to aim yourself on the timeline?"

"I think the talisman and the visualization are important components," I said, my eyes going to the ceiling as I thought it through. "But something Shasta said also gave me a clue about what I believe might be the very last component I need . . ."

I struck an exaggerated pose, sweeping my arms out, and paused for just a little longer than necessary—yes, I was totally milking the drama.

Because that's who I am, dammit.

"My feelings!" I proclaimed, giving one more expansive arm sweep. "Shasta was blathering on about how big and messy my feelings are, and I realized . . ." I paused, turning

the thought over in my head. "Every time I've time traveled, it's right after getting hit by a really gigantic, overwhelming emotion! I was consumed with sadness over me and Sam when I hopped to the week of my family's visit. I was terrified and drowning during the battle on the beach. And then wildly frustrated when I traveled to that Maui Christmas, freaked out and slightly elated when Sam's mom showed up at the family Christmas party, terrified again when I ended up back at the beach . . ."

"So you need to trigger a really big feeling?" Leah queried. "I can't help but think that for you, that won't be terribly hard."

"Excuse me, what are you saying?" I teased, sticking my tongue out at her and affecting a faux-indignant pose. "But no, seriously—I think it's a combo of all those things? So I'll hold my talisman, I'll visualize the beach moment, and I'll feel something *huge*. And once I get back to the beach, I can beat Shasta in whatever mental games she wants to play, successfully communicate with the kaiju—and I believe I can finally change things."

I cut myself off, my cheeks getting hot. This was where I couldn't tell her everything. Because I knew she'd only try to stop me.

"And you'll use the darkness!" Leah crowed. Luckily, she wasn't picking up on my sudden weirdness. "'Cause that's gonna give you an extra power boost against Shasta."

"Not just use it—I'm going to *embrace* it," I said. "All this time, I've been shoving it down, trying to get it to go away. Hell, I've tried to get my whole power to go away. But there was this moment during all my time-travel adventures where I just, like . . . felt it. Accepted it as part of me, and . . ." I trailed off, my eyes filling with tears as the memory flashed through me. Pancake whuffled inquisitively. "I traveled to this other moment, Lee, and you probably won't remember this since my sister got erased from the timeline. But I helped deliver her baby—that's Vivi. Oh yeah, Vivi's actually my niece!"

"The surprises, they just keep coming!" Leah exclaimed, index finger swooping through the air.

"I used my power in that moment," I continued. "Evie actually asked me to use it. She *needed* me. I felt that Otherworld darkness melding with my power, and it didn't just feel good—it felt so *right*, Lee. Like the glittery goth rainbow disco ball I've always wanted to be. The *hero* I've always wanted to be. And . . ." I swallowed hard, visions of Evie's face floating through my brain. But this time, that pale, pinched look morphed into a different memory, her looking at me as she had during her fashion emergency—grateful and moved and like she was no longer trapped in the painful prison of that one moment in time. "I helped my sister. For the first time in my life, I was the strong one for her. I thought I wasn't supposed to be there, I thought I was totally messing up the timeline . . . but I actually made things better for her, in that moment."

I thought back to what Doc Kai had said about time travel, how all of our choices became part of our path, an undeniable piece of our story. That's how I felt about Evie's birth moment—it was a crucial piece of my story now, and I couldn't imagine a life where I'd never experienced it.

"Sounds like your sister really trusted you," Leah murmured.

"She did! And maybe I'm finally learning how to trust myself, too. Like I don't have to be afraid of my power and everything it can do. I think . . ." I frowned, long-past memories surfacing. "When I was dealing with all that stuff with Mom-Demon, I guess I drew the conclusion that anything that felt good was automatically *bad*. And that the only way for me to grow up was to be as boring and basic and *blending in* as possible."

"And now . . . ?"

I ruffled Pancake's ears. "Now I'm ready to be the glittery goth rainbow disco ball of my motherfucking dreams!"

"*Yes!*" Leah crowed, jumping up and down. "This glorious self-actualization is *happening* and you have so reclaimed your essential Bebe-ness! Oh wait—I have something for you. Something that might help with your latest mission! Stay right there!"

I leaned against the counter as she scurried into the book-store's back room, stroking Pancake's fur.

"Your mom is kind of the most wonderful person I know," I said to him, my voice very soft. "Take care of her, okay?"

Pancake let out a concerned little yip, flicking his ears at me inquisitively.

"It'll all be okay, buddy," I promised. "You'll get a happily ever after, too—I'm gonna make sure of it."

"Here it is!" Leah declared, emerging from the back room and triumphantly waving a very battered book around.

With great fanfare, she presented it to me. It was a copy of our favorite dragon-shifter lady book, the one we'd bonded over in the first place. This was the treasured, much-loved ancient copy that my mom had given to me when I was younger—I'd gifted it to Leah right before I left for Maui, telling her I didn't want her to forget about me.

"This is yours now, though!" I exclaimed. "It was a gift—"

"A gift that belongs to both of us," Leah insisted, pressing the book more firmly into my hands. "It's like *Sisterhood of the Traveling Pants*, it should live with whoever needs it most at the moment. And I thought, Bebe, that this could be an-other talisman. I know you've got other things you've picked up along the way, but . . ." She shrugged, a knowing smile spreading across her face. "You're so extra, you definitely need all the talismans you can get!"

"Thank you," I whispered, tears falling freely down my cheeks. "I'm gonna talisman so hard. Oh, and Lee, I have something for you, too—an early Christmas present."

I dug around in my dress pocket, pulled out a folded-up piece of paper, and passed it over to her. She started to read the words inscribed on the paper, her expression morphing from quizzical to downright confused to pure disbelief.

"Bebe . . ." she whispered. "Is this . . . ?"

"It is. An official letter from Charlotte, declaring her intent to sell you the store—I talked to her earlier today, before I came over here. It's Lit is finally yours."

"Oh . . ." Leah's eyes filled with tears as she studied the document I'd handed her. "How?"

"I was very convincing," I said, waving a hand. "Um, convincing without using mind control, I promise. There may have been an all-new posterboard involved. To be honest, I think I motormouthed so much and for so long, she gave in due to sheer exhaustion."

"Bebe . . ." Leah swept me into a bear hug. "I don't know what to say."

"You deserve your dream," I managed, my voice choked with sobs. "Go live it, okay? Live it as hard as you can."

"Thank you," she said fervently. "I'm gonna paint that mural on the wall as soon as I can—with those mermaids who look like us!"

"It will be beautiful," I said. "And thank *you*. You're the best friend I've ever had. And you *always* believed in me. Even when I—"

"Kidnapped my girlfriend and tried to drag her to an evil demon prison dimension?" Leah filled in, a snorty giggle piercing her sobs. "Yes, I know. Can we just put that one behind us, finally? I'm over it—you should be too!"

"Deal," I whispered, hugging her even harder.

We stood there for a moment, me holding her as tightly as I could. I was painfully aware that this might be the last time I ever got to do that.

Because here was the part I couldn't tell her, the piece of my plan I wasn't going to reveal to anyone. Yes, I was going to go back to the beach. Yes, I was going to fend off Shasta and connect with the kaiju. And in the version I'd described to Leah . . . well, after that, I'd been purposefully vague.

But there was something else Shasta had said that stuck in my brain—the prophecy.

The child born of two worlds will wield unique power and heal all wounds.

Yes, that could be Vivi.

But it could also be *me*, couldn't it?

While I was not *quite* "born of two worlds," I did have the whole biracial thing going on, and that's a stereotype everyone just loves applying to mixed-race people. But perhaps more importantly, Shasta had mentioned that Vivi had "some of the Otherworld in her."

Well, so did I.

The big kaiju had told me to look at the prophecy differently. Perhaps this was what it had meant.

Because, look: when I'd been trying to put a plan together, I always got to a point where there was a big question mark. Say I managed to deflect Shasta's advances and sweet-talk the kaiju into *not* sucking any humans into its gaping maw. That still left a huge piece of things unresolved. The kaiju had assured me the prophecy was real—and that meant the second part needed to be satisfied.

But only once the destroyer has been fed and fulfilled, after which this evil shall vanish.

If the big kaiju wasn't "fed and fulfilled," it might go back to attacking everyone once I broke our connection. And what about all of the portals, all of the demons that were still getting through to our world, and Shasta's dogged determination to claim her granddaughter? None of this would ever end. Not unless I did something about it.

So that was the *other* part of my plan. I was going to connect with the kaiju—and then I wasn't simply going to sweet-talk it, I was going to convince it to take *me*, just as it had taken Sam and Evie. Just as Shasta wanted it to take Vivi. I was going to tell it about how I fit the prophecy so perfectly, how *I* was the thing it needed. And I wasn't going to try to mind-control it—I was going to use my darkness to project all those calming feelings and give it a safe space of sorts. I was going to strengthen our connection as much as

I could, so the kaiju could see this was the best course of action.

Of course, there were still things I didn't know, variables I wasn't sure how to account for. Like what *other* lies had Shasta told me? I was trying to sift through all the information, see what made sense with the data I'd collected throughout my time-travel adventures.

And okay, I was also doing a little of the "try the most outrageous thing you can think of" mode of experimentation I'd once pitched to Nate.

If my various hypotheses were correct, the kaiju would disappear from the beach, sated, the prophecy fulfilled. I would vanish from the timeline. And before we did any of that, I'd ask the kaiju to please, for the love of god, boot Shasta's sorry ass back to the Otherworld for good. That would certainly fit with the "evil shall vanish" part of the prophecy.

I didn't know what would happen to me after I went through the portal. Sure, everyone would forget I'd ever existed, but would my darkness ensure that I survived, that I ended up back in the Otherworld, as Vivi would have? Or would I simply cease to exist like Sam and Evie?

I didn't know. But I was sure that Shasta was right about at least one thing: happily ever after always requires sacrifice. That's what I'd learned, time and time again, from both completely made-up stories and my own real life.

I'd watched Evie worry about and take care of everyone, even when she was suffering the most. I'd watched Aveda throw her body in front of our family more times than I could count. I'd heard Nate insist that he'd give his own life before losing the woman he loved.

And now, I was ready to make *my* impossible choice—just like Thomas in *A Kaiju for Christmas*. I would sacrifice myself, so everyone I loved could get their happy endings.

I was finally feeling like a hero. And that's what heroes do.

I hugged Leah more tightly, allowing myself to luxuriate in the gentle, soothing atmosphere of It's Lit. This place that kept me cradled and sheltered and safe. I savored my last moment with her, my best friend in the whole world, the person who always made me feel seen.

And I tried not to think too much about how being a hero hurt like hell.

CHAPTER THIRTY

THIS WAS MY last Christmas forever. And there was someone I desperately wanted to spend it with. I'd wanted to run
to him even *before* I'd known it would be my last Christmas,
as soon as Leah had revealed he existed again in the world.

Sam. My Grinch of an ex-boyfriend who hated Christmas
down to the depths of his very soul.

My desire wasn't entirely selfish, I reasoned. After all,
wasn't Sam also the most likely person to produce a big, giant emotion in me, thereby sending my ass back through
time?

And okay—if this *was* my last Christmas, I also just really
wanted to enjoy it. Even if he acted like a Grinch, I needed
to spend the limited time I had left on Earth memorizing as
much of him as possible.

I of course hadn't told Leah that this was my last Christmas, but I had explained I was going to track Sam down in
an attempt to trigger the big feeling I needed. And that yeah,
I was kind of dying to see him after living in a timeline where
he wasn't there.

"You go, Bebe!" she'd said, waving Pancake's paw at me
encouragingly. "Live out all your holiday rom-com dreams!"

After I left It's Lit, I aimed myself toward Sam's parents'
place, remembering that Leah had told me he'd moved in
there full-time.

The Fujikawas still lived in the same ground-level apartment Sam had grown up in, a modest two-bedroom that contained every possession and scrap of ephemera his parents

had ever owned. The refrigerator was covered with drawings and art projects all three Fujikawa children had crafted throughout elementary school. I always wondered if they'd melded to the fridge door over the years, that thick, uneven layer of scraggly paper becoming one with the stalwart kitchen appliance. I knew Alex and Emily kept pushing for their parents to move to a "better" place and had even offered to pay for it, but Mr. and Mrs. Fujikawa always demurred. Sam had noted on more than one occasion that it would mean way more to his parents if his siblings simply visited for Christmas instead of trying to show off all their accomplishments by buying a big, fancy house they would never actually set foot in.

My heartbeat sped up as I approached the Fujikawa residence. The apartment was on the lower level of an old Victorian similar to the one where my family lived. But this Victorian had been split into several separate apartments; one of the residents on the upper level actually had to walk through the Fujikawa apartment to get to their place, since the main entrance led directly into Sam's parents' living room.

I bolted up the front steps, then paused when I reached the door, rocking back on my heels. A sliver of doubt pierced my urgent need to see Sam. According to Leah, we were still very much broken up and hadn't really talked or interacted since the beach. Would he be angry at me for showing up out of the blue? Would his mother greet me coldly? Would—

My spiral was interrupted by the door flying open, Mrs. Fujikawa staring back at me with a gigantic smile.

"Bea-chan!" she exclaimed. "You are here!"

Then she swept me into an enormous bear hug.

"Oof!" I blurted. Her tiny form was surprisingly strong, the iron grip of her arms squeezing the breath out of me.

"*Sam!*" She bellowed. "Your girlfriend is here! Isn't that nice?"

"Um," I said.

Girlfriend?!

Before I could process that, he was in front of me and all thoughts fell right out of my head.

"Bea?" he began, his face a mask of confusion.

I launched myself at him, flinging my arms around his neck and burying my face against his chest. I breathed in his familiar scent, luxuriating in the completely wonderful feel of his worn cotton t-shirt rubbing against my cheek. Tears pricked my eyes, and for a moment, I just let myself revel in the feeling of him, the warmth of his body against mine. His presence, his vibrance. His *life*.

"Hey," he murmured, resting a tentative hand on my back. "You okay?"

I pulled back, swiping at my eyes. Of course this was all weird to him, since the last time he'd seen me, we'd probably been fighting.

"I am," I managed, my voice a minuscule squeak. "I am right now, anyway."

"Sammy-chan, why did you not tell us that your girlfriend was coming over?" Mrs. Fujikawa scolded.

"Um," I said again. I'd gotten so swept up in the miracle of Sam's existence, I'd forgotten that his mom apparently thought I was still his girlfriend? Was this Asian Mom denial? (Which I'd heard a lot about from Aveda, but had never actually experienced myself. I wondered how closely Evie would hew to ultimate Asian Mom-ness—once I restored her to the timeline.)

"Yeah, Mom," Sam said, spending an inordinate amount of time on each syllable. "I forgot to tell you Bea would be stopping by."

Huh. So not Asian Mom denial, then.

"I have raised you better than that," his mother said, patting him on the arm. "But this is a great thing, ne? Since Emily and Alex cannot join us for the holidays this year, we have plenty of food!"

"I don't think Bea's staying," Sam said hastily, his gaze meeting mine. It looked like he was trying to send me some sort of complicated telepathic message, but since I didn't know what all he and Past Bea had last discussed, I had no idea what he might be trying to tell me.

And honestly, even if I had? I probably still would've done what I did next.

"I am so totally staying!" I sang out, pasting a big, cheesy smile on my face. "I can think of *nothing* I'd rather do right now!" I linked my arm through Sam's and followed his mom as she bustled into the house, muttering to herself about place settings and whether she needed to pop out to the market for more mochi-making supplies.

"Hatsu!" Mrs. Fujikawa chirped at Sam's dad. "Look who is here!"

"Ah, Bea-chan, joining us for Christmas Eve dinner after all!" Mr. Fujikawa enthused, jumping up from his threadbare pea-green recliner. "I hope you brought your biggest appetite!"

"Of course I did," I responded, returning his jovial grin. "And wow, I love all your decorations!"

The Fujikawa living room looked like Santa's Village had thrown up all over it. Garlands were festooned everywhere, from floor to ceiling. Decorative wreaths were affixed to every available surface. A Christmas tree that was just a little too tall for the space stubbornly pushed its way into the ceiling, the sparkly star at the top sparkling extra hard to compensate.

It was perfect. The exact right setting for my last Christmas.

"Finally, someone who appreciates the holidays!" Mrs. Fujikawa crowed, slapping me on the arm. "I'll get out the extra leaf for the dining table!"

"Oh, I can just squeeze in," I protested, eyeing the table positioned to the left of the too-tall tree. It looked like there was plenty of room for four people.

"It's not for you, it's so she can put out all the holiday treats she got at Trader Joe's," Sam muttered. "You are merely providing an excuse for her to go full Christmas."

"I knew I should have gotten *four* boxes of the special Joe-Joe's!" Mrs. Fujikawa declared, stabbing an index finger in the air. "Every cookie is enrobed in chocolate, ne? Extra festive!"

"Ooh, I love those!" I exclaimed, clapping my hands together. "You know the hack, right? Where you take 'em all apart and then mix up the different cookie pieces so you have infinite flavors—"

"Bea, come with me for a minute," Sam interjected, reaching out to cradle my elbow. Warmth from his palm seeped through my cardigan and spread across my skin. "I want to show you something."

I allowed him to guide me out of the living room and down the hall to his bedroom, the sound of his mom chattering on about Joe-Joe's and all the other things she needed to pick up for dinner wafting behind us.

Sam's bedroom was the one he'd shared with Alex when they were kids. Once Alex left for college, Sam had claimed sole ownership. And even after he'd moved out, his room had stayed his—the perks of being the favorite child. I saw signs of his adult life mixing with markers of the past: the mechanic's coveralls draped over the chair in the corner contrasting with a stack of old textbooks and a small collection of beat-up toy robots perched on the dresser.

"What did you want to show me?" I said, unable to squash the flirty tone that crept into my voice. "And how did neither of your parents object to that embarrassingly transparent line?"

"So obviously I kind of, sort of didn't tell them we broke up," Sam said, his eyes shifting to the side.

"And why didn't you do that?" I demanded, swerving easily into mild indignation. I sat down on the bed and crossed my arms over my chest. "How long were you planning on continuing this charade—was there going to be a whole fake wedding with a thoroughly unconvincing Bea Tanaka cut-out?"

"I . . . I don't know," he sputtered, sitting down next to me.

His broad shoulders slumped as he scraped a hand over his face. "I guess I didn't want them to see me failing—again. They were so happy when we started dating. They thought me being serious about someone meant I was finally settling down and becoming respectable or something. Especially since that someone was as wonderful as you."

My face flushed, and I stared down at his basic blue bed-spread, picking at a loose thread on the corner.

"You're their favorite," I finally said. "Always. It doesn't matter how many fancy degrees Emily and Alex have be-tween them—you're the one they love the most."

"I'm the one they feel like they have to take care of the most," he corrected. "Because I don't have Emily or Alex's skills or ambition or . . . whatever it is that makes them inca-pable of visiting. What I do have is a long list of under-achiever fuck-ups to my name, despite scoring astronomically higher than either of them on the math section of the SAT."

"You're taking care of your parents now, though," I said, fiddling with the loose thread. "You're the one who stayed."

He laughed, but there was no humor behind it.

"Bea. Why did you come here? After Maui, I thought we agreed we needed to stay away from each other."

"What happened to us in Maui?" I blurted out before I could stop myself. "It was all so chaotic, my memory of that time is a little . . . fuzzy. Like, I know there was the big battle with the kaiju—"

"Which I missed, since you ordered me to stay in that beach shack," Sam said, his expression turning grim. "Which then led to us getting into another huge fucking fight because you apparently thought it was okay to approach a gigantic monster without warning anyone first—"

"I decided that *in the moment*," I retorted. "Which is what superheroing is all about sometimes, you have to be ready to self-sacrifice! If it's down to me or the world, Sam, I gotta choose the world every time."

"I wouldn't," he growled, his voice unnervingly forceful. "I'd choose you."

You already did, I couldn't help but think. *And it was the wrong choice then, too.*

I looked up from the loose thread I'd been pulling at and met his dark gaze. There was a storm brewing in his eyes, so intense I couldn't look away. Heat licked up my spine, making the back of my neck burn.

God, why was this so impossible? Why couldn't we have each other? Why did superheroing require so much damn sacrifice?

I'd made my decision, yes. And I'd certainly felt all noble and selfless in the moment. But now that I was getting to see him again, to bask in the mundanity of slight shifts in his expression, to study every single one of his features until I'd committed them to memory . . .

A prickle of irritation ran over my skin. There were parts of being a hero that definitely sucked.

But no matter how much I wanted to be with him, I still had to choose the world. Fate had decided a long time ago that I wasn't built for a happily ever after. The least I could do was make sure everyone else got one.

"To answer your original question: I came here because I don't think I'm going to be able to return to, ah, San Francisco for a very long time," I said, the words triggering bitter memories of him saying something similar to me the past Christmas. "I'm going back to Maui soon, and that's where I'll be for the foreseeable future." I slid my hand across the covers, brushing my pinkie against his. "I know this is silly, but I miss you so much . . ." My throat thickened, and I hastily cleared it. "Can you give me one day? Where we pretend like we're *us* again. No bad feelings, no complications—a last perfect memory before I have to go away."

My gaze went back to the bedspread, my heart fluttering as rapidly as butterfly wings. I felt so exposed, so *raw*. What if he said no? I'd have to go into my big heroic sacrificial moment carrying the sting of rejection and regret, which would definitely not put me in the right headspace to take on Shasta and converse with a kaiju.

"Bea." His pinkie brushed against mine again. He paused for another long beat of silence, our fingertips tangling uncertainly. "Is this perfect day going to involve extremely Christmassy activities designed to convince me that I need to reject my Grinch side and embrace the 'fa-la-la-la-las' unironically?"

"What?!" I slapped his hand away, choking out a surprised laugh.

"I'm just saying, I'm pretty sure that's the plot of one of your movies," he shot back, warm amusement creeping into his voice.

"It's the plot of several of them, to be fair," I huffed, straightening my spine and giving him a look. This felt better—the teasing, the needling, the jostling to one-up each other. "But no, I'm not trying to Christmas-entrap you. I want both of us to enjoy ourselves. And anyway, we already have another very popular trope going."

"Which is?"

"You want us to pretend we're still dating, because of your parents!" I crowed triumphantly. "Which, by the way, was a scenario you totally mocked when I asked you to do it for me back in Maui."

"Oh, right." One side of his mouth tipped into a rueful grin. "So I guess we might have to pretend to kiss again."

"Count on it." I cocked a challenging eyebrow. "In fact—"

"Hey, kids!" Mrs. Fujikawa burst into the room, her eyes lit with excitement. No knock, of course. "I just had the best idea, ne? The city opened one of those temporary ice rinks next to the Trader Joe's! What do you think about—"

"Ice skating?!" I shrieked, leaping to my feet. "Ooh, and I bet they have one of those snack stands with roasted chestnuts and hot chocolate, although that's only a plus if they don't put a cap on how many marshmallows you can add—"

"Yes!" Mrs. Fujikawa cried, pumping a fist in the air. "See, Sammy, Bea-chan gets it! Bundle up, kids—and then we can stop for the chocolate-enrobed Joe-Joe's afterward!"

I clapped my hands together, my grin stretching so defiantly across my face that my cheeks hurt. This was exactly what I'd wanted. My last Christmas was already shaping up to be amazing.

As Mrs. Fujikawa bustled out of the room, Sam cleared his throat behind me. I turned to see him raising an amused eyebrow.

"I thought you weren't trying to sell me on Christmas," he said.

"I'm not," I claimed, putting my hands on my hips. "But if the natural festive air that comes with gliding across the ice, feeling the cold sting your nose, and then warming up with a hot drink that's mostly sugar sounds so terrible to you—"

"Stop, you've convinced me," he said, not even trying to hide the grin that was spreading across his face. "Fa-la-freakin'-la-la-la."

♨

The temporary ice rink was a spacious rectangle smack-dab in the middle of Union Square, surrounded by the old-fashioned façades of San Francisco's stately department-store buildings—Macy's and Saks and everything in between. A majestic fake "tree" wrapped in glowing lights towered over the proceedings on one side, casting scatters of glittering brightness across the smooth sheet of ice. Another side of the rink was lined with white canopies over bleacher-style seats where people could warm up with hot chocolate after a bout of skating, or simply observe their loved ones falling flat on their asses.

Tourists thronged around the rink, weighed down by piles of shopping bags and ostentatiously wrapped packages, many of them bundled in plush coats trimmed with fake fur and Santa hats tipped with tiny pom-poms. The whole scene evoked the shiny cheese of a postcard-worthy holiday movie, artificial nature jammed into the superficial fanfare of the city's most touristy destination.

I absolutely loved it.

"You know how to skate, Mrs. Fujikawa?" I asked, lacing up my rental skates with gusto.

"Oh, not very well," she demurred, waving a hand. "Emily was the one who loved it, I thought maybe she'd become a little Olympian. But once she got into her teenage years, well . . ." She gave me a smile that seemed a tad forced. "You know how the teenage girls are, ne? Hanging out with Mom was suddenly very uncool!"

"Mom," Sam interjected, tying up his own skates. "Can you not . . ."

My cheeks warmed as I realized he was trying to protect me—because no, I didn't know how teenage girls were in that particular way. I'd been twelve when my mom died; I would have committed several blood sacrifices in order to spend even a second with her again.

But that didn't mean I had *no* idea how teenage girls could be. You know, just in general.

"It's okay," I said quickly. "I do know what you're talking about, Mrs. Fujikawa—I made my sister Evie's life actual hell the moment I turned thirteen. Some would say I'm still doing it! Evie herself would probably say that."

"Sister?" Mrs. Fujikawa's brow furrowed. "I didn't know you had a sister. Sammy-chan, why you never mention this!"

Oh, right. I'd gotten so wrapped up in my perfect last Christmas, I'd forgotten—in this timeline, I was an only child.

"I meant my, um, good friend," I improvised. "I have a friend. Named Evie. Who's like my sister. You've never met her," I added, turning to Sam. "'Cause she lives in, uh, Canada."

"Interesting that you made your sister-friend's life hell all the way from here!" Mrs. Fujikawa exclaimed, getting to her feet and tottering toward the rink. "A true talent, ne? Sammy-chan, you have definitely found your match!"

And then she stepped onto the ice and skated off, cackling all the way.

"Uh, damn," I said, watching as Mrs. Fujikawa swept into

a perfect figure eight. "Forget Emily the supposed Olympian—your mom's a regular Kristi Yamaguchi out there."

"Bea." Sam shook his head at me, a smile crossing his face. "Did you just make up a whole sister so my mom wouldn't feel bad about saying something awkward?"

"Given what I know of Asian Aunties, I don't think 'saying something awkward' is gonna be the benchmark for making her feel bad. But sure, if that's how you want to interpret it."

"Evie," he said, rolling the word around his mouth. I tried not to flinch. "That's a nice name."

My heart clenched. "Yeah, it is."

I brushed away the image of her face as it floated through my mind, those springy curls that could never be tamed bouncing around her sweet freckled face. Soon our positions would be reversed—she'd be vibrant and alive again, and I'd cease to exist. At least she'd be spared the pain of remembering me.

"Let's get on the ice," I said, my voice overly jovial. I grabbed Sam's hand and pulled him to his feet, dragging him toward the rink. He was wobbly on the skates, struggling to maintain balance, but I used my own momentum to propel us along. When we reached the entry point, I glided on, pleased to see that my body still remembered how to balance itself.

Behind me, I heard an epic *splat*.

"Ahhhh, Sammy-chan!" Sam's mom let out a hearty laugh as she skated by his prone form. "Barely make it onto the ice before falling on your ass! Need to practice, ne? Look at Bea!"

I skated up to Sam, biting the inside of my cheek to keep from laughing. Sam's mom had already skated off like the pro she was, and I saw his dad gliding over to meet her. Mr. Fujikawa wasn't quite as good as his wife, but he was definitely no slouch. When he reached her side, he grabbed her hand, and they sailed over the ice together. They looked like a greeting card.

"Let me guess," I said, crouching down next to Sam. "Your total distaste for all things Christmas means you've never actually ice skated before, but you figured it 'looked easy,' and since you're so in shape, you'd be able to pick it up right away."

"Please don't tell me we're awarding points for reading the other person for absolute filth," Sam groaned, easing himself up on one elbow. "Because then I would have to admit you just won forever."

"Nah, I'll give you this one," I said, extending my mittened hand. "You look too adorable and pathetic right now for me to do anything else."

He allowed me to haul him up and ease us over to the side of the rink, where he could hold on to the railing.

"Maybe I finally understand why Emily gave this up," he said, wincing as his feet stuttered forward. "Ice is very hard. And very cold."

"And yet, so magical," I insisted, sweeping an expansive arm out. "Close your eyes, feel that cold on your face, hear the sounds of the ice scraping beneath you, and smell that delicious pine needle and hot chocolate scent—"

"Which has to be artificially piped in because that tree is fake and the hot chocolate stand is way over there," Sam countered, jerking his chin toward the other end of the rink.

"It's all about the experience!" I protested, swatting him on the arm. "You need to turn your Grinch levels down to, like, minus a hundred."

"I'm here, aren't I?" He shot me an overly aggrieved look as he struggled to maintain his death grip on the edge of the rink.

"And look how happy your mom is," I said, nodding toward the far end of the ice, where Mrs. Fujikawa was executing yet another flawless figure eight as her husband watched in admiration. Her cheeks were flushed, her smile so big I could see it all the way across the rink. "She's about to Tiger Mom you into fulfilling all her Olympic dreams."

"Good luck to her," Sam chuckled. One of his hands

slipped from the edge of the rink, and he nearly landed on his ass again. "I don't think I'm medal material. It'll be a miracle if I can actually let go of the edge before it's time to leave."

"You're doing fine." I slowed my skating so I could stay beside him as he fumbled along.

"Is this your idea of a perfect day?" he joked, valiantly trying to maintain his balance. "My mom kinda hijacked whatever you had planned."

"I wouldn't have picked anything else," I said truthfully.

We traversed the ice in companionable silence, and I turned my face up to the sky, the biting cold air kissing my forehead. California cold was nowhere near *actual* cold, but San Francisco's brisk December temperatures coupled with the chill of the ice was enough to make me feel like I'd traveled to the North Pole.

I closed my eyes and tried to live in this moment—where everything was soft and festive and beautiful. Where I didn't have to think about the next day or the next hour or even the next second, and all the heroic sacrifices I'd need to make in the very near future. I could just be here in this idyllic setting with someone I loved.

And then something damp brushed my cheek.

I let out a little squeak, my eyes flying open to see delicate bits of white drifting from the sky.

"Snow?!" I shrieked, a gleeful smile spreading over my face. "For real?"

"Soap flakes!" Mr. Fujikawa called out as he skated up next to us. "They do this every hour, on the hour. Gives the skating rink that true Christmas feeling."

"Oh my god!" I bellowed, twirling around with my arms outstretched, delighting in the fluff dotting the sleeves of my sweater and melting into the threads of my mittens.

I twirled some more, my hair flying around me like a tornado. Laughter bubbled up in my chest, a giddy sensation I hadn't experienced in what felt like forever.

What is time? Especially when you're time traveling.

"Sam, look!" I cried. "Even you can't Grinch your way out of loving this!"

I slowed my twirl and brought myself to a gentle stop, arms still stretched out at my sides—and was surprised to feel someone take my mittened hand. My eyes popped open and I turned to see Sam, who had managed to wobble his way up next to me. He stood very still as he clasped my hand, so as not to upset his precarious balance.

"You're right," he said softly, his eyes meeting mine. "I can't. Consider the Grinch reformed."

My mouth was suddenly very dry as my gaze roamed his face, searching for sarcasm or teasing. But there was none of that; he was looking at me with deep and earnest sincerity. It was the kind of look that always ended me, because it meant he wasn't afraid to be completely vulnerable. To show his whole self, because he wanted me to know just how much he loved me.

At least, that's what that look used to mean.

The fake snow swirled around us, that hot chocolate and pine needle scent wafting in from the sidelines. It was the kind of magical moment that always popped up in Christmas movies, when our two devastatingly attractive leads are just about to kiss. My heart pumped against my breastbone, threatening to drown out the sound of holiday carols.

Sam reached over and brushed a wild lock of dark hair off of my face, his fingertips lingering just a touch longer than necessary against my cheek.

"I still miss all those colors in your hair," he murmured.

"Sam," I whispered. "I—"

"Watch out, kids, Mama's incoming!" a loud voice bleated behind me.

And then, before I knew what was happening, Mrs. Fujikawa was flying between us, grabbing Sam's hand and pulling him along behind her.

"Mom . . . *oof!*" he blurted out, pitching forward and nearly falling on his face.

I skated up behind him and wrapped my arms around his

waist, bracing him from behind as his mother dragged him across the ice.

"See, Sammy-chan, nothing to be frightened of!" she crowed. "Keep moving forward, ne? And watch Bea, her form is excellent!"

"Holy shit . . . I'm gonna die, I'm gonna die, we're all gonna die!" Sam gasped, windmilling the arm that wasn't caught in his mother's grasp.

I stifled a giggle as we careened over the ice, frosty air nipping more decisively at my skin. Wind whistled in my ears and I attempted to make my stance even more solid so Sam and I wouldn't end up toppling backward.

We must have looked completely ridiculous: one very tall, very hot Asian man being towed across the rink by his tiny daredevil mother while his hapless ex-girlfriend fastened herself to his back, trying to provide a modicum of stability. And the fake snow was still falling from the sky, coating us in a layer of fluffy white soap.

"Oh no, I did not calculate this move for three people. Only for one!" Sam's mom bellowed. "Sammy-chan, I have to let go! Try to fall forward so you don't crush Bea!"

"Oh, fu—"

Sam didn't have a chance to get that curse out before the two of us were crashing into the ice, him doing his best to wrap his body around mine.

"What are you doing!" I shrieked. "You're about to absorb the full impact—*ow*!"

We landed hard, him on his back and me on top of him, my hands clamping on to his shoulders. I pushed myself up and glared down at him, our noses inches apart.

"Your mom said to fall *forward*—"

"And then you would have been totally unprotected—"

"I don't need to be protected, *you're* the one who can't skate—"

"And that means you should let go and let me fall—"

"If I'd 'let' you fall, you would have ended up with multiple broken bones . . . oh." I leaned in closer, scanning his face. "Do you have any broken bones? Does anything hurt really bad?"

"Like . . . everything?" he said, wincing. "I may need to call it a day."

"Time for hot chocolate, Sammy-chan!" Sam's mom called out, gliding by us. Her left leg was extended in a perfect arabesque. "The Olympics will have to wait."

And then she skated off through the fake snow, cackling all the way.

"I'll make one single concession about ice skating," Sam said as we snuggled under a big plaid blanket in the bleachers. He lifted his mug of hot chocolate. "This part is pretty okay."

"Told you," I said airily, tossing my hair over my shoulder.

"Question, though: is there any actual hot chocolate under all those marshmallows?" Sam cocked an eyebrow and gestured at my mug, which was indeed topped off with an epic level of marshmallows, their fluffy white cloud formation obscuring the mug's other contents.

"That's the way you're supposed to drink it," I insisted, nibbling on my top layer of marshmallows. "Trust me, I'm an expert."

"That you are," he said, toasting me with his mug.

He leaned back in the bleacher seat, his shoulder brushing mine. Heat seeped into my sweater and raced down my arm, as if to alert me that we were engaging in casual touch. I wanted to snuggle closer, lean my head on his shoulder, close my eyes and exist once again in a perfect moment. I forced myself to train my gaze on his parents, who were still swooping all over the ice.

"Your mom looks great out there," I said, gesturing with my mug. "Seems like she's doing so much better after the fall last year."

"She really went all in on the physical therapy," Sam said, an affectionate smile crossing his lips. "It was like she was determined to be her doctor's best student or something.

And . . ." He trailed off, a shadow passing over his face. "To be honest," he continued slowly, "I may have been a little overworried about my parents. I thought moving in with them was what they wanted, what they needed. But these days, I mostly seem to be in their way."

"Aww, I'm sure they don't see it like that."

"My mom keeps trying to get me out of the house," he said dryly. "A couple weeks ago, she finally ran out of random errands to send me on and started ordering me to go spend more time with 'my beautiful girlfriend.'"

"I can see why you didn't want to tell her we broke up." I preened a little. "Your mom clearly thinks I'm the best thing that ever happened to you."

"Not really an exaggeration," he said with a sardonic chuckle. "But the worst part is not the fact that my own mother needs 'space' from me. It's *why* she needs the space. Which is because she's going through a 'time to rekindle the *romance*' phase with my dad. And I, um, walked in on them."

"Sam!" I shrieked, clapping a hand over my mouth. "Okay, awkward, but it's cute that your parents are still so horny for each other."

"I *know*," he yelped, sounding like a peevish tween. "But then my mom started talking about how we need boundaries, and how she learned about the 'sock on the door' signal from 'the TikTok' and . . ." He shook his head, like he was trying to rid himself of certain images. "I guess when our roles started reversing, I never imagined that I'd be the fuddy-duddy dad who's cramping their style."

"Then why not move back out?" I nibbled at my next layer of marshmallows. "You can still help them, like you were before. But sounds like y'all could stand to have some privacy back. On both sides."

"I . . ." He frowned down at his hot chocolate, as if searching for meaning in its murky dregs. "I get scared for them. It's like, if I can't see them . . . I don't know, I think they must be in danger or struggling, or that they need me. And I'm always trying to make up for Alex and Emily not being here.

I want them to know that I'd never abandon them like that. That I'll *always* be here. That if I just love them enough, maybe it will make up for the kids who *aren't* here."

"Sam." I leaned more decisively into his shoulder and reached a mittened hand over to clasp his. "Your parents know you love them. And whatever happens to them, whatever they might have to face in the future as they get older . . ." I squeezed his hand. "We'll always figure it out, okay? Your siblings suck, but you don't have to go through this stuff alone. You have me and Leah and Pancake, and you can always call Ev—Aveda and the rest of my family if you need to. I know we broke up, but . . ." I swallowed the lump in my throat. "But you'll always be my family. So, especially when it comes to the hard stuff . . ." I squeezed his hand again. "Don't be alone, okay? You don't have to be—ever."

I met his eyes, hoping he could see how much I meant every word. Even if I wouldn't be here after today, even if he wouldn't remember anything I'd said to him . . . it seemed important to say it now. He gazed back at me in that earnest, intense way—I always felt like I could see his entire heart when he looked at me like that. I squirmed as he studied me, looking like he was trying to figure something out.

"Bea," he said softly.

I was suddenly very aware of the warmth seeping from my mug into my mittened hand. The cold air that brushed my cheeks, making them flush. The heat of his shoulder that was still pressed against mine. I shivered as the air between us turned heavy and still, our gazes locked, neither of us willing to break.

I finally took a big swig of hot chocolate, wincing as it scorched my tongue.

"Anyway," I managed, "I'm totally up for spending all my free time with your mom, since she appreciates Christmas—unlike her Grinchy son."

"That she does," Sam said, his tone resetting to something more exasperated, more familiar. "Bea . . ." He hesitated, and I snuck a sidelong glance at him. He looked like he was wrestling with how to say something. "Why do *you* love Christmas so much?" he finally said. "Is it the pageantry? The movies? 'Cause whenever the topic comes up, you go on and on about how you had to play a tree in your school play, but that actually seems like more of a negative memory."

"Right," I said, grinning a little. "I . . . hmm." I bit the inside of my cheek, trying to distract from the ache of my burnt tongue. "I *do* love any excuse to go completely over the top. But I think it's more about . . ." I hesitated, calling up memories from long ago—things I usually tried to forget. "That time I played a tree—it was the Christmas after my mom got diagnosed with cancer. And I really, really wanted to do something to cheer her up. That's why I went so all-out with my costume, my *moves*. Well, okay, maybe I would have done that anyway because that's just how I am, but I definitely went *even more* over the top. And then after . . ." I gnawed on my lower lip, remembering my little Christmas-tree self emerging to the backstage reception area, still covered in glitter. All the parents were staring at me and whispering about how I was destined for a life of troublemaking.

But I hadn't cared—I'd been looking around for Mom and eagerly anticipating the big smile I just knew she'd be wearing. "Turns out, my mom had to go to the hospital that night," I continued, staring down at my hot chocolate. "My dad went with her, so it was just my, um, friend Evie backstage. And she was all stressed out and worried because of Mom, so . . . yeah. I think that's when I knew what was happening was serious. Like, I finally realized she wasn't getting better."

"You've never told me that story," Sam said softly. "I'm so sorry."

"It's not very fun," I said, giving him a humorless half-smile. "And as we've established, you and I are all about the fun."

"Mmm," he said. "Also, not to be weird, but . . . that doesn't quite explain why you're all in on Christmas? If anything, I'd think it would be the opposite."

"Right, that was just the beginning of the story. You know

how I tell stories, it's nonlinear as shit. Anyway, that was also the holiday season when I discovered my favorite Christmas movie of all time—"

"*A Kaiju for Christmas*," Sam said, sounding amused. "Which I now know all about, thanks to one of your epic holiday movie letters."

"I watched that thing on a loop!" I exclaimed, laughing a little. "It was like my escape from everything bad that was happening, and it made me feel like there was still joy in the world."

"Even though that movie has a sad ending."

"It's beautiful and romantic! A bittersweet tragedy!" I protested, waving my hot chocolate around at him. The remnants of my marshmallow tower teetered. "All of that led to the *next* Christmas, which was the one right after Mom died and Dad took off. There was all this festive energy in the air, but everything was so sad and blah in the beige little apartment Evie and I had moved into. I wanted to do *something*."

"Your friend Evie moved in with you after what happened with your parents?" Sam said. "Did I know that? It sounds familiar, but . . ."

"I've probably mentioned it once or twice," I said quickly. "Evie was always so exhausted, she was barely an adult herself, and she suddenly had to take care of both of us. She didn't really know how to 'do' Christmas—and anyway, I was past Santa age and we couldn't afford a tree."

I paused, poking at my marshmallows again. I could see all of it as if it had happened yesterday—our sad apartment, not a scrap of tinsel in sight. Evie passed out on the broke-down couch after pulling another all-nighter, dark circles permanent fixtures under her eyes.

"So one day, on my walk home from school, I saw something in a dumpster, perched on top of all the other trash," I continued. "It was this weird ornament that looked sort of like a misshapen dragon? It was wearing a scarf and a Santa hat, and for some reason, it was metallic pink. It was objectively ugly, but I thought it was one of the most beautiful things I'd ever seen." I smiled at the memory—finding my first talisman, all those years ago. "I took it home and proudly displayed it on the scratched-up coffee table. The only Christmas decoration in the whole entire apartment. And I remember Evie seeing it, and for just a moment . . . she didn't look as tired. She actually smiled. And she said . . ." My throat thickened, and I poked at the marshmallows again. "She said, 'Awww, Merry Christmas, Bea.' I know that sounds like such a small thing, but . . ." I shook my head. "Whenever I saw that ornament perched on our shitty table, it made me feel a little bit better about everything. I knew I'd be putting it out again next Christmas. And next Christmas? Maybe things would be better. Maybe Evie would be less sad and I'd be less fucked up, and we'd look back and realize how far we'd come."

"A symbol of hope," Sam said. "A tacky, hot-pink symbol of hope."

"I mean, the best kind." I chuckled. "And ever since then, I've seen Christmas as a time when those little symbols of hope exist everywhere, a time when it's impossible for me to not believe in them. And a beyond-perfect time to share that hope with the people I love—even the ones who are total Grinches." I gave him a pointed look and he just grinned.

"Ahh, just like last Christmas," he said, bumping my shoulder with his. "I loved watching you with all your Maui friends. You'd only been out there for a couple months, and you'd already made this little family unit for yourself. Even grouchy old Pika—"

"Aw, Pika," I said, a soft smile crossing my face. "He still wants you to come back and help him with all his old cars."

"He was ready to bah humbug it up for the entire day, and you totally made his year by getting him that *Columbo* Christmas book."

"*A Christmas Killing*!" I crowed. "Never made into an episode of the TV series, but I figured he'd get a kick out of it anyway."

"He did," Sam said. "Especially when you read it to him

in your best Peter Falk voice. Which I will admit to finding disturbingly sexy."

"Mmm," I mumbled, my cheeks heating.

Sam's gaze drifted back to the rink, where his mom was engaging in some complicated-looking spiral action.

"I also remember that that's when things started to go wrong with us," he said, his voice very soft. "And Bea, I . . . I'm sorry. I don't think I knew how to have you *and* my parents in my life—I thought it was impossible. And I guess I thought I had to keep you separated or something because . . ." He blew out a long breath and gazed at the rink.

"Because I'm basically an orphan and mentioning any kind of family is obviously going to mess me up?" I said, trying to make my voice light.

"Kind of. Like we've said, we try to keep things fun. But I should have seen that you literally build these family structures around you, wherever you go. That you accept people into your heart so readily, and . . . and that you and Leah have always been my family, too."

"And Pancake," I murmured.

"And Pancake," he agreed. "I think all that was more about me, though. I felt like both you and my parents deserved to have my . . . my everything, you know? But since I was also sectioning you all off into different parts of my life, that was impossible and I always felt like I was failing. I think . . ." He trailed off again, a muscle in his jaw twitching. "I think me taking care of my parents, me being the kid who stayed . . . I made that into my whole identity. I hid behind it because it made me feel needed and valued and gave me purpose—since I'd kind of failed at everything else."

"I don't know why you think that," I said fiercely, my protective instincts flaring. "But I get what you're saying. I'm still trying to figure out how to be all valuable myself. Like, I took that job and moved out to Maui to make my world bigger, but . . ." I shrugged.

"Are you kidding?" he shot back. "You're doing that every

day. I could see that during my visit, too." He gave me an admiring smile that I felt I absolutely did not deserve. "I got scared of making my own world bigger. And I'm in awe because you just keep expanding yours—finding new friends and having new experiences and trying to figure out what kind of hero you want to be and what kind of life you want to live. You're so, like . . . endlessly curious. About *everything*. When you learn something new, you are always over-the-top thrilled, even if it's the most mundane factoid ever. And you live life so fully—it's beautiful to see. And I think it means your world's gonna be infinity-sized."

I raised my eyes to his, my heart beating very fast. I suddenly felt both too hot and too cold, the freezing air that was turning my nose numb contrasting sharply with the heat rolling off his big body, the warmth of the mug clutched in my hands. His dark eyes were searching, so vulnerable and open to me that I wanted to cry.

"We wanted to make our world bigger together," I said, so softly he leaned in closer to hear. "The together part . . . that was also important."

His eyes continued to roam my face as his fingertips grazed my cheek, little electric sparks igniting on my skin.

"Sammy-chan! You need this!"

We jerked apart just in time to see Sam's mom throwing a bit of greenery directly at our heads.

"What the . . ." Sam reached out and caught the greenery, then uncurled his fist to reveal . . .

"Mistletoe!" I shrieked, clapping a hand over my mouth.

Mrs. Fujikawa skated off, laughing heartily.

A faint blush suffused Sam's cheeks. "I guess she's expecting us to . . ."

"We did say we'd have to fake kiss at some point," I said, my own face flaming.

He met my eyes again. "Well, then . . ."

The air between us had grown charged, heat sizzling across my nerve endings as my mouth went dry. His hand curled gently around my jaw, his thumb stroking my cheek. I gazed back at him, frozen in place.

He leaned in and carefully pressed his lips against mine—every movement deliberate and so very tender, as if he was handling something breakable.

I gasped at the heat of his mouth, an irresistible contrast to the cold air brushing my face. And when he teased my mouth open and I tasted the intoxicating sweetness of hot chocolate . . . I was gone. I lost myself in the kiss, forgetting where I was and when I was and that a fake kiss probably shouldn't feel this good.

But it did. It felt *right*.

I wanted to stay locked in this kiss forever: a perfect moment, a perfect Christmas, a last perfect day on Earth. I even managed to forget, just for a moment, that none of it was real.

CHAPTER THIRTY-ONE

SAM'S PARENTS FINALLY got tired of skating circles around everyone else on the ice, so we made our pit stop at Trader Joe's and headed back to their place. Once we arrived, however, Mrs. Fujikawa produced a single red sock from her giant purse and slapped it on the doorknob.

"Your father and I need privacy after all that, ah, stimulation," she said, winking broadly at Sam. "Sammy, you go spend time at Bea-chan's place. Come back tomorrow!"

Neither of us had a chance to respond before she dragged Mr. Fujikawa inside and shut the door.

"Oh my god," Sam said, looking like he wanted to melt into the sidewalk. "Did my own mother just kick me out so she can . . ." His eyes went to the sock hanging on the doorknob, a vivid red symbol of his mortification. "Sorry," he continued, running a hand through his hair. "I can, um, find somewhere else to . . ."

"Don't be silly." I elbowed him in the ribs. "We have plenty of room at the Victorian. Come back with me. We'll eat all the holiday Joe-Joe's and get drunk enough for you to totally forget any uncomfortable images that might be invading your brain right now."

"I'm too disturbed to even try to come up with a clever excuse," Sam said, his eyes still glued to the sock. He finally tore his gaze away and turned to me, a tentative grin pulling at his mouth. "And honestly, that sounds pretty damn good."

We made our way back to the Victorian, silence falling between us as we maneuvered through icy streets. It wasn't exactly an awkward silence, but it definitely wasn't what I'd call comfortable, either. It crackled with the unpredictable energy that was now flowing between us, as if our kiss had been a promise—but a promise of what? Neither of us knew. My brain was still telling me it hadn't been real.

My body wasn't so sure.

I was kind of surprised the kiss hadn't sent me time traveling—it had certainly produced an overwhelming flood of emotion. But I was confident that a projection-level feeling would find me in Sam's presence. And in any case, I was definitely having the perfect last Christmas I'd hoped for.

I couldn't help but wonder if he would remember me, would realize that something—*someone*—was missing. Just like his mom and Pika had known he was supposed to be here.

Would he occasionally get a slight chill that reminded him of kissing a ghost girl by the ice? Would he briefly taste hot chocolate on his tongue and feel around for a memory that was just out of reach?

Hopefully he would find someone else, someone who could make him forget.

Tears sprang to my eyes, and I swiped them away as we entered the Victorian and silently tromped up the stairs to my bedroom. We were on autopilot, robotically going to the spot where we'd spent so much time together.

"Um, you can leave your coat in here," I said, sweeping in front of him to deposit my own coat, cardigan, scarf, and mittens on the chair by my tinkering table. "I don't know what food we have around, but we can always order something—or just eat chocolate-enrobed Joe-Joe's for Christmas Eve dinner." I smiled slightly, my back to him. "And I'm pretty sure there's plenty of booze. Ooh, we can figure out the best pairings for each individual Joe-Joe flavor! I know you hate all the holiday movies, but perhaps I can take it as my own personal challenge to find one you'll tolerate. And whenever you want to go to bed . . ." I flushed, and forced myself not to turn and face him. "Like I said before, there are plenty of empty rooms. And couches. Or if it'll make you most comfortable, you can stay in my room and I'll take one of the empties—"

"Bea."

I turned to see him stepping toward me, his eyes roaming my face.

"I don't want to stay in another room," he said.

"Oh, okay!" I responded, my voice twisting into a desperate squeak. "Then I will! No problem at all, I'll just—"

"*Bea.*"

He stepped even closer and took my hands in his, his gaze very serious. I noticed his hands were shaking a little.

"I don't want you to stay in another room either."

All the air left my lungs.

"I was wrong," he continued, gazing at me in that deeply earnest way that always made me melt. "When you asked me if love was the most important thing—"

"And you said no," I murmured, my cheeks heating at the humiliation.

"I was wrong," he repeated, squeezing my hands. "And I only just realized that today." A slight smile played over his lips, and he shook his head in wonder. "I guess I kept thinking of the love between us as this thing that was separate from the rest of our lives—that it existed outside of stress and worry and me trying to do whatever I imagined was my responsibility to my family. But the truth is . . ." He shook his head again. "When you love someone like that, it weaves itself into every piece of your existence. Even when we were apart, I thought of everything in relation to you—how you would probably laugh at a funny thing my mom said that day or love something she made for dinner, how the only thing I wanted after a particularly hard doctor's visit with my parents was to fall into your arms. You never stopped being part of my life."

I thought of the timeline without him, how there had been so many things I wanted to tell him and show him and experience with him. How he was the person I wanted to confide in about my disastrous dating exploits, the one I wanted to cry to when something went wrong. Even when he literally hadn't existed, he'd still been part of my life, too.

"I've realized that a lot the 'duty' I felt toward my parents was more about me than them—and you saw them on the ice today, they clearly don't need me as much as I thought they did," he said.

"But someday they will," I said, my voice very small. "And you should know—"

"That you'll be there—I do know that." He squeezed my hands again. "When you talked about that today at the rink, us being family no matter what . . ." He smiled. "It made me realize that we can tackle this stuff together. And if the shoe was on the other foot, if something happened to Pika or he just needed extra help—I'd drop everything to be with you. To help however I could." His smile warmed, his dark eyes gazing at me with unabashed adoration. "Your love is so . . . *big*. Wherever you go, you build these little communities around you. You already had, like, nine best friends after being in Makawao for only a couple of weeks. You would do anything for them. And that's the kind of love that can never really be separate from anything because it's the reason for *everything*."

He let go of my hands so he could cup my face, his gaze locked with mine.

"I love you, Bea. I love you in that big way, where it seeps into everything. It's a piece of who I am. And my life is bigger and brighter and just *more* when you're in it." He tapped my forehead, that spot that always got crinkly when I was thinking extra hard. "And god, I missed this crinkle. I don't think I can live without it."

He touched his forehead to mine, closing his eyes and speaking with fervor. "Please tell me we can figure something out, even if I have to be here and you have to be across the ocean. Because regardless of everything else, that kiss today told me that you feel the same way."

I closed my eyes and breathed, a tear slipping down my cheek as I reveled in the warmth where our foreheads touched.

Of course I felt the same way. I loved him so much, I hadn't been able to bear a world where he didn't exist. But he had no way of knowing that I'd actually had the opposite realization—love *wasn't* the most important thing. Love wasn't enough. Love didn't mean you got to have everything you wanted, or that you lived happily ever after with the person you adored. Not when you have to sacrifice yourself for the greater good. Not when being a hero means erasing yourself from the entire freaking timeline.

My big love had led me here—to a place where I could hopefully save everyone I cared about in return for never seeing any of them ever again.

I opened my eyes and studied every single one of Sam's features. His face was the one I'd see right before I threw myself directly at the kaiju.

"I love you too," I blurted out. "In that big way."

His eyes flew open, sparks of hope lighting his gaze. "So you're saying . . ."

"Yes." I nodded emphatically. "I want to be with you. I want to figure out how to make it work. I want to . . ." My throat thickened, tears pricking my eyes. "I want to have every Christmas with you. Go ice skating and drink hot chocolate under a blanket and kiss you until our lips are swollen. That's all I want, forever."

It was the truth, even though it was impossible.

He pulled me into his arms, his hands sliding down my back as his lips met mine. I let myself get swept up in it, even as my heart broke and tears streamed down my cheeks.

This is part of your last perfect day, your last perfect Christmas, I told myself. *Let yourself feel everything now. Let yourself love him the way you want to. You might not get tomorrow—but today's not over yet.*

I wound my arms around his neck and let everything

consume me, the heat of his mouth on mine, the way his fingers toyed with the straps of my slip dress, sending those sparks of electricity racing over my skin.

"Hey," I murmured against his mouth. "I need to give you your Christmas present."

"If that means I have to stop kissing you, I don't want it."

I pulled back and raised an impish eyebrow. "Oh, you will. I told you about this one—it's designed to put both of us on the naughty list."

I disentangled myself and strode to the bathroom, putting a little extra sway in my hips. Maybe he didn't remember my description of this particular present. He would soon.

I closed the bathroom door behind me and rummaged around in the cupboard below the sink until I found the box where I kept odds and ends from my various tinkering and craft projects. Past Bea had saved up a bunch of long, wide red satin ribbons for this exact purpose.

I shucked off my clothes and proceeded to strategically wrap myself in the ribbons, taking care to cover my various bits 'n' pieces. This ended up being much more difficult than I'd thought it would be, particularly since I didn't have anyone to help. But when I finally assessed the results in the mirror, I was satisfied. I'd managed to loop the ribbons all around myself, revealing swaths of tantalizingly bare skin in between the silky slashes of red.

I definitely would have enjoyed unwrapping myself, just saying. I hoped Sam would feel the same way.

I emerged and struck a pose in the bathroom doorway, tossing my hair over my shoulder and narrowing my eyes into what I hoped was a sultry gaze.

"Merry Christmas," I purred. "Want to unwrap your present?"

I was gratified to see his eyes widen, and he even stumbled backward a little bit, grabbing on to my bed frame for support.

"Buh . . ." he managed, his breathing going all heavy and uneven.

"I'll take that as a yes," I said, striding toward him.

He managed to stay standing, his eyes roaming my body like he'd never seen anything better.

When I finally reached him, his hands went to the small of my back and he pulled me into a deep kiss, palms flexing against my skin.

"Jesus Christ," he groaned, breaking the kiss so he could take me in. "The thoughts I'm having right now . . . I'm *never* getting off that naughty list."

"Honestly, it's more fun here," I said, trailing my fingertips down his neck.

His Adam's apple bobbed furiously, his pupils dilating until his eyes were nothing but black. I stood on my tiptoes so I could whisper in his ear.

"Do you remember *how* you're supposed to unwrap your present?" I nipped lightly at his earlobe and felt a rush of giddy satisfaction when his breath hitched.

One of his hands slid from my back to my shoulder, his fingertips slipping underneath the ribbon positioned there like the strap of a dress. I expected him to just rip it off, to proceed with getting me naked as quickly as possible. Instead his fingers drifted to a different ribbon, a long piece I'd tied around my waist as I was getting to the end of my gift-wrap journey. A few flicks of his fingers untied that piece, and then he held it in his hands for a moment, sliding the silky ribbon over his palm contemplatively.

"Get on the bed," he said, his voice low and charged.

Now I was the one who was off balance, my knees going weak.

"You don't want to finish unwrapping me first?"

He met my gaze, his dark eyes heating with desire.

"I want to unwrap you very slowly." He reached down with his free hand and cupped my breast, his thumb flicking over my ribbon-covered nipple. I gasped, feeling like I might pass out on the spot. "I want to make you sound just like that—over and over and over again." He bent his head, his lips brushing my ear. "So get on the bed."

I did as I was told, excitement bubbling up in my chest like champagne.

He eased himself onto the bed with me, rolling me onto my back as he took my mouth with his. He stroked one of my arms and kissed my palm, then gently maneuvered it above my head before following suit with my other arm.

Then he wrapped that single red ribbon around my wrists and tied me to the bed frame.

So he *did* remember some of my instructions.

He checked the bonds to test my circulation, then pulled back and surveyed his work, his gaze sweeping over my half-naked, half-restrained form. The way he was looking at me was so probing, so raw in its desire, I thought I might come before he'd so much as touched me.

"You need a safe word," he said, trailing his fingers over my waist and leaving goosebumps in their wake. "Since you're tied up and all."

"Gingerbread," I said, trying not to let my about-to-explode level of anticipation show in my voice.

"Gingerbread," he agreed, leaning in to kiss me again.

He feathered kisses along my jawline, so light and teasing I squirmed. I wanted him to really *touch* me, dammit. But I knew if I tried to make a demand, he'd only go maddeningly slower.

He finally moved to my neck, grazing his teeth against my collarbone and drawing a guttural moan from deep in my throat.

I felt him smile against my skin. "See? My way of unwrapping a gift is pretty fucking good."

"You could stand to unwrap a little *faster*."

"No way." His hand drifted up my side, fingertips sliding under the ribbons for a few tantalizing seconds before he withdrew them again. "Do you know how much I've missed you, how I've been in total hell without you? I want to make this moment last as long as possible."

Heat flashed through me, desire curling low in my belly.

If this was the last sex I was ever going to have, at least it was going to be mind-blowing.

His mouth continued to explore my collarbone as his hand slid up my side again, toying with the ribbons—lips and fingertips both getting very close to my nipples, neither making the full commitment. I released a cry of frustration and tried to wiggle closer, to get his mouth and his hands where I wanted them.

"Stop that," he ordered, his lips lingering on the slope of my breast. "I need to take this slow so I can see how much you missed me, too."

"I definitely missed you!" I squeaked, my voice ragged with need. "So much! Just . . . please, can you . . ."

He finally sucked my nipple into his mouth and I moaned. The ribbon was still firmly positioned over that delicate bit of flesh, but that made it even better, the silky material and the wet heat of his tongue rubbing against my nipple in tandem.

"Sam," I sobbed, trembling against him.

"God, just like that," he growled. "I *love* making you sound like that."

And then—fucking *finally*—he yanked the ribbon aside so his mouth could fully claim my nipple.

I drowned in the chills rushing through me, overwhelming all of my senses. My arms flailed and fought against their silken bonds as he moved lower, tasting me everywhere. But I never came close to my safe word, to *gingerbread*. Because all I wanted was *more*.

He untied various ribbons as he went, freeing up more bare skin for his appreciation. He was still fully clothed, but I felt the hot, hard length of him pressing into my thigh through his jeans as he moved downward—and I couldn't help but shudder. He smiled and pressed more firmly against me, so I could truly feel just how much he was enjoying this.

My legs shook when he moved to my inner thighs, trailing kisses along the sensitive flesh. He raised his head and studied the bit of ribbon still covering that crucial point between my legs, the area I *needed* him to touch before I lost my mind.

"Please . . ." I whispered.

Very slowly, he lowered his head to lightly flick his tongue over the ribbons—once, twice. The silky material pressed against my clit, the heat from his tongue sending shivers racing through me once more. My arms strained against their bonds, and I bit back another frustrated sob.

"Shhh. It's okay, Bea—forget the naughty list, I think you've actually been a *very* good girl," he said, his voice dripping with positively pornographic promise. "And that means you deserve to be rewarded."

Then he finally undid that last ribbon and put his mouth on me and . . . oh *god*.

I closed my eyes and gave myself over to sensation, the sweep of his tongue against the most sensitive part of me. He threw one of my legs over his shoulder to get better leverage, his mouth working to a relentless rhythm and drawing cry after cry from my throat.

It was so fucking good. But I still wanted more.

"Sam," I breathed, barely able to get that single syllable out. "Please, just . . . *please* fuck me. I need your cock."

He drew back and grinned up at me, all lazy-eyed and smug.

"You know, for someone who's supposed to be the gift *giver*, you're very bossy," he said, running a fingertip over my inner thigh. I tried not to squirm. "You keep telling me how to unwrap *my* present."

"I'm just trying to *help*," I said, attempting to make my voice haughty. It still trembled a little. "Since the way you unwrap the gift benefits you as well."

"I dunno . . ." He slid his hand up to stroke my breast, rolling my aching nipple between his fingertips. "I think I'm doing pretty good."

He pulled himself up and sent my head spinning with another long kiss. Then he moved between my thighs, and undid his jeans. That unmistakable hardness I'd felt against my hip broke free, his cock more than ready for me. He found a condom in my bedside table (luckily Past Bea had stocked up), tore open the package, and rolled it on.

Time seemed to freeze as he slid inside of me, making me moan with long, hard thrusts. My desire spiraled into the stratosphere as he built up a rhythm—the silky, half-untied ribbons sliding against my skin. Every nerve ending in my body felt like it was standing at attention, on fire, *alive*.

He brought me close to the edge again and again, until I was practically sobbing with need. Then, just when I felt like I couldn't take it anymore, he leaned down and kissed me—a very thorough, surprisingly gentle kiss. He pulled back and gazed at me, his expression so tender that the tears in my eyes started to stream down my cheeks.

"I love you," he said, his voice shaking with emotion. "This is the best Christmas I've ever had. The best gift I've ever gotten. You finally got me to love a holiday I've spent the past two decades hating—because you're *you*, and that's what you do." His voice cracked, his eyes glassy with tears. "I want to have every Christmas with you, too. Forever."

Then he buried his face in my neck and thrust into me even more relentlessly, rocking our bodies together until I screamed his name, finally going over the edge.

CHAPTER THIRTY-TWO

AFTERWARD, HE UNTIED me and we kissed, touched, just enjoyed being with each other for what seemed like hours. Time lost all meaning as I sank deeper into our blissful cocoon. We had sex again, slow and sweet and delicious. Then we drifted off to sleep with *A Kaiju for Christmas* playing on the TV in the background, his body wrapped around mine.

I'd never felt so warm, so perfectly happy—as long as we stayed in this moment, everything was wonderful.

I woke up just as the movie was ending, the Christmas kaiju emerging in all her glory. I watched Thomas make his impossible choice, knowing I would soon have to make my own.

I rolled over and studied Sam's sleeping face, all of his features I loved so much. It would all be okay. He would never know I'd existed. He would find someone else—maybe they would make up their own weird little competitions, too. Maybe he would record his "YOU JUST MATHED SO HARD" victory declaration for someone else. He would find a way to make his world bigger, to live the life he deserved.

I grabbed the remote, switched off the TV, and sat up in bed. Sam mumbled something in his sleep and shifted closer, throwing an arm around my waist and nuzzling his face against my hip—as if reassuring himself that I was still there. I stroked his hair absently, luxuriating in this gentle bit of affection I'd never get to experience again. His body softened back into a deep slumber, but his arm stayed locked around me.

My gaze drifted to the nightstand, which was usually a snarled mess of books, random papers, mugs, and hair ties. Right now it contained a single item—a copy of the *A Kaiju for Christmas* novelization. Apparently Shasta-Dahlia had gifted it to me in this version of the timeline as well.

I picked it up and idly flipped through. I'd always wanted to read this, but had never been able to find a copy. There was no digital version available, and my obsessive combing through used bookshops and thrift stores—and yes, the occasional charming old curio shop—had yielded nothing. My skimming revealed that the plot was basically the same, though there were quite a few flowery passages that went deeper into the inner monologues of both Thomas and Sandrine. I got to the end and relived Thomas's impossible choice, his melancholy as he watched Sandrine go on without him. Tears filled my eyes. It all felt so *unfair*—for them to find each other, overcome so much, and then be forced apart. But that was how heroing worked—sometimes the right choice felt wrong, but you always had to make it in the end.

Then I turned the page and realized that *wasn't* the end.

I frowned, flipping the page back and forth. It looked like there was a whole other chapter after the final scene.

I homed in on the Author's Note that preceded this new-to-me chapter.

Dear Reader,

The scene you are about to read is not part of the motion picture version of A Kaiju for Christmas. *It was, however, included in the original script, but was cut when studio executives decided it would be "more meaningful to end on a note that's bittersweet and melancholy." The idea that two people who love each other more than anything could find a way to turn an impossible situation into one filled with* endless *possibilities was deemed "unrealistic," and these executives claimed no one would be invested in these lovers unless they were tragic, suffering grandly, and forced to make the ultimate sacrifice.*

This author disagrees. Quite strongly.

We leave it to you to read this original ending and decide for yourself which you like better.

Happy holidays!

Wait . . . *what?*

I almost ripped the book in half trying to turn the pages too fast.

My eyes kept getting bigger and bigger as I read this lost final scene, a feeling I couldn't quite name growing in my chest.

In this new-to-me ending, Sandrine realizes what's happened—that the warlock who cursed her forced Thomas to choose her fate. That Thomas went with what he thought would make her most happy. And that she can't decide if she wants to run to him in order to kiss him or totally kick his ass.

Meanwhile, Thomas realizes he loves Sandrine no matter what, and he can't bear the thought of life without her. The two end up both going to their favorite spot, the place where they first kissed—a gigantic Christmas-tree display in some unnamed but magical city where snow falls right on cue and everything smells like cinnamon. Once there, they reunite just as the giant Christmas tree lights up and the snow begins to drift from the sky.

And then Sandrine is like, "Hey, wait a minute! Fuck that musty old warlock!"

Sure, he's the one who got her to turn into a kaiju in the first place, but all the really fucking powerful stuff she's done since then—like becoming the world's first official Christmas kaiju and merrily stomping through various waterfronts and falling in the kind of epic love that we usually only see in movies . . . all of that was *her*. She did that shit. And now she's the kaiju, the one with all the magic, so she's going to make her own fate.

She tracks down the warlock and tells him she's going to remain a kaiju forever, because she's discovered she loves it and it's her preferred form. But she's also going to be with Thomas, curse be damned. She's going to be *happy*.

The musty warlock tries to convince her this is impossible, getting more and more desperate—and Sandrine realizes this is because he totally lied and manipulated Thomas into making his impossible choice, and has been siphoning off her kaiju magic the whole time. The warlock's own magic has diminished in power over the years, and he was hoping to use her power as his own forever. The warlock's magic grows even weaker once Sandrine makes her own choice to be with Thomas and fucks up his stupid curse. She breaks his medallion in front of him, chomping it between her massive kaiju fangs.

Thomas, meanwhile, has discovered that he actually finds Sandrine *extra* hot in kaiju form—because that is when she is the most herself.

The two of them return to the giant Christmas tree and kiss, and Thomas cheers Sandrine on as she Christmas kaijus herself around the world. And they live—you guessed it!—happily ever after.

I shut the book, tears streaming down my face.

One of my favorite movies had *totally lied to me*.

I set the book back on the nightstand and carefully disentangled myself from sleeping Sam. Then I stalked into the bathroom and started to pace the small space, unsure of what I was even doing. My mind was racing and I couldn't get it to slow down, couldn't grab on to all the sparkly thoughts that were trying to affix themselves to my mental posterboard.

I kept coming back to the warlock's lies. It was Sandrine's magic all along, Sandrine's seemingly monstrous abilities that scared her so much until she learned how to embrace them. Sandrine's *power* that so many wanted to deny and take from her.

screp screp screp

A tiny sound buzzed in my ear, a noise that was like something scraping across the floor.

I stopped in my tracks and looked down. And actually wasn't terribly surprised to see a tiny kaiju running in a loop around the room, like it was training for a marathon. It noticed that it had gotten my attention and ran up to my foot, jumping up and down and waving its little claws around.

"Hey," I murmured, sitting down on the edge of the tub. "What is Shasta doing *now*? What could possibly be gained at this point by sending y'all to pester me?"

The mini kaiju waved its claws even more frantically, working itself into a tizzy.

not her not her I am . . . me

Its thoughts beamed out at me, loud and clear—it felt like we were establishing a deeper, more mind-meld-esque connection. Just like the one I'd had with the big kaiju at the beach.

Hmm. What was going on here?

I took in its general state of anxiety. The emotional projection it was sending my way conveyed a certain urgency, like there was something it desperately needed me to know.

Maybe I could just . . . ask?

My darkness pulsed and I took a long, slow breath and made space for it, that sparkly disco-ball feeling thrumming through me as it mingled with my power. They were now impossible to separate from one another. I closed my eyes and felt all of that, reveled in it. Then I reached deep inside of myself and gathered up feelings of calm and empathy, which I projected at the mini kaiju.

"What do you want?" I prompted, inclining my head at the little creature. It paused in its jumping around and made a swoopy gesture with its claw, pointing to where I was sitting. "Oh, up here?"

I reached down and held out my hand, palm facing up. "Hop on, li'l kaiju. I have no idea what's happening, I'm just doing what feels right."

The mini kaiju hopped eagerly into my hand. I brought it closer to my face, staring into its glowing eyes.

"What is it?" I urged. "I sense there's something big I'm

supposed to be getting—maybe something I was supposed to get this whole time. Can you help me figure it out? I'm listening."

I beamed out as much warmth and empathy and gentle listening energy as I could. My darkness hummed, luxuriating in the sensation. And there was that sense of *rightness* again, that very natural feeling that we were working together as one.

And then I felt the mini kaiju's voice in my head once more, a single word emerging as a tiny-voiced squeak.

creator

I studied the kaiju in my palm. It was standing very still, head tilted to the side, as if concentrating extra hard. I couldn't help but smile—that was kind of cute.

"Creator," I repeated back to the kaiju, sounding the word out carefully. "What does that mean?"

creator . . . you . . . you ARE creator . . .

"Who, me?" I pressed a faux-modest hand to my chest. "That seems like a really cool thing to be, but creator of *what*, exactly?"

The mini kaiju closed its glowing eyes and furrowed its spiky brow, as if concentrating even harder.

creator . . . of us . . .

"What!" I shrieked, so loud that the mini kaiju jumped. I clapped my free hand over my mouth. "Sorry. You're saying *I* created the kaiju?! The little ones? The gigantic ones? All of them?!"

The mini kaiju nodded, its glowing eyes full of glee.

"Is that why I can sense what all these kaiju are feeling, why I was able to connect in a deeper way to the big one on the beach—and now, to you?"

The kaiju nodded again.

you . . . after you felt . . . dark magic in you . . . your power changed . . . your projections created us . . .

"B-but *why*?!" I sputtered.

protection

"What, really? Because I haven't been doing a super great

job of protecting anyone lately—and that big kaiju on the beach keeps trying to kill my family!"

protection . . . of you

I opened my mouth, closed it. And stared at the mini kaiju, trying to figure out what it meant.

"What were you protecting me from?" I finally said. "Or maybe I should ask . . . *who*?"

the evil one . . . big hats, small guitars

I smiled, amused in spite of myself. That was an interesting way of describing Shasta, in her many forms.

"Were you trying to protect me from her mind control?"

in a way . . . hey, look, my words are getting . . . better?

"Yes, very nice!" I complimented the kaiju. "Perhaps our mental link is feeding you more human-type phrases or something. What do you mean by 'in a way'?"

she kept trying to take your mind . . . and failing . . . your big emotions would push her away and take the form of . . . us . . .

Holy fucking shit.

So in addition to sending me time traveling, my power/darkness super-combo had merged to construct *entire freaking supernatural monsters* out of my more extreme feelings. I thought back to that first mini kaiju, the one who had appeared during my dumpster-side meltdown and beamed my terrified feelings right back at me. The distraught, sobbing horde that had appeared in my bathroom when I'd been so broken up over Sam. The tiny monsters I'd spied in the bookstore and near the Victorian's Christmas tree when I'd been in high-stress situations, the army invading my family's party when Sam's mom had passed me the eraser . . .

And of course there was the big motherfucker on the beach.

"Wait, the big one!" I said to my new mini-kaiju friend. "Is it different than the others? Like, why is it so big? And is it the only one that's a portal?"

big kaiju is portal! the mini kaiju said, nodding emphatically. *and yes, different . . . not one feeling, but many . . .*

"Many," I murmured. "So, like, *all* the feelings I had on the beach?"

no ... go back further ...

"All the feelings I've ever had?!" I shrieked.

not that many, the mini kaiju said, sounding downright amused. *more like ... since darkness found you ... feelings you wanted to take away ... those of us who ... disappeared*

I leaned back against the bathroom wall, frowning into space. I remembered the curious way the big kaiju had referred to itself when we'd communicated: always *we*, never *I*. A Borg collective of emotions.

"Since the darkness came to me—so, after the power combo spell. All the big feelings I kept trying to push away and deny—those were the mini kaiju that disappeared? Like, whenever I tried to shove something down?"

I flashed back to that first mini kaiju, the one by the dumpster—how it had vanished when I'd cowered and attempted to suppress everything inside of me.

"But then, they didn't exactly disappear, they formed a *mega-kaiju* in the freakin' ocean?! That then turned into a portal ... hmm, I'm guessing because of that super-special piece of Otherworld magic that lives inside of me now?"

The mini kaiju beamed at me, looking something like proud.

big one tried to protect you too ... on the beach! but ... evil one tried to take over ... made it more scared ... made it attack!

Ah. So that's why the big kaiju had seemed so conflicted and distressed and had lashed out—when she hadn't been able to take over my mind, Shasta had attempted to control the big kaiju. But it had fought back, too.

My darkness had not only created monsters out of my feelings, it had used them to fend off Shasta's mind control. And it had tried to get me to listen every time and to trust myself, but I'd responded by shoving it down and trying to fight against both the darkness and the kaiju.

I'd been fighting *myself.*

And here was yet another lie Shasta had told me, something I'd just believed because I'd been in such a vulnerable
spot, unwilling to trust my own judgment and all too eager
to believe every bad thing I'd ever thought about myself.
Shasta had claimed *she'd* created the kaiju. And that she'd
done it using a similar method as she had for the other monsters she'd menaced Evie and Aveda with—the ghosts, the
vampires. She'd said she'd used humans' emotional energy . . .
but she hadn't exactly explained the rest, had she? I shook
my head, my glittery mental posterboard rearranging itself
so fast, I almost couldn't keep up.

Shasta had manipulated me even more than I'd thought.

That fucking asshole.

I met the mini kaiju's eyes and saw it nodding its head
emphatically, like, *That's right, girl!*

"What *is* true?" I blurted out. "What else did she lie to me
about?"

*peace is a lie . . . she will not rest . . . she needs control of
this realm . . . invasion . . .*

"I knew it!" I snarled. "Shasta's planning on taking over
this supposedly disgusting human dimension after all. But
does that mean the prophecy's not real—is that another one
of her semi-entertaining fictions?"

prophecy is true, but . . .

The mini kaiju regarded me shrewdly. I swore I saw it give
me a tiny eyebrow raise.

*more than one way to hear the words . . . more than one
way to speak them*

I studied the mini kaiju for a moment as it gazed at me,
turning that over in my mind.

"Do you mean, like—there are multiple ways to interpret
the prophecy?"

The mini kaiju clapped its claws together and nodded
vigorously.

Huh. I supposed I'd already been trying to give the prophecy a different meaning by substituting myself for Vivi. But

what about the second part—the piece about the portal closing once it was "fed and fulfilled"?

I thought back to the lost ending of *A Kaiju for Christmas*. Just like that shitty warlock, Shasta had convinced me I needed to sacrifice and suffer, that I had to give up someone I loved. And then I'd convinced myself that that someone should be me.

"Fed and fulfilled" could mean *so many things*. Why had I assumed I had to turn into some self-sacrificing stereotype of a hero? Was that the only way I could conceive of doing good in this world? Was that what I thought I *deserved*?

Another big, giant feeling took root in my chest.

"I'm so angry, I'm about to have a rage blackout," I said to the mini kaiju. "How about you?"

It stomped its tiny foot and held up its little claw.

"Oh, you want to fist-bump?!" I exclaimed. "Well . . . okay!"

I gently tapped its claw with my pinkie finger.

"Solidarity. Now if you'll excuse me for just one second, I need to gather my time-traveling materials."

The mini kaiju nodded and allowed me to set it down on the ledge of the tub. I went back into my bedroom and grabbed the dragon-shifter lady book Leah had given me and my cheesy #1 eraser. And then I searched the entire Victorian until I found my tacky pink dragon ornament—which was located in what was usually Evie and Nate's room. In this version of the timeline, it was just Nate's, his sad twin bed swathed in black sheets, his room completely devoid of excess decorations. Except for that ugly beacon of an ornament, which was perched on his bedside table. I wondered if he kept it there because he could feel Evie's presence echoing across the timeline.

I took all of my talismans back to the bathroom, where the mini kaiju was waiting patiently on the ledge of the tub.

"Let's do this," I said, giving it a determined nod. It scrambled to its feet and raised its claws in a power pose.

I clutched my talismans and reached deep inside of me, connecting with my darkness once more, allowing that sparkly rainbow feeling to flow through me. And I thought about how completely fucking pissed I was at Shasta.

"Man, fuck you," I growled. "Oh, not you!" I exclaimed, as the mini kaiju brought a scandalized claw to its chest. "You're great. I was talking about Shasta—er, big hat, small guitar lady." The mini kaiju gave me a decisive nod.

I took a deep breath and visualized the spot I wanted to travel to on the timeline. I felt my darkness-enhanced power rising up, its irresistible magic flaring through my chest. I thought about how Shasta had tried to make me feel— powerless, destined for suffering, an undeniable fuck-up. How she'd gone after everyone I loved, how she knew exactly where to hit me to make it hurt.

How she'd almost ruined *Christmas*.

I felt that rage coursing through me, a fire enveloping my entire body.

I let it burn.

Then I closed my eyes and felt myself falling and falling and falling, everything turning to darkness.

CHAPTER THIRTY-THREE

WHEN MY EYES snapped open this time, I was in my Makawao bungalow, tangled in my bed sheets. And maybe it was my imagination, but my usual time-travel headache didn't feel so bad this time.

I sat up slowly, getting my bearings, and looked down to see that I was wearing my MATHLETE tank. My gaze turned to the armchair, where Sam was sleeping, all wrapped up in his quilt. The window behind him revealed pitch-black night outside.

Perfect. I'd time traveled to the moment I'd been aiming for—the night before the battle on the beach. I'd picked this spot for many reasons, one of which was that I had a very important task to accomplish before day dawned and everyone woke up.

I slipped out of bed and shut myself in the bathroom, rummaging around in my cabinets for the necessary supplies. My task took several hours and involved many mistakes and a boatload of ruined towels, but I got it done. When I was finally finished, I faced myself in the mirror.

And a huge smile spread over my face.

There I was—Bea Tanaka, in all her rainbow-haired glory. Pink, blue, purple: shimmering through my waves, as bright and vibrant as the glittering hide of the big kaiju.

I was *me* again. And now I was truly ready for battle.

I exited the bathroom to sun streaming through the window and Sam stirring from his slumber.

"Bea," he murmured, blinking the sleep from his eyes.

"Your hair . . ." A sweet, bleary, not-quite-awake smile spread across his face. "God, you're so beautiful."

My heart felt like it was about to explode.

I catapulted myself across the room and launched myself into his lap, curling into him the way I'd wanted to when I'd experienced this moment the first time around. I inhaled his familiar scent like it was oxygen itself, tears springing to my eyes as he stroked a tentative hand down my back.

"Are you okay?" he asked, sounding a tad more awake. "Because last time I saw you, you were furious with me and storming out the door. And . . ." His gaze shifted, his eyes widening. "What the hell is all that?!"

I shifted in his lap and saw that my collection of talismans was littered all over my bed. And the mini kaiju who'd been helping me figure things out was snoozing away on top of my battered dragon-lady book, adorable snores drifting from its tiny fanged mouth.

"Whoa, the mini kaiju came with me—and it didn't vanish," I said. "Maybe because I finally trusted myself and accepted my feelings and figured out all the necessary steps for time travel—"

"Bea!" Sam shook his head in exasperation. "Please. What's going on? *Time travel?!*"

"Right, let me explain. But first, I have to tell you something really important." I reached up and brushed his sleep-mussed hair off his forehead, treasuring the feel of touching him.

"I love you, Sam. It's big and wild and it scares the fuck out of me sometimes, but it also makes me feel more alive than I ever have. I love that you feel everything so deeply—I know you're scared to show that to most people, but when you care about someone, you never hesitate to go all in. I love that you're always up for being completely ridiculous with me, in a way that absolutely no one else will. I love that you make me laugh so hard my face hurts—and then take my breath away two seconds later by doing something heart-stoppingly romantic."

I slipped my hand into his, tangling our fingers together. He was still looking at me in a dazed sort of way, as if wondering if any of this was real.

"I love you," I repeated. "And I know you're going to try to tell me that because we're *us*, we're not cut out for the whole long-term stable relationship thing. But seriously: who *is* cut out for that? I mean, just naturally. Humans are fucked-up, messy, wildly imperfect people. I refute your argument that we are somehow *more* fucked up than anyone else. In fact, I think the particular ways in which we are fucked up means we fit together perfectly." I snuggled closer to him, tears pricking my eyes. "So many things in this world seem impossible. So many things are hard for me to believe in. But I believe in us. And you actually made me see why I should."

"I did?" His hand drifted to my hair, and he plucked at one of the vibrant blue strands, running it through his fingertips.

"Yes. And now I'm going to tell you all about it—and about my little friend over there."

I went back to the very beginning and launched into my tale. I told him everything: the darkness that had terrified me so much, the sudden time traveling, the Christmas where he'd disappeared. I described my various experimentations, my jumps to the Maui of last Christmas and Evie's birth moment. I told him about our last perfect day together, his declaration of love to me, and the very special holiday gift I'd given him. He looked like he wanted to ask me many, many more questions about that last thing in particular, but I forged ahead, taking him through my discovery of the real *Kaiju for Christmas* ending and my most recent time jump.

"So I know there's lots more we have to talk about," I said. "And I still have a world to save and all, but assuming we make it to the other side of this: I want to be with you. I think we both got wrapped up in the idea that we had so much fun together—which, by the way, is an awesome thing! But we thought we could *only* be fun—and that growing up definitely meant an end to fun, period. It's like you said to me in the future: when you love someone the way we love each other, it weaves itself into every piece of your existence. I don't think we have to give up fun—being an adult doesn't mean we have to turn all sad and boring, and we should celebrate fun as much as we can! But the thing is, we can also have everything else. And we can do that by being exactly who we are—by *embracing* who we are instead of running away from it."

He gazed down at me, now looking fully awake, his fingertips still toying with my hair. I held my breath, hoping he'd truly heard everything I'd put out there.

"Wow," he finally said, shaking his head. Complicated emotions played across his face, and he looked like he was trying to solve the most intense of quadratic equations. I watched intently as his features shifted, his expression morphing into a signature cocky Sam Fujikawa smirk. "That speech I gave in the future *was* pretty amazing, huh?"

"That's all you took from it?!" I yelped, socking him in the arm.

"Not *all*," he protested, pulling me closer. He studied my face, that sweet tenderness that always brought tears to my eyes surfacing in his gaze. "You are incredible. I don't know how I ever talked myself into being without you, but thank god Future Me had way more sense. I love you too—in that big, wild, completely fucking scary way." He tapped my forehead. "And I can't live without this crinkle."

He pulled me in for a kiss, his hands cradling my face, his thumbs brushing tears from my cheekbones. I forgot where I was, *when* I was. All that mattered was this.

He broke the kiss and brushed his lips against my jawline, my neck, then moved to graze my earlobe.

"You just mathed so hard," he murmured in my ear.

I exploded in a fit of giggles, tears streaming down my cheeks.

"So what do we do now?" he asked, hugging me tight. "I

should probably be mad at you for thinking even for a second that sacrificing yourself was a good idea, but . . ." He ran his fingers through my rainbow hair again. "I'm so happy to just . . . *be* with you right now, I don't want to waste any more time arguing. And after hearing about all your adventures, I really want to focus on making sure we both make it to next Christmas so you can give me the best present I've ever received."

"Stop," I said, laughing as he raised a suggestive eyebrow at me. "And I'm sorry about the whole self-sacrifice thing. I got a little too wrapped up in this super emo idea of what a hero should be." I snuggled closer to him, overjoyed to be back in his arms. "As for how we're going to beat Shasta, I have an idea—well, the beginnings of one. But I want to talk it through with my family, because they're all going to need to be involved—"

We were interrupted by a light knock on the door.

"That's probably Aveda!" I exclaimed, leaping to my feet. "In the past, she showed up right about now. Although I remember her knock being way more forceful."

I crossed the room and heard the skitter of the mini kaiju following me. For some reason, that brought a huge grin to my face. I reached the door, threw it open, and saw . . . no one. I stuck my head out further, looking back and forth. Where was Aveda? Was she already at the bakery, loading up on malasadas?

"*Caw!*"

My gaze traveled downward, following the sound. And there, perched on the porch near my feet, was Roger. My best chicken friend.

"*Rog!*" I shrieked, crouching down so I could be at his eye level. "What are you doing here?! Do you want malasadas or gingerbread or—"

it's time

I reeled back, my mouth falling open. Had I just heard *Roger's* thoughts?

yes yes yes!

I turned and saw the mini kaiju dancing up next to me, waving its claws around in jubilation.

one of us! the mini kaiju thought, waving a claw at Roger. *one of us! one of us!*

I turned back to Roger, my eyes wide as dinner plates.

"Rog!" I exclaimed. "You're a kaiju too?! I created *you*?"

In response, Roger puffed out his chest—not an unusual move for a rooster. But then he fully extended his wings and they transformed before my eyes, morphing into shiny green and gold mecha attachments. And his eyes shifted so they glowed—just like the other kaiju.

"Damn," I murmured, shaking my head in awe.

it's time, Roger thought at me more fervently. *let's go!*

"Unless she changed a lot overnight, I don't think that's Aveda," Sam said, shuffling up behind me. He regarded Roger curiously, which only made the mecha-chicken puff out his chest even more.

"It's not," I said, grinning at my best chicken pal. Who I had apparently created. "Sam, this is my very good friend, Roger. And I think he's ready to fight this battle with us."

🔥

I kicked off my plan by assembling the Avengers. Which, honestly, I should have done from the very start.

I sent out an emergency summons to my family—*all* of my families—and asked everyone to gather in the Demonology Research Group's office. We had to cram in since said office was built for three, and I took a moment to look around the room, my heart warming at the sight of everyone being so *themselves*.

Aveda stood at attention next to Doc Kai's desk, posture ramrod straight and power ponytail twitching with determined energy. As usual, she was ready for anything. Doc Kai had graciously offered Evie her desk chair since it was the most comfortable. My sister was barely awake, her hazel eyes cloudy and cranky—still not a morning person, not even a little bit. Nate positioned himself next to her, a protective hand resting on her back. Doc Kai, Tosh, and Carmelo clustered around Tosh's desk. Doc Kai had her iPad out and ready, eager to take notes and make plans with her big science brain.

Keala and Giselle had crammed into the doorway of the kitchenette, and Pika was plopped down in my desk chair, complaining incessantly about how he was already behind on the morning's pancake-making marathon and missing one of his favorite *Columbo*s.

I perched on the end of my desk—Sam standing next to me, Roger pacing around at my feet. The mini kaiju had parked itself on one of my fidget-spinner toys and looked like it was about to take another nap.

And then, because I really did want to assemble *all* of the Avengers, we had an iPad set up on my desk, beaming in a signal from HQ back in San Francisco. Scott, Lucy, Rose, Shruti, and Team Tanaka/Jupiter's young charges were clustered around a single screen, jostling for space. A second FaceTime window revealed Leah and Pancake, calling in from their shift at It's Lit.

"The gang is seriously all here!" Leah exclaimed, waving Pancake's paws around as he stared balefully at her. "This feels like some real epic shit."

"It's about to be some real epic shit!" I confirmed, grinning at her. "And I'm gonna need every single one of you."

"Bea, what is this?" Aveda demanded, impatiently tossing her ponytail over her shoulder. "There will be plenty of time for family gatherings later. I really want to get to the beach early to catch those waves!"

"Oh, you will," I said. "And you're gonna look absolutely amazing while doing so."

She cocked her head at me. "What?"

"So there's no easy way to say this," I began. "I've been time traveling."

"Caw!" Roger agreed.

I took a deep breath and launched into my story. I edited out the more pornographic parts involving Sam, but attempted to convey everything else, even when it was hard. I caught Evie's eye when I told the tale of Vivi's birth, her expression a mix of horror and awe. I didn't want to scare her, but I also knew I couldn't hold anything back. I needed my family to know everything, so we could come together and kick Shasta's annoying ass.

"Damn," Aveda said, shaking her head as I wrapped up. "That's a lot of Christmas, Bea. Even for you."

"Not gonna lie, kinda loved getting a couple of bonus Christmases this year," I countered. "As imperfect as they were."

"And you found the non-local boy!" Pika exclaimed, nodding at Sam. "Finally, he's here to help me with my Dodge Charger."

"As soon as we save the world, I'm all yours," Sam said, giving Pika an easy grin.

"Bea, you went through so much," Evie murmured, her eyes full of tears. She gazed at me, radiating that all-encompassing empathy that came to her as naturally as breathing. "I'm so sorry."

"Don't be, Big Sis," I said, giving her a gentle smile. "It was quite an adventure—and it's not over yet."

"Beatrice, I am ever so glad you decided to spill every single one of the beans to us," Lucy piped up from the iPad screen. "And darling, pardon me if this is rather rude, but why now? Aren't you still concerned with messing up the timeline? Isn't that why you kept us in the dark all this time?"

"Actually, no, I'm not worried about that," I said, tossing off a one-shoulder shrug. "It's like Doc Kai said during our Christmas feasting: not every choice is the wrong one. Bringing you all together like this feels like the culmination of all the choices I've made for sure, that undeniable piece of my story! And . . ."

I paused, a small smile playing over my lips. For some reason, the words I'd written on the It's Lit bathroom wall so long ago flashed through my mind:

I don't know exactly what I'm doing. I don't know exactly what I'll be. But I do know this.

I choose joy.
I choose love.
I choose hope.
And I can be anything I want.

Why hadn't I been able to see those words as clearly as I had the day I'd written them? It was right there.

I choose.

"This is the path I want to be on," I said. "Now I'm finally trusting myself to follow it."

"Let me see if I have everything right!" Doc Kai exclaimed, brandishing her iPad. She'd been tapping away nonstop while I told my story. "The big kaiju is actually one monster amalgamation of all the big feelings you denied—those mini kaiju that disappeared, yeah?"

"I think that's correct," I said as the mini kaiju on my desk nodded vigorously. "I was probably projecting mini kaiju way before I actually saw the one behind the dumpster—starting right after that Otherworld darkness took up residence inside of me. I wonder if all our supposedly hallucinating tourists actually witnessed some of those?" I bit my lip, thinking of all the reports I'd dismissed as fanciful imaginings. "Whereas this one stayed with me because I accepted the feeling, gave it space to breathe, and actually communicated with my new little friend here." I gestured to the mini kaiju and it preened, happy to be recognized.

"What about Roger?" Tosh asked, pointing to my chicken friend. "Did he come from a feeling you accepted as well? Because he's been chillin' in Makawao this whole time!"

"I think Roger must've come from my overwhelming anxiety or something, which was basically impossible to shove down," I said. Roger puffed up again, displaying his mecha wings. "Or he's the unexpected, unexplained, unknown variable no one can quite figure out. And actually, when I saw him this morning . . . well, thinking about that kind of unknown variable gave me an idea of how to go into battle today."

"So my mother will be at the beach," Nate said, setting his

mouth in a grim line. "And she'll be trying to take over the large kaiju so she can attack us—"

"Yeah, she'll likely attempt that again, since she can't mind-control me directly," I said. "She's failed every time. And she also thinks this time, I'll go along with her terrible plan and help her take Vivi. But *I* am the unknown variable, here. And I'm finally realizing that's a feature, not a bug."

"Question," Aveda said, holding up an index finger. "You know I'm not one to suggest hiding, but . . ." Her gaze shifted to Evie, who was rubbing a protective hand over her belly. "What if we simply don't go to the beach today? If Evie isn't there, won't Shasta's plan be foiled before it can even begin?"

"This version of her plan, maybe," I said. "But she won't stop—she'll just come up with a different version, and she'll keep trying to attack us and invade Earth no matter what. She's cycled through ghosts and vampires and every manner of hostile supernatural scheme, and now she's trying to use *me*. This is our chance to stop her for good."

"I agree," Evie said firmly. "And I'm not sitting this out."

I glanced down at my mini kaiju, who had gone back to sleep on top of the fidget spinner.

"Even if we aren't there, Shasta might still try to do something to my big kaiju," I said. "She knows it's a portal, one of the keys to her getting back to the Otherworld so she can get that full-scale invasion going. And I've started to feel pretty protective of these awesome monsters."

"Real-life friendly sea creatures!" Doc Kai crowed, tapping away on her iPad. "Well, potentially friendly. Bea, what did I tell ya? This could be one positive addition to the ecosystem! Just what I've been dreaming of, yeah?"

"I hope it can be that, too!" I grinned at her. "And here's what I think we have to do to get there." I looked around at each of them again, marveling at the sheer variety of talent and skill packed into one room. This was truly a superteam like no other. "Shasta thinks she can win by using *my* big kaiju to attack us, and then manipulating me to do her bidding. And she managed to convince me that this was the way it had to be—that there was only one way for a creature to feel 'fed and fulfilled.'"

I glanced down at Roger again, prancing around with his mecha wings extended.

"So back to that unpredictable variable—*me*. I needed to look at this dilemma the way *I* would: chaotic, unconventional, and pulling in all the different variables I can." I imagined my mental posterboard sparkling all around me, showing me every connection it could find. I felt my darkness pulse, that shadow that had lurked there for so long. The darkness I was no longer afraid of. The darkness I was going to *embrace*.

"I'm going to use my darkness enhanced power to connect with the big kaiju, just like I tried to do before," I explained. "And I'm going to talk to it, like I did with the little one: explain what's happening, make it feel safe and secure. I'm going to finally accept all those feelings I denied and let them flow through me—which will hopefully make the big kaiju feel 'fed and fulfilled.' Then I'll ask it to work with me to capture Shasta's consciousness, boot it back to the Otherworld, and sever the connection between realms. No superhuman sacrifice necessary."

"Gasp!" Keala exclaimed. "How are you going to do that—like, actual mechanics, please?"

"I'm sooo glad you asked!" I responded, giving her jazz hands. "I was thinking about the experiments Scott and I were doing with the power combo spell—before I got scared and started avoiding his texts at all costs." I met Scott's eyes on the iPad screen, giving him a regretful look. "I'm sorry. I loved working on a super-charged science/magic combo platter with you—and I've always loved how you support me so freely, how you've never made me feel judged. Even when I was a bratty little kid."

"It's okay, Bug," he said, gentle as ever. "Just remember that you can always talk to me. I mean, I never told Evie about the time you spilled red Kool-Aid all over that white carpet in your old apartment—"

"What?!" Evie yelped.

"No," I agreed, grinning at him. "And you spent three hours with vinegar, baking soda, and a toothbrush, helping me get it out."

"And again: what?!" Evie repeated.

"We don't need to rehash ancient history," Scott said hastily. "Anyway, Bug, I'm here for you now. What are you thinking?"

"I want to try a variation of the spell," I said, studiously avoiding Evie's gaze. "Because just like there are different ways of interpreting an old-ass prophecy, there are different ways of deploying the elements of a power combo spell. Instead of me hosting everyone's combined powers in my body, I want us to connect my power to everyone else—including the non-superpowered folks."

"So we'll all be able to project?" Aveda asked, her brow crinkling. "Will we all be beaming those calm feelings at the big kaiju?"

"Not exactly," I said. "I want you to beam all of your big, messy human emotions at *me*. I'll use my darkness-enhanced power to gather all of them together and project at the kaiju in one huge blob of feelings. And I'm counting on all these variables—the extra power of my darkness, the extra oomph of adding all your feelings to mine, the close connection I have with the kaiju—to pull this off."

"What about Mother?" Nate asked. "Won't she be deploying her spell on Evie as well?"

"I'm thinking we can throw up some mental protection around Evie as part of the combo spell," I said. "Since we'll all be connected."

"Yes," Scott said, his brows knitting together. "I believe I can direct the magic to help us form a bubble that will at least partially shield her."

"If we know that wretched Shasta is the woman in the sun hat, why not just neutralize that person, darling?" Lucy asked.

"Because there's no guarantee Shasta will stay in that woman's body," I said. "Her consciousness could simply escape—no, this battle has to be fought on *my* turf. The brain plane."

"But if Shasta has also been through this scenario several times, won't she have learned from those experiences?" Nate pressed. "Just as you have learned from yours? What if she attempts something new we are not prepared for?"

"That's another variable," I said. "But I'm also counting on the element of surprise. She thinks I'm all beat down and that I'm ready to sacrifice my precious niece—hell, maybe she even keyed into my plan to sacrifice *myself*. Little does she know that I now plan on doing neither." I drew myself up tall, purpose percolating in my chest. "Shasta wants me to be afraid of my power and everything it can do   because she knows I can beat her. But I'm going to embrace that power in a way I never have before."

"Is there a particular feeling you want us to summon, Bebe?" Leah inquired. Pancake inclined his head, as if repeating the question.

"Love." I cast a sidelong glance at Sam, who gave me one of his sweet, secret smiles—the one that said we were in this together.

"Just one feeling? Will that be enough?" Aveda asked.

"Yes." My voice was strong and sure. "Love is *always* enough—and it's more than that, even. It's kind of everything. You all showed me that, while I was on my time-travel adventures. Even when I was sad and broken and doubting myself, you were all there for me, in ways I didn't expect. If I can give the kaiju that . . ." I smiled slightly, my heart swelling in my chest. "I know it will feel fed, fulfilled. Because that's how I feel now, looking at all of you."

My eyes filled with tears and I felt Sam's fingertips brushing mine. I twined our fingers together and squeezed his hand, all that love rushing through me.

"I've been thinking about the big conclusion of my Mom-Demon adventures," I said. "And I remember that seeing all of you battling through fear and uncertainty was what inspired me then, too—I realized that choosing hope means fighting against impossible odds and impossible choices to do the right thing. That's the kind of hero I want to be."

"Bea . . ." Evie rose from her seat and crossed the room to me, her expression unreadable. She stood in front of me, studying me intently. She looked fully awake now, her gaze alert and clear.

I shifted uncomfortably as the silence stretched out between us. Was she going to scold me for all my questionable decisions during my time-travel adventures or tell me why my plan was totally bananas and couldn't possibly work or—

"Little Sister," she said softly. "That's the kind of hero you already are."

CHAPTER THIRTY-FOUR

IF THIS BATTLE was going to happen the way it had in the past, we had about an hour to prepare and get to the beach.

Everyone broke into little pods for some extra strategizing, and I sat at my desk, toying with one of my fidget spinners and gathering my internal strength. I'd been totally freaking floored by Evie's words to me—and I honestly hadn't known how to react, so I'd looked down at the floor, cheeks heating, and murmured a quiet thank-you.

Yes, I was reclaiming myself and getting that big ol' superheroine confidence going. But my sister being proud of me . . . yeah, I still couldn't quite wrap my head around that one.

"Bea, come with me," Aveda ordered, marching past my desk with purpose. "Evie and I need to talk to you."

"But I'm, like, gathering myself," I muttered, even though I was already standing up to follow her. Funny how instantly I reverted to the bratty little sister of Team Tanaka/Jupiter.

She led me into the teeny kitchenette, where Evie was leaning against the counter, and closed the door behind us.

"Is this some kind of intervention?" I held up my hands. "Because I've seen you two do this kind of thing way too many times at this point, and we're just about to go into a really important battle, and like I said before, I'm trying to gather myself—"

"Bea!" Evie interrupted, pushing off from the counter and throwing her arms around me. "Can you please stop talking for two seconds and let us take care of you?"

"I don't need to be taken care of," I protested, my arms hanging at my sides. "Didn't all my awesome time-travel adventures prove I've at least grown up a little bit?"

"That's not what we're talking about," Aveda said, pursing her lips.

Evie pulled back from the hug. "I still can't believe you went through all of that and didn't tell us until now," she said—and I was shocked to see tears brimming in her eyes.

"Yeah, yeah, I know I fucked up a lot," I said, trying to sound breezy. She did *not* need to be worrying about me right now. "I guess . . . Leah and I were doing a lot of hypothesizing about time travel based on fictional examples, and that 'don't do anything to mess up the timeline' thing always seems to be the rule that gets emphasized the most. Although . . ." I gnawed on my lower lip, remembering Doc Kai's musings about how Doc Brown's life had been saved because Marty had written that letter telling him everything. "If I really think about it, when these stories have happy endings, it's always because someone *did* fuck up the timeline—because they just couldn't seem to blend in and do exactly what they were told."

A small smile played across my lips. "You know, I thought a lot about this after reading the real ending of *A Kaiju for Christmas*. I've loved that movie for years, and one thing I never really thought about is the fact that Thomas doesn't talk to Sandrine—or anyone else in his life—about his impossible choice. Yeah, the shitty warlock tells him he *can't* talk to anyone or Sandrine is doomed. But why does he just believe it? And why did I believe Shasta?" I shook my head, memories of my talks with the conniving wannabe–demon queen floating through my mind. "I guess I've been afraid for so long of what I could become—and of messing things up everywhere I go—and she knew that and took advantage of it. I can be kind of a disaster, and I always seem to *cause* disasters, and I was terrified I'd cause them for all the people I love. And then also I think I just wanted y'all not to worry about me anymore. To know that I was actually growing up, and that I could handle my own problems without relying on you for everything. But I wish I'd told both of you sooner, I really do, because—"

"Bea!" Aveda crossed her arms over her chest, her face a mask of exasperation. "We're not bringing this up to scold you. We're bringing it up because we've both done the same thing."

I opened my mouth, then closed it, tilting my head at them in confusion. I probably looked like Pancake when he was puzzled as to why I wasn't petting him.

"My god, she's speechless," Aveda said, arching an eyebrow. "Is that a first?"

"It's true," Evie said, laughing a little and taking my hand. "Annie and I have both been through hard things where we just couldn't seem to *talk* to anyone. I started pasting on a big fake smile and telling everyone I was fine when I was freaked out over being pregnant—I also didn't want anyone to worry about me, and I don't think I could admit to myself how scared I was. Because that made it real."

"And I tried to take on absolutely everything while we were on that vampire mission in LA," Aveda said. "I convinced myself that I could fix every problem and take down every demon all by myself. But I was doing that because I felt completely out of control and like I had to act as a super-human shield for every single person in my life." She met my eyes, her voice sincere. "I needed to be taken care of, too—and I needed to trust the people I love to do that."

"We're telling you this because we wish we could've been there for you through all of your adventures," Evie said, squeezing my hand. "Asking for help, supporting each other—that's not weakness, it's the exact opposite. But Annie and I both had to learn that the hard way. We have a little too much experience when it comes to attempting to shoulder every burden and solve every problem—and freaking ourselves out even more in the process. Don't you remember how I was before I became a superheroine?" She shook her head ruefully. "I was terrified I was going to burn my entire life down, so I suppressed my fire power as hard as I could."

"We all have our *things*, right?" Aveda said, nodding sagely. "Qualities people or society or whatever have convinced us are inherently bad, but are often our greatest strengths. Evie's beautiful empathy, the way she cares so much for everyone and embraces her softer feelings—people perceive that as some kind of weakness. Or with me—how many times has someone tried to convince me that I'm an egomaniacal bitch because I'm ambitious and powerful and ask for what I want?" She drew herself up tall, crossing her arms over her chest. "It's such bullshit. And by the way, this particular brand of bullshit gets applied especially hard to women of color."

"I believed in the bullshit for way too long," Evie said wryly. "And I also believed I couldn't handle my own power, that it was too much for me—the same thing you were feeling, Bea."

"Another insidious stereotype!" Aveda hissed. "Why is it that we assume women who have power will inevitably turn into supervillains?"

"Seriously," Evie said, her eyes narrowing. "And Tanaka girls are badass. We should at least know *that* by now."

"You have an unconventional way of doing things, Bea," Aveda said, her piercing black eyes meeting mine. "You look at the world in a way that no one else does."

"And you do everything with such gusto," Evie chimed in. "You find joy wherever you are, you attract new friends like no one else I know, and you truly relish every moment of your existence."

"And that makes me . . . what?" I said. "Flighty, irresponsible, bad at commitment—"

"No!" Evie shook her head, laughing.

"Way to learn the wrong lesson," Aveda muttered.

"It means you don't get caught up in pointless rules or stuck in a pattern of doing what society or whatever is telling you you're supposed to do," Evie said, squeezing my hand more fervently. "You *live*, Bea. Fully and passionately and like you want to squeeze every drop of wonder out of the world. I love that about you, and you're becoming even more amazing every day." She beamed at me, her eyes going misty again. "I'm so proud of you."

"I . . ." I bit my lip, hastily swiping at my eyes. "Thank you—both of you." My throat clogged, tears spilling down my cheeks faster than I could wipe them away. "I can't believe I bought into that sacrificial bullshit—that I almost missed out on more time with the people I love because I thought I had to be all tragic and noble and shit to be a hero."

"Hmph," Aveda sniffed. "You know, I am sick to death of women-of-color heroines being most prized for suffering and sacrifice and so-called resilience. We're allowed to enjoy ourselves, we deserve to be treasured and cared for, and we don't have to struggle endlessly to be worthy of happily ever after. I am full up on resilience, thank you very much."

"Future You also had a lot to say on that topic," I said, grinning at her.

"So I'm fabulous in every part of the timeline," Aveda said. "Good to know."

"You really are. And I think . . ." I paused, my throat thickening again. I swallowed and forged on. "I want to be part of the team again. Like, officially. I mean, I keep butting into all your investigations, just like the annoying little sister I've always been—"

"Stop." Aveda rolled her eyes. "Bea, you haven't been anyone's little sister in quite some time—except in a purely affectionate sense. Like I said, we're not here to scold you. And like Evie said, we're trying to offer our support as co-heroines, as *colleagues*! I think the only person who still sees you that way is . . . *you*."

"I might still see you that way a little," Evie admitted. "But I'm also in serious awe of everything you've accomplished. And look how you just commanded that room in there: you rallied the combined forces of multiple superteams!"

I looked down at the floor, trying to process everything they were saying to me. I thought about those incredible superteams, how so many of the people in that room had believed in me when I hadn't been able to believe in myself. Nate, who had always seen my potential. Scott, who had gone along with my most bananas ideas. Leah and Sam, who managed to see pieces of me more clearly than I ever had. Doc Kai, who heartily encouraged my weird way of science-ing. Pika, who shared my bright light.

I'd been so set on seeing myself a certain way, I'd shut myself off from all other perspectives—the perspectives of people I respected, trusted, and loved.

"I guess I'm figuring out that growing up doesn't mean totally shutting myself off from everyone," I said slowly. I thought back to what Sam had said about our big love—how it could never be separate from anything because it was the reason for everything. "My very mature life needs all of you in it. So yeah, I want to come back to the team. But I'm not sure what to do, because I also really want to stay in Makawao, I absolutely adore the work I'm doing with Doc Kai, and I love all my friends here, they've become my family too . . ."

I trailed off, my mental vision board already attempting to come up with a plan that would make all of these impossible scenarios work.

"I'm sure we can figure something out," Aveda said, giving me a queenly nod. "I didn't ever feel like you left, either."

"What a freaking liar," Evie hooted, rolling her eyes. "She's missed you almost as much as I have." She smiled at me and took my hand again, the tears in her eyes matching my own. "I hope you can be there when the baby comes, Bea—even if the experience turns out to be as wild as it sounds. Actually, *especially* if it turns out that way." Her smile turned thoughtful as she studied me, so much emotion surfacing in her gaze. "I guess you already know the baby's first name—but did you ever hear her middle name on any of your travels? Because Nate and I have that all picked out, too."

"No, I don't think so," I said, scouring my memories. "What is it?"

"Constance," she said, her voice catching. "Vivian Constance Tanaka-Jones."

"Constance," I repeated, my own tears returning with a vengeance. "You're middle-naming her after *me*? Big Sis, I know you're already worried about this baby having demonic superpowers—"

"Did you see anything in the future?" Evie interrupted, worry flashing over her face. "*Does* she have superpowers?!"

"I didn't see anything," I said, smiling slightly. "But what I'm saying is: giving her my middle name is kind of asking for trouble, don't you think?"

"If she's the kind of trouble you were, I welcome it," Evie insisted, taking my hand. "Bea, I know you're always talking about how I had to raise you. But you raised me, too. You showed me how to be open, how to feel joy and rage so fiercely, and how to let all my feelings out. I wouldn't be who I am without you—and even if I could go back in time, I wouldn't change a thing. That is an undeniable part of *my* story." One corner of her mouth quirked into a slight, playful smile. "And just for the record, I don't think I'll ever stop worrying about you—but it's kinda nice to know that you worry about me, too."

"Always," I murmured, overwhelmed with so many feelings, I was surprised I hadn't fallen through time. "You know . . . maybe it's actually good that we worry about each other so much, Big Sis—it means we care."

She pulled me into another teary hug, and this time my arms went around her too. I let her hold me, gathering my strength for the battle ahead.

I couldn't help but flash back to another moment when she'd hugged me like this, comforting me backstage after my scene-stealing performance at that long-ago Christmas pageant. I'd broken down sobbing over Mom, and she'd held my sparkly little Christmas-tree form as the other parents sent scandalized looks our way.

"That Bea Tanaka," they'd said. "She's going to be *trouble*."

Damn right I am, I thought, hugging Evie even more fiercely. *And that's why we're going to win this thing.*

CHAPTER THIRTY-FIVE

I COULDN'T BE sure of what all Shasta had deduced, and I
didn't want to run the risk of alerting her to our plan. So I
asked everyone to act like we were still having a totally normal beach day, with the extra special additions of the San
Francisco crew joining us on FaceTime. Oh, and Roger and
my mini kaiju hid themselves behind a small rock formation,
so as not to arouse further suspicion.

We spread out the towels and the mochi as we had before—
minus the sexy bicker-fest I'd engaged in with Sam. I was
also able to stop Evie from stringing Christmas lights around
that long-suffering palm tree. And I added my talismans to
our towel setup, placing them all around me.

"That's Shasta," I murmured to Evie, subtly jerking my
chin at the tall lady with the giant sun hat. She was positioned where she usually was, a ways down the shore. "Or it
will be, at some point. I'm not sure if she's possessing that
lady's body just yet."

"So creepy," Evie shuddered.

"Should we go to the beach shack?" Sam asked. "If we're
replicating our previous movements and all."

"Let's do the power combo spell first," I said, my cheeks
flushing. "I want to make sure that link is strong before she
tries to control my big kaiju and gets it all riled up. Nate, Doc
Kai—can y'all keep an eye on Sun Hat Lady while Scott and
I get that going?"

"On it," Doc Kai said. "Bea, this is so thrilling! I've never gotten to see so much supernatural action live and in person!"

"Well, get ready," I said, giving her a wink. "If your beloved friendly sea monsters become a reality, we might be dealing with a lot more supernatural doings real soon."

I turned to the iPad Aveda had set up on one of the towels. The FaceTime window featuring everyone back home at Tanaka/Jupiter HQ was positioned right in the center, Scott framed in the middle of the gang and awaiting my cue. Leah and Pancake's window hovered next to them.

"You ready, Bug?" Scott asked, flashing me his easy grin. "You sure you feel okay about power combo-ing it up?"

"More than okay," I said firmly. "I am so freakin' *ready*."

He gave me a nod and we both closed our eyes, ready to connect. I felt his magic touch my mind, his spell fusing us together from across the ocean.

There you are! he exclaimed in my head.

And my glittery column of darkness pulsed with pleasure, reverberating through me. I felt that same intoxicating sensation I'd had when we'd done this spell a month ago—but this time I breathed that in, made space for it.

I'm using the spell to link us all together, Scott said. *And wow, Bug, I can really feel what you were talking about the first time round—this Otherworld magic . . . it's a part of you now. And it feels so fucking cool!*

Yay, me! I thought back. *I'm glad you finally understand the excellence of the supernatural rainbow disco ball. Now let's see about sharing my power with everyone . . .*

I reached deep inside of myself and felt that darkness again, that weird and wild energy. I let it swirl around my mind, allowed it to embrace my consciousness. I sensed everyone else's mind connecting with mine as Scott continued his spell.

A thrill ran up my spine when I realized I could actually *see* all of my family in my mind's eye, little individual lights flitting around that big rainbow disco ball. I visualized all of them coming together, fusing into one. Then I made that rainbow disco ball expand, surrounding every single person's consciousness with magic.

Are you all there? I called out.

Present! Aveda said officiously. *This is . . . wow. Incredible! I totally feel like I could mind-control someone right now!*

Except we're not *doing that!* Evie said, sounding exasperated.

Of course not, Aveda sniffed. *I'm just saying, I can see why that was such a temptation! Why, if I'd had this when I was dealing with that asshole Mercedes—*

Anyway! I interrupted them. *You should all feel that version of my power I'm beaming out to you. Start preparing your best emotions, because as soon as the storm begins and the kaiju rises—*

As if on cue, the sky darkened and the ground started to shake. I felt Scott directing some of our combined magic toward Evie, surrounding her in that bubble of protection. Beach-goers began to flee, just as they had before.

And then my massive kaiju burst out of the ocean, sending those tsunami-level tidal waves crashing toward the shore. A cacophony of screams echoed through the air as people started to run in earnest. I turned slightly, looking for the woman with the sun hat. She had her back to us, gazing out at the churning sea.

The kaiju roared. And the ground shook even more decisively, a rumble I felt down to my bones.

Now! I screamed in my head. *Project those emotions at me right fucking now! And remember: it's all about the love!*

I felt all of them do it at once, the collective power of my family's love flowing through me and making my darkness shine even brighter. I stumbled to my feet, shaky on the moving earth. But that love powered me forward, lighting me up from within. I focused on the kaiju, trying to get its golden gaze to meet mine, trying to get our minds to link.

Hey, I thought at it. *I'm here for you, okay? I* am *you, in a way. And I'm gonna get you to talk to me, but first . . .*

The big kaiju roared and lurched through the water as I

gathered all of those emotions in my chest, the darkness bolstering my projection and making it even more powerful.

Then I sent that projection spinning directly at the kaiju's roaring face.

It halted in the water mid-lurch, cocking its head to the side.

Yes! I thought at it, my darkness pulsing in triumph. *That's it! Can you hear me in your mind now? Because we have much to discuss—*

And then I felt that massive mental shove, the one I now knew had to be Shasta.

I pushed back against it, certain that all the dark magic flowing through me would keep her out. But I still felt that invisible wall coming down between me and my kaiju, locking me in my own brain, and why was this happening, why did it suddenly feel like she was so much stronger, why—

I gasped, falling to my knees as pain exploded around my temples. I was vaguely aware of voices yelling my name, but I couldn't tell if they were in my head or if my family was using their actual voices *outside* of my head or—

Before I knew what was happening, I was engulfed in darkness and the entire world was disintegrating around me and I felt like I was falling, falling . . .

I landed with a *whump* on something very soft, my eyes flying open as my limbs scrabbled for purchase. I was . . .

I frowned, looking around frantically. Where was I?

I was surrounded by shiny, sparkling surfaces, each one lit up with a cascade of rainbows. It looked like a hall of mirrors as designed by a really extra unicorn.

Or the inside of a rainbow disco ball.

"That's right, Beatrice," a smug voice purred. "We're in your mind."

I whipped around to find Shasta standing over me, arms crossed over her chest—now she looked like she had back when we'd first encountered her, embodying the humanoid form she'd initially chosen on Earth. A satisfied grin spread over her face.

"Wh-what are you doing?!" I sputtered. "Did you actually manage to possess me this time?! After failing every other time?"

"Now, now, there's no need to be rude," Shasta said, giving me an exaggerated pout. "Although I suppose you're already being rude, since you decided to betray me!" She shook her head, waving a scolding finger in my face. "Ironically, that's what gave me my opening." Her grin reinstated itself, ghoulish in its delight. "When I attempted my possession of you this time, I found your mind strangely . . . accessible. Like the door was unlocked and there was a big ol' welcome sign out front." She glanced around, feigning awe at my sparkly rainbows. "I believe it's because you'd opened your consciousness in order to connect with your family—and your darkness was too busy with all of that to protect you!"

"Dammit," I growled, attempting to scramble to my feet.

But . . . I couldn't move. I was frozen in place as the rainbows swirled around me—cradled on my back by the softness of my brain's apparently very cushy surface, but unable to get up.

"Mmm." Shasta smiled down at me. "My possession has almost claimed you fully. Soon you'll only be able to watch as I complete my mission."

"So you're not making with the baby-snatching right now?" I snapped, terror seizing my chest.

"That will come—once I'm able to possess you one hundred percent," Shasta said, waving a hand. "Your mind is still so . . . *resistant* . . ." She frowned into space, contemplating the inside of my brain. "Perhaps I have enough control to use one element of your power, though. Let me see . . ." She closed her eyes and concentrated while I flailed around, fruitlessly attempting to get to my feet.

I hadn't gotten very far before I was plunged into darkness once more, hurtling toward something I couldn't see.

I gasped for air, clawed at the empty space around me . . . and then suddenly, I was back in my body again.

And everything was all wrong.

I was sitting up very straight in a large, ornate chair with plush velvet cushions and way too many gold curlicue accents, and I seemed to be positioned in some kind of ... evil throne room? That was the only term I could think of to describe my strange, macabre surroundings. It looked like an extra goth version of a haunted mansion, flocked black velvet covering the walls and high ceilings, creepy candelabras and over-the-top sconces everywhere. I reflexively reached up to rub my temples, which were already throbbing away. Although ...

I felt my way up my head and discovered that perhaps the *gigantic fucking crown* I was currently wearing was contributing to the headache situation.

"What the fuck," I said out loud.

"Please!" a voice cried out.

I looked down and saw a beautiful young woman prostrating herself on the gray stone floor in front of me, her tangled snarl of hair covering most of her face. Her dark eyes flashed with desperation, her body was clad in rags, and ...

I frowned, studying her.

Why was she so familiar ...

"Please, Auntie Bea!" she wailed. "You have to remove Mom and Dad from your possession! I'll do anything ..." She broke down in inconsolable sobs.

"Vivi?" I breathed, unable to process what I was seeing.

That's right, Beatrice! a very smug, very annoying voice trilled in my head. *I've taken you to the future—your future! Don't try to move around very much, I have enough control over your body to make it hurt.*

I of course tested this anyway, trying to stand. I was immediately hit with a wave of pain so excruciating, I nearly vomited all over my weird goth throne room.

What is this?! I thought at Shasta. *What kind of demon trick are you trying to pull now?*

It's not a trick, she said, as Vivi continued to sob. *I have enough control over your mind to activate your time travel. Like I said, this is your inevitable future—wherein you are simply unable to resist all that beautiful temptation of Otherworld darkness and turn full supervillain. This is what happens after you refuse to help me, no matter how many foolhardy quests you embark on! I offered you the only chance you've ever had to be a hero! To help me in my noble mission to sever the link between our dimensions—*

Except you weren't going to do that! I thought back at her furiously. *You fucking lied to me about* my *kaiju! The little one told me all about your plan, how you were going to launch an invasion after you got back to the Otherworld with Vivi!*

So I was, Shasta said. *Even if the big kaiju closed all the portals, well! Me and those great scientific minds of the Otherworld just knew the power Vivi was about to bless us with would help me reopen everything so I could finally rule over both dimensions as I've always deserved! I would have been a much more benevolent ruler than you, though. It's disappointing you selfishly decided not to sacrifice anything, Bea— and all of that led to a series of even more selfish choices. Look where you end up—it's even worse than Earth being ruled over by demons, don't you think?*

"Please, Auntie Bea," Vivi sobbed, sprawling in front of me. "Mom and Dad love you! We all love you so much . . ."

So sad, Shasta *tsk*-ed. *Your darkness eventually consumed you and you hungered only for power—you have so much of the world under your mind control, doing your evil bidding. Except Vivi—you couldn't bring yourself to take away her free will just yet. But don't worry—that part's coming.*

No! I roared at her, helplessness overwhelming me. *That can't be true!*

You know it is, Shasta gloated. *You can still stop this—you can still give me full control and help me take Vivi to a place where she can thrive, instead of ending up here. And like I said, I promise to be a much kinder ruler than Queen Bea. But otherwise? This is who you really are, Bea—who you're going to become. This is your future you can't stop, your destiny you can't deny. This is where you were always going to end up.*

Don't listen to her.

My eyes widened, my posture straightening—which sent another wave of pain roiling through my body.

There was a new voice in my head now. And I swore it sounded like—

Yeah, it's Evie, Little Sis! Scott felt Shasta invading your mind right as it was happening and managed to section the rest of us off in that bubble he'd set up for me. We're all still linked to you through the power combo spell, and we're trying to figure out how to break her mental hold!

Wait, so everyone's in my head right now?! I squawked. *But Shasta . . . can she hear me talking to you?*

No! The bubble's holding strong, Evie said. *We can hear her, but she doesn't seem to detect us yet. And we can't see what you're seeing right now, whatever time you've ended up in, but it sounds . . . disturbing. I know it's hard, but you have to fight Shasta.*

But . . . I looked down at Evie's daughter, begging for my mercy. *Evie, this is really bad. I totally turned into a supervillain! Even after all our tearful moments and your inspiring pep talk and my dedication to all things hero! It's my destiny!*

Tears filled my eyes as I gazed down at Vivi's sobbing form. My worst fears had come true. My destiny was already written—no matter how hard I tried, no matter how many heroic quests I took on, no matter how much I embraced my darkness . . . I was still going to end up here. Totally evil and all alone.

That's not true, Evie said, her voice more fierce than I'd ever heard it. *You know that's not true! Remember what you told me about my birth moment—you showed up and changed it! You literally rewrote something that supposedly already happened! And you know what, the future hasn't actually happened yet. Your future will be determined by the choices you make!*

And not every choice is the wrong one, yeah? Doc Kai piped up. *You're writing your story right now, Bea! And we all believe in you!*

Yes, Bebe! Now Leah's voice was in my head, sunny and determined. *Remember what we talked about with Ms. Marvel! Good is not a thing you are—*

"It's a thing you do," I whispered, tears streaming down my cheeks.

Bea, another voice said, so tender my tears flowed even faster.

Sam? I thought back, my inner voice shaking.

You can do this, he said. *I love you so much—don't forget, you're the unknown variable! And I know you can math really, really hard.*

A laugh exploded from my chest, disrupting my tears. On the floor below me, Vivi looked up quizzically.

What's funny about this? Shasta said, suddenly suspicious.

Nothing, I thought back, willing my tears to retreat.

We're still projecting all that love at you, Bea, Evie said. *Shasta's hold may be dimming the effect, but—*

I feel it, I thought fiercely. *I feel it all.*

And I did, I realized. I could still sense their lights reaching for me, bright and sure.

My little bathroom wall message from long ago flashed through my mind like a beacon: *I choose joy. I choose love. I choose hope.*

I gritted my teeth and felt around in my mind, locating that darkness inside of me. It was still there, still thrumming away. And . . . hmm. I could feel it reaching for me, too, as if trying to wriggle free from Shasta's grasp.

What had she said to me right before sending me to this horror show of a future? Something about my mind being resistant. Something about not having full control of me just yet . . .

Right. Because if she had that . . . she wouldn't need to show me this shit. She wouldn't need me to give in, to offer her full power over my brain. She could just mind-control me into doing whatever she wanted.

Did she not remember just how much *trouble* I could be?

I closed my eyes and felt my darkness flowing through me,

reaching out for me, both of us craving that connection. I imagined it wrapping around my mind, protecting me, ready to summon an army of kaiju or project me through time to save me from the evil that wanted to claim my mind.

I told it what I wanted to do, even though I didn't have all the pieces figured out just yet. Doing things the Bea Tanaka way yet again. My darkness pulsed in response, those rainbows glowing more vividly.

Hey Shasta, I thought at her. *Are my talismans still lying next to me on that beach towel?*

Of course, she smarmed. *That's how I was able to bring you to this dystopian future in the first place!*

Great, I thought back. *Oh, and one more thing—fuck you!*

I squeezed my eyes shut, visualized myself clasping one of my talismans, and let all the love from my family flow through me, more powerful than anything I'd ever felt before.

And then I was falling through time all over again.

Chapter thirty-six

WHEN MY EYES snapped open, I was sprawled in a very familiar bathroom in a very familiar bookstore. I bolted upright, gasping for air, my temples throbbing . . . but hey, I could move again! And I didn't sense Shasta in my head.

I scrambled to my feet, my gaze scanning the collage of affirming notes written all over the walls of It's Lit's most peaceful enclave. I zeroed in on that bathroom wall message to myself, those words that had flashed through my brain, the mantra I'd scribbled right before leaving for Maui. The letters were now all faded and patchy. But still there.

I moved closer and ran my fingertips over the message I'd written so long ago, lingering on the two little words that repeated over and over again—the simple phrase I'd finally realized was the key to everything.

I choose

I took a deep breath and exited the bathroom, taking in my surroundings. The store was empty, but had been decorated for what appeared to be an important event. There were flowers everywhere, twinkly lights strung over the ceiling, and all of the furniture had been moved to make way for a petal-strewn aisle leading up to the stage area where the store usually hosted events. It looked like a fairy wonderland.

My hand flew to my head and found . . . more flowers. I felt around some more. I seemed to be wearing an elaborate flower crown. And I was in a dress of the softest pink, its gauzy layers floating around me.

"Auntie Bea!"

I whipped around to see . . . oh my god. It was Vivi again, all grown up and bustling into the store. But now she was beaming, glowing, lit up from within. Her long dark hair fell in loose waves around her, festooned with a cascade of white flowers. She was clad in a very chic white silk suit, perfectly tailored to her form, those piercing eyes she'd gotten from Nate sparkling with joy.

"What do you think?!" she crowed, spinning around. "Shruti did amazing work, right? I'm so excited!"

She towed me over to the pink velvet couch, still bouncing with unrestrained happiness.

"You're getting married today," I said, the pieces clicking into place as we sat down.

She cocked an eyebrow, giving me a confused grin. "Well, yeah! And listen, I'm soooo grateful that Auntie Leah let me use her store! I can't imagine a more magical place!"

My gaze drifted to the wall behind the counter, and I saw that beautiful mural Leah had wanted to paint, the mermaids that looked like us floating against a serene blue backdrop.

Vivi clasped my hands with hers, bouncing in place. Her nails, done up with glittering silver polish, twinkled in the light. "Thank you for everything you've done! You're the best maid of honor I could have asked for! Or is it 'matron of honor,' since you're married to Uncle Sam? Eh, I don't like the way that sounds, though! How about super sparkly magical person of honor?!" She giggled and threw her arms around me, pulling me into a bone-crushing hug. "I love youuuuu!" she cooed.

"Vivi," I murmured, completely overwhelmed. "You're okay."

She pulled back and grinned at me, pulling a goofy face. "Of course I am! And seriously, thank you for everything—you're the only one I could trust to really see the full rainbow of my vision!" She gestured to the store, in all its fairyland glory. "Don't get me wrong, I adore Mom, but she can be kind of a stick in the mud—oh! Speaking of, looks like everyone's here!"

Vivi leaped up from the couch and bounded toward the door.

And then I saw them all, spilling into the store. Every single member of the extended Tanaka/Jupiter family. I saw Evie, beaming with pride, silver threading through her hair, Nate at her side. Aveda, marching purposefully as ever, power ponytail swinging behind her. Scott was whispering in her ear again, probably telling her to slow down.

And Sam . . . still so handsome and giving me one of those secret smiles . . .

There were others too, people I hadn't met yet, people who only existed in the future.

I closed my eyes, tears streaming down my face.

This time, I wasn't at all surprised when my surroundings dissolved, and I felt myself tumbling through time.

🔥

"Bea!" Sam's strong hands gripped my shoulders, his face swimming into view above me.

"I'm okay!" I shrieked, bolting upright and throwing my arms around him. I was back on that Maui beach, sitting on my towel, my talismans by my side. Roger and the mini kaiju had emerged from their hiding place and Roger was nudging my foot, making concerned little *caw* noises. "Where's Shasta?" I looked around, trying to find the woman in the sun hat.

But I only saw my family, clustering up around me. And on the towel next to mine, Scott, Leah, and the gang back at HQ were still on the iPad screen.

"She's gone!" Evie was flinging herself at me and Sam now, trying to wrap both of us in an unwieldy hug. "The woman in the sun hat . . . Shasta must have jumped from her head to yours. When we tried talking to her, it was pretty clear she was no longer possessed. Man, she was *so* confused. Bea, I'm not sure what happened, but . . . ."

"I time traveled!" I sang out. "I mean, again. And on purpose. The future Shasta showed me was this wretched dystopia where I was some kind of evil queen—"

"Okay, that sounds kind of cool, though," Leah murmured.

"And kind of hot," Sam added.

"And at first it gave me this sick sense of inevitability—it was exactly what I've been so terrified of, my total descent into supervillainy. But hearing you all in my brain, remembering everything I've been through during all my time-traveling adventures . . ." I shook my head, a slow smile spreading over my face. "I started to realize just how completely impossible it is for me to picture that kind of future now. So I asked my darkness to help me find a future where I trusted my path and my choices—where I trusted *myself.* I knew it had to exist out there somewhere."

"And . . . ?" Aveda raised an inquiring eyebrow.

I beamed at her. "It does. And it's beautiful."

"Beatrice, you mentioned previously that you need to visualize the spot on the timeline you're traveling to," Nate said. "But given that this is a piece of the future you haven't experienced yet, how did you do that?"

"I pictured that message I left to myself on the It's Lit bathroom wall," I explained. "And I focused on those two very important words: *I choose.* Because I wanted to go to the future I'm writing for myself."

"I love that!" Doc Kai enthused, clapping her hands together. "Marty McFly would be proud, eh?"

"I hope his amazing mentor would be, too," I said, giving her an affectionate pat on the shoulder. "'Cause he definitely couldn't have done any of this without her—she's gotten him . . . er, her? Sorry, my metaphor's totally breaking down now. What I'm trying to say is: thank you for encouraging me to always look at things from an unexpected angle. You altered the course of *my* life in the most incredible way, too." Doc Kai blushed, reaching up to cover my hand with hers.

"Bug, our power combo connection to you broke when

you time traveled to this other future," Scott said. "And we think that's also what broke Shasta's partial hold on your mind."

"Perhaps she could not follow you because she could not visualize where you were going," Nate said. "And although you did not know either . . ." He grinned at me. "As you said, you trusted yourself and took a risk on a very innovative experiment."

"You basically *escaped through time*!" Leah crowed. "How cool is that?"

"I realized she was trying to manipulate me again," I said slowly, trying to recall my train of thought. "To make me think I needed to reject my darkness and my power and give her everything. But knowing all of you were there, listening to everything you were saying to me . . ." I smiled at my families, my eyes misting over. "It helped me figure it all out. The power combo spell may not have worked *exactly* as intended, but the love I felt from you all—it gave me the strength I needed."

"So your plan worked, just not the way you intended?" Doc Kai said. "Seems very *you*."

"Seriously." I grinned at her. "And then I remembered what the mini kaiju said to me about both the time travel and the kaiju being protection—oh! What about my big kaiju?!"

"Weelllllll . . ." Doc Kai said slowly.

I followed her gaze to the ocean—and saw that my big kaiju was there still. But now it was simply floating in the water, gazing at us from afar, its golden eyes glowing with curiosity. No more massive waves coming our way.

I stood and made my way down to the shore, my eyes locked with the kaiju's. I stopped right where the ocean lapped at my feet, the water as warm and soothing as it usually was.

I gathered all of those feelings of love in my chest, everything I'd felt from my family. I let my darkness reinforce them, and sent them spinning toward my big kaiju, hoping it felt safe at last.

Hello, I thought tentatively. *I just want you to know: I accept every feeling you're made up of. I accept every bit of myself. And I'm not sure how it all works, but I think that means . . . you can exist here peacefully?*

Yes, the big kaiju thought back at me. I felt our minds touch, connecting us in that special way. The kaiju's feelings flowed through me: all of its contentment, its wonder at being set free. Even the way it was speaking was so much calmer—and way more coherent.

But you still have something to decide, the kaiju continued.

Oh no, I thought at it. *What now?!*

The evil one, it said. *You pushed her from your mind when you leaped to your beautiful future. And now . . . she is here.*

What?! Like Shasta's consciousness is inside of your *mind?*

Something like that, it said. *My connection to you allowed me to trap her—*

I winced. *I'm sorry. She is* so *annoying! Oh, and look at you, no longer speaking in 'we' terms like the Borg!*

Indeed, the big kaiju thought. *Because I am now . . . fed. And fulfilled. So I can—*

"Boot her back?!" I cried out loud. "Oh my god, yes. Do it!"

This will also close all the portals, the big kaiju said. *Just as the prophecy says.*

"So I did get to be the 'child of two worlds,'" I crowed, vamping a little. "But what will happen to you? Will you be able to stick around? You just won't be a portal anymore?"

I believe so, the big kaiju said. *But all of this is not certain—as you know, prophecies have a way of being open to interpretation.*

"Cute," I said. "Was that a little joke?"

I am from you, the kaiju said, its voice something like sardonic. *I can be cute. But what I am saying is this: it is not certain that this severing of dimensions will be forever, or will work the way we think it might. The Otherworld and your world have touched and mingled for many years now, and that cannot be undone. You may see those effects continue, morph, and grow—just as I have already morphed so much during my existence. And your enemies may return someday . . .*

I turned and looked back at my sprawling, extended, interconnected family, laughing and talking amongst themselves, celebrating and stuffing their faces with mochi. Roger and the mini kaiju flitted about, attempting to snag crumbs for themselves.

"You know what?" I said, facing the big kaiju again. "I think that's okay. We have gotten good things from the Otherworld, after all. Nate. Superpowers. My beautiful darkness. Who knows, maybe someday we'll be able to make contact with some friendlier demonic types. And if the evil forces from that dimension decide to come for us again? We can handle it."

My darkness surged, that glittery rainbow disco ball lighting me up from the inside, making me feel like I was radiating the same incandescent glow Vivi had on her wedding day.

I met the big kaiju's golden eyes again and smiled.

"Turns out, we're all pretty good at causing trouble."

EPILOGUE

Christmas Eve, Nine Months Later

"NO!" I YELPED, gently moving Vivi's chubby little hand away from a heaping plate of gingerbread. "You just started solids, I'm pretty sure the most decadent of holiday treats aren't on the menu yet."

"Not *yet*," Sam echoed, sitting down next to me at the kitchen table, which was laden with just about every form of sugar and spice imaginable—including five boxes of Mrs. Fujikawa's prized, chocolate-enrobed Joe-Joe's. "But if she's going to match the rest of the Tanakas, she'll be scarfing this all down in no time."

"How's everybody doing out there?" I asked, jerking my head toward the den. An uproarious burst of laughter seemed to answer my question.

"Great," Sam said anyway, breaking into a playful smile. "My parents are loving every second of Christmas karaoke with Lucy and Rose. But Pika's getting cranky because they're hogging the TV, which means no *Columbo*."

"I'll set him up with my iPad," I said, bouncing Vivi in my lap. "Right after I get this one settled in for a nap."

"And I better get back out there," Sam said, wincing as someone in the other room started yelling about whose turn it was. "Who knew the combined Tanaka-Jupiter-Fujikawa-Maui-fam Christmas would be so rowdy?"

"Aww, look at you, enjoying the season!" I said. "I love that I've finally reformed you of your Grinchy ways."

"You know, you haven't actually accomplished that in this version of the timeline yet," he said, getting to his feet and giving me a lazy smile that sent butterflies parading through my stomach. "That's later tonight, right? I finally get to open my present?"

"You do." I stood on my toes and kissed him, the butterfly parade intensifying. I trailed my fingertips down his arm, cocking a suggestive eyebrow. "But you better listen to my extremely detailed instructions this time."

"We'll see," he said, his voice going all husky.

I grinned at him, holiday warmth swelling in my heart.

As I headed toward the stairs that led up to Nate and Evie's room, I paused and peered into the den, where everyone was gathered. It had been my idea to get all the people I loved together, flying my Maui family to my San Francisco family for a big ol' Voltron of a Christmas. So far, it was working out perfectly.

I sighed happily as I watched Pika try to hide the remote from Rose and Lucy while Aveda serenaded everyone with her rendition of "Santa Baby." Leah and Pancake both winced when she tried to hit the high note.

I smiled to myself as I climbed the stairs, Vivi cooing in my ear.

The last nine months had been an adventure of another sort—but no time travel had been involved.

Sam and I were finally working on making our world bigger together. We weren't sure if we had it right just yet, but we were definitely having fun figuring it out—half a year in Makawao, half in San Francisco, always together. Doc Kai had actually been super delighted to work out a plan for me to be the Demonology Research Group's first dual-city member, someone who could look at things from a big-picture perspective, doing fieldwork in both locations. She was also endlessly happy that my big kaiju had continued to hang out, at last fulfilling her dream of friendly sea monsters bolstering Maui's ecosystem. My mini kaiju were still running around as well, integrating surprisingly well with the

Makawao chickens. Roger had emerged as their de facto den mother, gathering dropped malasada bits every morning for his charges and then leading them on expeditions to gobble up pampas grass—another thing for Doc Kai to be delighted about.

And while the Otherworld portals seemed to be closed for now, we knew the magic from the demon dimension had still touched our world in ways we probably weren't even aware of yet—making this one of the most exciting times for supernatural research that Doc Kai and I could remember.

Sam, meanwhile, was loving the opportunity to hang more with the Car Uncles, and had started apprenticing at Pika's café. Pika, of course, acted put out, like he didn't need any help—but I'd overheard him tell Tosh that he was hoping maybe Sam could become a full partner at the restaurant one day.

I still felt my beloved darkness inside of me, wrapped around my power to form that beautiful rainbow disco ball—they were now truly fused as one. Once I'd embraced it and accepted all of those feelings I'd been trying to deny, I could feel my power stabilizing a bit, leveling out. I found I could control my projections better, and that I wasn't prone to accidental time travel or creating tiny monsters whenever I was stressed. But my darkness still felt undeniably powerful, and Nate and I had planned a series of experiments while I was back in San Francisco to see if we could figure out what all it could do.

What all *I* could do.

I was finding my superheroine path, diving headfirst into all the supernatural experimentation and exploration I adored so much, and loving every minute.

In other words, I was finally living the future I wanted to write for myself.

I made it to Nate and Evie's room, humming Christmas carols to myself as I carefully settled Vivi in her crib.

"You're so lucky, kid," I said, grinning down at her as she

cooed back at me. "Look at all this family you're gonna have—Aunties and Uncles freaking everywhere! Although I guess that also means you'll have a metric fuckton of people all up in your business." I leaned in closer, lowering my voice to a whisper. "Just remember: you choose *me* as your maid of honor."

"Talking to her about the future again?" a wry voice said from the doorway.

I turned to see Evie striding into the room, wearing a sleepy grin.

"Just one potential future," I said with a wink. "Though I'd like to think I'm her favorite Auntie in every possible version of the timeline."

I hadn't told my family every detail of all the possible futures I'd seen—and not because of any lingering worries about timeline interference. Just . . . some things deserve to be experienced in the moment. It was interesting to see how things had played out since the battle on the beach. There were certain memories I had of the various Christmases I'd been through that happened in similar fashion, but the details ended up being different. Like Sam and I had still enjoyed a beautiful afternoon of ice skating with his parents, but since we'd never broken up, all our kissing had been totally real. And Leah, Pancake, and I had participated in a much less fraught version of the gingerbread-house competition, but this time we'd been on the same team—and we'd won.

Evie's birth moment had still unfolded in similar dramatic fashion—there were no french fry demons, but it had still been unexpected, messy, traumatic. And I had still swooped in to assist, making the moment better for her. I'd never figured out exactly how I'd time traveled to Evie's birth moment in the first place, since I hadn't been physically present for it in my initial version of the timeline. Yes, one could chalk it up to the darkness making my power super unpredictable, to unknown variables and all that. But I couldn't help but feel that it was because I was always supposed to be there.

Sometimes I couldn't remember which memories of mine were from the current timeline and which were from something I'd experienced during my adventures. They kind of melded together, a beautifully imperfect mosaic of my thrilling life. I figured all these memories were part of me now anyway—my path, my story.

"You *are* Vivi's favorite," Evie said, bringing me back to the present. "Don't tell Annie."

"Need a break from the festivities?" I asked, reaching out to squeeze her hand.

"It's a little loud." She squeezed back. "And someone needs to take the mic away from Annie."

"Couldn't be me," I said, holding my hands up in surrender.

Evie leaned over the crib, smiling down at Vivi. "I also just like to watch her sometimes, you know? She's so . . . perfect." Her eyes turned glassy. "Is that creepy?"

"Not at all. You're supposed to be kinda obsessed with your baby. And I can't really blame you, she's such a little angel . . ."

I reached down, waiting for Vivi to wrap her chubby fist around my index finger.

She reached out for it . . .

And the tiniest flame sparked in her palm.

"Whoa!" I shrieked, jumping backward.

Vivi giggled and cooed, waving her little flame around.

"Evie!" I goggled at her, not sure what to think. "Has she . . . has that happened before?!"

"A couple times," she admitted, smiling down at her tiny daughter.

"And you're not scared? I thought you were all freaked out about this baby inheriting superpowers or demon powers or . . ."

"I was," she said, stroking Vivi's hair. "But when it actually happened, you know what I felt?" Her smile grew wider. "Pride. Excitement. *Hope.* My power . . . I used to be so afraid of it. But over the years, I haven't just accepted it—I *love* it. It's part of who I am. Why wouldn't I want to give that to her?"

Vivi cooed again, clapping her hands together until the flame winked out.

"Is she testing that fire again?" Aveda asked, striding into the room.

"You knew about this, too?" I demanded.

"Of course," Aveda sniffed. "I'm her favorite Auntie, after all."

Behind Aveda's back, Evie shook her head at me. I suppressed a grin.

I watched them as they both turned back to the crib, watching Vivi as her eyes started to drift closed. They looked exactly as they had in the beautiful future I'd seen, where everyone piled into Leah's fairyland of a bookstore for Vivi's big day.

I knew that future wasn't written yet. That the choices we made every day would determine our path. But I also knew that no matter what, all the love I'd felt in that moment would guide us through.

"God, Vivi has so much amazing family!" I said. "And that's something you and I *didn't* have for a long time, Evie. Not until now. That family's what's helped us become who we were meant to be."

"And that's another reason I'm not worried," she said, beaming at Aveda and me. "Whatever Vivi decides to do in life—whether that's being a superheroine or something else entirely—she has all these incredible people to guide her and love her and be there for her."

"It's like Doc Kai said: we change each other's lives all the time, simply by being in them," I marveled. I remembered the vibrant, glowing young woman I'd seen in the future, flowers strewn in her hair. "I think no matter what happens, Vivi's going to embrace who she is, always."

I thought back to those words I'd written on the bookstore bathroom wall so long ago, the ones that had guided me to that future I'd so desperately needed to see.

I choose

I was going to keep choosing joy, love, and hope every day—for me, for Vivi, for our beautiful sprawling family.

I leaned my head on Evie's shoulder and reached out to take Aveda's hand. We all gazed down at Vivi, her soft snores echoing through the room. I felt my heart open, dreaming of destinies still unwritten.

We would write them together—and I couldn't wait to see what the future held.

ACKNOWLEDGMENTS

I am a glittery rainbow disco ball of gratitude. I decided long ago that this would be the final book in the *Heroine* series—my characters felt like they were truly coming full circle in their journeys, I'd said everything I wanted to with this story, and I could truly envision Evie, Aveda, and Bea (and their sprawling found family) finally thriving off the page in their happily ever afters. I am ridiculously proud of this series and the complicated, messy, joyful Asian American heroines I've been able to bring into the world. And I am endlessly grateful to all the fans and readers who made this series so special—I love your fan art and your cosplays and your passionate support for my girls. Thank you for loving these characters and helping me live my dream.

Thank you to Jeff Chen for holding me together this whole time—I love you so much, and I love spending every Christmas with you.

Thank you to my superteams: The Girl Gang(s), the Shamers, Heroine Club, the incredible Asian American arts community of LA (and beyond!), Team Batgirl, the Millsies, and all the writing sprint support threads, hilariously named group texts, and convention crews. As always, I am honored to be in your company.

Thank you to my warrior of an agent, Taylor Haggerty—you kept reminding me there was a finish line, and you helped me cross it. I would not be writing these acknowledgments if not for you! And to Jasmine Brown and everyone at Root Literary for your steadfast support.

Thank you to everyone at DAW Books and Penguin Random House—especially Betsy Wollheim, for acquiring this series and believing in it in the first place! And to Katie Hoffman, Josh Starr, Alexis Nixon, Jessica Plummer, Leah Spann, Lindsay Ribar, Sheila Gilbert, and everyone who helped bring *Heroine* to such beautiful life.

Thank you to Jason Chan for covers that always capture my girls in all their vibrant glory—you set the tone for this series, and this one is my favorite yet. And to Emily Woo Zeller for giving each and every one of my heroines a distinctive voice—you are the audiobook MVP!

Thank you to Amber Benson for reading this book almost as many times as I did—your support, kindness, and love for Bea (and me) mean the world. Thank you to Keala Kendall for the deep reads, conversations, and insights—Musubi Monday is in our future, no time travel required! Thank you to Erik Patterson for breakfast burgering with me during crunch time, to Tom Wong for helping me break and re-break this stubborn story, and to Jenn Fujikawa for twin-style emotional support and introducing me to many of the delicious eateries mentioned in this book.

Thank you to Mel Caylo, Christine Dinh, Javier Grillo-Marxuach, Liza Palmer, Rebekah Weatherspoon, and Jenny Yang for some extra deep talks while I was working through this book—you are all bright lights, and I am so happy to know you.

Thank you to Amy Ratcliffe for revealing the lovely cover, to Sara Miller for some true schedule wizardry, and to Bea and Leah Koch (and the late, great Fitzwilliam Waffles) and The Ripped Bodice for continued inspiration—I am honored to work with all of you.

Thank you to the wonderful people who also fed this book in some way: Alyssa Cole, Andrea Letamendi, Christy Black, Nick Brandt, David Perkiss, Betty Woo, Colleen Miller, Janet Eckford, Jenny Bak, Jane Sussman, Michi Trota, Michelle Chong, Keiko Agena, Will Choi, Julia Cho, Naomi Hirahara, Naomi Ko, Maryelizabeth Yturralde, and Scott and Geri Okamoto (and the extended Okamoto fam).

Thank you to my family for being my family—Dad, Steve,

ACKNOWLEDGMENTS   439

Marjorie, Alice, Philip, and all the other Kuhns, Yoneyamas, Chens, and Coffeys. Special shout-out to Rocky—the real Littlest.

It was a delight to feature fictionalized versions of some of my favorite Maui eateries in this book, so thanks to them for the inspiration: Maui Specialty Chocolates, Geste Shrimp Truck, Restaurant Matsu, Sam Sato's, Honokowai Okazuya & Deli, Fukushima Store, and T Komoda Store & Bakery (which was a little extra fictionalized, thus the different name!).

Thank you to G. Willow Wilson for writing that *Ms. Marvel* line that is the cornerstone of so many modern superhero narratives: "Good is not a thing you are. It's a thing you do." I thought about this line so many times while writing this series—and while writing this last volume especially.

Thank you again to everyone, from the bottom of my heart—I love you all. Please do good.